Praise for Kathleen Barber's Novels

FOLLOW ME

"Soul-cycling, Pilates-perfected, media-savvy readers will devour [*Follow Me*]. Barber's narrative, like social media itself, is as addictive as it is disturbing."

—*Booklist*

"A cautionary tale about the perils of social media . . . [that] keeps you guessing."

—*Kirkus Reviews*

"Fast-paced and au courant."

—*Publishers Weekly*

"A commentary on today's obsession with image and technology— and also a great pick for fans of Caroline Kepnes's *You*."

—*Glamour*

"A disturbing story that becomes even more so because of her [Barber's] restraint, understatement, and occasional humor . . . [It] feels like watching an automobile accident develop in slow motion and may serve as a cautionary tale for our times."

—*New York Journal of Books*

"A cautionary tale about the dangers of sharing too much online— this is one that will really make you rethink your social media use."

—*CrimeReads*

"Kathleen Barber's fast-paced writing and short, action-filled chapters make *Follow Me* an easy and enjoyable read."

—Bookreporter.com

"Pretty much perfect escape reading."

—Self.com

"A compelling cautionary tale about the lust for social media attention and the dangers of Internet exposure. A must-read!"

—Wendy Walker, *USA Today* bestselling author
of *All Is Not Forgotten*

"Addictive, disturbing, and frighteningly real . . . Barber ratchets up the tension in this spine-tingling thriller about the dangers of oversharing. *Follow Me* is one of those rare books that are creepy and suspenseful, while still managing to be a fun, unforgettable read."

—Christina McDonald, *USA Today* bestselling author
of *The Night Olivia Fell*

"A gripping, chilling, and relevant deep dive into the dark and scary side of social media. Kathleen Barber masterfully keeps the reader guessing until the mind-blowing conclusion."

—Robyn Harding, bestselling author of *The Party*

"In this twisty, propulsive thriller, Kathleen Barber is at the top of her game, plumbing the depths of female friendship and obsession, while showing us who we really are, #unfiltered."

—Kate Moretti, bestselling author of *The Vanishing Year*

"A chilling take on obsession, self-obsession, and the closing gap between the two in our hyperconnected digital age."

—Jessica Strawser, bestselling author of *Not That I Could Tell*

"Wow! More than just an addictive thriller . . . Kathleen Barber's chilling insights about social media and privacy will stay with you long after its last nail-biting pages."

—Angie Kim, bestselling author of *Miracle Creek*

"A thriller for the Instagram age, *Follow Me* had me looking over my shoulder, closing my social media apps with a shudder, and above all, flipping pages to find out what happened next."

—Amy Gentry, author of *Good as Gone*

"A sharp look at the downfall of inventing better online versions of our own realities. Absorbing, utterly addictive, and possibly the most riveting book I've read this year."

— Jennifer Hillier, award-winning author of *Jar of Hearts*

"In this twisty thriller about every woman's worst online nightmare, Barber expertly explores complex issues of privacy, voyeurism, and consent while keeping the pages turning with heart-pounding suspense."

—Layne Fargo, author of *Temper*

TRUTH BE TOLD

(Originally Published as *Are You Sleeping*)

"[An] inventive debut . . . The intense plot and character studies are enhanced by the emotional look at the dynamics of a family forever scarred by violence."

—*Publishers Weekly*, starred review

"A twisty tale that will grip readers as they follow Josie confronting a past she finally cannot escape. Highly recommended for fans of the podcast *Serial* and authors such as Ruth Ware and Paula Hawkins."

—*Library Journal*, starred review

"Showing how complicated the truth can be when people have different levels of investment in it. Dark. Moving. Timely."

—*Oprah.com*

"Josie's dark past becomes fodder for the podcast du jour—if that doesn't hook you, the twist will."

—*Cosmopolitan*

"My prediction: the book is destined for the *New York Times* bestseller list."

—*Chicago Tribune*

"I was completely hooked from the very first page. Who to trust? Who to believe? Barber is a fabulous new author to watch. If you like twisty psychological thrillers, this is your book."

—J. T. Ellison,
New York Times bestselling coauthor of
The Devil's Triangle

"A classic whodunit gets a very clever modern treatment that left this reader's heart racing right up to the last page."

—Liz Nugent, author of *Unraveling Oliver*

ALSO BY KATHLEEN BARBER

Truth Be Told (formerly published as *Are You Sleeping*)

FOLLOW ME

KATHLEEN BARBER

POCKET BOOKS

New York London Toronto Sydney New Delhi

Pocket Books
An Imprint of Simon & Schuster, Inc.
1230 Avenue of the Americas
New York, NY 10020

This book is a work of fiction. Any references to historical events, real people, or real places are used fictitiously. Other names, characters, places, and events are products of the author's imagination, and any resemblance to actual events or places or persons, living or dead, is entirely coincidental.

This Pocket Books paperback edition April 2022

POCKET and colophon are registered trademarks of Simon & Schuster, Inc.

For information about special discounts for bulk purchases, please contact Simon & Schuster Special Sales at 1-866-506-1949 or business@simonandschuster.com.

The Simon & Schuster Speakers Bureau can bring authors to your live event. For more information or to book an event, contact the Simon & Schuster Speakers Bureau at 1-866-248-3049 or visit our website at www.simonspeakers.com.

Manufactured in the United States of America

10   9   8   7   6   5   4   3   2   1

ISBN 978-1-9821-8996-9
ISBN 978-1-9821-0200-5 (ebook)

For Marc

The internet is a weird place, full of unexpected rabbit holes. Follow them at your own risk—you might discover something new and interesting, or you might find yourself reaching for the eye bleach.

One day I stumbled upon the latter while idly browsing the Legal Advice subreddit. It's one of my favorite places to kill time online: as a non-practicing lawyer, I enjoy the discussion surrounding the more mundane queries (landlord-tenant disputes, arguments with neighbors over property lines), and as a practicing writer, I can't get enough of the more outrageous tales (discovering gold in the walls of an inherited home, learning a spouse thought long dead is in fact alive). That afternoon, I came across a poster concerned that his boss was accessing employees' home security cameras.

How outlandish, I thought. *This post must be fake.* But no one else appeared to have the same reaction and instead casually rendered advice as though it were no more exotic than a speeding ticket. I saw references to another subreddit dedicated to "controllable webcams," and, intrigued, visited it. There I found post after post sharing links to what appeared to be live footage of restaurants, bars, doggy day cares, and more. I turned to the internet at large, attempting to discern what exactly a "controllable webcam" was, where they were located, and how these internet denizens were discovering them. Could anyone find them? Could I, for instance, find more puppy cams?

But my research took a hard left turn as I stumbled across an article with the chilling headline "Meet the men who spy on women through their webcams."*

I read in horrified fascination how someone, using only minimal technological skill, could secretly install a remote administration tool, or RAT, on another person's computer. With the RAT installed, the "ratter" then has almost complete access to the victim's computer, including their files, screen, and webcam. From that point on, whenever the victim uses their computer, a stranger might be monitoring their activity—both digital and physical.

I read about how some ratters toy with their victims, playing pranks like opening porn on their screens; some

---

* Ars Technica, March 10, 2013, https://arstechnica.com/tech -policy/2013/03/rat-breeders-meet-the-men-who-spy-on-women -through-their-webcams.

steal website credentials; and some are more invasive, scouring hard drives for compromising photographs or other blackmail material. I was far more disturbed, however, by the ratters who collect "slaves"—their name for the women they've spied on via webcam. In addition to watching their "slaves" in secret, these ratters gather in forums to share what they've observed their oblivious "slaves" doing and post screenshots of the women. When they're bored with a "slave," they might sell or trade her to someone else on the forum, further perpetuating the violation of privacy.

My skin crawled at the idea of a stranger electronically invading my home, riffling through my personal files, and watching me while I thought I was alone. And then for that stranger to be sharing my secrets on a forum filled with like-minded creeps? Petrifying. When I read that many victims involuntarily downloaded the RAT software while torrenting, I relaxed—I never use torrent sites—but I relaxed only slightly. After all, I had recently listened to an episode of the podcast *Reply All* titled "What Kind of Idiot Gets Phished?"—which made it abundantly clear that idiots are not the only ones getting phished. As that podcast proved, a minimally proficient phisher can quickly and easily gain access to your email—even with two-factor identification enabled—so who knows what else they could do?

I was so deeply unsettled by the thought of an anonymous ratter lurking around my computer that I did two things: first I covered my laptop's built-in webcam with a sticker, as Mark Zuckerberg and James Comey both reportedly do, and then I began writing this story.

FOLLOW ME

PROLOGUE

HIM

Everyone on the internet is a liar. Every last one of us. The difference is the magnitude of our lies. On one end of the spectrum are the scammers, the phishers, the lowlifes trying to convince your grandmother to bail you out of a fictional Thai prison. On the other end are those whose untruths are the smallest, the most inconsequential: those who click a box affirming they've read terms and conditions, who click "like" on a cousin's photograph of her pug-nosed child. In the middle are the rest of us: those who tell slightly bolder lies designed to make ourselves look better. We embellish our job descriptions. We smile in pictures even when our hearts feel shriveled and black. Because what's the harm in making our mediocre lives look and feel just a little less mediocre?

But the internet can reveal just as much as it can obfuscate.

Take Sabrina, for example. When I was sixteen, she was my whole world, my pocket-sized, red-haired princess. Every thump of my beating heart was an echo of her name. With her small hand in mine, I could do anything. But seven months into our relationship, her family moved across the country to California. Part of me wanted to drink bleach and die, and another part of me was certain Sabrina and I were simply enduring a test to prove our everlasting love and that fifty years later we would laugh about those years apart. The day she left, I found two strands of her strawberry-blonde hair on my pillow, and I placed them in an envelope beside my bed for safe-keeping.

At first, we talked for hours on the phone each night. I twisted those hairs around my finger and listened to Sabrina say how much she hated California and how much she missed me. She promised she still loved me. She promised nothing would change. She *promised*. But her calls gradually became less and less frequent. She started taking an hour, and then two or three, to respond to text messages. I assumed she felt as gutted as I did, so I mailed her gifts and flowers to cheer her up, sent her poems all but written in blood squeezed from my aching heart.

And then Astrid Marshall, one of Sabrina's bitchier friends, sent me a link to a YouTube video called "HOT-TEST GUYS AT NEWMAN HIGH RATED!" I felt sick as I watched Sabrina, her gorgeous hair hacked to her chin and streaked through with brassy blonde, sitting in some unfamiliar room in a circle of strange girls. The ringleader—a bleached blonde who was wearing so much makeup that her face was a different shade than her neck—screeched a greeting into the camera and then led the others in discussing which of the boys at Sabrina's new school were the "hottest." My stomach churned as Sabrina giggled and nodded in agreement, but the bile started to really climb my throat when someone asked her, "But you have a long-distance boyfriend, don't you, Sabrina?" She shook her head quickly, her alien hair swishing around her small face. "No, no. There's this guy who's, like, obsessed with me, but we're not going out. I just keep him around for the gifts." The entire circle cackled with cruel laughter, and I slammed shut the computer before that treacherous whore could take another bite out of my heart.

That night, I stole a lighter from one of my older brothers and watched those glimmering strands blacken and break.

When I confronted Sabrina about the video, she cried that she was sorry. But that was just another lie. She was only sorry that she was caught, that her duplicity had been exposed. After all, a quick search had shown me that there were more videos, and in them Sabrina didn't look sorry at all. That stone-cold bitch had moved on, leaving me completely and utterly destroyed. For years, I thought my heart had been broken beyond repair. I thought I would never love again.

But then there was Audrey.

Ironically, Sabrina is the one who brought me to Audrey. If it weren't for Sabrina and her lies, I never would have ended up on the Overexposed forums. That was where I took shelter, commiserating with other men who had discovered disheartening truths online about the women they thought they loved. The other commenters helped me gain perspective, helped me see that this was less a reflection of me and more a reflection of Sabrina and the grasping, unhappy women like her.

But the forums didn't just contain grievances and complaints about ex-girlfriends. They were also home to lively discussion about online women. You know the type: the bloggers, the vloggers, the Tumblrinas, the Instagram models. The women who peddle their bodies online like fruit at the supermarket. The consensus on those threads was that admiring these virtual women was better, easier than finding one in real life because all women lie, and at least these liars were up-front about it. It was no secret that their perfect bodies were Photoshopped, that their sultry eyelashes were glued on. Online women could never humiliate you. They couldn't carve a gaping wound in your soul because they didn't have souls themselves.

The thing that I would never admit to in those threads was that I missed the pulsating heart of a real woman. I missed burying my face in silky hair, inhaling the scent of perfumed skin. I missed the softness of feminine lips beneath mine. If only that bitch Sabrina hadn't broken me.

And then one night, I was lying in my extra-long twin bed, listening to my roommate snore and battling insomnia by browsing Overexposed. I was on a thread where users were posting screengrabs of their ideal woman when one of them caught my eye. I rocketed to a seated position, my chest clenched so tightly I could barely breathe. The thumbnail image was small, only an inch or two at most, but I would recognize that mane of shimmering, red-tinged hair anywhere.

Sabrina.

With trembling fingers, I tapped open the picture. Relief and disappointment coalesced as I realized it wasn't her. It was another flame-haired beauty smiling at the camera, her name discernible in the screenshot from her social media post: *Audrey.*

Her resemblance to Sabrina had initially taken my breath away, but the more I studied her, the more I saw the differences. Both were small and red-haired, but Audrey was sharper, more femme fatale. Aquamarine eyes flashed beneath thick lashes, heart-shaped face came to a point, pale breasts swelled beneath a plunging neckline. My mouth filled with saliva; heat surged through my body.

Audrey.

I found the rest of her online presence, from her Tumblr to her WordPress blog, and followed her wherever I could. For days, I binged on her. I went through her blog archives, committing every image to memory, parsing every chatty post for its deeper meaning. She was more adventurous than Sabrina ever had been, and funnier, too. I learned what she was listening to, what she was watching, what she was reading; I devoured every morsel she shared of herself.

Lucky for me, that was pretty much everything.

My favorite image was of her standing on a beach, her milky-white skin glowing against her black crochet bikini. She was partially turned away from the camera, her body angled toward the ocean behind her, her eyes looking straight through the screen into mine. One hand restrained her flowing hair, the other was extended to the camera, beckoning, as if to say, *Follow me.*

CHAPTER ONE

AUDREY

What doesn't kill you makes you more interesting. At least, that's always been my personal motto, and it was echoing through my mind as I tried to stave off a panic attack on a southbound train to Washington, DC. In this instance, though, it wasn't helping—largely because I wasn't sure that the logic held. What if this move actually made me *less* interesting?

I shuddered and once again considered petting the emotional support Chihuahua currently occupying a quarter of my seat. When I'd extended a hand to scratch behind his ears earlier, his owner—a ferocious woman with a French-tip manicure and wearing a lemon-yellow velour tracksuit—had practically screamed, "He's working!" The little dog looked to me like he was snoozing, but I was in no hurry to set his owner off again.

Instead, I fished a Xanax from my purse and took another surreptitious photo of the dog. I added "Hour 2" in purple text and a GIF of a small, yapping dog before uploading it to my Instagram Story. Almost immediately, comments from my million-plus followers appeared:

> Safe travels!
>
> That dog looks like he has it in for you!
>
> Hang in there, Audrey!

The tension that had ratcheted my shoulders up by my ears began to melt, and I finally relaxed into my seat. Comments from my followers were hands down my favorite part of living my life on the internet. My former roommate (and former best friend) Izzy used to say that was because I was a narcissist, but Izzy was the one who couldn't pass a reflective surface without checking herself out, so, you know, glass houses and all that. Anyway, it wasn't a love of myself that kept me sharing my world with my followers—it was my love of *connection*. With a million friends at your fingertips, how could anyone ever feel truly alone?

I started responding to comments about my clothing, nail color, and music in my headphones, but not the one query that kept reappearing: *Why are you leaving New York?*

Good fucking question.

It was the question that was raising my cortisol levels, the one that had me chewing benzos. I mean, I loved New

York. It was the most vibrant city in the world, the most exciting and unquestionably *best* place to live. For almost as long as I could remember, I'd dreamed about living there. I'd even collaged my childhood bedroom walls with images of the Empire State Building, Statue of Liberty, and dozens of other landmarks.

But now, seven years after I thought I'd found my home, I was speeding away from it on the Amtrak while my belongings simultaneously made their way south on a moving truck. I used to imagine that if I ever left New York, it would be for someplace almost as glamorous: Paris, London, Tokyo.

Washington, DC, had never made that list.

I fingered another Xanax and wondered whether I was making an enormous mistake.

You're doing the right thing, I told myself. *How could taking your dream job be anything other than the right move?*

Because the truth was that I had aspired to work in a museum even longer than I had wanted to live in New York. I'd graduated from college with a degree in art history and planned to take a year to work in galleries in New York before applying to graduate school for a museum studies degree—but one year turned into two, and then I kept finding reasons not to apply. I put it off even as I watched the plum museum jobs I coveted all go to candidates with master's degrees, and so I was stuck working part-time in a couple of privately owned art galleries and volunteering at museums like MoMA and the Whitney.

Last month, though, I had been browsing the job boards and spotted the advertisement for the Hirshhorn Museum's Social Media Manager position. *I could do that,* I thought as I read the description. *I could totally do that.* I *excelled* at social media. Seriously, how else did a random midwestern transplant construct a minor cult of personality out of thin air? I submitted an application before I could second-guess myself.

When Ayala Martin-Nesbitt, Director of Public Engagement, called to offer me the job, I had momentary cold feet. I'd fallen in love with the world-class museum—part of the Smithsonian system—during my interview, but I'd been less taken with the location. How could I move away from New York? Ayala gave me a day to think it over, and I'd decided to celebrate the offer and talk it out with Izzy. Izzy had been my best friend since grade school and had talked me through decisions ranging from whether to cut bangs to how to confront a former boss who made inappropriate jokes. She'd always steered me straight; I knew she wouldn't let me down.

But when I'd flung open the door of our East Village apartment, clutching a bottle of Prosecco and bursting with enthusiasm, I found Izzy sitting stiffly on the couch.

Frowning, I set down the bubbles and asked, "What's up?"

Izzy lifted a few strands of her long, dark hair and examined them for split ends. To her hair, she said, "Russell's lease is up at the end of the month."

"Oh, bummer," I said, hoping this meant that Izzy's terrible boyfriend and his annoyingly trendy beard would be leaving the city.

"Yeah, well." She dropped her hair and finally met my eyes. "He's moving in."

"What?" I gaped at her. "No way, Iz. You can't just *announce* that your boyfriend and his collection of fake Gucci sneakers are moving in."

Her hazel eyes darkened and she pursed her mouth. "Actually, I can. My name is the only one on the lease, because you were too busy working below-minimum-wage jobs and chasing Instagram fame to qualify as a renter. This is *my* apartment, and I decide who lives here."

Her words hit me like a fist in the chest. Over the course of our decades-long friendship, Izzy and I had fought infrequently, and never about money. I had no idea she was harboring resentment for covering a few rent payments years ago. I'd long ago paid her back, and it wasn't like I didn't fork out my share these days. Besides, she never objected to accepting the sheet masks, adaptogens, and slow fashion items I got from brands courting me to promote them on Instagram.

"Whatever," I sniffed, picking up the Prosecco. "I'm moving to DC anyway."

Izzy blinked, surprised. "You got the job?"

"Yep," I said, unwrapping the foil around the bottle's top.

Not too long ago, Izzy would have demanded to know all the details, would not have relented until she'd heard my conversation with Ayala recounted in excruciating detail. She would have stayed up all night with me, discussing the pros and cons of taking the job, thoughtfully helping me reach the right decision. Now, she merely nodded.

"Oh. Well. I guess this will all work out then."

"Yeah," I snarled, popping the cork and taking a swig. "Everything's going to be just fine."

And it would be. Better things awaited me in DC. That much was finally clear.

CHAPTER TWO

CAT

Every Saturday, I ran my hand along the rows of nail polish displayed on the salon wall, lingering on shades of cherry and coral and fuchsia. And every Saturday, I selected the same pale pink I'd been wearing for the last four years.

"Live a little!" Monet, my favorite manicurist, implored. "Go for something with a little pizzazz!"

"Maybe next week," I said, knowing I would not. "I have an important client meeting on Monday."

"You always have a client meeting," she clucked as she began removing the chipped remnants of last week's polish.

That wasn't strictly accurate but it was close enough. If I wasn't meeting with a client, I was seeing opposing counsel, having lunch with a partner, or accompanying a more senior associate to court. I needed to command respect, and I couldn't do that with "Showgirl Red" on my fingertips.

Monet nodded at my phone as it balanced faceup on the arm of the chair. "Must be an important client."

My phone usually stayed in my purse at the salon. My weekly manicure was one of the few bits of time I carved out for myself, and it was the only time I turned off my ringer. For a glorious forty-five minutes on Saturday afternoons, I was unreachable. Client emails had to wait; partner requests for more research were put on hold.

I had been using manicures for stress relief since freshman year of college, when Audrey first got me hooked on them. She'd found me in the library, unshowered and unraveling into a pile of textbooks. She'd grabbed me by the hand and physically dragged me to the nail salon, despite my protesting the whole way. I told her I didn't have the time for a break, that manicures were a waste of money. She just laughed like she knew better. And she did. There was something inherently soothing in having someone else gently shape and lacquer your nails. I was an immediate convert. Maybe now that Audrey was moving to DC, she and I would start going together again. I wouldn't mind sacrificing my weekly forty-five minutes of personal time for Audrey time.

Audrey and I had lived together in college, but after graduation seven years ago, she had moved to New York to live the glamorous life of her dreams and I moved to Virginia for law school. As many college friends do, we went from sharing secrets and Diet Cokes daily to catching up at the occasional wedding festivity or baby shower.

I missed her. Audrey wasn't a perfect friend, but she was the best one I'd ever had.

I could still remember, with brilliant clarity, the day we met. It was the first day of college, and I had been hopeful things would finally be different. After all, *I* was different. I had shot up in height since that disastrous summer at camp, and counseling and medication had nearly eradicated my stutter. I was no longer the girl Emily Snow had called "freak." My fantasies about college being tolerable were shattered when I met my roommate, a snub-nosed brunette who introduced herself as "Tiffani with an *i*" and regarded me with barely concealed disdain. When our floor assembled for a meeting that afternoon, Tiffani pretended not to know me, and I resigned myself to being at the mercy of mean girls for another four years. I took a place on the floor, sipped a Coke, and tried not to cry.

When Audrey sauntered in, perfectly fashionably late, everyone turned. With her shiny, red-gold hair and her infectious laugh, she was impossible to ignore. She was flanked by a pair of thin blonde girls, all three of them in denim cutoffs so short the pockets were visible, and as she sat down, she said something to the blondes that made them cackle like hyenas. I was captivated. Throughout the meeting, I watched Audrey from underneath my eyelashes, wondering what it would be like to make my way through the world so self-assuredly. She never so much as glanced in my direction.

But when Tiffani (purposefully, I think) kicked over my can of soda on her way out the door, it was Audrey who materialized by my side with a wad of paper towels.

"Here," she said, handing a few to me and dropping

the rest to the floor, using her sandaled foot to wipe up the mess.

"Thank you," I said.

She flashed a bright smile as she nudged the mass of soaked paper towels in the direction of the trash can before abandoning them in a pile at its side. "No worries. See you around."

That "see you around" shifted my entire perspective, made the entire college experience stretching before me seem doable. And, with Audrey by my side, it had been.

CHAPTER THREE

AUDREY

Other than the afternoon I interviewed at the Hirshhorn, I'd only been to Washington, DC, for an eighth-grade class trip. I had exactly one distinct memory from the visit—that of a classmate with food poisoning decorating a White House carpet during our tour—but it was otherwise a dim haze of monuments and museums.

I should have come down one weekend to apartment hunt, but after I accepted the offer, the reality of leaving New York hit me like a wrecking ball and I couldn't imagine wasting even one precious second of my remaining time there. My last two weeks in New York were a blur of indulgent dinners at favorite haunts; drinks upon drinks with friends, acquaintances, anyone I'd crossed paths with in my tenure there; and late nights roaming the streets, trying to commit every crowded, trash-heaped corner to memory.

One such night, buzzed on spicy margaritas and feeling the weight of my impending move, I'd gone home and inquired about a random apartment on Craigslist. When I awoke in the morning to an email from the landlady, I did just enough research about the neighborhood to convince myself it wasn't a scam listing and told her I would take it. But even my meager concern felt like overkill: the woman used an email signature that included a motivational quote in rainbow text, for crying out loud. How bad could one of her apartments be?

I arrived in DC the afternoon before my scheduled move-in, and so I crashed with my college friend Cat. I couldn't remember the last time we'd seen each other—two years ago maybe? At Amber's wedding? I vaguely recalled unsuccessfully trying to pull a blushing Cat up onto a bar with me at the after-party—but when I told her I was moving to DC, she immediately and enthusiastically invited me to stay with her as long as I wanted.

When Cat opened the door of the well-maintained, three-story brick row house where she lived, she looked exactly as I remembered: thick, blonde hair falling to her shoulders in an enviable natural wave; bare face; long limbs emerging from a preppy sleeveless chambray shirt and pink chino shorts.

"Cat!" I exclaimed, leaning in for a hug. "It's so good to see you!"

"You too!" she said, embracing me in a floral-scented squeeze. Until I was pressed up against her, I'd forgotten just how tall Cat really was; my head only hit her collarbone.

"Come in," she continued, pulling away and leading me up a set of interior stairs to her unit. "How was the train?"

"You mean aside from Chi-Chi the Chihuahua? It was—" I broke off when I saw Cat's confused expression. "You saw my Instagram Stories, right?"

She shook her head. "I don't really use Instagram."

"I forgot how weird you are about social media," I teased.

"I just—"

"Relax, Cat, I'm kidding. Anyway . . ." I trailed off as Cat opened the door to her living area. "Wow. Nice digs."

The entire second floor was one open space cast in a soft yellow light from the enormous front bay window. The seating area was anchored by a pale gray sofa I'd drooled over in the Restoration Hardware catalog and arranged around a brick fireplace filled with cream pillar candles. A full-sized dinner table made of rustic-looking wood separated the living area from her well-appointed kitchen with its shining stainless-steel appliances, espresso machine, and high-end blender. Behind that, a wrought-iron spiral staircase disappeared upstairs.

"This place looks great," I said appreciatively and a bit enviously, running my fingers along the supple fabric of the sofa. "I know you said you don't do Insta, but this living room—or even just this fireplace—could get you a thousand likes easy."

She laughed. "My decorator will be pleased to hear that."

"Oh, you hired someone?" I asked, instantly relieved but not surprised. Style was my domain. Cat was sweet, but she lacked imagination—she was the kind of woman who walked into J.Crew and bought whatever was on the mannequin. Besides, Cat had the money to splash out on interior designers. She worked at a fancy law firm, and she came from money. In college, she was the only one of us wearing real Burberry, and I'd often wondered why she—smart, ambitious, wealthy—went to a state school. I assumed she'd flubbed her interviews at the elite private schools. Poor thing could be so awkward.

"You think I have the time to decorate? Come on, let's put your stuff in the guest bedroom."

Impressed she had a guest bedroom—my guests had always been lucky if I could scare up an extra blanket for the couch—I followed Cat up the tightly coiled staircase.

"Whoa," I said, clutching the handrail. "This thing is an accident waiting to happen."

Cat smiled apologetically. "I don't recommend going down it in socks."

At the very top of the stairs was Cat's bathroom. Through the open door, I glimpsed gleaming white tiles and the edge of an old-fashioned bathtub. Cat pushed open the next closest door to the bathroom.

"Here we are. Is this okay?"

"Um, this is more than okay," I said, looking around the room. Like the rest of Cat's apartment, her guest bedroom had the obvious touch of a professional: clean lines, soft linens, thoughtful accents. Most of the room was occupied by a low Scandinavian bed covered in a gray duvet, accompanied by a minimalist nightstand topped with fresh flowers. But beside the flowers, one thing seemed out of place.

"You're kidding me," I said, laughing as I picked up the framed photo of Cat and me at a sorority formal.

We were the picture of opposites: Cat draped in a gauzy, powder-blue dress with her hair pulled into a severe bun, and me squeezed into a skintight black dress with my long hair flat-ironed within an inch of its life. I remembered consuming nothing more than lemon water for two days before the event just to fit into that thing.

"Look at us! We were such babies."

"I know," Cat said, smiling fondly. "We were juniors there. Can you believe it's been eight years since that picture was taken?"

"Unbelievable." I sank down onto the bed and slipped off my sandals. "Thanks again for letting me stay tonight."

"Stay as long as you want. Really. I rarely use this bedroom." She smiled shyly. "It could be like college all over again."

"You mean we could do shots of Goldschläger while watching *Gossip Girl*?" I laughed. "Sounds tempting, but my movers are arriving at the new place tomorrow."

Concern flickered across Cat's face. "I still can't believe you rented a place sight unseen. How can you be sure the apartment even exists?"

"Don't worry, I promise I didn't wire money to some offshore scammer. I searched Google Maps and checked out the landlord, who, by the way, is a nice old lady named Leanne—"

"You *think* she's a nice old lady. She could be anybody. She could be a he. She could be Ted Bundy!"

"Ted Bundy's dead, Cat."

"She could be *like* Ted Bundy. She could be worse than Ted Bundy. You never know."

I shrugged. "Sometimes you have to roll the dice. You know what I always say—"

"Whatever doesn't kill you makes you more interesting," Cat finished. "Let's just hope that apartment makes you nothing more than fascinating."

CAT'S INVITATION TO MOVE IN was generous, and for a hot second I even considered backing out of my lease, but ultimately I knew I couldn't live with Cat for more than a few days. It wasn't that Cat was a bad roommate. Rather, she was too *good* of a roommate. When we lived together in college, she was always doing my laundry or fixing me tea or checking on me when I was out late. It was like living with my mother but with less nagging.

I never said anything to her, of course. Cat meant well. She was just a little needy. My stomach bottomed out as I remembered the first day of sorority rush. I'd stood in front of the Kappa Gamma Alpha sorority house—my top choice and the house I would eventually pledge—sweating in the midwestern August heat and scanning the (pleasingly lackluster) competition. As I was doing so, I locked eyes with Cat.

I recognized her from my dorm and looked away quickly, hoping she wouldn't come over. There wasn't anything wrong with her per se, but her entire demeanor seemed a little forced. She walked around with this approximation of a smile on her face that verged on a wince, and she was always *lurking*. She would come up behind the rest of us and just stand there, nodding like she was part of the conversation and smiling that weird smile.

As the door swung open and singing sorority sisters paraded out, I glanced over my shoulder to make sure Cat wasn't going to glom on to me. She must have read my expression, because her face was red, her cornflower-blue eyes bright with hurt. My mouth went sour with guilt, but what was I supposed to do? I couldn't let some girl I barely knew torpedo my chance at getting into a good house.

If I'd known she was a legacy, I might have behaved differently.

At the bid day party, the KGA president stood at the front of the room in a size zero Diane von Furstenberg wrap dress and clasped her manicured hands together, gushing about how lucky they were to have us, how lucky our chapter was to consistently pledge such amazing women. Later, after we had dispersed into smaller circles, I noticed Cat standing alone. As she was nearly six feet, it was hard for her to fade into the wallpaper, but that's exactly what she was trying to do.

She's in way over her head, I thought unkindly.

But then I remembered her wounded expression from the first day of rush, and I felt a flicker of shame. Hadn't I promised myself I would be less of a bitch in college? And here I was, just a couple of weeks into the venture, already being exclusionary—and to one of my own sisters, no less! I excused myself from a conversation about sunless tanner with two girls named Lindsay and crossed the room to Cat.

"I'm Audrey," I said. "We live on the same floor."

"I know," she said shyly, ducking her head so that her thick hair curtained around her face.

Stop acting like some bashful fucking tween, I wanted to scream. Instead, I smiled brightly and said, "Looks like we're going to be sisters."

CHAPTER FOUR

CAT

I was perpetually astounded by Audrey's apparent belief in her own immortality and the risks she took because of it. I still felt queasy when I remembered the trip we took to Mardi Gras senior year, when Audrey disappeared with some guy she met on Bourbon Street. She laughed when I tried to stop her from leaving the group, calling me a worrywart and swearing to kill me if I told her boyfriend, Nick. Four anxious hours later, I was on the verge of calling the New Orleans Police Department when she stumbled into our hotel room, giggling and wearing her shirt inside out.

But even with Audrey's history of making reckless decisions, I was stunned she was foolish enough to rent an apartment blind. She scoffed at my concern and insisted she'd done her due diligence: googling her landlord, reverse image searching the pictures from the Craigslist ad, scouting the location on Google Maps street view.

I was reserving judgment on the actual unit, but I felt good about the location at least. The address she gave me was near Logan Circle, a neighborhood that was vibrant and largely safe. Most of the buildings in the area were either classic row houses or new construction, so her unit was almost certainly decent unless she was terribly unlucky. And Audrey was never unlucky.

Besides, her new home was only a few blocks from mine, and I was pleased with the idea of Audrey living so close to me. I envisioned us picking up our friendship where we had left off, getting manicures and brunch and dancing along to old Britney Spears songs in our pajamas. That night, we had opened a bottle of wine, and then another, as we caught each other up on our lives, and everything had felt so much like the old days that I thought I might burst with happiness.

In the morning, a hangover throbbing behind my eyes, I walked with Audrey to meet her new landlord. I crossed my fingers that this "Leanne" was truly who she claimed to be and that Audrey's laissez-faire attitude to apartment shopping wouldn't lead to trouble. We turned onto one of the neighborhood's quiet, narrow side streets, lined with leafy green trees and colorful row houses. It was the kind of street that made you forget you were in the middle of the city.

Audrey stopped midsentence and checked the address on her phone. "Here it is. Home sweet home."

I followed her gaze to a picturesque four-story row house, its brick painted pale beige and its shutters a crisp black. It was set slightly back from the sidewalk, a short path leading to the steps cutting through a small, grass-covered front yard. A couple of flowering bushes were crowded along the building at ground level, and window boxes dripping with flowers hung from the upper stories.

I exhaled with relief. "It looks nice. Which unit are you in?"

"B. I'm not sure which one that is. Maybe the second floor?"

I cringed, certain that "B" did not stand for second floor. I had seen enough "B" units during my own apartment search to know what it meant.

"Hey, check out the dungeon," Audrey said, nudging me and pointing to an iron gate underneath the front steps. Behind it, a bright blue door was partially hidden below street level.

"Um . . ." I murmured, pointing reluctantly to the letter "B" above the buzzer next to the gate.

"Oh. I guess it's *my* dungeon."

I tried to give her a sympathetic look but she wouldn't meet my eyes.

"Leanne said to ring the bell for Unit 1 when I arrived," she told me, then set her jaw and marched up the front stairs, platform sandals heralding her arrival. She depressed the buzzer and then looked back at me, offering a brilliant, obviously fake smile.

Her smile dropped when the door swung open to reveal a thin, wiry man in his twenties. He had greasy dark hair looped into a bun on top of his head and a tattoo of something with wings—an eagle? a dragon?—spreading out from beneath his wifebeater, and he clutched a canned energy drink in one hand with jagged, dirty nails.

"Sorry," Audrey said, obviously taken aback. "I must have pushed the wrong buzzer. I'm looking for Leanne Lo—"

"Grandma!" he hollered over his shoulder. Then he turned back to Audrey, running his jumpy, mud-colored eyes over her body. "You must be the new tenant."

His feral stare sent a shiver down my spine, but Audrey remained as composed as ever.

"Good morning!" a singsong voice called as a small, smiling woman with a creased face and vibrant maroon hair appeared behind him. "You must be Audrey. Let me grab the keys and we'll go down to the unit. This is my grandson, Ryan. He lives on the first floor here."

As Leanne bustled away, Ryan looked at Audrey and curled his mouth into a smile, revealing small, yellowed teeth. "Hello, neighbor."

This is why you don't rent apartments over the internet, I thought uneasily.

"Tell your grandmother I'll be waiting downstairs," Audrey said brusquely. She pivoted and hopped down the stairs, ponytail bouncing, mouthing *oh my God* to me.

"You don't have to do this," I hissed to her. "I can look at your lease. I'm sure there's an escape clause or—"

"It's fine," she interrupted. "Honestly, you should have seen some of my neighbors in New York. They'd make this guy look like Mister Rogers."

"Here we are," Leanne trilled, hobbling down the stairs.

She unlocked the gate under the stairs and then the door, and Audrey and I followed her inside. I held my breath as I ducked through the hobbit-sized door-way, prepared to see one of the dark and dreary "English basements" that were so ubiquitous in the city. To my surprise and delight, however, we stepped into a decently sized, recently renovated apartment with an open-plan living area. The faux wooden floors gleamed, the updated appliances in the small kitchen shone, and the whole space smelled like lemon-scented cleaner. Sunlight streamed in, despite the living area's only window being partially blocked by an overgrown bush and covered in iron bars.

"What's with the bars?" Audrey asked, pointing to the window.

Leanne pulled open a closet door. "Did I mention this unit has a washer and dryer?"

She then proceeded to hit the rest of the highlights—dishwasher, rain-style showerhead, ample closet space—before pressing two keys into Audrey's palm ("The big one is for the gate, the small one is for the door," she explained) and telling her to call if she needed anything. As Leanne gave us a final, cheery wave and pulled the door shut, I noticed there were three locks on the door.

"You should ask her about those other keys," I noted, pointing to the pair of keys Audrey held. "But otherwise this place is incredible."

"There's no need to be hyperbolic," she said, laughing drily. "But it'll do until I find something a bit more upscale . . . or, you know, aboveground."

"You know you're always welcome to stay with me."

"Thanks, hon." She threaded one of her Pilates-toned arms through mine and tugged me toward the bedroom. "Come on, help me decide where to put the bed."

As we entered the bedroom, I noted how bright it was—even brighter than the front room. Row houses traditionally have all the windows on the fronts and backs of the buildings; the sides remain windowless because they share walls with neighboring row houses. But Audrey's bedroom had *two* windows: one small, slit-like window at what was the back of the building, and one larger one to the side.

I peered through her side window and frowned. "This bedroom looks out onto an alley."

Audrey shrugged. "Yeah, I saw it on the way in. But it's a skinny little alley. It's not like there are going to be cars driving up and down it all night or anything."

"It's not cars I'm worried about," I murmured, pressing my face against the window to better view the alley. "At least it looks like there's a gate on either end. But you should definitely get a curtain ASA—"

Bang!

Audrey and I both jumped at the sound of her front door whipping open. We exchanged a look and returned to the living room, where we found her skeevy upstairs neighbor standing in the doorway, his fingertips drumming an irregular beat on the can he still clutched.

"You ever hear of knocking?" Audrey demanded, hands on hips.

He looked at her without blinking. "Grandma wanted me to tell you that the dumpster and recycling are behind the building."

"Thanks. Knock next time."

He lifted a bony shoulder in a noncommittal response.

"By the way," Audrey said, "can you tell your grandmother she only gave me one key for the front door?"

"There's only one key."

"But there are three locks," she said, pointing.

He barely concealed the amusement on his face as he repeated, "There's only one key."

CHAPTER FIVE

AUDREY

'd never lived alone. I moved from my parents' suburban home to a shared dorm room at OSU to a crowded sorority house to New York City, where I couldn't have afforded to live alone even if I had wanted to. I met my first New York roommates—a pair of eating-disordered PR assistants looking for a third for their soulless, cramped Upper East Side convertible—on Craigslist, and I cheerfully abandoned them and their empty refrigerator when Izzy announced she was moving to the city. The fact that we hung sheets to partition that first apartment—a tiny one-bedroom in Chinatown—didn't faze me at all; there was something comforting in hearing someone else sleep. I would die before I admitted it, but I was a little sad when we upgraded to our two-bedroom in the East Village.

As the movers stacked my boxes in my living room, I worried I had made a mistake and should have taken Cat up on her offer. I wasn't cut out for living by myself. The silence alone would kill me. I thought of my Granny Wanda, who took to leaving the television on all day after my grandfather died. My mother chastised her for it, argued she was wasting electricity, but I understood. Granny Wanda had needed those soaps and game shows to keep her company; she needed their voices so she didn't go completely mad.

AFTER THE MOVERS LEFT and I'd made an inaugural trip to Trader Joe's to stock up on necessities like cheap wine, frozen Indian food, and animal crackers (my favorite snack food, something my ex-boyfriend Nick had mercilessly teased me about, often quipping, "Can you really call yourself a vegetarian if you eat animal crackers?"), I collapsed onto the only piece of furniture in the apartment—my bed—and, too tired to locate glassware, began swigging wine directly from the bottle.

I scrolled through Instagram, double-tapping gorgeous nature shots, pictures of internet-famous dogs, and candids of my sister Maggie's children with their chubby faces smeared with food, until I stumbled upon one of Izzy's posts. It was a softly filtered, overhead shot of a meal for two: two plates of green salad topped with slivers of rare steak, two glasses of bloodred wine, and a partially sliced artisan baguette on a wooden cutting board. I recognized the dinner plates as the mismatched blue and green ones we'd found at the Brooklyn Flea. Izzy and I had picked them out together, but she'd insisted on paying for them, later claiming that made them hers when I tried to take half of them with me. I rolled my eyes and continued, seeing more celebrity pets, some gorgeous shoes I couldn't afford, and then my friend Hannah's attempt at an artsy shot of what appeared to be a bourbon old-fashioned. I cringed with secondhand embarrassment. The poor thing would never learn. She had been running a small lifestyle blog called *Hannah in the City* for almost four years now, and she hadn't gained any traction or improved her skills. Most of her images were just like this one: poorly framed, poorly lit, with poor attention to detail. The stained, crumpled napkin in the corner of this shot might have read as a style choice from another photographer, but from Hannah it just looked amateurish. I'd always deflected when Hannah asked to write a guest post for my old blog or suggested that she "take over" my Insta for a day.

I couldn't blame her for asking. She had almost no audience while I had over a million followers. But it had taken years of hard work to cultivate that following, and I wasn't about to entrust it to someone as careless as Hannah. A woman has to zealously protect her brand.

I hadn't always been so meticulous about what I posted. Like every other basic white girl on the planet, I'd started a blog in the late 2000s with a free WordPress template and very little to say. I wrote terrible poetry and posted memes and thinly veiled gossip columns about my friends. (*Lavender slept with yet another member of the worst fraternity on campus*, I wrote, as though Jasmine wouldn't be able to tell that her code name was "Lavender" or, for that matter, that she had been the one sleeping with the terrible guy.) Despite being a shameless scandalmonger, I never lost any friends over it—almost certainly because no one was reading that blog. I had, like, two unique visits per day. I was essentially shouting into a black hole.

Then I moved to New York and started copying some of the more popular lifestyle bloggers. I splurged on a fancy camera and began posting "outfits of the day" and photos of my "meals" (in reality I only posted about 30 percent of what I actually ate, since the rest was popcorn and cheap wine). For more than a year, I diligently posted and received no engagement. I was discouraged, but it turned out to be the best thing that could have happened to me. I stopped posting the things I thought I was *supposed* to post, and instead started posting the things I *wanted* to post: bizarre art installations, thrift store finds, my favorite hole-in-the-wall dim sum place.

And then I met Elle Nguyen, a top-tier fashion blogger, at the art gallery where I worked. We bonded over a series of mixed-media sculptures and our disdain for a particular D-list blogger who posted nothing but sponsored content. Elle took me under her wing, and she gave me a primer on best blogging practices, introduced me to some of her contacts, and, most important, linked to my blog in one of her posts.

My readership exploded overnight. No one was flying me to Milan, but I suddenly had offers of representation from management companies and an inbox full of emails from brand reps who wanted to work with me. I seriously considered quitting my job and devoting all my effort to becoming a major influencer—those girls could rake in some serious cash—but the idea of writing glori-

fied ad copy drained my soul, and I couldn't bring myself
to give up a steady paycheck. I still believed I'd made the
right decision. I'd stayed true to my vision and developed
the engaged, loyal following that I craved—all without
having to resort to shilling personal care products, like a
not-small percentage of my blog friends.

I took another pull from the bottle and snickered.
Swilling wine atop a half-made bed was hardly aspirational, but that was the magic of the internet: my followers saw only what I wanted them to see.

I was answering comments on my latest post when
my buzzer rang, a wholly unpleasant sound that called to
mind a dying cat. I made a mental note to ask Leanne if
anything could be done about it and turned back to my
phone. After all, I wasn't expecting anyone. Someone
must have hit my buzzer by mistake.

Scraaaaape.

I paused, tilting my head toward the sound. Was someone opening the gate outside my door? Fear shot through
me as I remembered Cat's warning about the alley, and I
glanced uneasily at the curtainless window. I wrapped one
hand firmly around the neck of the wine bottle and grasped
my phone—unlocked and ready to dial 911—in the other,
and then I eased off the bed. Just as I stepped into the living
room, the front door swung open. I was already raising my
makeshift weapon when I recognized the intruder as my
upstairs neighbor and landlady's grandson.

"What the *hell*?" I demanded, letting my arm drop to
my side. "*Knock*, remember?"

He blinked bloodshot eyes at me and glanced around
my apartment. "I heard noises down here."

"I don't think so," I said, moving to block him from entering.

He ignored me and strolled into the apartment, surveying my boxes and making his way to the kitchen.

"Hey," I said, roughly setting the wine bottle down for emphasis. "You can't just come in here uninvited."

"I rang the bell," he said as he reached one hand into the open tub of animal crackers on the counter.

"And I didn't answer because I didn't want guests. Or unwelcome neighbors." I stuck out my hand. "Now give me your key to this door and show yourself out, or I'm going to call your grandmother."

He smirked. "Hey, man, I'm just being neighborly. Checking on the new tenant and all. You're the one who left your door unlocked."

"Bullshit."

"Let me give you some free advice," he said, popping an animal cracker into his mouth. "That door and gate don't lock automatically."

Could that be true? I had never lived somewhere where doors didn't lock behind me; it hadn't occurred to me to manually secure them.

"You're welcome," he said, his eyes gleaming with cruel amusement. He put another animal cracker in his mouth and meandered toward the door. In the doorway, he turned around and gave me a toothy grin caked with partially chewed cracker. "Have a good night, neighbor."

I shuddered. *Creep.* Determined not to show him how rattled I was, I made my face a stony mask and followed him out the front door. I yanked the iron gate firmly shut behind him, locked it, and gave it a good rattle to ensure it was secure.

"There you go," he said with a condescending sneer.

I flipped him my middle finger and stepped back into my apartment. He was still watching me as I slammed the front door. My hands shook slightly as I twisted the lock until I heard its angry, satisfying click.

CHAPTER SIX

CAT

After the unpleasantness that summer at Camp Blackwood, my parents sent me to a doctor who diagnosed me with social anxiety disorder. I resented the diagnosis at the time (there was nothing wrong with *me*), but as the panic I sometimes felt around my peers began to diminish with treatment, I was forced to admit the doctor might have been right. Eventually, I realized that, while my anxiety might've been more extreme than most people's, it wasn't unusual to feel unsettled at times. Lots of people feel tension around social interactions, and everyone gets nervous occasionally. Even people like Audrey, who hid her fears behind false bravado and a biting sense of humor, experienced anxiety sometimes.

If you'd just met Audrey, you'd think that she was

unflappable. It wasn't until I shared a room with her in the sorority house that I realized her carefree persona was just that: a persona. I started to recognize her tells, like the way her cheek sucked slightly inward when she chewed on it and how her true emotions would show briefly on her face before being remolded into a smile. I was loath to admit it, even to myself, but I found comfort in knowing that even someone like Audrey wasn't perfect. She was a real person just like me under all that flash and charisma.

You had to know her to see the cracks in her veneer. For example, when she realized she'd rented an English basement, concern flickered through her blue-green eyes for a fraction of a second. She blinked it away so quickly that most people wouldn't have noticed it, but I did. That was part of being a best friend.

I didn't need that minute slip to know she was anxious, though. Sometime around three that morning, I'd been walking to the bathroom when I heard a voice coming from the guest room. I eased open the door and peered inside. There was Audrey, stretched out on the bed with eyes closed and mouth moving. I strained to hear what she was saying, but it sounded like nothing more than gibberish. I was turning to leave when she clearly said, "I'm scared."

I knew little about somniloquy, my entire experience limited to the times Audrey talked in her sleep during college. Her nighttime utterances were usually indiscernible, but often included some variation of the phrase *I'm scared*. At first, I thought Audrey was having nightmares, but I later realized they corresponded with a particularly stressful time: midterms, finals, the weeks leading up to graduation. That was the only clue that Audrey was nervous; she hid her anxieties well. I would have sold my soul for a poker face half as good as hers.

I wished that for once she could allow herself to be a bit vulnerable and admit that she was scared. She didn't have to stay in that basement apartment with its window opening onto an alley and its sketchy upstairs neighbor. She could move into my guest room instead. I could help her. Back in college, Audrey had offered me a hand, had given me hope when no one else did. Her friendship saved me. She had guided me through a tough transition, and I was determined to repay the favor in kind.

CHAPTER SEVEN

HIM

Like all of Audrey's followers, I knew she moved to Washington, DC. I'd seen the announcement during one of her Instagram Lives. I had been so captivated by her pale, freckled shoulders, visible from underneath a white, spaghetti-strap dress, and the way that her beautiful red-gold hair curled around them, that I almost missed what she said. For days, she had been teasing "exciting news" and I'd guessed she had a trip planned—the last two times she'd done a Live reveal of "exciting news," it had been for trips to London and Miami. So when her glossy lips revealed that she was moving *here*, my brain short-circuited. I rewatched the Live twenty times or more, my pulse thundering more loudly and powerfully each time, until I realized that it was true: Audrey would soon be here.

I marked my calendar with her moving day, and I began checking her Instagram every hour, often more frequently, hoping for updates. My bones rattled with anticipation as the days until she arrived dwindled to three, two, one. And then she was here. Her Stories showed her buying coffee at Columbia Brews, a hipster coffee shop near Logan Circle, and captured a team of men in matching T-shirts carrying boxes into her apartment. The evidence was indisputable. She was really here, and I could think of nothing else. With every inhalation, I knew we were breathing the same thick air. With every sunrise, I knew the sun was creeping across our rooms at the same time. With every passing second, I wondered if she was nearby. She obliterated every other thought, leaving me a stammering mess during dinner with my family, an ineloquent scatterbrain on work emails.

I couldn't go on like this. She was in my city, within my grasp. I had to do something.

CHAPTER EIGHT

AUDREY

Capturing the scope of the Hirshhorn's monumental building—an elevated, concrete wheel rising among the other, more sedate museums on the Mall—was impossible from my phone. After a few failed attempts, I settled for snapping a picture of the distinctive sculpture by the entrance: a black '92 Dodge Spirit being crushed by a boulder with a painted-on face. I tagged the location, added an animated heart, and uploaded the image to my Stories.

I slid my phone into my bag and looked up to see my new boss, Ayala, waiting for me just inside the glass-walled lobby. She looked as glamorous as she had at my interview, wearing a crisp white sheath, her black hair slicked into a ballerina bun and her lips painted candy-apple red. I nearly shot my arm up to excitedly wave but forced myself to offer a restrained nod and smile instead. Projecting a cool exterior was imperative even though I felt anything but cool. For starters, the temperature was in the upper nineties with what felt like 1,000 percent humidity. The outfit I'd chosen with such care—cropped, wide-leg black pants with a slinky black camisole and a gauzy kimono covered in a cheeky bird print—had felt damp as soon as I stepped outside, and my hair felt enormous.

Moreover, I was a mass of nerves. Here I was, about to fulfill a lifelong dream of working in one of the country's top museums. What if I couldn't hack it? Maybe I really *did* need that graduate degree; maybe without it I was woefully unprepared. What if they realized right away what a fraud I was? I couldn't return to New York a failure, couldn't beg Izzy for my old bedroom back. I wished I could dip a hand into my bag for the Xanax I'd stashed there alongside some animal crackers, but Ayala was holding the door open for me, so I didn't dare. Instead, I swallowed my anxiety, pasted a smile on my face, and channeled the confident, chic woman I pretended to be online.

"Audrey," Ayala said, her long, neon-green nails pressing into my flesh as she clasped my hand. "So nice to see you again."

"It's wonderful to see you, too. I'm so excited to be here."

"We're *thrilled* to have you on board," she continued, the warmth in her voice melting some of my nerves. "A friend who owns a gallery in New York introduced me to your Instagram account years ago, and I absolutely just fell in love with your voice. It's so *irreverent*. When I saw your application, I knew immediately that you were the woman for the job. You don't take yourself too seriously."

She paused, frowning slightly, and I glanced down at myself as surreptitiously as I could, wondering what she had seen that was out of order.

"You should know, however, that not everyone agreed. There were those who felt we should go with a more *traditional* choice. Someone with an advanced degree and proven museum experience." She placed a hand on my shoulder and squeezed, just tightly enough that I squirmed. "I advocated for you, Audrey."

I swallowed hard and cranked up the wattage on my smile. "I really appreciate that. You won't regret it. I have some ideas about—"

"I'm dying to hear them," Ayala said, holding up a hand. "*Truly*. But first, the official tour."

AFTER AYALA HAD LED ME through the permanent collection and the new exhibitions, she stopped in front of a gallery blocked off with plain gray screens. A small black sign was posted to it, reading GALLERY CLOSED.

"I have exciting news," she said dramatically. "You've heard of Irina Venn, I presume?"

"Of course. I was volunteering at MoMA when they hosted *Missed Calls*—that exhibit of hers with all the deconstructed phones?"

"Yes, yes." She nodded encouragingly. "What did you think of it?"

"I think she's fucking brilliant."

Ayala paused, her head cocked slightly to the side like

a cat who's just spotted a bird, and my stomach plummeted. *You moron*, I chastised myself. *Way to drop an f-bomb in front of your new boss within the first hour on the job. Überprofessional.* My fingers itched to reach for that Xanax, but I kept them at my side and my face as blasé as possible. *Pretend you've done nothing wrong. Be as if.*

She broke into a sudden, toothy grin. "Then you're going to love this."

She swept one section of the screen aside and slipped behind it, beckoning me to follow her.

"Here it is," she said reverently, cheeks flushed as she gazed around the dimly lit room. "The future home of the newest Irina Venn installation."

I looked around to see a gallery still under construction, with no signage or labels of any kind. A number of pedestals had been erected in the room, and glass-encased dioramas stood atop several of them. At first glance, it reminded me of the miniature rooms at the Art Institute of Chicago. My family had taken a trip to Chicago when I was in elementary school, and I had been captivated by those rooms' lush details. Back home, I had "curated" my own collection of miniature rooms by assembling doll furniture in a series of shoeboxes, an "exhibit" that lasted until Maggie demanded to know why her meticulously arranged dollhouse had been ransacked.

"Dollhouses?" I guessed.

"In a sense," Ayala said, a smile teasing the corners of her mouth. "Come with me."

She strode to the far end of the gallery and gestured to one of the final dioramas. At her urging, I peered inside. Unlike the pristine rooms in the Art Institute's collection, this one featured a little bed with rumpled sheets, tiny cosmetics bottles strewn across a miniature vanity, and a doll-sized dress hanging off the back of a diminutive chair.

"It's—" I started.

Then I noticed the dark red stain on the furry rug, coming from underneath the bed. I tilted my head to get a better view. Beneath the tiny bed, I spotted something pale and . . .

I jumped back, surprised.

Ayala laughed. "Meet Rosalind."

"Is Rosalind . . . dead?" I asked, my skin breaking out in gooseflesh as I leaned forward again to examine the bloody doll.

"She is, yes. Poor Rosalind. It's called *The Life and Death of Rosalind Rose*," she said, gesturing in the air with her hands as though she were unfurling a banner. "Rosalind and her story are fictional, but the artist was inspired by the murder of a real French woman named Colette Boucher."

"I remember reading about her," I said, still staring at Rosalind's motionless face. "She was that actress who was murdered by an obsessive fan, right?"

"Indeed. As you can see, poor, dear Rosalind meets the same fate. When all the dioramas are installed, visitors will see our girl leaving her hometown for Los Angeles, striving for and finally achieving her big break, discovering the fame she'd dreamed of isn't all she'd imagined, and ultimately meeting her untimely demise."

"The artistry is incredible," I said, marveling at the miniatures. "Even if the story is a bit gruesome."

"Exactly. Between the artist's celebrity, her incomparable work, and the provocative subject matter, I'm expecting this exhibition to draw crowds." She clasped her hands together and smiled at me, her teeth glittering. "This is where you come in. It'll make great social media fodder."

"When does it open?" I asked, looking around the gallery and trying to imagine what still needed to be done.

"Two months. I'll need you to hit the ground running and lean hard into the promotion on our social media channels." She paused and frowned. "I won't bore you with the details, but there have been some hiccups and we find ourselves *extremely* behind schedule. Making Rosalind a success is our number-one priority. I'm sure you can imagine how devastating it would be for us to have an exhibition of this caliber falter."

"Totally. You can count on me."

"I'm glad to hear that." She leaned in close and said, "And just between you and me and the doll, if you can pull this off, there might be a promotion in your future."

"A promotion?" I repeated, unsure I'd heard her correctly. Less than an hour ago, I had been worried about being let go on my first day and now we were talking about promotions?

"I know it's unorthodox," she continued, vibrant lips smiling. "But a little bird told me the Director of Digital Content will be moving on soon, and I have a good feeling about you. If you impress me . . ."

"Prepare to be wowed," I said, my voice assured even while my nerves twitched. If I had learned anything from working with social media, it was that *pretending* to have confidence was just as important as—if not more so than—actually having it.

CHAPTER NINE

AUDREY

I could already *taste* that promotion, could hear myself saying "I'm Audrey Miller, Director of Digital Content for the Hirshhorn Museum." *Director* was obviously more impressive than *manager*, and *digital content* sounded far more mature than *social media*. I couldn't wait to tell my mother, who always asked why I was "wasting my time" on Instagram, about how what she called my "internet addiction" had earned me not only a sought-after job but a promotion in record time.

But to get that promotion I would have to knock the social media campaign for the Irina Venn exhibit out of the park. I was so excited to get started that, after spending the morning on paperwork and training, I decided to work through lunch. Grabbing my phone and animal crackers for sustenance, I returned to the closed gallery.

The glass cases stretched before me in the darkened room, the fatal story line they contained both intriguing and repulsing me. I approached one diorama at random and peered inside: there was Rosalind, her blonde hair pinned up in tiny curlers, reading a miniature script on a small, threadbare couch, a little can of Diet Coke on the shabby coffee table in front of her. My stomach twisted slightly. Rosalind wasn't real, but knowing she was based on a real woman made me feel like a voyeur to tragedy.

I shook off my uneasiness, popped a couple of animal crackers in my mouth, and began snapping pictures on my phone. As I captured Rosalind's tiny face, a dreamy smile that was totally innocent of the horrors yet to come, I felt the hair on the back of my neck rise.

Stop letting this get to you, I chastised myself. *This is just art.*

I moved to another diorama, looked into the room, and shrieked.

A pair of flat, dark eyes were staring at me through the glass.

I stumbled backward in surprise, and the owner of the eyes straightened, revealing himself to be a blocky man in his early twenties, his black clothing blending into the dark and his face shadowed by a baseball cap.

"What are you doing in here?" I demanded, affecting my best authoritative voice as I placed a hand over my heart in an effort to control its panicked rhythm. "This gallery is closed."

He cocked his head at me. "Do you know who I am?"

I faltered, suddenly unsure whether he was a fellow museum employee.

He smiled at my unease and took a step toward me. "Which scene's your favorite?"

The predatory look in his hooded eyes sent shivers down my spine, and I was suddenly certain that this man was no colleague of mine.

"You need to leave," I said firmly. "Now, before I call security."

"Relax," he said, holding up meaty palms in mock surrender. "I'm going."

I crossed my arms over my chest and sternly watched as he ambled to the exit. Before he passed through the screens, he paused and looked over his shoulder. A slow smile spread across his face and he said, "I like the one where the guy's outside the girl's window with a hatchet."

I stretched my lips into a tight smile to conceal my fear. "Enjoy the rest of your visit."

He smirked and waved. "Later."

Heart jackhammering inside my chest, I followed him out and stared hard at his back, not looking away until he disappeared down the escalator and out of view.

I READILY ACCEPTED an invitation to grab a drink with my new colleague Lawrence. He'd amused me with his collection of dad jokes, and, besides, Cat had canceled on me and I was in no hurry to return to my lonely apartment. But just as Lawrence and I were heading out, someone called him back to address something.

"This'll just take a minute," he promised.

"Take your time," I said. "I'm going to wander around outside."

The lush oasis nestled between the Hirshhorn and the Art and Industries Building had caught my eye on my way to work that morning, and I headed over to check it out. The vibrant shrubbery, tumbling vines and attention-seeking flowers were even more beautiful than they'd seemed that morning, and I began snapping photos of them on my phone.

Perfect, I thought as I paused to check my work. Later, I would increase the saturation to make the colors really pop, and then I'd choose the best image to upload to my Instagram grid. It would make an excellent advertisement for my collection of presets—assuming I ever got my act together to finish them. Every day, I got dozens of messages from followers asking when my presets, which would allow them to easily adjust their own photos in Lightroom to match my aesthetic, would be ready. *Soon*, I kept telling them. *And they're worth the wait!*

My stomach growled as I circled the exquisite central fountain, an audible reminder that I had skipped lunch. *I hope Lawrence takes me somewhere with food*, I thought, digging the animal crackers out of my bag. I was lifting one to my mouth when I felt a crawling sensation on the back of my neck. I glanced uneasily around, but I was alone in the garden, save a pair of sparrows frolicking in the water.

I turned my attention back to my snack, but almost immediately had the same, unmistakable feeling of being watched. I froze in place, holding my breath and straining my ears.

And there it was: the sound of a footfall behind me.

I spun around just in time to see a dark sleeve disappearing behind a hedge.

I hurried to the hedge and peered around it. The National Mall sprawled before me, thousands of people strolling along, taking photos, chasing children, walking hand in hand. My eyes quickly jumped to the handful of dark shirts I saw: a tall woman rushing away, a man in a Washington Nationals baseball cap hunched over his phone, a man zooming by on an electric scooter. I blinked and realized there were dozens more dark shirts, moving quickly all over the Mall. It was impossible to tell who—if anyone—had been in the garden with me.

You're just jumpy from seeing that weirdo in the Rosalind exhibit, I told myself. *No one was watching you.*

Still, I shivered despite the oppressive heat.

CHAPTER TEN

HIM

I regularly fantasized about the demise of my immediate family. Sometimes I imagined a terrible accident, like a carbon monoxide leak or an electrical fire, and driving up to the sprawling suburban home to find it consumed by flames, every single member of that detestable group trapped inside. Other times I envisioned doing the deed myself, lacing a meal with rat poison and watching as they all choked to death.

More than a little unnerved and worried I might end up emulating Ronald DeFeo Jr., I sought the advice of a licensed therapist. Within the first five minutes, he told me everything I needed to know: having occasional inappropriate thoughts (or *intrusive thoughts*, as he called them) was normal and didn't necessarily mean I would slaughter everyone in their sleep. He then told me I had unresolved feelings of resentment toward my family and wanted to schedule weekly sessions at nearly two hundred dollars an hour to work through them. I declined. I didn't need a professional to tell me I resented them, and I certainly didn't need to sit there and listen to a stranger's advice on how to "resolve" that resentment. My family, particularly my parents, had the emotional capacity of cats. They knew how you felt; they simply didn't care.

If not for my weakness for creature comforts, I would have walked away from them years ago. But I took their money and continued to suffer through the weekly dinners at my parents' home, where my brothers, their families, and I dutifully assembled to pay homage to the idea that we were a functioning family unit.

Surviving these dinners without stabbing myself or someone else was a herculean task. Inevitably, my father played back-seat quarterback with my career, while my mother preferred to focus on the shortcomings of my personal life. Every week, when she mentioned my failure to produce children, my middle brother, Tag, considered that his cue to say, "No kids we know of, at least," a bawdy joke that somehow never lost its appeal. Every time it was uttered, my father and oldest brother, Simon, laughed appreciatively while my mother looked scandalized, and I wondered if I was stuck in a time warp.

The dinners were so formulaic that I could predict the menu, conversation, and how much my mother would drink down to the smallest margin of error. So when Simon's wife, Leigh, turned to me and asked whether I was seeing anyone, I wasn't surprised and had my standard answer about focusing on my career ready to go.

Before I could open my mouth, Leigh's seven-year-old daughter, Esther, interjected, "Why do you always ask this? You know he just drives everyone away."

Those were almost certainly Leigh's words that Esther was parroting, and Leigh had the decency to look mildly embarrassed, while everyone else simply nodded in agreement.

"Actually," I said, slicing my steak and dreaming of instead slicing off one of Esther's fat fingers, "I'm sort of seeing someone."

Silence descended. I put the steak in my mouth and chewed.

"That's great," Leigh finally said, her tone a little too earnest.

Beside her, Tag's wife, Arielle, smirked, her expression calling me a liar.

She was wrong. I was, technically, *seeing* Audrey. Maybe I wasn't seeing her in the precise sense that Leigh meant, but it wouldn't be long until things changed.

"Oh yeah?" Tag said, cutting his eyes at Arielle.

"Yeah," Simon echoed. "Who's the lucky lady?"

I shook my head resolutely. I couldn't trust my family with so much as a crumb of information. I knew they'd find a way to ruin things.

"Come on, Peanut," Arielle taunted, using the infantile nickname I had repeatedly requested they retire. "What's the big deal?"

Underneath the table, I balled up my fists and squeezed, nails digging into my palms. The pain steadied me and made me less inclined to grab Arielle by her yellow hair extensions and smash her face into the good china.

"Yeah," Tag agreed. "You can tell us."

"Come on now, everyone," Leigh said. "Let's leave poor Peanut alone. Look how embarrassed he is. His cheeks are so red!"

She smiled at me sympathetically, and I hated her. I hated all of them, my smug brothers with their sycophantic wives and horrible children and my disinterested, image-obsessed parents. I dug my nails deeper into my palm and blinked back dark, rage-filled thoughts.

"We're just having fun," Tag said. "Peanut can take a little fun. Can't you, Peanut?"

I couldn't open my mouth or a primal scream would come out. My nails bit through my flesh and I smiled tightly at my brother as blood trickled from the wounds.

At the head of the table, my mother rose. "Can I get anyone another drink?"

AS USUAL, the family retired to the back porch for after-dinner cordials and dessert. Also as usual, Leigh and Arielle declined dessert and disappeared to watch the children, while my mother fell asleep in her drink and my father and brothers dissected something they read in the *Wall Street Journal*. As they debated financial terms with which I had no familiarity, I excused myself to the restroom. No one even looked up.

Passing the open door to the family room, I heard Arielle's nasally voice say, "It's just so obvious that he's making it up."

I halted, veins alighting with anger.

"Oh, come on," Leigh said. "That's not fair. Why shouldn't he see someone? He's a good-looking guy. I really thought things were going to work out with—"

"Yeah, but they didn't," Arielle interrupted. "And his looks will only fool a girl for so long. You know as well as I do that there's something *off* about him. You remember what happened when . . ."

Blood roared in my ears and I clenched my fists, briefly indulging in the fantasy of putting my hands around Arielle's spray-tanned throat and squeezing until there was nothing left in her. I imagined her face turning red, and then blue, as she gasped and choked, pleading with me. Maybe she wouldn't dismiss me so easily when I held her life in my hands.

But I wouldn't do that, of course. It was just another totally normal, inappropriate thought, the kind born of healthy resentment. With my head held high, I walked past the family room, past the bathroom, and out the front door.

CHAPTER ELEVEN

CAT

I had been eyeing the partnership ever since I first walked through the polished mahogany doors of Barker & Liu, LLP, four years ago. I knew reaching its pinnacle would be no cakewalk; across all offices internationally, the law firm made fewer than twenty partners annually, and only one or two were women. The road to the top was steep and packed with obstacles, but as my father always said, nothing worth having is easy.

"Not easy" was putting it lightly. Being named partner would require an almost inhuman dedication to the job. The hours were so long and unrelenting that I ate most of my meals at my desk and worked through the night a few times per year. Most people couldn't handle it. They burned out; a lucky few escaped to cushy corporate jobs while the majority moved to government work or smaller firms, taking the substantial pay cut in exchange for a good night's sleep and time with their families.

That wouldn't be me. I could sleep when I was dead, and I had no family clamoring for my presence. I had exactly one social obligation: I joined my friends for bar trivia on Thursday nights. We'd been going to the same cheesy sports bar since the summer I graduated from law school, when my friend Priya suggested its trivia night as a much-needed sanity break from studying for the bar exam. The idea of drinking pitchers of domestic beer and thinking about trivialities when I should be studying the rules of evidence made me break out in hives, and so I planned to skip it . . . until Connor asked if he would see me there.

Of course I said yes. I had been attending ever since, although my participation flagged the year Connor lived out of state for a clerkship. Since he had returned, I rarely missed trivia. Even though we now worked at the same law firm, those Thursday-night excursions were the only times we saw each other outside of work, but remembering my vow to help Audrey acclimate to the city, I invited her to join us.

I ARRIVED AT THE BAR ten minutes later than promised and found Audrey perched on a barstool, dressed in short black shorts and a white eyelet lace shirt. She was sipping a glass of rosé and laughing with the bartender, a babyfaced guy adorned with tattoos. From his leering expression, I could tell he was wondering the same thing I was: whether she was wearing anything underneath that shirt.

Her glossy mouth twisted wryly as she said something to the bartender that made him throw his head back in exaggerated laughter. He then said something and she ducked her head coyly, twisting a lock of her long, red-gold hair with her white-polished fingers. I hesitated, unsure whether I should interrupt their flirtation.

Suddenly, she swiveled on her barstool and called out to me. "Cat! There you are!"

"Sorry," I said, hurrying to her side. "I got stuck at work. Have you been waiting long?"

"I haven't minded," she said, throwing a kittenish smile at the bartender.

"Let's—"

"Hey," one of the regular waitresses, a young woman with emerald-green hair and the inability to make it through a shift without spilling at least one drink, said as she stepped between me and Audrey. With a tray of empty glasses balancing precariously on one hand, she said to Audrey, "You're Audrey Miller, aren't you?"

Audrey smiled beatifically at her. "I am. And you are . . . ?"

"Jody. I've been following you for, like, ever." She set the tray down on the bar with a loud rattle and handed her phone to me. "Here, take our picture."

Audrey offered me a shrug and a small smile before casually tossing an arm around Jody's shoulders and grinning for the camera. It was magic: somehow Audrey managed to make it look as though she and Jody were great friends, rather than strangers who'd met only seconds before. I knew that photo would be plastered all over Jody's social media the second we walked away.

The bartender smiled crookedly at Audrey. "Should I be following you, too?"

"*Everyone* should follow me."

"Maybe I will," he said, winking at her.

The way he said it turned my stomach, but Audrey was already plucking a business card from her purse. I restrained myself from snatching it out of her hand and warning her about picking up strangers in bars, particularly strangers who had a giant, bloody skull tattooed on one hand.

"Come on," I said sternly instead. "The game's about to start. We should find the rest of the team."

"Absolutely. Just let me settle up here."

"No worries," he said. "It's on the house."

"You're a doll," Audrey said, spinning off the barstool. She collected her wine and a plastic bag of animal crackers from the bar.

I smiled and pointed to them. "I see your favorite snack hasn't changed."

"Guilty as charged," she said brightly, holding the bag out to me. "Want some?"

I took a few and led her through the bar to where our team, the Fertile Octogenarians (a property law joke that had seemed hilarious when we were neck-deep in bar prep), traditionally gathered in a large, rounded booth. I quickly made introductions: my friend Priya from law school; Jessa, Priya's coworker at Planned Parenthood; Lamar, Jessa's boyfriend; Harry, a friend of Lamar's from college; and Lon, who worked with Harry at the DOJ.

"Hi, everyone, thanks for letting me crash your trivia party," Audrey said, smiling and sliding into the booth beside Harry. She tossed the bag of animal crackers in the middle of the table. "Help yourselves."

Lon, who had a nasty habit of digging around in his

ears with his fingers, immediately reached a hand into the bag, and I decided I'd had enough animal crackers.

Audrey pulled me into the booth beside her and raised her arm, her phone angled toward us, taking a selfie. I forced a smile onto my face, already knowing what the image would look like: Audrey grinning coquettishly, her eyes widened and her chin tilted just so, while I sat woodenly beside her, my face inevitably captured with one eye partially closed. I had hundreds of such pictures from our college years.

"Where's Connor?" I asked, striving for casualness even as my throat closed over his name. I had walked past his office on my way out of work, but his door had been shut and I couldn't tell whether he was inside or already gone.

"Right here."

Connor had the kind of deep, authoritative voice that all lawyers dreamed of having, and the sound of it always made my heart contract. I turned to see him standing at the edge of the booth, smoothing his thick, sand-colored hair with a hand. He grinned and my heart squeezed again, dangerously tightly. I loved his smile in its imperfect perfection, the way it lifted slightly higher on the left and the way it displayed his chipped front tooth.

"Hey, Harrell," he said, sliding into the booth beside me. "Who's your friend?"

"Hi," Audrey said brightly, leaning around me, "I'm Audrey."

"Connor," he said, directing his smile at her in a way that made me bereft. I intensely wished that Audrey were wearing something more substantial than a doily.

Feeling shamefully territorial, I leaned forward to

interrupt their eye contact, saying, "Audrey, Connor went to law school with Priya and me, and he works at Barker & Liu with me now."

"Ah," she said, eyes twinkling mischievously. "So I should probably keep the lawyer jokes to myself?"

"No, I love a good lawyer joke," Connor protested. "Here, what's the difference between an accountant and a lawyer?"

"I don't know, what?"

"Accountants know they're boring."

"Ba-da-bum-ching!" Lon said, laughing loudly and rapping his brawny hands on the table.

I glared at him. Lon had wormed his way into the team by following Harry to trivia enough times that we felt as though we had to let him play. He was a wealth of sports knowledge, but he was a lecherous boozehound. He'd been ousted from the bar more than once, and a girl from another trivia team once claimed he had followed her home and pounded on her door until she called the police. I didn't want him even looking at Audrey.

But Audrey ignored him, saying to Connor, "That's pretty good. But I have a better one: What's the difference between a mosquito and a lawyer?"

"Somehow I doubt this will be a flattering comparison."

"One's a bloodsucking parasite," Audrey said with a smirk. "The other is an insect."

"Burn!" Lon announced, extending his body across the table and offering Audrey his open hand for a high five. She gamely slapped his palm.

"Ow," Connor said, faking an injury to his heart, and then said to me, "Harrell, your friend is cruel. Did you know what she thinks of you?"

Words failed me, as they often did around Connor, and I ended up saying stupidly, "She's just kidding."

Connor blinked slightly, and then placed his hands on the table. "Okay, guys. I'm going to grab a drink before things get started. Anyone else need anything?"

Lon pounded the rest of his beer and slammed the empty glass on the table. "Another Bud Light."

"Sure thing, Lon," Connor said, smiling tolerantly. "Anyone else?"

"I need a drink," I said, sliding out of the booth after him. "I'll come and help carry."

Connor smiled down at me, sending my heart galloping again. Even more than that smile, I loved the fact that he could smile *down* at me. I'd towered over every romantic prospect since the age of fourteen, and it was refreshingly novel to feel small and feminine for once. I envied women like Audrey, pixie-sized women who would never have to worry about being taller than their partners.

As I stood, Audrey caught my eye. She winked ostentatiously, and even as I died of embarrassment, I felt a rush of warmth in the center of my chest. Audrey got it. She got *me*. It was going to be great having my best friend around again.

CHAPTER TWELVE

AUDREY

Sorry, there's a fire drill here at the office. 😞 Rain check?

I read Cat's text with dismay. I'd nabbed us last-minute reservations at the Michelin-starred Bresca, and was really looking forward to the evening. The menu looked incredible, even for a plant-based diner like me, and there was a living wall of moss that would make for amazing photos. In anticipation of a fun and picture-ready evening, I'd carefully selected an only minimally wrinkled outfit—I had yet to unpack anything other than my laptop and prized record collection, and was cherry-picking increasingly rumpled clothing from boxes as needed—and applied a full face of makeup, including false eyelashes. And now Cat was abandoning me, expecting me to spend the night alone? It wasn't like there was anyone else I could call.

That's not entirely true, I reminded myself. There was someone else I could invite to join me for dinner, but I hadn't told him I'd moved to DC yet and didn't want to call him with a whole evening planned. It would just go to his pretty head.

Instead, I poured some Riesling into a recently acquired wineglass and reminded myself that, with my healthy social media following, I was never truly alone.

I checked my already immaculate makeup, opened Instagram, and switched to Live view.

"Hey, friends," I said brightly.

Izzy had once criticized the sunny voice I used in my videos. "You're presenting a false reality," she said. "I thought you claimed to have this 'authentic' persona." I'd fired back that being cheerful wasn't inauthentic—it wasn't like anyone told you how they *really* were after a polite "how are you." Besides, there was research to support the idea that smiling even when you felt low could put you in a better mood. I smiled harder and hoped that was true.

"Confession: I have yet to unpack from my move." I flipped the camera around and slowly panned the mountain of boxes before turning back to my face and slapping a hand to my cheek in mock embarrassment. "I know, I know, it's *shameful.* I decided I could not live another minute like this, and so tonight I am finally tackling this totally hideous task."

I started chatting about my day—the new glassware I'd purchased, the barre class I'd attended, and the uniquely DC experience of getting stopped by a motorcade on the way home from work—and comments began appearing at the bottom of the screen.

I love DC! You're going to have the best time there!

Great earrings!

I felt my smile stretching, becoming more genuine. *This* was why I shared my life online. The free products were fun, but it was the connection with real people that kept me turning on my phone. It made my heart sing to know that at that moment, tens of thousands of people across the world were taking time out of their lives to hear about mine, to send me comments.

Of course, while the comments were usually evenly divided between fawning praise and questions, there was the occasional slimy one. *Nice rack* seemed a perennial favorite. I ignored the more depraved comments, knowing they were almost certainly posted by some weirdo living in his mother's basement. (The irony of mocking anyone else for living in a basement did not escape me.)

"Having a serene living space is really important to me," I said, telling them not the truth but rather something I *wanted* to be the truth. "So these boxes have been driving me bananas! I've been far too busy since I moved here to unpack, so I made the decision to stay in tonight and finally just do it! I've got everything I need: a box cutter, a glass of wine, and a Talking Heads record cued up. Wish me luck!"

good luck, audrey!

Good luck!

You have the best taste in music!

goooood luck xxx

"Bye for now, lovers," I said, tossing a wink at the camera and disconnecting the livestream.

I dropped the phone to my side and let the smile fall from my face. I *really* did not want to unpack those boxes. I poured another glass of wine and began rearranging my records instead. My sister mocked me mercilessly for living a digital life while collecting something so hopelessly analog (but Maggie worked as an accountant for a paper company, so, really, who was she to criticize something for being analog?), but I loved the tangibility of records. My infatuation with them had started on a whim, when I'd come across a secondhand (or, more likely, third- or fourth-hand) copy of the *Sgt. Pepper's Lonely Hearts Club Band* album at the Brooklyn Flea and had decided it would look fun in a frame. Then Nick gifted me a record player so I could actually listen to it, and I became a vinyl convert.

My ringing phone interrupted my thoughts, and I glanced down at the screen and smiled. It was as if thinking about Nick had actually conjured him, like some sort of sexy Beetlejuice.

"Nicky," I purred into the phone. "I was just thinking about you."

"And here I was, thinking you didn't care at all. You didn't even bother to tell me you were moving to town."

"You seem to have found out."

"You're not exactly discreet, you know. Although I did expect you to call."

"The phone works both ways, babe. You could have called me."

"I *am* calling you."

"Well, you have my most heartfelt apologies for not

alerting you to my relocation." I dropped my voice slightly. "Maybe you want to come over so I can show you just how sorry I am."

"I think that might do the trick," he said, a smile in his voice. "Text me your address."

"Doing it now. See you soon."

TWENTY MINUTES LATER, Nick was ducking through my stooped doorway. Warmth flooded my body, and I had to bite my lip to keep from smiling too broadly. I would die if Nick knew that his presence still melted me, even seven years after we had officially broken up.

"I like what you've done with the place," he said, clear blue eyes twinkling as he surveyed my boxes, half-empty wine bottle, and open container of animal crackers.

"Oh, shut up, Nick," I said, playfully punching him in the arm. "I've only been here two weeks. Which I'm sure you know since you've been stalking me on social media."

"It's not stalking when you put it out there, Aud."

"Whatever you need to tell yourself."

He flashed me the same teasing smirk that had won me over sophomore year in college. When I first met Nick, he had been upside down, his hands clenching the sides of a keg and a hose in his mouth. It hadn't been a flattering angle, but even then I could tell he was handsome. With my arms crossed over my chest and one eyebrow arched, I'd waited for the guys holding his legs to right him.

"Wow," I had said drily. "That's hot."

Totally unfazed, he had brushed his golden hair from his eyes and smirked. "I assume you're next?"

It was the first and last time I attempted a keg stand.

"Well, this isn't exactly the Castle, is it?" Nick said, referencing the nickname for my old sorority house.

"Not exactly. But it'll do for now. I think the place just needs a little bit of light."

"And some furniture. Are the movers bringing that later or something?"

"Or something," I admitted. "I don't actually own any."

"What about all that stuff in your apartment back in New York?"

"It was all Izzy's. I'm going to have to buy new stuff, but I haven't gotten around to it yet."

"Well, you know there's an IKEA over in College Park, right? It might not be glamorous enough for a social media star like yourself—"

I stuck my tongue out and poked him in the ribs; he lightheartedly batted me away.

"—but let me know if you want a ride over there or need my help assembling furniture or anything. I don't like to brag, but I'm pretty handy with an Allen wrench."

"I may take you up on that, considering I don't even know what an Allen wrench is."

"Of course you don't," he said with a laugh, and shook his head. "Someone's always built your furniture for you, haven't they?"

I shrugged. "When you're this pretty . . ."

"Modest, too."

"You know me."

"I do," he said softly, reaching out and wrapping a lock of my strawberry-blonde hair around his fingers, tugging slightly. "You're letting your hair grow again. I like it."

"You don't look so bad yourself," I said, surveying his athletic build, tan skin, and neat blond hair. Teasingly, I pinched the flesh on his tight midsection. "You've put on a little weight, but you carry it well."

"Shut up, Audrey," he said throatily, wrapping a strong arm around my waist, pulling me close, and lowering his lips onto my smiling mouth.

Kissing Nick was easy, comfortable. Even though our relationship had come to an end when we graduated, Nick always called when he was up in New York and we saw each other a few times a year. I once told him that being with him was like riding a bike—no matter how much time passed, I could always remember how our mouths, our bodies, fit together. He had given me a strange look, mildly perturbed at being compared to a man-powered vehicle, but hadn't disagreed.

I snaked a hand up underneath his T-shirt, tracing his muscles and lingering on the left shoulder blade I knew was marked by a poorly conceived tattoo. I felt a little bad about that. I had been with him in the Fort Lauderdale tattoo parlor, both of us slightly buzzed on rum and sun, and I should have told him not to take the tattoo artist's word that the Chinese character he pointed to meant "brave." I should have told him that getting a tattoo he couldn't read was a terrible idea.

But Nick should have told me not to tattoo a random line of poetry on the inside of my wrist. He should have pointed out that my obsession with Edna St. Vincent Millay was new and likely fleeting, and he would have been right.

"So," Nick said, pulling away slightly, his lips swollen.

"You got a bed in here anywhere, or have you just been sleeping on a pile of boxes?"

"Let me give you the grand tour," I said, tucking my fingers into his waistband and pulling him toward my bedroom.

CHAPTER THIRTEEN

HIM

At home, I sat on my couch, staring at Audrey's most recent Instagram post while holding a newly acquired container of animal crackers on my lap. One by one, I pressed the misshapen beasts against the roof of my mouth before crushing them between my molars, savoring the taste, knowing that the inside of her mouth tasted just like this: bland, slightly sweet, faintly lemony. I closed my eyes as I chewed, rolling my tongue through partially masticated cracker, thinking of the warm, wet interior of her mouth and her perfect rosebud lips.

The thought ignited a series of explosions beneath my skin, miniature bursts that toed the line between pain and pleasure. I focused on the glimmer of Audrey's hair, the pale glow of her skin, and then dragged a hand up my bare arm. My overstimulated flesh crackled and burned, just the way it did when I was near her.

Her physical perfection captivated me, and her sparkling personality spoke to my very soul. Still, there was something faintly dangerous about her, a warning in her flame-streaked hair and seductive turquoise eyes. *She will ruin you*, a voice deep in my subconscious cautioned, but it was too late. She had ruined me already.

I wanted nothing other than her, wouldn't, *couldn't* stop until the drumbeat of her heart reverberated against my own chest for all time.

For now, I put another animal cracker in my mouth.

CHAPTER FOURTEEN

AUDREY

The first time a follower recognized me, I was half-naked in the Equinox locker room. I'd just finished an intense HIIT class, and I was so sweaty that my skin felt slick and my eyes stung. As I peeled my soaked Lululemon tank from my body, a pony-tailed, college-aged woman in neon-pink exercise pants bounced up to me.

"You're Audrey Miller!" she announced, beaming.

"That's me," I said, offering an exhausted smile and desperately wishing I'd taken more care with my hair that morning. I'd tied it up in a sloppy topknot before class, and I could feel the weight of it tugging against the elastic, surely pulling strangely across my scalp.

Pink Pants turned to a pair of women across the

locker room and called, "Danielle! Reina! Come over here! I told you it was Audrey Miller!"

Her friends in similarly bright-hued workout gear surrounded me, telling me how much they *loved* my blog, *loved* my hair, *loved* my Stories. They pulled out bedazzled iPhones and pleaded to take selfies with me; I made them wait until I'd showered. I half expected them to have vanished before I emerged in my towel, but there they were, eagerly waiting, phones in hand. Their enthusiasm was overwhelming.

I fucking loved it.

When I'd relayed the encounter to Izzy, she'd smiled lightly and said, "Ladies and gentlemen, my best friend, the narcissist." She'd claimed she was just joking, but I knew she wasn't. I didn't care, though. Being recognized like some sort of celebrity was the best high I'd ever experienced.

So when I was rushing to a spin class one evening and heard my name, I thrilled. I adjusted my ponytail, pasted my most welcoming smile on my face, and turned to greet my fans. I was surprised to see Cat's friend Connor waving at me from one of the sidewalk tables outside Columbia Brews. A white coffee mug sat on the table in front of him, and the sleeves of his light blue button-down shirt were pushed up in the sweltering heat.

"Audrey, hi," he said, smiling genially and rising to greet me. "I thought that was you. I'm Cat Harrell's friend Connor. We met at trivia the other week, remember?"

"Sure, of course I remember," I said, omitting the fact that I *also* remembered the moon eyes Cat made at him. The poor girl practically had a flashing neon sign above her head advertising that she was in love with him. When

I'd called her out on it, she had turned a vivid fuchsia and wildly shaken her head. "The lady doth protest too much," I had joked, but not even my lame Shakespeare could jostle loose the truth. I didn't believe her repeated denials for a second. Connor was precisely her type: tall, smart, and falling just shy of handsome with his prominent Adam's apple and wide-set, drooping eyes. They would make an adorable—if slightly awkward—couple.

Cat will thank me later, I thought as I decided to play Cupid.

"It was so nice of Cat to invite me to trivia," I said. "It's so hard moving someplace new, but Cat's really gone out of her way to make me feel at home. She's just so thoughtful."

"Yeah," he agreed. "Harrell's great."

I frowned at his tepid response. This was going to take more effort than I'd thought. "She really is. She—"

"Hey, why don't you sit down? Let me buy you a latte."

"Thanks, but I have a bike booked in twenty minutes. Besides, I can't have caffeine this late in the day. It'll keep me up, and then I'll have to take a sleeping pill, and then I'll be so tired I'll drink more coffee, and it's this whole vicious cycle."

He gestured to his cup and lowered his voice conspiratorially. "This is decaf."

"Is there even a point to decaf? Seriously."

He smiled slightly and shrugged. "There is when you're meeting someone for coffee late in the day."

Alarm bells rang in my head. He was meeting someone for coffee? As in a *date*? Perhaps I should stick around to check out Cat's competition. But before I could say I had changed my mind, another thought occurred to me: Why would he invite me to have a latte if he had a date?

"Meeting someone?" I asked faux breezily. "Is that code for 'Tinder date'? Are you meeting someone from online?"

His cheeks colored, and that told me all I needed to know: he was definitely meeting a woman there, probably a first date. So the situation wasn't ideal—I didn't like that he was actively dating while referring to Cat as "great"—but it wasn't completely hopeless. I was an excellent matchmaker—I'd introduced Jasmine to her now-husband, Hannah to her boyfriend, and Tatiana to her girlfriend. (I couldn't—and gladly didn't—take credit for Izzy and Russell.) I knew I could do the same for Cat. She was a good friend, and I wanted to help her.

My phone buzzed, my reminder to get to spin class.

"I have to run, but it was nice bumping into you. We'll have to get together with Cat again," I said, fully intending to make plans and then bow out at the last minute, leaving the two of them on a surprise date.

"That would be great. See you around, Audrey."

I waved goodbye and walked to the intersection. While I waited to cross, I felt eyes boring into the back of my neck. I glanced over my shoulder at Connor, but he was preoccupied with his phone. I turned my attention back to the intersection, but as the light changed, I felt the same sensation once more. I hurried across the street and then whirled around, fully expecting to catch some creep ogling me.

Instead, I found my face just inches from Nick's strong chest.

"Nick!" I squealed, laughing with relief even as my heart continued to pound. "You scared me! Don't sneak up on me like that."

He smiled impishly. "You know how much I like to make you scream."

"You're bad," I said, socking him lightly in the stomach. "But what are you even doing over in this neighborhood? And don't say you're here to see me."

"Of course Little Ms. Vain thinks I'm here to see her," he joked, ruffling my hair. "Nah, babe. I'm meeting a buddy for a drink down the street. Want to join?"

"No way. The last time I joined you on one of your bro dates, I was subjected to two hours of nonstop fantasy football bullshit."

"I can assure you that won't happen this time," he said seriously before breaking into a huge grin. "It's fantasy baseball season."

"How tragic that I've already booked a bike and will have to miss out," I said with a roll of my eyes. "Have fun with your fake sports, nerd."

"Speaking of nerds," Nick said, nodding toward Connor, who was still engrossed in his phone outside Columbia Brews. "Who was that?"

"Just a friend of Cat's. You remember Cat from college?"

He snorted. "That weirdo? How could I forget?"

"Don't be an asshole, Nick. Cat's been good to me."

"Not as good as me," he said, wrapping a thick arm around my midsection and pulling me close.

"Don't," I protested, wriggling out of his grasp.

He blinked, his normally overly confident smile wavering. "Audrey—"

"Spin class, remember?" I danced a few steps away and then winked at him. "But maybe I'll see you tonight?"

His smile slowly returned. "I'll definitely see you."

CHAPTER FIFTEEN

HIM

Audrey stopped at Columbia Brews for an almond milk latte, her long-standing drink of choice, every morning on her way to work. I knew this both because I regularly posted the coffee shop to her Instagram Stories and because I was sometimes waiting for her there. I sat in the back with a book of poetry propped in front of my face, my hair concealed beneath a Nationals baseball cap. I was hiding, yes, but I was also daring her to notice me. Observing her like this was dangerous, I knew. If caught, I could be risking our entire future. But I couldn't help myself. I loved seeing her move through her daily routine.

I watched as she waited for that morning's almond milk latte, her elegant fingers tapping on her phone, pausing only to tuck some fiery strands of hair behind her ear.

A collection of tiny gold earrings glittered in the light, and my mouth ached to kiss her soft earlobes, to work my tongue around each and every one of those delicate golden rings.

When are you going to realize how much I love you?

Being this close to her and not telling her how much I worshipped her was sometimes so painful I could feel my bone marrow sizzling, and yet I continued to torture myself. Someday soon I would find the words to tell her how I felt, to tell her that we belonged together, hearts beating in tandem, forever.

I watched in despair as she walked out the door, drink in hand, head bent over her phone.

She was gone.

For now.

CHAPTER SIXTEEN

CAT

"Come on, Cat," Audrey's voice pleaded. "All work and no play makes Cat a dull girl."

Unbidden, Emily Snow manifested before me. Still a leggy thirteen years old and wearing her green-and-white Camp Blackwood T-shirt, she placed one dainty hand on a thin hip and used the other to toss corn-silk hair over her shoulder. *As if*, she sneered. *You're so dull.*

"Go away," I whispered to the apparition, squeezing my eyes shut.

"What did you say?"

I cracked an eye open and exhaled with relief. Emily was gone. She couldn't hurt me anymore. She couldn't hurt *anyone* anymore.

"Nothing," I said to Audrey, tucking my phone under

my chin and glancing at the stack of cases on my desk. "I was talking to my assistant. Anyway, I'm really sorry, but—"

"No way. I'm not taking no for an answer. You *have* to come celebrate me. A girl doesn't get featured as an 'Influencer to Watch' in *Glamour* every day."

"I know, and I'm thrilled—"

"Did you know I gained five thousand new followers today? *Five thousand.* This is huge, and, honestly, I think it's partially because you're rubbing off on me. All those nights you blow me off to work have inspired me to do the same. I totally owe you a glass of champagne or five. Hell, I owe you a whole bottle."

I didn't point out the irony in her logic that she was encouraging me to slack off on my assignments in order to celebrate her newly acquired work ethic. Instead, I said, "Let's have that bottle this weekend. Right now, I'm staring at a draft of a filing that's due on Friday and—"

"Friday?" she repeated. "That's four whole days away! Come on, Cat. Please? Celebration is nonoptional, and I can't do it alone. Meet me after work at Le Diplomate for a drink, okay? Just one, I promise."

My resolve crumbled. I knew how much Audrey hated being on her own. If I was a good friend, I should do what I could to spare her that discomfort. After all, she had always looked out for me. From that first day in the dorm's common room to that awful Bid Day to any number of times Audrey had made sure I was included, she always took care of me. She was a good friend, the best friend. The least I could do was have a drink with her.

* * *

HOURS LATER, I felt guilty as I hurried uptown. I'd gotten stuck on a conference call, and Audrey hadn't responded to my texts telling her I was running late. I imagined her sitting alone at the bar, glasses of champagne quickly losing their carbonation in front of her.

I should have known better.

When I stepped through the doors of the bustling French bistro, I glanced instinctively toward the bar but didn't see Audrey's vibrant hair. My stomach sank; I was too late. I scanned the rest of the room quickly, and there she was: seated in a corner booth with two glamorous women with impossibly perfect makeup, and a man in round tortoiseshell glasses who had his arm thrown around her. They were talking animatedly, each of them clutching a cocktail glass. One of the women lifted her drink in a toast, and, over the din of the restaurant, I heard her say in a British accent, "To Audrey!"

"Hi! How many are in your party?" the hostess asked me.

I stared at the hostess dumbly. I didn't know whether I should join Audrey's group or whether I should turn around and walk out. Audrey obviously didn't need me. I was a fool to think she ever did.

"Miss?" the hostess pressed.

"I'm just—" I began, backing away.

"Cat!" Audrey shouted suddenly, half standing and waving me over.

I felt impossibly unhip as I walked over to their table, suddenly very aware of the coffee stain on my faded Brooks Brothers shirt and the fact that my eyes were red and bleary from reviewing documents all day.

I reached up to pat my hair into place and found a pen stuck behind my ear. Blushing furiously, I shoved it into my bag.

"Hi," I said, forcing brightness as I approached the table. "Sorry, I got stuck at work, and—"

"Here," Audrey said, grabbing a martini glass filled with pink liquid from the table and pushing it into my hand. "Catch up."

"Thanks," I said uncertainly, checking the rim for lipstick marks.

"Everyone, this is my friend Cat," Audrey announced to the table. "Cat and I have been friends for, like, a million years. Cat, this is Lawrence, who works with me at the museum. And here's Keisha and Georgia, who are travel bloggers visiting from London. We connected over Instagram this afternoon."

"I love London," I said politely.

One of them took that as her cue to begin telling me about the best places to shop in London. I nodded along, hoping she couldn't tell I barely recognized any of the brand names she was dropping, and was glad when the conversation moved on to the bloggers' American itinerary. When the conversation then shifted to posting schedules and Google analytics, I felt my mind drifting to the pile of work in my shoulder bag. I was plotting my exit when Lawrence leaned toward me, eyes twinkling behind his glasses, and asked, "Has Audrey told you about the president of her fan club?"

I shot Audrey a glance. "You have a fan club?"

"It's a joke," she said with a forced-sounding laugh.

"There's this gallery closed for installation, right?" Lawrence said. "And on Audrey's first day, she found this rando in there. She kicked him out and gained a major fan in the process. Dude's been back *every single day* since. He just lurks around the halls, hoping for a glimpse of her. The rest of us have made spotting him into a game."

I raised my eyebrows in alarm. "Has anyone alerted security?"

"It's okay, Cat," Audrey said. "He's not dangerous. Just a little weird."

"You don't know that."

The table fell silent. Lawrence exchanged a look with one of the bloggers, a look that clearly implied I was no fun. Fine. Maybe I was no fun, but I also wasn't going to stand by while my best friend fell victim to some stalker just because everyone thought it was a *game*. Women were murdered by seemingly harmless "admirers" all the time because they were conditioned to not make a fuss.

"Promise me you'll talk to security," I insisted, ignoring Lawrence's rolling eyes.

Audrey patted my hand gently and effectively changed the subject by asking the bloggers when they planned to travel to New York. Twenty minutes later, Lawrence called it a night, giving Audrey a lingering kiss on the cheek, and Keisha and Georgia took off just after him. I was reaching for my bag, assuming Audrey would be ready to leave, too, but she flagged down the waiter and ordered us another round.

"Thanks for coming, Cat."

I released my bag. "Well, it's not every day your friend gets national recognition. Congratulations."

"It's more than that, though," she said, swirling the dregs of her drink. "I really couldn't stand the thought of being in that apartment alone another night, and I don't want to have Nick over again. It'll just inflate his ego, and you know it's big enough as it is."

"Wait a second. You've had Nick over? *Nick* Nick?"

Audrey tossed her hair and flashed me a devilish smirk. "That's the one. He lives here, you know."

"So do half a million other people," I said with a frown. I had never understood Audrey's attraction to Nick. He was good-looking, sure, but he had never been any more interesting or engaging than any other beer-bonging, pot-smoking frat boy. Audrey could have done so much better.

"Relax, Cat," Audrey said as the waiter placed fresh drinks in front of us. She seized hers and lifted it. "Anyway, let's not talk about Nick and my lack of love life. Let's talk about yours instead."

"There's not much to say about my lack of love life."

"Oh no?" she asked with a smirk. "What about Connor?"

My cheeks burned. "I've already told you. Connor's just a friend."

She laughed triumphantly. "Cat, you have the worst poker face! Every time you talk about him your eyes go heart-shaped. So what's the story?"

The story was that I had been helplessly enamored of Connor since first semester of law school. I'd just concluded an argument in torts class when this tall, handsome man in the back of the room raised his hand and began, "But to play devil's advocate . . ." I met his warm hazel eyes across the room, and all reason left me. I stopped listening to his counterargument and started planning out the next few decades of our lives.

But as long as I had been nurturing that crush,

I'd never admitted it aloud, and so I automatically said, "There's no story."

"Like hell there isn't. Come on, Cat. If you can't tell me, who can you tell?"

I looked into Audrey's open face and realized she was right. She was my best friend. Finally, I had someone I could confide in again.

"We kissed once," I admitted, a flush warming my chest as I remembered the soft pads of his fingers caressing my jawline, the wet warmth of his mouth.

"Just once? What happened after that?"

"We sobered up. It was at a party celebrating our law school graduation. We'd both had too much to drink and . . . it just happened. But then we were consumed with bar studying, and then Connor moved to Idaho for a clerkship."

"Okay, but *now* you're both here. Working in the same office, even. And you're *obviously* still into him."

"We're just friends, Audrey."

"Yeah, currently," she said with a giggle. "But did I tell you what he said about you?"

"What?" I asked, heartbeat suddenly pounding in my ears. "No. When did you talk to Connor?"

"I ran into him the other day on the street. We got to talking, and he said he thinks you're great."

I sagged, pulse still racing. "That doesn't mean anything."

"It was the *way* he said it," she said confidently. "Trust me. So what are you going to do about it?"

"What do you mean?"

"Cat! He clearly wants you. And you clearly want him." She laughed and shook her head. "Hon, you are so lucky that we're best friends."

Audrey began laying out a plan to help me "land" Connor, a plan that seemed hinged upon heavy spending at Nordstrom, Sephora, and the salon, but I was fixated on her word choice: *best friends.* I'd always considered Audrey my best friend, but she always reserved the honorific for her childhood friend Izzy. Hearing her say we were "best friends" warmed every corner of my heart.

"Trust me, Cat," she said. "You're going to be like a different person when I'm through with you."

CHAPTER SEVENTEEN

AUDREY

Smudging a new home with a clump of burning sage was painfully trendy and more than a little woo-woo, but still I found myself circling the basket of smudge sticks at Urban Outfitters. I had spent an hour wandering around inside the Georgetown CB2, testing out different couches and lusting after light fixtures, but had walked away without purchasing anything. My lack of furniture was getting ridiculous, I knew, but I still couldn't commit to a couch. It was an anchoring piece, something that set the tone for the entire room—and since I planned to escape my basement apartment as soon as possible, it would need to be something that wouldn't look out of place in a larger apartment. Overcome with indecision, I put a pin in the furniture buying and popped into

Urban, ostensibly to look at some patterned pillows I saw featured on another woman's Instagram. I wouldn't buy the same pillows, obviously—I was no follower—but I thought there might be something else I would like.

I was underwhelmed by the pillow selection but intrigued by the smudge sticks, imagining how dramatic the smoke would look on camera; it would make for a great series of photographs. The smudging itself would make good blog content, too—people were really into Wicca and other mystic shit. I got at least a dozen comments each week inquiring whether I had tried crystals or had my chakras aligned.

Why not? I thought, picking up a smudge stick and carrying it to the register.

I'd thus far avoided filming much inside the apartment. I didn't want my followers to see how little progress I'd made on unpacking—especially after I'd done that Live where I talked about getting started on the boxes. I couldn't bring myself to unpack, though, because I knew I could find someplace better as soon as I marshaled the resolve to spend a day sifting through ads on Craigslist and Zillow. Besides, style was the bedrock upon which I'd constructed my whole image, and I knew my followers expected me to live somewhere more chic than this bare basement apartment. With that in mind, I returned to CB2 and purchased a matte-black table lamp and a polished silver side table I had been eyeing.

At home, I wiped down the walls and baseboards in the sunniest corner of my subterranean living room, arranged my new purchases, and topped the table with a bright bouquet of flowers from Whole Foods. The tableau made the apartment look charming and inviting . . . so long as you narrowed your field of vision to that one portion of the apartment. The rest remained crowded with boxes, but I would address that later. My more immediate concern was generating new content for my followers, an inclination that gave me pause. I'd watched so many of my online friends become fixated on polishing their lives to attract lucrative sponsorships only to lose their authenticity—and their followers. I was careful to remain myself online—an amplified version of myself, sure, but *myself*—and I was rewarded by a devoted fan base. I knew I could make bank if I started aggressively monetizing my online presence, but there was no way I was selling my soul to corporate sponsors. I wanted to remain true to myself, and, more important, I wanted to have a shred of dignity left when the influencer bubble inevitably burst.

I cast an appraising eye over my handiwork. Something was still missing. I thought for a moment and then dug through a box until I'd found my grandmother's ashtray. Granny Wanda had smoked like a chimney—as a girl I'd been convinced she was part dragon—and her beautiful cornflower-blue ashtray with its inside crisscrossed with delicate gold lines was always within arm's reach. It was the only thing I had wanted after she had passed on, and I had kept it by my bed as a catchall ever since.

I reverently placed the ashtray on the table in front of the flowers and then balanced the smudge stick on the ashtray. I snapped a few pictures with my DSLR, then ignited the stick and took a few more. I reviewed the images on the camera and smiled. I had been right; there was something alluring and beautiful about the smoke curling up from the shot. The brilliant blue of the ashtray provided a necessary pop of color in an otherwise mono-chrome setting. It was an arresting image.

I put down my camera in favor of my iPhone and shot some video of myself wafting the smudge stick through the air—carefully keeping the angle tight so as not to reveal the mound of boxes. I checked the results. All good. I fluffed my hair and went live.

"Hey, everyone! Guess what I'm doing!" I held up the smoldering sage and wafted it back and forth in front of my face. The smoke made my eyes water, and I blinked as I set it back down in the ashtray. "I'm smudging my new apartment. Have any of you ever smudged your homes? I'd love to hear about it!"

I grinned as comments started rolling across the screen.

> Love smudging!
>
> Great lamp!
>
> hi audrey!

"Shoot me a message and let me know if you have any great smudging tips!" I continued. "I'm a newbie."

> I like the table. Much better choice than that marble one.

I caught my breath. In the years I'd been sharing my life on the internet, I had received hundreds, if not thousands, of creepy, weird, and downright disgusting comments. I was largely immune to them, including the truly upsetting ones (even "your eyeballs would look perfect on my nightstand" had only bothered me for thirty minutes), but this one sent a real chill down my spine. I *had* been admiring a marble end table at CB2. Had someone been *watching* me?

I suddenly realized I hadn't said anything for several seconds and forced myself back into action. Smiling hard to conceal my uneasiness, I said, "All right, guys, I've got to go and drive the negative energy out of this place! But send me your smudging stories! Talk soon."

Hands shaking, I disconnected the livestream and watched the Stories I'd made about my shopping trip. There I was, meandering around the store without a care in the world—completely oblivious to someone who might have been following me—and giving a running commentary on pieces I liked. I relaxed when I saw myself trail fingertips along the smooth marble surface of a low-slung coffee table. So that was it. The commenter had seen it in my Stories.

But I didn't say anything about that table, I thought uneasily. *How would they have known I was seriously considering it unless they'd been there to overhear my conversation with the salesman?*

I brushed the concerns aside, certain I was being paranoid. Just because I hadn't specifically mentioned a table didn't mean a commenter couldn't have an opinion on it. Or, who knows, maybe that commenter really had seen me in the store—that didn't mean they were *watching* me. I had followers all over the world; I was sure I had several thousand here in DC. Maybe one of them happened to be there at that moment.

Maybe.

I went to extinguish the smoldering sage but hesitated. I didn't believe for a second that the bundle of herbs had mystical cleansing properties, but waving it around couldn't hurt. Just in case. I carried it around the apartment, self-consciously exorcising any lurking bad vibes.

TWO HOURS LATER, I arrived home from a Reformer Pilates class feeling strong and energized. I loved working out on Reformer machines, but at around forty dollars per class, they weren't part of my normal routine. After the weird comment about the table, I'd decided to treat myself and then bonded with the studio owner over the fact that we'd both lived in New York before moving to DC. I walked out with a verbal agreement for fifteen sessions in exchange for an Insta post featuring her studio and the possibility of additional classes for more publicity. Like the professional I was, I promised to send her a contract later that night.

I was mentally modifying my standard contract as I unlocked my front door, and so I didn't notice it at first. It wasn't until I reached my bedroom that I smelled it.

The sage.

It was burning.

I looked wildly around the room and spotted the smudge stick balancing precariously on a wineglass set atop the cardboard box beside my bed, smoke curling from the dwindling bundle. My heart leaped as I snatched it and rushed to the kitchen sink. I dropped the smoldering herbs inside and turned on the faucet, extinguishing it.

Still shaking, I returned to the bedroom and stared at the small pile of ash beside the wineglass. On the *cardboard. Jesus Christ.* I could have caused a fire. I could have burned down the entire fucking building. Why would I even leave the sage there in the first place?

I hadn't, had I?

I tried to retrace my steps. After I turned off the livestream, I had carried the sage around the apartment, swirling the smoke in corners and generally acting like a loon. I had finished the bogus ritual in the bedroom; I remembered that. I also remembered setting the sage on the wineglass—*momentarily*—while I fielded a quick FaceTime from my mom, who'd wanted help deciding which shoes to wear to her book club.

But then I had picked it up.

Hadn't I?

I was sure I had. I was sure I had picked it up and carried it back into the living room, stubbing it out in Granny Wanda's ashtray.

At least I thought I had.

CHAPTER EIGHTEEN

CAT

I've often thought of myself as something of a Franken-
stein's monster. My individual pieces might be fine on
their own—my thick hair, my long legs—but the overall
effect is off-putting. I *should* be pretty, but I'm not.

I used to assign blame to specific characteristics: my
teeth weren't straight enough; my skin was bad. My parents took me to an orthodontist and a dermatologist, as
well as an aesthetician to address what my mother called
my "masculine brows" (a feature I hadn't thought to
worry over until that moment), and I still wasn't satisfied.
When I hit a growth spurt the summer before ninth grade
and rocketed up six inches in the span of three months,
baby fat distributing in the process, I was relieved. My
face might still have its flaws, but my newly convention-

ally attractive body would surely be my ticket to popularity. Boys would ask me out; girls would no longer torment me for sport.

I was wrong.

I didn't understand how my body's metamorphosis could fail to translate into increased social standing until I met Audrey. Objectively, she was no great beauty. She was unusually short, with red hair, freckles, and a sharp chin; there was something foxlike in her appearance. She had one bicuspid that turned inward and a crooked smile to conceal it, and she was quick to develop dark, bruise-like circles under her eyes. If you were to score us on discrete physical attributes, I might rate more highly than Audrey.

And yet she captivated people. Audrey turned every head in every room she ever entered, and people fell all over themselves to be in her presence. I studied her, trying to understand what made her so utterly bewitching. After weeks of careful observation, I finally concluded it was indefinable. Audrey *sparkled* and that was all there was to it.

Knowing I would never possess even a fraction of Audrey's innate charm was somehow freeing, allowing me to stop trying to emulate her and to instead focus my energy on things that were in my control, like my education and my career. I was proud of what I'd accomplished, and greatly enjoyed updating my LinkedIn page with new achievements: big cases on which I'd worked, articles I'd written for legal journals. I might not ever hold a roomful of people in my thrall like Audrey could, but I would impress the right audience.

Still, I wanted more. I longed to be the delicate,

romantic heroine setting my prince's heart aflutter. So when Audrey suggested doing my hair and makeup before trivia, I agreed with only the briefest hesitation. I left work at five o'clock for the first time in my professional life, leaving my office light on and sneaking into the elevator when no one was looking, and was waiting with a stomach full of nerves when Audrey arrived at my apartment thirty minutes later. It was silly to expect she could transfer some of her je ne sais quoi to me through a swipe of mascara, and yet I was hopeful.

She greeted me with a frown. "That's not what you're planning on wearing, is it?"

I glanced down at the gray J.Crew sheath I'd worn to work, trying to see it through Audrey's eyes. It had always been one of my favorite dresses, an understated, easy piece with a matching suit jacket, but now I realized how boring it was.

"Of course not," I said.

Her light eyes twinkled as she laughed. "Liar. But don't worry. I'm here to help."

From her bag, Audrey produced a black T-shirt with a plunging neckline.

"I can't wear this," I told her. "There's no way I can pull it off."

"You absolutely can."

"No, Audrey—"

"It'll look great on you," she interrupted. "Come on, Kitty-Cat. Trust me."

I eyed the shirt nervously, imagining my thin, pale chest exposed by the expansive V-neck. How would that be appealing to Connor?

"You trust me, don't you?" she pressed.

I *wanted* to trust Audrey. I *wanted* to believe she could work a miracle.

"Of course," I finally said. "I trust you."

AUDREY SET UP her laptop on my bathroom counter and began searching for YouTube videos on eyebrow shaping. Shame burned in my chest as she clicked through video after video, a pair of neon-pink tweezers in her hand.

"Sorry about these masculine brows," I murmured, running my fingers over them self-consciously.

"Are you kidding? You have *amazing* brows."

I searched her face for signs of sarcasm, but saw none.

"I would *kill* for strong brows like yours. That's why I'm looking up these videos—I want to make sure I'm doing you justice. I only have these little scraggly things to work with."

I studied Audrey's eyebrows, realizing with surprise that they weren't the perfect, tawny arches they appeared to be. They were sparser than I thought, filled in with pencil and powder.

"Your eyebrows look great," I said honestly.

"It's all smoke and mirrors," she said, taking hold of my face in one hand. "Now don't move."

AS AUDREY SMOOTHED creamy foundation over my skin, I couldn't help but think of Emily Snow daubing Cover Girl on my face in our cabin. *Look at you*, she'd chirped. *Just like a model.*

I shuddered.

"Hold still," Audrey said. "Unless you want makeup in your eye. Then you do you."

"Sorry."

"Suck in your cheeks," she ordered, picking up a peachy-pink blush and a fluffy brush.

I complied, contorting my face and closing my eyes as Audrey dusted me with color. Next came contouring powder, multiple eye shadows, eyeliner, false eyelashes, mascara, brow pencil, brow gel, highlighter, and lip gloss, after which she turned to my hair. She smoothed a glossy serum through my mane and then twisted a few face-framing pieces with a curling wand.

She took a step back and studied me for a moment before breaking into a huge smile. "Take a look! What do you think?"

With trepidation, I rose and turned to the bathroom mirror. I gasped. Audrey had used so many products I'd expected to look like a pageant contestant, but I didn't. I looked like myself, only better, as if I were lit from within.

"You're a magician," I said, astonished at the subtle changes to my face.

"I know, right?" she said, raising her phone and pointing it at me.

Instinctively, I twisted away and shielded my face. "What are you doing?"

"Posting my handiwork on Insta," she said as if it was the most natural thing in the world. "Come on, move your hand."

"Don't."

"Really?" she asked, sounding annoyed. "You're not seriously still that phobic about social media, are you?"

It was the same tone of voice she'd used the first time

I stopped her from posting my image on social media. All throughout college, I'd let her paper the internet with pictures of me, pictures in which I looked less than perfect while she was smiling flirtatiously. But then, during Jasmine's bachelorette party, I'd gotten a notification that Audrey had tagged me on Facebook. I'd looked at the photo and choked on my pink champagne.

"Take that down!" I had demanded. "I'm interviewing with law firms next month. I can't have a picture of me wearing a penis necklace on the internet."

"Relax, Kitty-Cat. It's obviously a bachelorette party. They're not going to think you'll, like, show up in court wearing it or something."

"Law firms are conservative," I'd insisted, ripping off the flimsy necklace as my panic grew. "I need you to take it down. *Now.*"

Audrey had made a show of rolling her eyes, but she complied. After that, I stripped my Facebook profile and locked it down. I knew Audrey didn't mean any harm; she just didn't understand why I wouldn't want that picture online, just as I didn't understand her seemingly pathological need to share every detail of her existence. How could I explain to someone like Audrey that social media reminded me of a high school cafeteria, a place where you and your vulnerabilities were on full display for the jackals who were your compatriots? I couldn't release my hopeful, made-up face for their consumption. I couldn't put myself through that again.

"You're being silly," she said, aiming the phone at me once more.

"Don't!" I shouted, the alarm in my voice surprising us both.

She lowered the phone. "What's going on?"

I drew a shaky breath as I gathered myself. "I . . . I don't want people to make fun of me."

"What?" she asked, looking genuinely puzzled. "Cat, no one's going to make fun of you. You're a total babe."

I shook my head. "You don't get it. How could you? Everyone loves you."

"Everyone loves me?" she echoed in disbelief. "That's a joke, right? Have you ever read the comments on my Insta posts? Did you know there's an entire thread on Reddit devoted to what a self-obsessed airhead I am? Here, let me pull that up for you."

"Don't," I said, putting out a hand to stop her from typing on her phone. "I get it. But, Audrey . . . that's different. So a handful of people on the internet are giving you a hard time. You still have, what, thousands of followers—"

"A million," she corrected me.

"Right. Exactly. You still have a million followers hanging on to your every word. And that's just online. Wherever you go, people love you. That's not how it is for me." I took a deep breath and turned my eyes to the ceiling, trying to stop the tears from ruining my flawless makeup. "It's never been that way for me."

"Cat, you have plenty of friends. I mean, we're going to trivia to see a bunch of them right now."

I leveled my face at her. "I have a few friends because I work hard at it. Social graces don't come easy to me. They never have. You know that."

"Cat—"

"Stop pretending otherwise, Audrey. It's disingenuous." I put my thumb in my mouth and bit down hard, the pain drowning out the aching memories. "Don't you remember when we met?"

"Sure. What about it?"

"You didn't think . . . ?" I tasted blood suddenly and removed my thumb from my mouth, tucking it inside my fist. "Come on, Audrey. Why did you decide to be friends with me?"

"Cat . . ."

"Tell me. You and I both know how awkward I was. Why did you decide to be friends with me? No one else did."

Audrey's aqua-blue eyes flashed briefly, a dare, and then she looked away. "Just remember you asked for this, okay?"

I nodded and steeled myself for the worst.

"I went to high school with this girl named Tara. She was . . . well, she was *weird*. She never washed her hair and she shopped at Goodwill, but not in a cool way, you know what I mean? She was a punch line for our whole class." Audrey paused and studied her nails, frowning at a chip in the gold polish. "Senior year, my biology teacher, this vindictive troll of a woman who'd always had it out for me, I swear to God, assigned Tara to be my lab partner. And . . . I mean, I just lost it. Trust me, I know how it sounds now, but at the time I really couldn't imagine anything worse. What if we, you know, had to study together outside of class? What if people saw us? What if they thought we were *friends*? God, it would have *ruined* my social life. Or, I mean, I thought it would have. I was being dramatic, I know, but I was seventeen years old, so cut me some slack." She glanced quickly at me, ready to defend herself, but I said nothing. She sighed and continued.

"Anyway, Tara was nothing but nice to me, and I . . . I just was *mean*. Like, I barely spoke to her, would only answer direct questions. Mostly, I just rolled my eyes at her and called her stupid. And . . . um, well, I started spreading these rumors. I told everyone that her parents were cousins and that was why she was so stupid."

My heart clenched. I knew what it felt like to be the Tara of the story. I knew the desperation, the feeling that you would do anything—*anything*—to escape the torment.

"I don't know what I was thinking. I was just . . . well, anyway, Tara took an overdose of her mother's sleeping pills." Audrey noted my shocked expression and quickly added, "She's fine. I saw her on Facebook a couple of months ago, and she's an executive with some tech company out in California. She's doing well for herself. But at the time, I felt *awful*."

"You should have," I said, still aghast.

"I know. Trust me, I know. And so I decided to be different. I wasn't going to be that sort of mean girl anymore."

Suddenly, I remembered why Audrey was telling this story, and sour saliva filled my mouth.

"Wait a second. So what you're telling me is that you're friends with me as a way to atone for bullying some poor girl into attempting suicide?"

"Jesus, Cat. No. That's not what I meant. I just meant that the thing with Tara made me more aware of other people's feelings. I started to pay more attention to those in the room who might need a friend." She looked at me baldly. "And you, Kitty-Cat, needed a friend."

"What about now?" I asked hesitantly. "Is that why we're friends now? Because you think I need someone?"

Audrey looped an arm around my shoulders and grinned. "Don't be silly. You know why we're friends. Besides, you have more people in this city who love you than I do."

CHAPTER NINETEEN

HIM

If you asked the regular commenters on the Over-exposed forums, no worse place exists to meet a woman than in a bar. To an extent, I agreed: the floors are sticky with spilled drinks, the music drowns out any chance of meaningful conversation, and the air of desperation hangs heavy. But I disagreed with the party line that the only women you'll meet in bars are promiscuous binge drinkers who use alcohol as a substitute for personality. I knew that wasn't the truth. After all, Audrey frequented bars and she wasn't promiscuous or a binge drinker. She was just social.

Bars and parties had always been part of her life, for as long as I had been following her. Her college blog had been chronicles of one party after another, and when she lived in New York, her Instagram feed involved a regular rotation of artistic craft cocktails, mint sprigs sticking jauntily up from highball glasses, rocks glasses with enormous square ice cubes. The images were so impeccable that if they had been posted by anyone else, I would have sneered, imagining them selecting their drink to match a color scheme and micromanaging the bartender in order to obtain that perfectly coiled lemon peel garnish. I knew that wasn't how Audrey operated, though. Beauty simply came to her. Like attracts like.

Now that she lived in DC, however, the fashionable cocktails in her feed began giving way to Stories showing draft beers and house wines from trivia night. Those images might not have been as photogenic as the cocktails of the past, but they didn't dim her sparkling persona one bit. She remained the brightest light in the room, the sun around which the rest of us orbited.

I watched her standing at the bar, her small, bejeweled hands toying with the stem of her empty wineglass. I knew I shouldn't stare, knew that it would be all over if she caught me, but I was powerless to drag my eyes away from her. Her skin, glistening faintly, looked as though it were covered in millions of tiny diamonds. She shook her head and her glorious mane rippled, shimmering like it was spliced through with spun gold. She was stunning, a physical punch in the gut. It took all the strength I had to not seize her around her dainty waist and bend her sylph-like body backward as passion overtook us both.

I swallowed hard and pressed my hands firmly against my sides to prevent them from reaching for her.

Soon, I promised myself. *Soon*.

CHAPTER TWENTY

AUDREY

I tried to hide my aggravation as I stood up from the booth. I couldn't sit there and watch Cat stare down at the scratched tabletop all night and offer meek, monosyllabic answers whenever Connor spoke directly to her. That wasn't why I'd painstakingly glued individual false lashes to her eyes.

"Where are you going?" Cat asked, panic threading her voice.

"To the jukebox," I said faux breezily. "If I hear 'Tiny Dancer' one more time, I'm going to murder someone."

I stalked away, silently adding that the *someone* I would be murdering would be Cat if she couldn't get her shit together. Honestly, sometimes she had the personality of a baked potato.

Be nice, I admonished myself. I didn't know why I expected anything different. Cat had never been good at flirting, not even at college parties that were little more than Bacchanalian mating rituals set to pop music.

As I stood at the jukebox, considering the Tom Petty offerings, a large hand clamped down on my shoulder. I whirled around to find Connor grinning broadly at me. I glanced behind him in the direction of the booth.

"Where's Cat?"

"She had to go to the restroom."

Of course she did. It was literally painful not to roll my eyes at Cat's cowardice.

"Here, let's get some Journey in there," Connor said, leaning around me to touch the screen. "'Don't Stop Believin'' is my karaoke jam of choice."

Despite myself, I groaned. "Oh, man, we have to find you some new material."

"What's wrong with 'Don't Stop Believin''?" He sang the first couple of lines for my benefit, as though I had mistaken it for another song.

"Nothing. It's just *everyone's* karaoke song. I mean, be a little more basic, Connor."

"Ouch, that hurts," he said teasingly. "But I'll let it slide. You know, even though you wound me with that sharp tongue of yours, I'm glad you came tonight."

"Yeah, without me, your team wouldn't have gotten that answer about Kanye," I joked. "You're desperate for someone up on Kardashian-adjacent trivia."

"That's not the only reason," he said, his voice going husky and his eyelids lowering.

Too late, I realized he intended to kiss me.

"Connor, no," I said, pushing him away.

"Wait, Audrey, I—"

"I'm going back to the table," I said firmly, stepping around him. "Cat's waiting."

"Audrey," Connor started, putting his hand on my arm. I shook him off and walked briskly to the booth, where Cat sat alone.

"How was the jukebox?" she asked.

I glanced uneasily at Connor, who smiled guilelessly. I knew I had to tell Cat that Connor made a pass at me. She was my friend—right then, she was my *best* friend— and she deserved to know that the man she was interested in was pressing himself against other women in bars.

But how could I tell her that after she'd laid bare her insecurities? After everything she'd said about her low self-esteem and her mistaken belief that everyone loved me, how could I tell her that Connor had tried to kiss me?

For her protection, I swallowed my bitter discontent and said, "Great. The music selection should improve shortly."

She smiled, and I felt like a traitor as I smiled back. But what else could I do? I knew how fragile Cat was.

I INVENTED A HEADACHE as an excuse to leave the bar. I couldn't spend another minute there, couldn't watch Cat pine after this guy who wasn't into her and who, frankly, wasn't that attractive anyway. And I couldn't tell her that he wasn't worth her time, not without having to tell her about what had transpired at the jukebox, and I really, really didn't want to tell her that.

I couldn't break her heart like that. Not again. Even though this thing with Connor was decidedly *not* my fault, I worried that Cat would see parallels to the Bruce Gellar incident from sophomore year. Back then, Cat had a crush on this guy Bruce, who was cute in a very Jim-from–*The Office* way, but who also was an idiot who kept a three-foot bong named after a porn star in his room and who had a broken arm from jumping off the frat house roof two weeks prior. He was a bad match for sweet, studious Cat, and I told her so. I assumed she agreed, so later when Bruce went to kiss me at a party, I didn't think twice. Like I said, he was cute, and I was soaked through with spiced rum and THC. It was one dumb little kiss, but the way Cat reacted you would have thought I'd married the guy. For weeks afterward, I'd felt the fury pulsating off her in waves. If Cat could generate so much anger over some dopey stoner, I could only imagine how enraged she would be about Connor, this man whom she'd been obsessed with for something like seven years.

As I stalked home, I grew more and more frustrated with Connor for ruining the evening. Why couldn't he have responded to Cat's overtures like a normal man? She was textbook hot—maybe a little awkward, sure, but so was he—and she was plainly into him. So why had he come on to me instead? I hated him for reinforcing Cat's stupid theory that everyone fell at my feet and was repulsed by her. It wasn't true, and I worried it was driving us apart. And I couldn't lose Cat, not when she was the only real friend I had in this city. It was so unfair that *Connor* was the one who had made a mess of everything, and yet *I* was the one who had been chased from the bar, who would now have to spend the rest of the night alone and angry.

Or, I thought as I reached my gate, *I don't* have *to be alone. Cat might be my only real friend here, but she's not actually my only friend.*

FIVE MINUTES LATER, Nick was sauntering through my front door, toothpaste-commercial smile gleaming.

"That was fast," I observed.

"When the lady beckons," he said, tipping an imaginary hat to me. "Actually, I was already in the neighborhood."

"Lucky me," I said, wrapping my arms around his torso and burying my face in his chest. I inhaled, filling my nostrils with the familiar scent of Nick's musky, slightly spicy cologne and the faintest hint of beer. It was a combination that reminded me of simpler times—sitting on Nick's lap at football games, cuddling in his bed on lazy Sunday mornings and watching DVR-ed *SNL*—and made me glad I had called him.

"I'll show you lucky," he said, voice low as he captured my face in his hands and covered my mouth with his, ending all conversation.

LATER, NICK AND I lay side by side in bed on our phones. Nick was texting with his friends about some sports something or other, and I was composing an Instagram Story about the night, trying to figure out how to share the evening with my followers without revealing how it had ended in disaster—or how I had salvaged it by calling my ex-boyfriend.

"Oh, hey," Nick said, looking up suddenly. "I just remembered. My mom wants to see you."

"Your mom?" I asked, putting down my phone. "Why?"

"She always liked you," he said with a shrug. "She knows you moved to town, and she thought you might come over for dinner sometime."

"Oh," I said noncommittally. The last thing I wanted to do was have dinner with Nick's family, his mother especially. I'd met her a few times when Nick and I were dating, and the elegant but frosty woman had seemingly taken an uncomfortable shine to me. She'd run her hands through my hair, leaving it lightly smeared with her rose-scented hand cream and getting the strands caught on her cocktail rings, and begun talking about future holidays spent together. She'd thought our relationship was more serious than it was back then; I didn't want to know what she thought about it these days.

"I'm pretty busy with work right now," I added, "but maybe sometime."

Nick nodded and returned to his phone. Relieved I had dodged that bullet, I lifted my own phone and went back to work on my Stories. My heart twisted when I saw an image of Cat's happy, hopeful face, and I sighed heavily.

"Something wrong?" Nick asked, glancing over at me. "Is this about my mom? Because, Audrey, you don't have—"

"No, it's just . . ." I started, then trailed off. "Nick, do you think I'm a bad friend?"

"Babe, I'm in your bed," he said, smirking. "I think you're the very *best* kind of friend."

"I'm serious," I said, lightly punching his arm. "My decades-long friendship with Izzy just completely disintegrated. And then there's this thing with Cat—"

Nick interrupted me with a groan. "I can't believe you're friends with that girl. She's so weird."

"Don't be mean. Anyway, you haven't seen her in years. She's changed a lot since college."

"I'll believe that once I see it. What's this 'thing' that happened?"

"I went to trivia with her tonight—"

Nick laughed. "Is *that* why you're always at trivia night? I've seen you post about it and wondered if you'd been taken hostage." His voice turned slightly mocking. "It seemed a little *off-brand* for Audrey Miller."

"You're right, okay?" I said, pinching him playfully. "But I've been going for Cat. She has this crush on some guy on her trivia team, but . . . well, tonight he tried to kiss *me*."

Nick's golden eyebrows arched. "Did you kiss him back?"

"Of course not."

"But what? Cat thinks you did?"

"No," I said, shaking my head. "I don't think that Cat even knows he tried to kiss me."

"So what's the problem?"

I wrapped a lock of hair around my finger, pulling it tighter and tighter as I considered how to articulate what was bothering me. As the tip of my finger turned red, I said, "I guess the problem is that I don't know *why* he tried to kiss me. Like, why did he think I would reciprocate? Did he think I had been flirting with him? *Had* I been flirting with him? Am I the kind of woman who flirts with her friend's crush?"

"You think too much," Nick said, gently unwinding

the hair from my finger and twisting it around his instead. "He tried to kiss you because you're hot. Full stop."

"Yeah?"

"Yeah," he said, tugging lightly on my hair. "But I don't like the idea of other guys trying to put their filthy mouths on you."

I laughed and pushed him away. "Oh, come off it, Nicky. I don't belong to you."

He growled low in his throat and rolled on top of me, pinning my hands down to the bed. "Tonight you do."

"YOU'VE POSTED about this coffee shop so many times I feel like I've been here myself," Nick joked as we joined the queue at Columbia Brews. "Are they paying you for all that publicity? Should I alert the FCC?"

"You know, that's not a half-bad idea. If I could work out a partnership with them, then maybe I wouldn't have to spend half my paycheck just to sustain my caffeine addiction."

"Have you considered investing in a coffeemaker?" he asked wryly.

"Considered and rejected. Come on, how aspirational is brewing your own coffee? I've got to think of my followers!" I teased.

He chuckled and shook his head. "You're a real piece of work, Aud."

Out of the corner of my eye, I saw the door swing open and a tall man stride in. My laughter caught in my throat. Even with his face partially concealed by a Nationals baseball cap, I recognized Connor.

Clutching Nick's arm, I hissed, "Don't look now, but the guy I was telling you about last night just came in."

"Where?" Nick asked, immediately twisting toward the door.

"Dammit, Nick," I muttered as Connor looked up and directly at us. Our eyes met, and he smiled. He removed his hat and ran a hand through his thick, sandy blond hair as he approached.

"Audrey, hi. How's your head feeling?"

I ignored Nick's questioning look and touched my forehead lightly, squinting as if the light hurt. "Better, thanks."

"Great, I'm glad to hear that." He glanced at Nick and then back to me, clearly expecting an introduction. I had no intention of prolonging our conversation and was about to dismiss him when he took matters into his own hands. Turning to Nick, he said, "Hey, I'm Connor."

"Nick," Nick said, throwing a casually possessive arm around my shoulders. Any other time, I would have knocked Nick's arm away—I hadn't liked that proprietorial move when we were dating, either—but I didn't want Connor to think I was doing it for his benefit. For all I cared, Connor could think I'd been up all night, clawing at Nick's back with him pulling my hair—which, of course, was exactly how I had spent the evening.

Connor remained in front of us, smiling dopily, like he was waiting for an explanation or something. I felt myself growing angry. *Cat* was the one who deserved an explanation. It was *so obvious* she was in love with him, so outrageously obvious that even my four-month-old nephew who was just discovering his own feet would have been able to recognize it. I was gearing up to say something biting to him when the barista called, "Next!"

Relieved, I offered Connor a fake smile. "See you around."

"*That* was the guy who tried to kiss you?" Nick snorted, making no effort to lower his voice as I tugged him toward the counter. "Babe, you're so far out of his league."

I elbowed Nick sharply in the ribs and cast a quick glance over my shoulder to see if Connor had heard him. He was looking at me with an unreadable expression on his face. For reasons I didn't totally understand, I shivered.

CHAPTER TWENTY-ONE

CAT

I turned over a bottle of shimmery nail polish to read the name. *Kiss Me Coral.* I shuddered and could hear Audrey's voice in my head, instructing me to get the brighter color, to be bold, be someone different. Easy for her to say. Audrey didn't have to be someone different to get what she wanted.

Or what anyone else wanted.

I should have known better than to invite Audrey to trivia. How could I have forgotten what it felt like to be compared to her? Audrey eclipsed everyone within a hundred-foot radius; she always had. How could I have expected Connor to notice me with Audrey in the picture?

I didn't tell Audrey that I saw her with Connor. I'd

just returned to the booth, fresh from reapplying the lip gloss Audrey had lent me and giving myself a pep talk, only to find Connor missing. I'd glanced toward the juke-box, looking for Audrey, and that's when I saw him lean-ing toward her. Tears blurred my vision, and I had averted my eyes. When I dared look again, she was shoving him away, and I was pleasantly surprised to see she was doing the right thing. I couldn't have always said that about her.

It was stupid of me to think I could have Connor. We had known each other for years, had weathered plenty of all-nighter study sessions and work-related fire drills together. If Connor thought of me as anything more than a friend, he'd had ample opportunity to make that known. Our relationship had remained strictly platonic, aside from that one drunken kiss.

It had been four years ago, the night we finished the last of our law school finals. Too many of us were crammed into our friend Betsy's tiny apartment, giddy with having survived law school and drunk on cheap beer. Things had started innocently enough: Connor and I had been sitting beside each other on Betsy's cat hair–covered couch, as we often did, when his leg brushed against mine. Normally, I would have adjusted to give him more room, but that night everything felt different. School was over; the possibilities were endless. And so I kept my leg where it was, our denim-clad thighs touching. Connor's leg pressed more firmly against mine, and he threw his arm along the back of the couch, resting his fingertips on the back of my neck. He gently traced small circles on my skin, and I was so thrilled I nearly blacked out.

I shifted slightly so that we were sitting even closer, our arms now touching, and he abruptly rose from the couch. Immediately, I felt sick, sure I had misread something and had weirded him out. *Stupid*, I thought to myself. *Stupid, stupid, stupid. This is why no one likes you.*

But then Connor's hazel eyes met mine and he raised his eyebrows ever so slightly before walking to the bathroom. I glanced around the room, and once I had confirmed that no one was paying attention, I stood and followed him. My hand on the doorknob, I paused. What if I had imagined his silent message? What if he was just using the bathroom for its intended purpose? I almost backed away, but the magic of the evening compelled me to twist the knob.

The second I did so, Connor thrust open the door and grabbed my arm, pulling me inside and shutting the door behind me. Suddenly we were kissing, his tongue colliding with mine and his hands on my body and all I could think was *It's happening, it's finally happening.*

But then someone was trying the knob, and we broke apart, panting and smoothing our clothing back into place. Without a word to me, Connor opened the bathroom door and loudly said, "Thanks for getting that out of my eye, Harrell."

He didn't look at me again as he strode back into the thick of the party, falling easily into a conversation about baseball with some of our classmates. I stood there, unsure what had just happened, unable to process the knowledge that Connor's tongue had been inside my mouth, and that it no longer was.

Look at me, I thought desperately. *Just look at me and give me some sign that we're in this together.*

He didn't look at me, not even when I gathered my belongings and left the party without saying goodbye to anyone. I didn't see Connor for weeks after that, and then he acted like nothing had happened. In the years since, we hadn't once discussed that evening.

It was obvious I shouldn't continue ascribing meaning to that night's kiss. The only thing that mattered from that party was the aftermath: the way he had brushed me off then and every night since then. Pursuing Connor was a waste of time, and I knew it. I shouldn't squander another second on him, and should instead focus on things I *could* achieve: like securing a spot on the team for the Phillips trial. The high-profile case was going before the Southern District of New York in a couple of months, and Bill Hannover, one of the firm's most prominent partners and head of the litigation group, had announced that one of the associates would have an opportunity to argue in court. Even though the very idea of speaking in court made me break out in hives, I desperately wanted that to be me. I needed the experience to progress my career, and I wanted to prove myself to Bill, a man who could almost single-handedly guarantee my future at the firm.

I promised myself that, going forward, I would clean up my act. I would stop wasting time on Connor, I would stop letting Audrey jerk me around like a pet, and I would stop trying to be someone different. Instead, I would be true to myself, be the ambitious, hardworking woman I knew I was. It had been working for me thus far.

I replaced the bottle of coral nail polish on the shelf and selected instead my usual pale pink. Handing it to Monet, I said by way of explanation, "Client meeting."

CHAPTER TWENTY-TWO

AUDREY

Two months before college graduation, Nick and I were sharing a joint in his bed on a Tuesday morning when he lazily asked me, "So, did you want to move to DC with me?" I had laughed in his face, and that had been the beginning of the end of us. Rather, it had been the explicit beginning of the end—I'd always known our relationship came with an expiration date. Nick was fun, but it wasn't like we were going to get married or anything. I mean, how could I spend my life with a man who counts Maroon 5 among his favorite bands? If Nick were moving to New York, we might have squeezed another couple of years out of things, Adam Levine and company notwithstanding, but at the time I couldn't fathom moving to DC—not for Nick, not for anything.

Against all odds, though, DC was starting to feel like home. It would never be New York, but that was true of all cities that weren't New York. Now that I'd been here a month, I was starting to appreciate the things that made DC unique: the slightly slower pace of life, the ambiguously patriotic feeling I got when I saw the Capitol Building each day. I missed the 24/7 vibrancy of New York, but there was something to be said for rolling up to a restaurant without a reservation and not facing a two-hour wait. That very night, I had ignored Cat's protestations about work and dragged her out to sample some kale nachos at a place I'd seen written up in the *Washington Post*, and we had only had to wait fifteen minutes. I was so busy thinking warm and fuzzy thoughts about the city—*The food is top-notch! The drinks are reasonably priced! Even my street is charming!*—that I was halfway through my gate before I realized I hadn't yet pulled out my keys.

I frowned, scouring my mind for a concrete memory of locking it. All I recalled was a text message from my mom: Have you seen Nick lately? she'd asked, subtle as a sledgehammer. I always liked him. I'd lied through my teeth, responding as I left that no, I hadn't seen him for a while. I must have been so distracted that I didn't remember to lock the gate.

Good work, Audrey, I thought as I deliberately pulled the gate shut and twisted the lock behind me. I turned around and put my key in the front door, only to find it was unlocked as well.

My stomach hit the pavement. It was conceivable I'd spaced out on locking the gate, but I was certain—*certain*—I had locked that goddamn door.

Hadn't I?

I stood as still as stone, my heart beating loudly in my ears while I tried to determine whether I should open the door. What if someone was in there?

Thump.

Fear shot through my body. Had that been my galloping heart, or had that noise come from within the apartment? Scarcely daring to breathe, I listened for other noises, but heard nothing. *It's just your imagination*, I told myself, but I nevertheless wrapped my hand around my key ring, pushing the keys through my fingers to form a spiky weapon.

Once I was semi-armed, I carefully pushed open the door. My apartment was dark, the faint glow from the streetlight throwing sharp shadows across the small space. So frightened I could taste it, I looked wildly around the room, searching for signs of an intruder.

The apartment was a disaster—which is to say, it was exactly how I left it. Sagging with relief, I was reaching for the light switch when I heard someone cough.

Fuck.

I wanted to turn and run, but my feet felt glued to the laminate, and so that's where I was standing when a shadowy figure appeared in my bedroom door. A montage of scenes from horror movies flashed through my mind, and I swallowed a scream while tightening my hand around my key ring.

Then I noticed the man-bun looped atop the intruder's head, and my terror began to ebb. *Ryan.* Ryan was a class-A creep, but I doubted he made a habit of murdering his grandmother's tenants.

Fear morphing into anger, I turned on the overhead light and demanded, "What are you doing here?"

Ryan flinched, shading his bloodshot eyes.

"*Answer me*," I snapped, digging in my purse for my phone. "What are you doing in my apartment?"

He dropped his hand and rolled his head so his neck cracked. "I got confused."

"You got *confused*?"

"Yeah. I used to live in this unit before you," he said, looking past me to the open front door. He took a step in that direction, his grungy fingers tapping an irregular rhythm on the bulging pocket of his baggy jeans.

"What's in your pocket?" I asked suspiciously.

"Nothing. Cigarettes."

"Show me."

"Huh?"

"Show me what's in your pocket. Show me these 'cigarettes.'"

He smirked at me. "No smoking in this building. Grandma's rules."

Now certain that he was concealing something of mine in his pockets, I brandished my phone and said, "Maybe we should call Grandma. Maybe she wants to see these 'cigarettes,' too."

"Maybe she wants to see your weird-ass blunt," he countered.

"My *what*?"

"That weird-ass blunt you were smoking in here." His voice turned mocking. "No drugs allowed."

"You mean the smudge stick? How did you . . ." I trailed off as it dawned on me. "You came into my apartment while I was out and lit the sage, didn't you? Did you try to *smoke* it?"

He scowled deeply, and I had to laugh.

"You moron. That was *sage*."

"Fuck off," he grumbled, trying to step past me.

"Not so fast," I said, blocking his exit. "What's in your pocket?"

He rocked back on his heels and sucked his teeth in consideration. Finally, he said, "What if I give 'em to you?"

"The 'cigarettes'?"

"Yeah. Or, you know. Whatever. What if I give 'em to you? You won't call her?"

I held out my hand. "Show me what's in your pocket, Ryan."

"Don't call her," he warned, reaching into his pocket and producing a handful of costume jewelry, my bottle of Ambien, and the fifty dollars in five-dollar bills I had on hand for tipping manicurists.

I snatched my belongings from his grimy hands and struggled not to scream. "Is that all?"

"Yeah."

"If anything else is missing, you know where I'm looking, right?"

"That's all," he sneered, turning his pockets inside out, their contents nothing more than a crumpled pack of Camels and a jumble of keys. "See?"

I pointed to the keys. "Give me the key."

"I don't have a key."

I blinked, amazed by the brazenness of his lie. "You're a terrible liar. Give me the fucking key and get out of here, or I'm calling the police."

"Bitch," he muttered, unwinding a key from the ring. He threw it onto the floor and then stalked past me and out the front door, pausing only to spit in my entryway.

* * *

OUR LANDLORD IN NEW YORK had been a faceless corporation to which we mailed a check every month and otherwise interacted with infrequently. When something broke, we submitted a maintenance request and waited for a contracted handyman to come. Response times varied, and some requests were simply ignored, but dealing with the corporation had been easy. There was a defined method for communication, we knew exactly the level of apathy to expect, and we never had to tell the corporation that its grandson was a shiftless loser who burglarized her tenants' units.

I almost waited until morning to make the call—as annoyed as I was, I didn't relish the idea of breaking the elderly woman's heart—but in the end, I couldn't sleep until I called Leanne.

"Good evening, dear," she greeted me pleasantly. "Is everything all right?"

"Not really," I said. "Your grandson has come into my apartment *multiple times* without permission."

"Oh, he *did* tell me he gave you a fright the other week," she said apologetically. "He didn't mean to scare you. You see, he heard some strange noises coming from your apartment, and he thought he should check on you. A young woman like you, living alone . . . he just wanted to make sure you weren't in trouble."

I bit my tongue instead of telling Leanne that I, *a young woman living alone*, was fully capable of protecting myself and didn't need her twitchy, drug-addled grandson to be my knight in shining armor. Saying it would have felt therapeutic, but it would have only distracted from my point, which was that *there was no reason for Ryan to be in my apartment*, the other week or that night or any other night.

"Leanne, there were no strange noises that night. I was sitting alone in my room, not making a sound. I didn't even have any music on. There was nothing he could have heard that would have made him think I was in danger, nothing that would have made it reasonable for him to *come inside* without my permission."

"Well, maybe he heard something outside. All I know is he rang your doorbell, and you didn't answer. So he wanted to—"

"Rob me," I interrupted. "He wanted to rob me."

Leanne let out a small gasp. Her voice hardened as she said, "That's a serious accusation."

"I know," I said, adding steel to my voice to match hers. "And I'm not making it lightly. Ryan didn't come into my apartment that night because he heard noises; he came in because he heard *no* noises. He thought I was out, and thought my not answering the buzzer confirmed it. He thought he could walk in and help himself to whatever he wanted."

"That's not what happened."

"I'm sorry, but it is. I came home tonight to find Ryan in my apartment, his pockets stuffed with my jewelry, cash, and medicine. He was robbing me, Leanne, and I caught him in the act."

"Are you sure?" she asked faintly. "Maybe there was a misunderstanding . . ."

"I get this is hard for you," I said sympathetically. "I do. But I'm your tenant, and you have responsibilities to me. I need the locks changed immediately—all three on the door and the one on the gate."

"Oh, I don't think all that's necessary. I'll just talk to Ryan, and—"

"My lawyer thinks it's necessary," I broke in, sending off a mental apology to Cat for dragging her into this without her consent. "Unless you'd rather discuss this with her?"

"No, no," she said quickly. "There's no need to involve lawyers. I'll have the locks changed first thing tomorrow. Ryan won't bother you again."

LEANNE SPOKE too soon.

Shortly after two in the morning, my buzzer rang. Startled awake, I vowed to ask Leanne to replace that thing when she changed the locks. No doorbell should sound like a crow being electrocuted. As it continued shrieking, I dragged myself out of bed to investigate.

I pulled open the door and nearly jumped out of my skin when I saw Ryan on the other side of my gate, face twisted and leaning maliciously on the buzzer. Without letting go of it, he growled, "You said you wouldn't call her, bitch."

I shrank back in momentary fear before I gathered myself. I wasn't afraid of some halfwit who smoked *sage*, for God's sake. What could he really do to me while I was behind a locked iron gate, anyway? Annoy me to death?

"I never promised that," I shot back. "Now get your filthy hand off my buzzer and get lost."

Ryan lunged suddenly, rattling the bars of the gate like a gorilla at the zoo. I recoiled, heart thundering in my chest, and wondered whether I had miscalculated the potential for danger. How strong was that gate really? And what might he do once I was no longer behind it?

My mind flashed back to a night in college: me,

screaming at some incredibly large, exceedingly drunk guy who had grabbed my ass while I waited at the bar, and Nick, holding me back and saying sharply in my ear, "Audrey, goddammit, someday you're going to get yourself killed."

I shivered.

Still clutching the bars, Ryan pressed his face against the gate so his bloodshot eyes and snarling mouth bulged like some nightmarish gargoyle. He barked once, then smacked chapped lips together in an exaggerated kiss and said, "Sweet dreams, Audrey."

CHAPTER TWENTY-THREE

AUDREY

I scrutinized the image I was about to post—a close-up of Rosalind's dreamy doll face as she gazed out the window of her Los Angeles apartment, her golden hair pinned up in miniature curlers—and then, satisfied, uploaded it to the museum's Instagram feed. The opening of *The Life and Death of Rosalind Rose* was still a month away, but I had been stoking interest by sharing one carefully cropped image each week. The tactic was working—the posts got tons of engagement.

I knew people were genuinely excited about the art—as they should be!—but I personally thought the series was doing so well because of the images I had curated. Before I'd posted a single photo, I'd spent hours thinking about how to frame the exhibit. It didn't lack for shock value—between the inspiration from a real murder and the rumor that Irina Venn had painted the scenes with actual human blood, there was plenty to scandalize the audience—but I'd chosen to focus on Rosalind's humanity. When I looked at the dioramas, the doll herself was what grabbed me, the rawness of the emotions etched on her tiny face. Rosalind was the star of the show, and I wanted our followers to connect with her just as I had.

I was reviewing the first wave of comments when a notification popped up that I had a direct message from Irina Venn.

My heart skipped a beat. Why was the artist sending the museum—sending *me*—a direct message? Had I made a mistake in my last post? Quickly, I reviewed the photo and the spare caption (*Meet Rosalind on August 28*), but nothing was out of order. I took a deep breath and opened the message.

> Whoever is running this account is brilliant. Rosalind thanks you from the bottom of her cold, dead heart. Please contact my assistant Lisa Zimmerli at 212-555-1981.

I had to read the message twice before I fully comprehended its contents, and then I gasped aloud. *Brilliant.* Irina Venn, a visionary artist whom I had admired for years, thought I was *brilliant.*

The word "brilliant" was still echoing through my mind as I called the number Irina had given.

"Lisa Zimmerli," Irina's assistant answered.

"Lisa, hi," I said, my voice sounding unnaturally shrill.

"My name is Audrey Miller, and I'm the Social Media Manager of the Hirshhorn Museum and Sculpture Garden. As you know, we're exhibiting Irina Venn's *The Life and Death of Rosalind Rose*. I just received a direct message from Irina on Instagram asking me to contact you."

"Of course, yes. Thanks for calling. Irina has been *obsessed* with your Instagram posts. She thinks you really *get* Rosalind."

"I'm so glad to know she's pleased," I said, striving to keep my voice professional while every cell of my body shrieked with triumph.

"Very pleased. In fact, Irina has decided to create a video especially for your institution. In it, she'll discuss her inspiration and process for creating the pieces. She says you're free to use it however you wish, but she suggests as a complement to the exhibit."

I had to swallow my scream of victory. Irina Venn was creating something special for our museum? More to the point, she was creating something *because* she liked my social media coverage? That promotion was as good as mine.

I promised to connect Lisa with the appropriate person on our end and then hung up, still smiling so hard my face hurt. I spun around, pumping my fist in the air in celebration, and jumped when I found Lawrence standing directly behind me.

"Lawrence! I didn't know you were there."

"I didn't mean to frighten you," he said. He adjusted his round glasses and gave me a quizzical look. "You look awfully pleased with yourself."

"That's because I just got off the phone with Irina Venn's assistant, and Irina likes what I'm doing with

Rosalind on Instagram so much that she's creating a special video for us to exhibit alongside the dioramas!"

"Wow," Lawrence said, widening his eyes. "That's incredible."

"I know!" I exclaimed, deliriously happy, and threw my arms around him.

If he was put off by my lack of professionalism, he didn't show it. Instead, he squeezed me back and said, "Congratulations, Audrey."

I SAW THE BRIGHT ORANGE from half a block away. I squinted, confused, as I tried to make sense of the color attached to my gate. Were those . . . flowers? I had been certain I would come home from a late spin class to find Ryan had broken through the new locks and trashed my apartment, but instead . . . there were flowers? As I drew nearer, I was able to confirm that yes, there were in fact flowers—a gorgeous bouquet, bursting with orange roses, brightly colored zinnias, and sprigs of wildflowers—fastened to my front gate.

Carefully, I untied the bouquet and turned it over in my hands, looking for a card. Nothing. I inspected the flowers again, more cautiously this time, searching for evidence that Ryan had booby-trapped them. I stopped short, laughing at myself. What a ridiculous notion. Ryan was the sort of brainiac who thought ringing my doorbell at two in the morning was cutting revenge; he wasn't clever enough to lure me in with an expensive bouquet of flowers and somehow sabotage them.

Who could have sent them? Nick? In college, he'd had some sort of pathological aversion to flowers, but maybe he'd grown to appreciate their charms. Maybe Cat? I'd told her about the incident with Ryan; maybe she had sent them to cheer me up? But no—Cat's answer had been that I should move in with her; it wasn't sending flowers. Besides, Cat surely would have mentioned it.

As I fingered the orange blossoms, I suddenly remembered a conversation I'd had with Lawrence the other day. I had been walking by his desk when he stopped me and pointed at his computer screen, where a collared shirt from J.Crew was on display.

"Audrey, you have great style. Help me out. Should I get this shirt in blue or in orange?"

"Orange, definitely," I'd told him. "It's more distinctive. And it's my favorite color."

He had smiled and clicked, adding the shirt to his shopping cart. "Done."

Lawrence knew how much I loved the color orange, and he knew about the win with Irina Venn. Besides, with his on-trend glasses, neatly buffed fingernails, and penchant for bow ties, Lawrence seemed like the kind of man who could pick out a killer bouquet. Could he have sent these?

It doesn't matter, I thought, pressing my face into the bouquet and inhaling the floral scent as I carried it inside my apartment. *Never look a gift bouquet in the mouth.*

I AWOKE WITH A START, uncertain what had roused me. As I blinked my eyes open in the dark, I strained my ears, listening for something amiss. I heard nothing other than the bright sound of silence. At first, I had found DC's nighttime quiet unnerving—New York, after all, was never anything less than noisy—but now I relished it.

Convinced I had awoken over nothing, I closed my eyes and rolled over, nestling beneath the soft new sheets I'd received from a start-up linen company in exchange for a review that I had yet to write. *Comfortable even when your sleep isn't*, I drafted in my head. *No, that's terrible. It should be something more like—*

Scratch.

My eyes flew open. *What the hell was that?* I was almost certain it had been a footfall in the alley, and I lay still as a corpse, listening closely. I heard nothing—which, rather than reassuring me, made my skin prickle. Someone was out there and they weren't moving *through* the alley. No, they had stopped right outside my window. The window that overlooked my bed.

With my pulse thundering in my ears, I carefully turned to face the window, pretending I was flipping in my sleep. I opened my eyes as much as I dared and peered up at the glass. I'd covered it with curtains in a cheerful yellow-and-cream chevron pattern, and in the space where they gapped, I saw the outline of something dark. I caught my breath. *A shoe. Jesus Christ.*

There was no reason for someone to be in that alley. It wasn't a through street—just a narrow gap between two buildings. There was a gate at each end, ostensibly to keep people from using it as a footpath, but the gates were rarely latched and I'd seen plenty of people using it to cut through the block. *That's all that it is*, I told myself. *Someone trying to take a shortcut.*

I remained perfectly still, watching the shoe, waiting for it and its owner to move on.

They didn't.

Goddammit.

Don't freak out, I told myself. *It's probably Ryan, casing the apartment again.*

"Go," I whispered fiercely at the window.

And still the feet remained.

With a sinking feeling, I realized I was going to have to do something unless I wanted to lie awake all night, worrying about my creepy neighbor outside.

My first thought was to call the police. I imagined how satisfying it would be to see red and blue flashing lights arrive and Ryan caught in the act. It wouldn't be so easy for Leanne to ignore his deplorable behavior then. But my grin faded as I thought about what would come afterward: more middle-of-the-night buzzers, more illicit entries into my apartment, more of me feeling unsafe in my own home.

And what if it's not Ryan? I challenged myself. *What then?*

I pictured myself calling the police, reporting a suspicion that someone was outside my window. I saw the officers rolling their eyes about silly women living in basement apartments and losing their pretty little minds over any passersby. How long would it take them to respond to a nonemergency like that? By the time they arrived, whoever it was could be long gone. Or what if the officers arrived and found it was nothing other than a homeless person looking for a safe space to sleep? I would feel awful.

Having talked myself out of calling the police, I climbed from bed, slipped my feet into flip-flops, and armed myself with a high-heeled bootie. It wasn't the most conventional of weapons, but it would give me something to threateningly swing should Ryan—or whoever it was—

lunge at me again. I gripped the shoe tightly and hoped I wouldn't have to use it.

I quietly made my way through the front door and gate, and began inching toward the alley. The night air was hot and sticky, and still a shiver ran down my spine.

Come on, Audrey, I chided. *Let's do this.*

Keeping as close to the front of the building as possible, I crept to the corner, where I paused and listened. I heard someone breathing—panting, really, a disturbing sound that both convinced me this was no innocent party and enraged me.

I jumped around the corner, brandishing the shoe over my head, and shouted, "Hey!"

A shadowy form leaped up from a crouched position and sprinted down the alley away from me. I lowered the shoe as I processed what I had just seen.

He jumped up. *That sick fuck was crouched down, looking through my windows.*

Trembling with righteous fury, I ran back into my apartment, where I paced the floor.

Had that been Ryan? I couldn't tell; it had been dark and I'd been blinded by adrenaline.

All I knew was that I couldn't stay in that apartment any longer. I grabbed my purse and took off.

CHAPTER TWENTY-FOUR

HIM

Is this what a heart attack feels like? I wondered as I sat on my couch, clutching at my chest as I struggled to breathe normally. My entire body felt clammy, my pulse a runaway train. How could I have screwed things up so completely, so irreparably? *Had Audrey seen my face?*

I shouldn't have been outside her window. I knew that. Of course I knew that. I told myself I was just there to see if she liked the flowers I'd left her, but that was a lie. I knew she liked the flowers: she had Instagrammed the bouquet that very night, captioning the image *Surprise flowers are the best flowers.* She'd appended the caption with an emoji of flowers and one of a face surrounded by hearts, and then a string of hashtags, ranging from *#flowers* to *#someonelikesme.*

No, the truth was that Audrey was a drug to me, her small, heart-shaped face a high I couldn't stop chasing. Once I had been able to control myself, but now that she was here in DC, breathing the same air I was every single day, I had fallen completely off the wagon.

And so I stood outside her window for hours. My stomach rumbled and my legs cramped and still I didn't leave. I was mesmerized by her sleeping form, could have watched her chest rise and fall all night long. She was so perfect, so dizzyingly, heartbreakingly *perfect*, that part of me longed to wrap my hands around her delicate throat and press a thumb against her windpipe gently, lovingly, until she stopped breathing, so she would stay just like this forever.

I wouldn't, of course. It was just another intrusive thought. Utterly harmless.

And then disaster had struck in the form of a stray cat. It had sauntered into the alley and begun rubbing its thin, flea-ridden body against my leg. Repulsed, I had swatted at it, and it had retaliated by hissing and lunging for me. I jerked out of the way and my knee smacked against the glass of Audrey's bedroom window.

I froze, the *thump* as loud as a foghorn. I readjusted my position and cautiously looked down through the window to see her stirring.

I should have run. I should have fled before she could see me, but I was caught in her thrall. I remained in place, half of me thrilled at the inevitable confrontation, half of me aware it was tantamount to suicide. *Go!* I screamed at myself. There would be no happy ending if Audrey found me outside her bedroom window. It was Audrey herself who snapped me out of my reverie. Her objection—

Hey!—had broken through to me, smacked my sense back into me. I leaped to my feet and ran.

PATHETIC, I CHASTISED MYSELF. *Utterly pathetic. It's no wonder Audrey isn't yours. You don't deserve to even tread the same ground as her.*

I punched my fist into my thigh, hard enough to make myself wince. This couldn't be who I was. In all other aspects of my life, I was more than competent: I had a decent job with benefits and a healthy 401(k); I maintained a carefully researched program of running and lifting weights; I laundered my sheets and towels with regularity. But where a woman—where *Audrey*—was concerned, I morphed into an embarrassing, irredeemable mess. I couldn't do anything right, couldn't even pull off sending flowers without turning it into an international incident.

Pathetic.

Oh, but she had loved those flowers. Seeing her smell them, lightly touching the blooms with a pleased smile, had been worth it. I was glad I had insisted upon the completely orange bouquet. The florist had urged me against it, had suggested I add in some different colors "for interest," but I had held firm. I wanted Audrey to know I knew her favorite color. I wanted her to know that I understood her.

And then I had gone and screwed it all up.

Stupid, pathetic idiot, I thought, punching myself again, harder. *No wonder you're alone.*

As my thigh throbbed, I realized that wasn't true. I wasn't alone. I had the Overexposed forums. The men there had never let me down; they'd been there for me as I agonized over Sabrina, Aly, and the other women I'd used as substitutes for Audrey. They would help me.

I grabbed my laptop and logged into the forums, but then hesitated, unsure where to post. Like dozens of other top-tier bloggers and social media influencers, Audrey had her own thread. I'd visited it on occasion and always regretted it. None of the men who posted there truly understood Audrey or even wanted to. All they wanted to do was share screen-captured images with disgusting, filthy captions and upload pictures they'd created by pasting Audrey's face onto the bodies of various adult actresses.

Her dedicated thread would be the absolute worst place to post, and so instead I clicked through to the Relationships subforum within the Off-Topic forum, the same place where I had written about Sabrina and Aly. There, I posted a lengthy confessional about where things stood and what I had done. Instantly, I felt lighter. Help would come.

I read the comments as they began appearing. Some encouraged me; some gently ribbed me for being such a disastrous fool about the whole thing. *Okay*, I thought, nodding. *I deserved that.* But as the comments continued to pile up without a single actionable suggestion, I began to get frustrated. Where was the help I needed? The help I was counting on?

I was about to close my laptop when I received a direct message from a user calling himself pm-me-nudes:

Hey bro. Saw your post, thought you might find this interesting. https://www.objectofaffection.com/vip -forums/2017041825 You have to be VIP to see it.

If you're not already registered as a VIP, click here:
https://www.objectofaffection.com/vip-forums
/register and use my invite code: pm-me-nudes
-inviteARQ573. Good luck.

VIP section? I'd been reading this site for years and
had never heard of a VIP section. I hovered my cursor
over the registration link and then paused. Even though
this place had seen me through some tough times, I was
ashamed to frequent it. Becoming a VIP was doubling
down on it, falling deeper into the rabbit hole.

But what if this was the one thing that could help me
with Audrey? Shouldn't I just get over my humiliation and
do it? After all, didn't I always say that I would do anything for her?

With a sharp nod of resolve, I clicked the link and
entered the invite code. Almost immediately, a smaller
window popped open, reading: *Welcome! Congratulations on becoming one of the elite.* I keyed in the URL from
the direct message and found a post in the VIP Forums
titled "Full Access."

Fellow Exposers, there's been a lot of discussion about
RATs here. If you're looking for that information, or if
you're just wondering what the fuck a RAT is (remote
administration tool, for the uninitiated), you're in the
right place. Below is my guide for setting up a tool on
a slave's computer so you can watch them all the time.
So easy a trained monkey could do it.

I reread that paragraph, my skin slowly alighting in
flames. *You can watch them all the time.* In my mind's

eye, I saw Audrey in her apartment, slowly shedding her clothing in an unintentional, unself-conscious striptease. Twisting that long, fire-laced hair up to expose her thin, pale neck. The temptation was almost too much. My palms sweat; saliva filled my mouth.

Heart pounding, I slammed the computer shut.

CHAPTER TWENTY-FIVE

CAT

"Catherine."

Panic shot through my already rattled body when I heard Bill Hannover's voice booming from my office doorway. Bill had requested that a memo on a complex procedural issue be on his desk by the time he arrived this morning, and I was still working on it at almost noon. I couldn't believe I had blown this deadline. I'd never been late with work product, not ever, and certainly not when it mattered this much. If I dropped the ball on this, Bill would never put me on the Phillips trial team, let alone select me as the associate to argue in court.

"Where's that memo?" he asked, an undercurrent of impatience belying his otherwise calm voice. "The deadline to file our motion is Friday. I need that research."

"I know," I said, nerves making my voice squeak like a cartoon character. "You'll have it within the hour. It's almost finished."

It really was almost finished. The problem was that it had been *almost finished* all morning. Over the last two days, I had read dozens upon dozens of cases, plus all the applicable statutes and legal treatises, and had compiled a highly detailed outline highlighting the most relevant issues. Writing the memo itself should have been a breeze. At midnight, with all but the last section drafted, I had decided to take a break. I'd set my alarm for five o'clock, thinking that a few hours of sleep and a clear head would let me finish the memo in just an hour or two. My plan was solid. I should have handed in the memo on time and still felt refreshed for the rest of my day.

But then I'd been awakened around two o'clock by insistent banging on my front door. Half certain I was dreaming, I closed my eyes and waited for the noise to stop.

Then I heard my name.

Bewildered, I dragged myself from bed and carefully descended my spiral staircase. I peered cautiously through my peephole, almost expecting to see the apparition of Emily Snow, eyes cold, mouth sneering, face bloodied. Instead, there was Audrey, wearing pink cotton pajamas and flip-flops, hair in a sloppy ponytail and a purse strung incongruously across her body. As soon as I opened the door, she flung herself into my arms, jabbering incoherently about someone outside. It took me five minutes to get her calm enough so that I could understand what she was saying: she had awoken to find someone spying on her from the alley. I shuddered. I'd *known* that alley was bad news. That whole apartment was bad news. Audrey should have taken my advice and moved in with me. But I wouldn't dream of rubbing it in, not when she was in such a state, so when she moaned that she couldn't sleep there, I simply patted her on the shoulder and assured her the guest room was all hers.

Thinking the matter resolved, I yawned and returned to my own bedroom, but Audrey followed me like a lost puppy and sat on the edge of my bed. She twisted her hair around her fingers as she repeated how frightened she was. I sympathized; I did. It must have been terrifying to find someone watching her while she slept, and I could only imagine how vulnerable she must feel. But she was safe now, secured in my home on an upper level behind a solid door. She could rest.

But instead she rehashed the night's events again and again, embroidering the details slightly with each pass. As my agitation grew, I remembered one night in college when Audrey and Nick had had some fight, the cause of which had long been forgotten, and Audrey had kept me awake all night, asking on a loop what she had done wrong and what she could do to win him back. My answers (that she had done nothing wrong and that she should *not* attempt to "win him back") did nothing to console her. She seemed so distraught that I had prioritized her personal crisis over studying for my Biology 101 midterm the next day, and I had done so poorly on the exam my grade wasn't able to recover. I got a B instead of an A in the class, ruining my perfect 4.0 GPA. Later, when I was rejected from Harvard Law, I couldn't help but wonder if it had been because of that blemish on my record. To add insult to injury, I'd returned from that bio exam to find Audrey and that slimeball Nick making out in our shared room.

You're not twenty years old anymore, Cat, I told myself. *Just tell Audrey you have to go to bed.*

But I couldn't. Every time I opened my mouth to do so, fresh tears welled in her eyes and I was reminded that this wasn't like the thing with Nick. This was my best friend having a truly terrifying experience. She needed me, and so I stayed up most of the night with her, falling asleep only an hour before my alarm went off. Now I was paying the price as I struggled to finish the memo, feeling as though my eyes were coated in sandpaper and my mouth was stuffed with cotton.

"I'll be waiting for that memo, Catherine," Bill said with a frown.

I nodded feverishly and turned back to my computer, fingers flying over the keys as I raced to finish it. Just as I was hitting my stride, my phone buzzed. I glanced away from the screen and saw that it was a text message from Audrey: I forgot to ask! Did you send me flowers yesterday?

I stared in disbelief at the message while resentment flooded my body. No *Thank you for listening,* no *Sorry I kept you up,* no *How's that memo going?* Just Did you send me flowers? Audrey might've been my best friend, but she was also the most self-obsessed woman I'd ever met.

CHAPTER TWENTY-SIX

AUDREY

I began having trouble sleeping in my apartment. Every time I put my head on my pillow, I heard phantom footsteps and faint scratches outside my window. I hung thicker curtains to shield myself from the prying eyes I assumed were out there, but then realized the opacity went both ways—no one could see in, but I couldn't see out. If someone was truly out there, I might not know—and so I began routinely leaving the curtains slightly cracked.

I was already on edge, and then I started having nightmares about Rosalind. I dreamed of being stuck inside her tiny doll world, hurtling toward an unpleasant but inevitable end. One of the dioramas in particular haunted me: Rosalind, blinded by a silky sleeping mask, tucked snugly beneath a fluffy comforter while her future murderer stood outside her window, his face obscured by a balaclava and his gloved hand wrapped around a miniature hatchet.

I like the one where the guy's outside the girl's window with a hatchet. I shuddered as I remembered the words of that dead-eyed creep I'd caught in the Rosalind exhibit on the first day. It had been weeks, and I was still turning corners in the museum and finding him there, loitering with his gaze hidden by his baseball cap. I wanted to demand to know who the hell he was and why didn't he ever seem to have a life to get to, but I didn't want to cause issues at work. I wanted that promotion, and there was no way I was going to allow him to ruin it for me.

Don't let it get to you, I chastised myself. My situation was wholly dissimilar to Rosalind's, or Colette's before her. So some guy who lacked social skills hung around a free museum too much. That didn't make him a stalker. I didn't *have* a stalker; at most, I had a random Peeping Tom who, as far as I knew, had never come back and probably didn't even own a hatchet.

But still I struggled to get a good night's rest. I had talked in my sleep since childhood—something that had made me a peculiarity at middle school slumber parties—and suddenly I began talking so loudly I woke myself. In the small hours of the morning, I would shoot bolt upright in bed, looking wildly around for the source of the voice that had awakened me, only to find the room empty. It had only taken a few nights of that before I downloaded an app called Luna Listen, which proclaimed, "Set yourself free from insomnia!" It promised to do this by tracking my sleep and recording irregular noises. The idea was that a person could use it to figure out what was disrupting their sleep, be it a snoring partner, a barking dog, or their own relentless tossing and turning. In my case, *I* was the only thing disrupting my sleep—when I woke up petrified with fear, I only had to listen to the most recent recording to reassure myself that the loud voice shouting *I'm scared!* or sometimes *Go away!* was only me.

I RESOLVED TO MOVE OUT of that apartment soon. Leanne could change all the locks she wanted, and that basement unit would still be vulnerable to her grandson or any other miscreant skulking through that alley. Every day over lunch, I scrolled through apartment listings on Craigslist and trolled the Zillow app. I was in a hurry to leave, but I didn't want to be in such a hurry I found myself in a similar—or worse—situation, and I didn't want to let moving distract me from work.

Cat said I could stay in her guest room as long as I wanted, but there was an unfamiliar edge to her voice. If I didn't know better, I might think Cat was annoyed with me. I was sure, though, that she was just stressed about work. Still, staying with Cat while she was in that kind of mood seemed unappealing, and so I declined her invitation and called Nick instead. Nick cut an imposing figure; he could intimidate my unwelcome visitor, should he return, much more successfully than I could, with or without expensive footwear in hand.

HAVING NICK OVER eased my paranoia, but I hated needing him. The damsel in distress was my least favorite trope, and I disliked embodying it. I tried to keep Nick on the back burner and to find other, healthier ways to distract myself from worries about the alley: I voraciously sampled exercise classes, testing a new Reformer or spin class every day; I spent hours on my Instagram presence, editing photos, crafting Stories, and working on the pre-set filter collection I hoped to soon launch; and I even FaceTimed my sister, Maggie, something I usually avoided because her kids seized her phone and started spinning it around in their chubby hands, leaving me dizzy.

And I threw myself into my job. Two months in, I still felt like I was learning the ropes, although I grew more confident every day. After all, who had so impressed Irina Venn that she'd created a special video for the museum? *This girl.* I knew the next several weeks would be demanding: *The Life and Death of Rosalind Rose* was opening later that month, and there was an exclusive member preview before that. Just that afternoon, I had been working on a posting schedule when Ayala had hovered over my shoulder, her breath sharp with the scent of bitter coffee, and had reminded me how important it was for the Rosalind exhibit to succeed. I was determined to not let her down—and to snag the promotion she was dangling.

But between my uneasiness in my apartment and the pressure with work, I began to feel like I was dragging. I was getting a late-afternoon coffee—my third of the day—in the Hirshhorn's sleek lobby with my colleague Lena, a Margot Tenenbaum clone who worked in public engagement, when she pointed out the dark circles under my eyes.

"I would bite someone's head off if they told me I

looked tired," she said. "And you're well within your rights to do so to me. But, honestly, Audrey, are you okay?"

"I've been having trouble sleeping," I confessed. "I think the Rosalind exhibit is getting to me. And, you know, that thing with the guy outside my window didn't help matters."

"What?" she asked, kohl-rimmed eyes going wide. "No, I don't know. What thing with what guy outside your window?"

Briefly, I recounted the shock of finding someone peering through my apartment window. To my surprise, Lena didn't look horrified—instead, she nodded knowingly.

"That's the worst. I lived in an English basement when I first moved to DC, too. Once I forgot to close my curtains and woke up to find some perv literally jerking off on the other side of my window."

"*Gross.* What did you do?"

"Closed the curtains and called the police. First things first, right? Then I signed up for a self-defense class." She curled her pale lips into a proud smile. "Ask me how to break a nose."

"That's a great idea," I said as wheels began to turn in my head. A self-defense class would help me feel less helpless, sure, but think of the content! Instagram Stories from a lively, empowering class—I could recruit Cat to help with the filming; me wearing this cute new Outdoor Voices workout set I'd been looking for an excuse to buy and adding swipe-up affiliate links; a serious post and perhaps some videos about the scourge of violence against women and opportunities to take action.

Take that, I thought to the stranger outside my

window. *You think you're going to take advantage of me? I'm going to monetize the hell out of you.*

Lena interrupted my thoughts with a low groan. "Don't look now, but here comes Lecherous Larry."

"Who?" I asked, looking around the lobby, expecting to see the usual creep, but he wasn't there. Neither was anyone else who looked particularly unsavory. I glanced back at her and realized with a start that she was looking at Lawrence, who was heading toward us with a coffee in his hand, wearing the orange shirt I'd helped select.

"You mean Lawrence?"

"I can't *stand* that guy. He's so *grabby*," she muttered, while smiling at him as he approached. "Hi, Lawrence."

"Ladies," he said, dropping into the chair beside mine and throwing an arm across my seat back. "How's the day treating you?"

"No complaints," I said. "At least, not now that I have this caffeine."

"We should really get back to work," Lena said, standing abruptly. "Come on, Audrey."

I could feel Lena's pointed stare even without looking at her, and I was baffled. Lawrence had never been anything other than friendly to me. He'd certainly never been "grabby." But I didn't want a scene in the lobby, and I actually *did* need to get back to work, so I rose to follow her and offered Lawrence an apologetic smile. "See you around."

He waved languidly, but then looked up as if suddenly remembering something. "Oh, Audrey? Your friend is here."

"My friend?" I repeated, surprised. Cat was here? Had we had a coffee date that I'd forgotten about?

"You know the one," he said, smirking slightly. "President of your fan club."

My stomach churned. I felt unsafe at home; I shouldn't have to feel unsafe at work, too. A self-defense class was exactly what I needed.

CHAPTER TWENTY-SEVEN

HIM

I couldn't get the post out of my mind. *You can watch them all the time.*

All the time.

The allure of having access to her even when she was alone, even when she wanted to remain private, was hard to ignore. I knew that installing a remote administration tool—or RAT, as they called it—on her computer was an inappropriate thing to do, but I had lost all sense of reason when it came to Audrey. Her thin, flawless fingers had burrowed an opening in my skin, and she had slipped into my bloodstream whole. She coursed through my body; every heartbeat echoed her name. I couldn't even close my eyes without seeing her perfect face carved into the backs of my eyelids.

Midway through another sleepless night, the siren song of the forums became too insistent to be ignored. I grabbed my laptop and logged on, refusing to admit my intentions to myself even as I navigated straight to the "All Access" thread in the VIP forum.

All the time. I could see what she was doing that very minute. My fingers itched, scrolling quickly through all seventy-six responses, looking for the pertinent information. Maybe it was the lack of sleep catching up with me, or maybe it was simple depravity, but I found myself nodding along as I read. Installing the RAT began to seem reasonable. After all, it wouldn't hurt Audrey in any way. She would never even know.

Besides, Audrey shared so much of herself online. She invited this. She *wanted* it.

It seemed so simple. All I had to do was download the desktop program onto my computer, and then have Audrey download another program onto hers. Once both were in place, I could control Audrey's computer remotely. I could look through files, view her screen, and, most important, turn on her camera and microphone so I could observe her in real time.

Simple, maybe, but far from easy. Everything was predicated on convincing Audrey to download the program, and she was much too savvy to fall for some amateur attempt at spam. Navigating this would be like walking a high wire, where any misstep could prove fatal. If Audrey recognized the attempt to gain access for what it was, or even just recognized it as something suspicious, and was able to connect it to me, everything would be lost. All the stars in our universe could align and there still wouldn't be any help for me then.

I knew I had to be cautious, and so I vowed not to act until I had a solid plan in place. I began combing through Audrey's accounts, and thirty minutes later, I found my opening on a two-day-old Instagram post. It was about something called microblading, and I had initially skimmed the post because I didn't completely understand. Tattooed eyebrows? That didn't sound right. Surely I was missing something.

But I didn't miss the last couple lines of her post: *Have you had microblading done? I'd love to see your results!*

There it was, as near to an engraved invitation as I was going to get. Hiding behind a VPN, I started a new message in an email account I'd created under the name "Aria Williams," the kind of upper-middle-class millennial white-girl name that I imagined belonged to her followers. I pasted in Audrey's email address, prominently displayed on her blog.

Subject: Fan letter + microblading vid
Audrey! I'm a huge fan! I would DIE for hair like yours! Anyway, I saw you ask for pictures of micro-bladed brows. I've had mine done and love it—my coloring is similar to yours, too! I attached a short video of the process for you to see. xx

Then, hands shaking with a potent combination of nerves and excitement, I added an attachment. I had named the attachment "microblading-vid," but that's not what it was. Rather, it was the program that would install the RAT on her computer. I hesitated, wondering if the attempt was too clumsy. File name aside, if Audrey paid the slightest bit of attention to the file size, she would realize it was far too large to be a "short video."

But I was desperate.

I inhaled deeply, filling my lungs to their capacity, and hit "send."

CHAPTER TWENTY-EIGHT

CAT

I had told Audrey I couldn't join her at some self-defense class she'd found, and still she appeared on my porch on Sunday morning, wearing a cropped, emerald-green exercise shirt that exposed her taut stomach, tricolor leggings, and a high ponytail.

"Good morning," she sang, handing me a to-go cup from Columbia Brews. "Ready to kick some ass?"

I frowned, trying to recall the exact conversation I'd had with Audrey. I was certain I told her about the new memo Bill had assigned me. Bill had a reputation for being ruthless; a chance to redeem myself and still earn a spot on his trial team was an unexpected gift, and I couldn't squander it.

"No," I said slowly. "I have to work. Remember?"

She rolled her eyes dramatically, giving me a view of the new lash extensions I'd heard so much about. "How could I forget? You *always* have to work. But I remember you said your thing isn't due until Wednesday, which is *three whole days* away. I'm not taking no for an answer."

You and your not taking no for an answer is the entire reason I'm in trouble at work, I thought irritably.

Before I could say anything, though, her demeanor changed, a flicker of fear showing through her veneer of carefully applied makeup and wide smile. "Please, Kitty-Cat? I'm just so sick and tired of feeling helpless."

How could I say no? After all, Audrey was right. There was more than enough time to finish the memo over the next three days. I could spare an hour or two for my best friend in her time of need. She would do the same for me.

Would she? a nasty little voice inside my head asked. *Isn't it always about what Audrey wants?*

Shut up, I told myself. *Shut up, shut up, shut up.*

IN LAW SCHOOL, a so-called self-defense expert had given a presentation to the student body. He had been a short, muscle-bound man wearing a gray sweat suit, and he had demonstrated several quick motions before unloading a case of pepper spray to sell us. I still had the canister rattling around the bottom of my purse; I had no idea if it had an expiration date.

The class Audrey had selected, however, was nothing like that uninspiring display. It was much more of a workout class, led by a pair of energetic instructors who introduced themselves as "Samantha and Samuel . . . but you can call us Sam!" When they turned on a soundtrack of electronic music, I thought I'd made a grave mistake in coming, but soon I was enjoying myself. Typical exercise classes made me feel shy, but because the focus of this class was self-defense rather than vanity, no one was looking at my body.

Which is not to say that vanity didn't enter the equation. Audrey kept pressing her rose-gold iPhone into my hands and instructing me to record her, then pausing to ask if her facial expression had been right or if her arm had looked weird. If I hesitated for even a split second, she'd insist on redoing the whole thing. Sam and Sam seemed oblivious, but the other class participants were plainly annoyed. "I didn't know there was a *celebrity* in our class," one woman said in a loud, sarcastic voice. I shrank a little, embarrassed, but Audrey merely beamed in the woman's direction.

Once things got moving, though, Audrey relaxed on the constant filming, and we had a good time.

"Amazing, right?" Audrey asked when class ended, not waiting for an answer before wrapping one of her damp arms around me and taking a selfie. The class had left me sweaty, spent, and euphoric, and I smiled widely, for once not remembering to be self-conscious.

"Amazing," I agreed. "Thanks for insisting I come."

"Remember that next time you try to weasel out of something because you have to work," she said with a laugh, and kissed me on the cheek. "I always know what's best for you."

I HAD PLANNED to turn back to the memo, but, still high on endorphins, I let Audrey drag me back to her apartment for brunch. It was the first time I'd been over since she moved in, and I was surprised to see not much had changed. One corner of the living room held a trendy table and lamp, pieces I had seen posted on her Instagram account (I'd started checking the app in order to keep up with Audrey) and had assumed were indicative of the rest of her decor. The only other furniture in her living room was incredibly incongruous: one slouchy, bright pink beanbag chair; one small, cheap-looking desk cluttered with mail, makeup, and cords; and one folding chair. The rest of the space was filled with open boxes, the contents spilling out onto the floor.

Once I had recovered from my shock, I asked diplomatically, "Do you need help unpacking?"

"Oh, I'm not unpacking," she said. "Unpacking would mean I'm staying here, and I am definitely *not* staying here."

"What are—"

"Ugh, no," Audrey said, covering her ears with her hands. "I absolutely do not want to talk about the problems with this place or my uninspiring apartment search. I'm taking the day off from it, and instead we're having brunch in bed."

"Brunch" turned out to be animal crackers, a container of slightly past-prime strawberries, a carton of orange juice, and two bottles of sparkling wine. I looked at the spread and laughed because we'd often enjoyed the exact same meal, also eaten in bed, while in college. To really drive that point home, Audrey set up her laptop at the end of her bed and put on a playlist full of our old favorite pop stars from college (Katy Perry, Lady Gaga, Rihanna) and the older artists Audrey always played in our room (Blondie, the Talking Heads, David Bowie), cut through with the obscure indie bands she enjoyed. Between the nostalgic songs and the homemade mimosas, an onslaught of warm, fuzzy memories beset me: late-night "dance breaks" as we crammed for finals, getting ready for sorority formals together, clutching hands as we walked home from campus bars in the dark.

"Come stay with me," I said impulsively. "My guest bedroom is all yours while you look for a new apartment. You shouldn't stay someplace where you're afraid."

She groaned. "I told you, Cat, I don't want to talk about this today."

"I know, but that doesn't make the situation go away. I hate the idea of someone looking at you through this window."

Sighing heavily, she said, "You and me both. But, as far as I know, no one has been in the alley again. There have been some random scratches that have been freaking me out, but I think it's just this mangy cat I keep seeing around the dumpster. I haven't even had any problems with Ryan from upstairs lately. Honestly, the only thing getting to me now is my own imagination. Have I told you I've actually been waking myself up at night?" She tapped at her phone and tossed it to me. "Here, press 'play' and see what I mean."

Obediently, I pressed the moon-shaped "play" button on the star-bedecked app open on Audrey's phone. There was some static and then Audrey's voice clearly said, "I'm scared," followed almost immediately by a loud gasping noise.

I looked up with alarm. "What was that?"

"Exactly what I'm talking about," she said wryly. "I've been scaring myself awake."

"Then come stay with me," I urged. "Audrey—"

Her phone buzzed in my hands, interrupting me. I looked down to see a text message from Nick: Tonight?

"Um, Nick wants you," I said, handing the phone back to her.

She smirked and waggled her groomed brows suggestively. "You bet he does."

Tongue loosened by the mimosas, I said, "I don't understand what you're doing with him. There was a reason the two of you broke up."

"Yeah, because he was moving here."

"And now because you're here, you guys are dating again?"

"No, I'm not trying to *date* Nick. He just, you know, comes over to keep me company."

"Somehow I doubt he's coming over to play Scrabble or watch *Jeopardy!*"

She giggled. "Not exactly."

I shook my head in disgust.

"Oh, come on, Cat, lighten up. It's just *Nick*. We're just having fun."

"But why are you wasting your time with that sleaze? You could have anyone you wanted."

Anyone, I thought bitterly.

"Sleaze?" Audrey echoed, eyes widening. "Have another drink, Cat, and tell me how you really feel."

I flushed. "I'm just—"

"Forget it," Audrey said, pouring more champagne into my plastic cup. "Let's not talk about my boring sex life."

I laughed shortly. "At least you have one."

"Well, let's do something about that. So things are

kind of stalemating with Connor. Who cares? There are tons of other guys out there, guys who will actually appreciate you. Have you considered online dating?"

She wants Connor for herself, a little voice hissed as an image of Connor pressing Audrey against the jukebox flashed through my mind. *She's trying to dissuade you from pursuing him so that she can have him.*

No, I reminded myself. *I saw her push him away.*

Didn't I? My champagne-muddled mind suddenly couldn't remember.

"I saw you and Connor," I blurted.

Audrey's glossy mouth dropped open, and I derived a small amount of cold satisfaction from striking my effervescent friend speechless. I held her eyes, challenging her to defend herself.

"I don't know what you think you saw," she finally said, "but I did *not* kiss him."

"But he tried to kiss you."

"Cat—"

"Don't," I interrupted, a bubble of hysteria rising in my chest. "I know what happened. Connor fell in love with you, just like every man you've ever encountered."

"That's ridiculous."

I laughed bitterly. Leave it to Audrey to not even *notice* the men piling up at her feet. "It's not. But it doesn't matter. What matters is that you should have told me. You're supposed to be my friend. How could you not tell me?"

"Because I wanted to protect you!" she exclaimed, flinging her arms in the air. "I know you like Connor, but he's a moron who doesn't realize what a catch you are."

I snorted. "Sure. I'm a real catch."

"You *are*. You're—"

"No," I said, shaking my head firmly. "Once a freak, always a freak."

"What are you talking about? You're not a freak." She reached for my cup. "Maybe I should cut you off . . ."

"You know I'm right," I said, yanking the cup out of her reach, sloshing juice and wine on her bed. "You remember freshman year. And before that . . . Audrey, I haven't always looked like this. I used to be shorter, chunkier. I had bad skin and a stutter. I couldn't make eye contact without breaking into a full-body rash."

"So? That's not who you are now. You're beautiful and smart and confident—"

"Tell that to Emily Snow."

"Who?" Audrey blinked.

I caught my breath, suddenly sober. I hadn't meant to mention Emily Snow. I'd made it all these years without once telling Audrey about that summer at camp, and I hoped to make it many more. I swallowed hard and shook my head. "Just some girl who used to torment me."

"Forget her," Audrey said, putting her hands over mine. Until that moment, I hadn't realized mine were shaking. "You're a striking woman, a brilliant lawyer who owns her own gorgeous apartment in a vibrant city. What do you think that Emily Snow bitch is doing these days? Shilling some pyramid-scheme yoga pants out of her suburban tract home?"

My stomach tightened. If only Emily Snow were doing that.

"Listen to me, Cat," she said, blue-green eyes shimmering earnestly as she squeezed my hands. "You have everything going for you. *Everything.* So one dumb guy doesn't get it. Who cares about him?"

I wanted to agree with her. I wanted to wash my hands of my unrequited obsession with Connor, to be free of the way he made me feel like I wasn't good enough. God knows I had tried. But for some reason, I just couldn't let go.

I hung my head and whispered, "I care."

Audrey dropped my hands and sighed. "Fine. I ask you not to judge my choice in male companions, so I'm not going to judge yours."

"At least you can *have* Nick. You're not—"

"Stop that negative self-talk right now. You're a babe, and you can have whomever you want, Connor included." She paused and smiled slowly. "And I'll prove it to you."

"How?"

Her smile widened and her eyes sparkled. "I have an idea."

Against all reason, I felt a flicker of hope in my chest. Everything Audrey touched turned to gold. Why shouldn't I?

CHAPTER TWENTY-NINE

HIM

The three days after I sent the RAT-laced email were excruciating. My entire being vibrated with anticipation; I couldn't eat, couldn't drink, couldn't sleep. I could hardly bring myself to step away from my computer in case I somehow missed her, and so I called in sick to work. Even taking a shower was too much time away from my post, and I sat in my own filth. I sustained myself on my dwindling supply of animal crackers and berated myself for fouling this all up. Audrey wasn't going to download the program. Of course she wasn't. What person in their right mind would download a random file from a stranger? I was an idiot to think it would have been that easy, a lovesick *idiot*.

My constant vigil overwhelmed me, and I must

have fallen asleep, because I awoke with a start, my neck cricked and a half-chewed animal cracker stuck to the roof of my mouth. Blearily, I turned back to the computer.

And there it was.

On my RAT desktop, I could see the icon indicating I had access to her computer. I blinked once, twice, wondering whether I was still asleep, whether wanting something so much had made me delusional. Holding my breath, waiting for the icon to vanish before my eyes, I navigated my mouse to it and clicked. My stomach lurched as I did so; I was terrified that, if this was real, she would notice the green light suddenly appearing beside the eye of her laptop's camera. I'd read all about how that light had spelled disaster for other "ratters."

But Audrey gave no indication she noticed it. She wasn't even looking at the screen. She was sitting cross-legged on her bed, her exquisite body clad in form-fitting exercise clothing. She held a plastic cup in one hand, while the other was digging around in a tub of animal crackers. My face tingled, and I swallowed the lump of saliva-soaked cookie in my mouth. *She's eating animal crackers at this very moment, too.* It was a sign. It had to be.

I reached out to touch my screen, tracing a finger along that gorgeous hair that I loved so much, imagining that I was actually twining my fingers through the locks, inhaling the scent of her coconut shampoo. I was so captivated by Audrey's shimmering aura that I barely glanced at the other woman in the frame. When I finally noticed her, I paused and frowned. What a strange pair these two were. One fire-haired sprite, one awkward dormouse.

And then Audrey looked up and directly at me, her brilliant, jewel-colored eyes staring right through the screen and into the farthest reaches of my aching heart. It swelled within my chest, constricting my lungs, my throat, choking me. I gagged painfully, but oh, what a way to go, asphyxiated by love.

She frowned, and every cell in my body froze. She *knew*. She knew I was there, staring through the virtual peephole.

"Hmm," she murmured, looking at the screen. "That's weird."

No, no, *no*. How could I have been so stupid? So goddamn *greedy*? I'd ruined everything already. If only—

But then, instead of slamming her computer shut or running a spyware program, she took a sip of her drink and shrugged. Turning her face away from the screen, she said, "I really need a new computer. This old thing can't even open a simple file anymore."

I exhaled, sagging with relief. My clumsy attempt had been, against all odds, successful. I was in.

CHAPTER THIRTY

AUDREY

Three champagne-heavy mimosas deep, I hadn't been able to take Cat's plaintive sobbing any longer and had come up with the idea to put both Cat and Connor on the list for the museum's exclusive preview for *The Life and Death of Rosalind Rose*. I thought it was inspired. Cat seemed doubtful, but I had finally convinced her that the problem wasn't that she was some sort of hideous, unlovable troll, as she seemed to believe. Rather, the problem was that Connor had only ever known Cat as a classmate, colleague, and trivia buddy. For him to consider her a potential romantic partner, he needed to see her through a different lens. The preview was the perfect location for that: a little glamorous, a lot out of their comfort zone, and with a built-in topic of conversation.

On the night of the event, as museum members and donors began arriving, I worried I hadn't properly counseled Cat on what to wear. I wouldn't put it past her to come straight from work in her usual ink-stained suit and unflattering pumps with their ground-down heels, which would totally defeat the purpose of removing her from her normal environs. I was about to text her some last-minute ideas when she entered the room. I relaxed. She'd traded her frumpy work wear for a pair of slim, cream-colored pants that showed off her long legs and a cadet-blue tunic that matched her eyes. Her hair fell in loose waves around her shoulders, and her lips were painted a subtle rosy hue. Even her fingernails, usually a shade of pale pink so boring I wanted to die, were a punchier rose. She was standing erect, her neck elongated as she looked around the room.

"Hey, gorgeous," I greeted her. "You look stunning."

"Really?" she asked anxiously. "Thanks. You don't think this is a little much?"

"Not at all. It's exactly the right amount of much for a first date."

"This isn't a date," Cat said quickly, flushing.

"Sure it isn't. Speaking of, where is Connor?"

"He got stuck on a call, but he's on his way." Her mouth trembled slightly, and she started to raise her hand to her mouth. "That's what he said, at least. I went home to change."

"Then we'll see him soon. Listen, I wish I could stay and chat, but I promised my boss I would be on social media all night, so I have to get back to work. You'll be all right until Connor gets here?"

Cat nodded the affirmative even as her expression said otherwise.

"You'll be fine," I assured her. "Have a drink. Meet some new people. Have fun!"

FIFTEEN MINUTES LATER, I could only hope Cat was having fun because I decidedly was not. Midway through a Live chat with the Director of Exhibitions, my phone had flashed a low-power warning. My stomach sank—I had plugged in my phone that afternoon; had the cord been bad? I wrapped the Live up as quickly as I could, and then rushed out of the gallery toward the office space.

Don't be such a fucking amateur, Audrey, I thought angrily as I dug through my desk drawers in search of an external battery. I sorted through various ephemera—pens, paper clips, loose bobby pins, a mostly empty package of Orbit—my panic growing with each moment.

I know there's a battery in here, I thought, and sent up a quick prayer to whichever body might be listening. *Please, please let it be here.*

I exhaled a sigh of relief as my fingers closed around it. *Thank you.* As I attached the battery to my phone, I heard someone enter the room behind me. My skin prickled, and I had the sudden thought that the creep whom Lawrence always jokingly called the president of my fan club had followed me in here. That was irrational, though. I hadn't seen him all day, and certainly not that night.

I spun around and relaxed when I saw it was only Lawrence, looking dapper in a polka-dot bow tie and with his light hair carefully combed and gelled.

"You scared me!" I exclaimed with a relieved laugh.

"Sorry. That wasn't my intention."

He was smiling, but the intense way he held my eyes

and the studiously casual way he was leaning against the doorframe sent a warning flare up my spine. Honestly, I was so paranoid these days that even *Nick* was giving me the creeps.

I shook it off and asked, "What are you doing in here?"

"I saw you come this way and didn't know if you needed help with anything."

"Nope," I said, holding up the battery. "I was just looking for this. All good now, thanks."

Lawrence straightened and licked his lips. "Audrey, now that we're alone—"

The warning flare transformed into full-blown alarm. Nothing good ever started with the phrase "Now that we're alone."

"I really should get back to the gallery," I interrupted, taking a step toward the door.

"Just a second," he said, catching me by the arm.

I looked uneasily at his hand. It was resting lightly on my forearm, an ostensibly friendly touch, and yet it felt vaguely threatening. *Lecherous Larry.* I shook his hand off me.

"Not now, Lawrence."

"I need to talk to you about something," he continued as though I hadn't spoken, still making extreme eye contact. I fervently wished we weren't alone in this space, out of earshot from everyone else.

"Later," I said firmly. "I'm busy right now."

"Come on, Audrey," he said softly, reaching out to touch my hair. "Let's stop dancing around the obvious. I've seen the way you look at me."

"Excuse me?" I recoiled, wincing in pain as some

strands tangled in his fingers and were yanked free from my scalp.

"There's no point in denying it," he said, closing the short distance between us and breathing heavily on my face.

"I haven't been looking at you like anything," I snapped, rubbing the sore spot on my head and taking a step backward. Annoyed, I added, "Except maybe with ridicule because that bow tie looks like some sort of bad joke."

His expression flickered through irritation, anger, and finally settled into amusement. "I've always liked that you're not afraid to say what's on your mind."

"This conversation is over," I said, and moved to step around him. He shifted his body to block mine, and even though he wasn't a particularly large man, the motion forced me backward. I stumbled, surprised when my shoulders hit the wall behind me.

I'm literally cornered, I thought. A glimmer of fear ran through me before it gave way to anger. There was no way I was letting some grabby jerk ruin one of the most important nights of my career.

"Back off!" I ordered, planting my hands on his tangerine-colored shirt and shoving him away from me.

Lawrence recovered quickly, laughing as he grabbed my bare upper arms tightly. "Come on, Audrey—"

I jerked my arms from his grasp and brandished my cell phone. "Don't touch me again or I stream this live."

He smiled playfully as though this was all one big joke. "Audrey—"

"I'm serious," I said. "Get out of my way, or I go live in three . . . two . . ."

His grin faded and he straightened his bow tie. "What's gotten into you? I was just messing around."

"Ha ha," I said sarcastically before stomping around him and out the door.

I WAS STILL trembling with anger as I pushed my way through the crowded gallery, searching for Cat. Sequins scratched at my bare arms and I caught elbows to my collarbone, but I pressed on, muttering apologies as I stepped on people's feet. I *needed* Cat. Where was she? For the ten millionth time in my life, I wished I were just a few inches taller so I would have a better vantage point.

In the center of the gallery, a crowd had formed around the diorama where Rosalind first arrived in Los Angeles. It was one of the more hopeful scenes in the otherwise dark series: a tiny spotlight simulating the sun shone down on Rosalind, her red lips grinning and blonde ponytail high as she stood proudly beside a doll-sized U-Haul truck. In one of her tiny hands, she clutched a miniature tabloid, its headline—"Dead at 24!"—hinting at the horrors that would come. I paused my search for Cat and lingered on the crowd's edge, eavesdropping— *immaculate details, how about the use of lighting here?, God I hate knowing how this ends*—and searching for the best candidate for a quick Live. My eyes had just settled on Lena, who was engaged in a deep conversation with a pastel-haired woman dressed completely in white, when I felt the sensation of being watched.

I whirled around, expecting to find Lawrence staring at me from across the room. Instead, I saw only a sea of unfamiliar faces, none of which were looking in my direction. I scanned them anyway, paranoia growing as I searched for someone, anyone, who might have been paying me undue attention. I froze as I caught a glimpse of a bulky figure wearing an incongruous baseball cap. *That creep always lurking around the halls.* Still riled up from my encounter with Lawrence and spoiling for a fight, I curled my hands into fists and started toward him. I was going to tell that loser to leave me the hell alone once and for all. I was *not* going to let another stupid man intimidate me at my workplace.

"Hey," I said, my voice crackling with anger as I tapped him sharply on the shoulder.

He turned around, licking his lips when he saw me. "Hello there."

"What the hell are you doing?"

He adjusted the brim of his cap and cocked his head at me. "Checking out the exhibit. You know I've been interested in this one."

A memory of the shock I felt when I saw him in the gallery on that first day flashed through my mind, and I tightened my fist. "I seem to remember you helping yourself to an early glimpse. Now, as this preview is exclusively for donors and members, you'll need to leave."

He laughed slightly. "I'm not leaving."

Furious, I jabbed a finger at him—the second man to ignore my request to leave me the hell alone in the last thirty minutes—and snapped, "Listen, I don't know who you are, how you got in here, or what it is that you want, but I am sick and tired of you showing up and ogling me when I'm just trying to do my goddamn job."

A large, vaguely familiar-looking man with a ruddy complexion lumbered up to the creep's side and placed one of his hefty hands on his shoulder. Glowering at me from underneath bushy gray eyebrows, he asked, "Is there a problem here?"

Suddenly, I recognized him as Senator Adrian Potts, whom Ayala always praised as a generous patron of the arts. *Shit.* Upsetting Senator Potts was a serious enough offense to cost me that promotion, no matter how many special videos Irina Venn created for us.

"No problem, Dad," the creep said.

"Good. Don't make a nuisance of yourself, Brandon," the senator said, lifting his hand from his son's shoulder. He then looked to me, clearly expecting cheerful concurrence.

Rage bubbled inside me while I smiled brightly and echoed, "No problem."

With a heavy nod, Senator Potts moved on. As soon as his broad back was turned, I dropped the smile and shot Brandon a cold look, silently warning him that I was over his bullshit, no matter who his father was. He tugged at his cap and smiled smugly.

"Leave me alone," I spat at him before spinning around and pushing myself once more through the crowd.

"Audrey."

I whirled at the sound of my name, every last one of my frayed nerves screaming.

"Hey," Connor said, looking at me with concern. "Is everything all right?"

I forced myself to rearrange my features into a pleasant smile. "Everything's perfect. Glad you made it."

"Yeah, thanks for the invite. I've always wanted to come to something like this."

"You haven't seen Cat, have you?" I asked, casting another glance around the gallery.

"Not yet. I just got here." Connor stretched his neck and looked over the crowd. "Aha, there she is. Come on, I'll lead the way."

He took my arm and began guiding me across the room. As we made our way to where Cat was standing, talking to a blond man I didn't recognize, my neck crawled once again with the feeling of eyes on me. This time, I didn't turn around.

I'm not giving you the satisfaction, Brandon, I thought as I gritted my teeth.

CHAPTER THIRTY-ONE

CAT

I checked the time on my phone. Connor said he was on his way twenty minutes ago. Our office was less than a fifteen-minute walk from the museum; he should have arrived by now. I tightened my grip on my wine as scenarios ran through my mind. Maybe he had stepped off a curb and been hit by one of the ubiquitous tour buses. Maybe he had been struck by someone texting while operating a motorized scooter. Maybe he had been denied admittance by the door staff.

Or maybe he had changed his mind about spending the evening with me and gone home. My cheeks grew hot as I considered this last, and most likely, possibility. I shouldn't have let Audrey talk me into inviting him here. Connor had no interest in me beyond friendship;

he never had. I decided to give it another ten minutes. If he hadn't made an appearance by then, I was leaving. I wouldn't subject myself to this humiliation much longer.

"Cathy? Cathy Harrell?"

My blood froze in my veins. I hadn't gone by "Cathy" in years, not since middle school. Not since I'd become a different person. Apprehensively, I looked up from my phone.

"Cathy? It is you, isn't it?"

I struggled to place the man standing before me. Handsome in an unassuming way with a mop of loosely curled blond hair and warm brown eyes, he looked vaguely familiar.

"It's me," he said, offering a dimpled smile. "Max Metcalf. From Camp Blackwood."

My mouth filled with acid as images of bloodstained rocks swam before my eyes. *Don't panic*, I told myself, summoning every ounce of self-possession I had. *Remember, it was an accident.*

"Max," I said, my anxiety turning his name into a question. I struggled to modulate my tone and added, "It's been a really long time."

"It sure has been," he said, reaching out for a half hug, to which I submitted reluctantly. "It's been, what? Fifteen, sixteen years?"

"Longer, I think."

"Cat!"

I turned in the direction of Audrey's voice and saw her approaching with Connor, still in the gray slacks and light blue shirt he'd worn to work that day, at her side. My jaw clenched suspiciously. How long had Connor been here, chatting it up with Audrey, while I waited and agonized over whether he would show up? And why was his hand on her arm? I searched Audrey's face for indications of guilt, but she gave nothing away. Then again, she'd shown no contrition the night Connor tried to kiss her, nor had she when she kissed Bruce Gellar, or any of the dozens of other times Audrey had waltzed off with something she knew I coveted, whether it be a leadership position or just the last slice of pizza.

"Look who I found!" Audrey exclaimed, presenting Connor to me as though he were hers to give.

Still, I was grateful for the interruption. "If you'll excuse me," I started to say to Max, but Audrey had already aimed her glossy smile at him and was introducing herself. Stomach tightening, I thought to myself, *This can't end well.*

"Sorry," Connor said to me, smiling apologetically. "I got hung up at work."

"It's no problem," I lied. "I haven't been here long."

"Who's that?" he asked, nodding to Max, who was laughing at something Audrey had said.

"Someone I used to know. Come on, let's go see the exhibit."

"Shouldn't we wait for Audrey?"

"She's busy." I took a step away and beckoned him. "Come on, before it gets too crowded."

With one final glance at Audrey and her form-fitting black dress, Connor followed me to the start of the exhibit. I could feel all my muscles unclenching and a wave of relief washing over me as I put distance between myself and Max Metcalf and whatever memories he might have from camp.

* * *

AN HOUR LATER, I had just returned to the gallery after a restroom break and was looking for Connor when Max strolled over, smiling pleasantly.

"Hey, Cathy. What do you think?"

I think you should leave me alone, I thought as my palms prickled with sweat.

Aloud, I said, "It's interesting."

He laughed. "That's a lukewarm response. Not your thing, huh?"

I shrugged, a forcedly casual motion I hoped would communicate the depth of my disinterest in speaking with him. It had taken hours upon hours of therapy and a lot of hard work to put that devastating summer behind me, and I would kill Max Metcalf before I let him reveal a single second of it to Connor.

Oblivious, Max continued. "Do you come to many museum events? I feel like I would have run into you."

"No," I said, shaking my head. "I'm just here to support my friend."

"That's nice of you. What was her name? Audrey? She seemed cool."

I nodded tightly and looked around for an exit from the conversation. My gaze landed on Audrey standing near one of the dioramas, her head bent over her phone, and I nodded in her direction. "Speaking of, I really should be getting back over to her, so . . ."

Max followed my line of sight, and as we both watched, Connor approached Audrey, touching her lightly on her exposed shoulder to get her attention. She looked up, startled, but then offered him a beaming smile, one that showed every dazzlingly white tooth, even the crooked one. My stomach shifted unpleasantly.

"Is that her boyfriend?" Max asked.

"*No*," I said more forcefully than I intended.

Max looked at me curiously.

"I mean, no," I tried again. "Connor is my friend."

"Got it. So, is she dating anyone else?"

I was so relieved by the question I almost laughed. Max wasn't hanging around because he wanted to reminisce about our shared past at camp. He was only interested in Audrey. Just like everyone else. If I hadn't been so thankful, I would have been insulted.

"She's not seeing anyone right now," I said, purposefully omitting mention of Nick. "Are you asking because you're interested in her?"

Spots of rose appeared in his cheeks. "I'm that obvious, huh? I'm sure she gets hit on all the time, but . . . I don't know. Earlier, we were talking about how it's always really hard to find something to eat at these things—you know, because we're both vegetarians—and I kind of thought we had a connection."

Everyone thinks they have a connection with Audrey, I thought drily. *That's part of her charm.*

"Maybe you could put in a good word for me?" he suggested. "We could double-date. Me and Audrey, you and your *friend* over there."

I shuddered as I imagined what an uncomfortable evening that would be: I would be pining after Connor like some sort of lovesick schoolgirl while he no doubt ogled Audrey in the same manner he'd been doing all night, and, across the table, Audrey and Max would be swapping stories about when they met me. *Well, I met Cat when she was an awkward wallflower during sorority rush, what about you? Oh, I met her at camp, back when . . .*

I pressed a fist into my stomach to stop the awful churning.

"I don't know," I hedged. "It's been a really long time, Max. I barely know you."

"You *do* know me, though," he protested, face imploring. "We shared that summer at Camp Blackwood together. A person never forgets camp."

My skin prickled with gooseflesh. *A person never forgets camp.* The words sounded too deliberate not to be a threat, but his expression was open, warm.

"I've changed since camp," I said hesitantly. "Audrey . . . she didn't know me then, and . . ."

"Say no more. I understand. You can trust me, Cathy."

"Cat."

He tilted his head. "What?"

"I go by Cat now."

"Okay." He nodded. "You can trust me, Cat. I promise."

I hesitated. *Could* I trust him? I had only known him that one summer, and we'd only spent minimal time together. I remembered him as being kind, willing to talk to the likes of me even though not an outcast himself. A few more fuzzy, pleasant memories surfaced, and I found myself relaxing. Of course it wasn't a threat. He was a nice guy. He would probably be good for Audrey, much better than her continued liaison with that Neanderthal Nick.

"All right," I said. "I'll help you with Audrey."

"Thanks, Cat," he said, face cracking open in a genuine smile. "That's really nice of you."

My gaze drifted across the room to where Audrey still stood in conversation with Connor. Her body was angled toward his, one hand toying with her long hair as she laughed about something. Connor smiled down at her, his expression covetous. *Of course.* If nothing else, putting Max in front of Audrey might dissuade her from flirting with Connor all night.

"Come on," I said, grabbing Max's arm roughly. "Let's go say hi."

"CAT, HEY," AUDREY SAID, dropping the lock of hair and beaming at me like she hadn't just been making eyes at the man she'd invited to be my date. "Connor and I are talking about the exhibit. What do you think?"

I looked to Connor, who didn't meet my eyes. I wondered what he had said to Audrey about the show. To me, he had said that framing women's deaths as art was a gross practice. From the way Audrey was smiling, I doubted that was what he had said to her.

"It was really something," I said noncommittally. "Audrey, I think you met Max earlier."

"Sure, hi," she said, then glanced down at her phone, thumbs moving as she responded to a comment on Instagram.

Max shot me a pleading look; Connor had yet to make eye contact with me.

If you don't do something, you're going to have to stand here and watch Audrey and Connor flirt all night, a small voice said nastily in my mind.

"Max and I were just catching up, and I think you guys have a lot in common," I said, my voice sounding false to my own ears.

"Yeah?" Audrey asked, looking up and scanning Max's body appraisingly.

I glanced over at him, trying to see him through

Audrey's eyes, and blanched. What had I been thinking? This would never work. Max Metcalf, earnest and slightly disheveled, wasn't Audrey's type. She went for men like Nick, choosing swagger and vanity muscles over things like intellect and character.

A person never forgets camp.

But what if that *had* been a threat? Max looked harmless, but what if he wasn't? What if he told Audrey or, worse, Connor about that hideous summer? Panic flickered in my chest. I couldn't give Max any reason to make good on that threat. It could jeopardize everything I'd worked so hard for. If all I had to do to protect my future was push a date on Audrey, I was more than happy to do it.

"Yeah," I said, hoping Audrey didn't hear my voice wavering. "Maybe you two should get together sometime."

"Any friend of Cat's is a friend of mine," she said with a shrug. From her purse, she produced a business card and handed it to Max. "Here."

He looked down at it and frowned faintly. "What's this?"

"My Instagram handle. Direct message me sometime, and we'll grab coffee."

"Oh," he said, fingering the card's edges. "Right. Sure. Okay, I'll just download—"

"Wait," Audrey interrupted, looking amused. "Don't tell me you don't have Instagram. Cat, are all of your friends technophobes like yourself?"

I faltered, but Max smiled easily. "I did have Instagram. Once. But I kept getting inundated with messages from Russian porn bots, and dealing with that didn't seem worth being able to post the occasional picture of coffee or cool album cover."

"Depends on how cool those album covers were," she said with a slight smile. She reached into her purse again and retrieved a pen, which she used to scrawl her phone number across the card she'd handed him. "Here. Let's leave the bots out of things. Text me."

My stomach turned sour with regret. I'd thought only of the short-term, and completely neglected to consider the long-term implications of setting them up. What if things went well? What if they started dating? How could I ever relax knowing that at any moment, Max Metcalf could be revealing my dark past to my best friend? But it was too late. The wheels were already in motion, and all I could do was hope to not get flattened.

CHAPTER THIRTY-TWO

AUDREY

I hadn't had a boyfriend since Nick. Izzy blamed Nick for emotionally scarring me (he hadn't), and my mother suggested I had never gotten over him (I had). My singledom had less to do with Nick and more to do with me enjoying being unencumbered. I liked not having to answer to anyone, liked being able to stay out until five in the morning without a boyfriend questioning my whereabouts. And I *really* liked being able to pour all my extra energy into building my online brand.

The first time Nick called me while he was in New York, I almost didn't see him. We were only eight months out from graduation, and the last thing I wanted was to fall back into a relationship with him—and a long-distance one at that. But Nick was Nick, and I was powerless against his clear blue eyes and orthodontia-perfected smile. The next thing I knew, I was waking up beside him and already looking forward to seeing him when he was in town again. I thought I'd finally cracked the code: I got to enjoy my favorite parts of Nick without having to endure his less desirable bits, like the way he used to passive-aggressively "like" comments I made on other guys' Facebooks or the way he never properly replaced the lid on anything.

Of course, I didn't let my pseudo-relationship with Nick keep me from exploring other options. I dated occasionally, sometimes seeing someone as many as six or seven times. Most attempts, though, never got off the ground. Far too many dates started with the guy trying to impress me by interrogating the server about the wine list, and then either flat-out ordering for me or making heavy-handed suggestions. ("The only real option here is the branzino," one particularly insufferable guy had told me, not long before he informed me that Paris was the only "real option" for a weekend getaway.) Depending on how the rest of the date was going, I might play along or I might rebel. The branzino guy earned my scorn for not listening to me when I'd mentioned I was a vegetarian; I mocked him (without including his name or face—I wasn't that cruel) in my Instagram Stories all night.

These dates often subjected me to a litany of reasons I should feel honored to be in their presence, and then gave me the opportunity to marvel at their wealth, intelligence, and interests—yet their eyes would glaze over when I tried to tell them anything about me. I was nearly always ready to leave before the entrées arrived, but it was obvious they believed they were charming me.

Almost without fail, they would casually ask "So where to next?" as they picked up the check. (It was always, *always* while they picked up the check, the subtext being that I owed them.) Eventually, I had mostly given up on dates. It wasn't like I was really missing anything in my life, especially not since I had Nick.

But my perspective had started to shift since moving to DC. Without Izzy in the next room and my coterie of New York friends, I often found myself alone, binge-watching Netflix and drinking wine. I kept up appearances on my Instagram—sometimes stretching pictures from nights out over several days—but the truth was that I was lonely. I had Cat, sure, but if she was busy—as she often was with work—I had no one to fall back on other than Nick. And maybe Cat was right; maybe the thing with Nick had run its course. Now that we were seeing each other more frequently, I was starting to remember why we had broken up in the first place. Nick could make my body quiver with a single glance, but he was selfish and jealous and could be self-absorbed to the point of being boring. Maybe it was time to consider finding someone else to share those lonely nights, someone with whom I could actually envision a future.

STILL, I HAD SURPRISED MYSELF by giving my phone number to Cat's friend Max. Based on looks alone, he wasn't the type of guy I was usually attracted to. That type of guy was—well, Nick. Genetically blessed gym rats with Kanye West–sized egos and possible drinking problems. Max wasn't bad-looking—far from it, actually—but he wasn't as glaringly handsome as Nick. He also didn't

have Nick's sense of style—the shirt and pants he wore to
the Rosalind preview were fine, although they could have
used a good pressing, but he had paired them with beat-
up Vans. *Vans*. Like some sort of mid-90s skater. But I'd
felt like he was really listening to me during our brief chat
at the museum, and when he called the day after the preview to ask me out, I found myself smiling at the sound
of his voice.

And now, as I finished dusting highlighter on my
cheekbones—using my favorite splurgy Guerlain Météor-
ites rather than the free highlighter stick I'd been sent by
a brand hoping to partner with me—I realized I was looking forward to the date. If nothing else, I knew it wouldn't
be another boring restaurant date. Max didn't seem the
sort to parade me to a high-end restaurant in order to
show off an encyclopedic knowledge of wine—*Vans*,
hello—and when I had specifically asked if we would
be going out to dinner, he said he had something else in
mind. His vagueness made selecting an outfit somewhat
difficult, but I had gone with my favorite black jumpsuit,
a piece that could read as dressy or casual depending on
the situation.

I struck a pose in my bathroom's full-length mirror—
one foot forward, hip angled, shoulders back, chin
down—and took a picture. I quickly filtered it and was
adding text reading *First Date!* when I paused. Did I really
want to share this with the world? For the last several
years, I had broadcast so much of my life that I no longer
stopped to consider whether everything merited sharing.
Maybe this was something that should remain private—if
for no other reason than I had no idea how this date was
going to go, and I didn't want a flock of virtual onlookers

watching and judging. I put my phone down. There would be plenty of time to recap the date tomorrow—by which time I would know how to spin it.

I returned to my laptop, open on my small desk, where I was streaming an eclectic Spotify playlist of some of my favorites from multiple genres. As I shut down the computer, my phone buzzed with a text message from Nick.

What time should I come over tonight?

I laughed. Of course Nick just assumed he was welcome whenever he wanted.

Tonight's no good, I typed in response.

Why not? You have a date or something?

I sent him a kissy-face emoji.

Immediately, my phone rang. I rolled my eyes as I answered, "Hi, Nicky."

"You're kidding," he said flatly. "You have a date?"

"It's true. I'm being wined and dined." I paused. "I think."

"You think?"

"I'm not sure what our plans are yet."

"Christ, Audrey. You can't just go off with some stranger without knowing where you're going, and telling someone where you'll be. Don't you ever watch *Dateline*?"

"I'm not going to get serial killed, Nick. Besides, this guy isn't really a stranger. He's friends with Cat."

He laughed. "Oh. *Oh*. Well. I'm sure he's a winner, then."

"Don't be a dick. Listen, as much as I would love to continue defending my choices with you, I've got to go."

"Text me later so I know your head didn't end up in this guy's freezer."

"Gross, Nick. I'm hanging up now."

FIFTEEN MINUTES LATER, I was stepping out of the Lyft in front of a four-story brick building—a four-story brick *mansion*, more accurately. We'd passed several embassies on the ride over to the address in Kalorama Heights, and, while I didn't see a flagpole, I couldn't help but wonder if this, too, was some sort of cultural destination. Maybe there was an event happening?

I rang the bell, all the while checking discreetly for plaques or other signage. I saw none, but was still surprised when Max, barefoot and wearing faded denim, answered the door. I stifled a smirk. The Vans were gone, but I wasn't sure this was an improvement.

"Audrey," he said, smiling warmly. "You look great."

"Thanks," I said, stepping onto the entry's shiny wood floor. Beyond Max, I could see a sitting room and, beyond that, what looked like a kitchen. Was this his *home*? Even I, who had almost zero familiarity with DC real estate, could tell this was a pricey location. Max clearly wasn't hurting for cash—despite his embarrassing shoe choice at the Rosalind preview, he must have been a donor to be there at all, and besides, he'd mentioned going to camp with Cat, and I knew Cat's family was loaded.

"Is this where you live?" I asked, unable to contain my awe.

"I wish," he said, flashing his dimples at me. "It's ours tonight, though."

"What, did we break in or something?"

He let out a surprised laugh. "Of course not. What kind of first date would this be if we ended up spending the night in jail?"

"The kind that makes a good story," I teased. "What doesn't kill you makes you more interesting, you know."

"I don't think that's how that saying goes," he said, eyes twinkling. "But I was thinking something a bit more tame for the evening. Less criminal activity, more home-cooked dinner and wine."

"Ah, well, there's always next time," I said, stepping farther into the home and peering into the sitting room. A midcentury-style teal couch and two wood-framed, mustard-colored armchairs sat around a low, modern coffee table. A large Rothko-style painting was on the wall. I raised my eyebrows, impressed. "So who *does* live here?"

"No one right now. This place is on the market. My dad's real estate firm is handling this property, and I borrowed the space for the night."

"It's incredible. How much would a place like this set a girl back?"

Scratch.

Max opened his mouth to reply, but all I heard was the scratching—not unlike the noises I often heard in my alley—coming from the side window. I whipped my head in its direction, staring hard at the drawn curtains and wondering just what might be on the other side.

"What was that?"

"What?" he asked, following my eyes to the window.

"That scratching noise."

Max shrugged. "I didn't hear anything, but I'm sure it's just a tree branch or something."

I nodded even while my pulse raced. Could it really have just been a tree branch? It had sounded too deliberate, too *human* for my comfort.

Stop being paranoid, Audrey, I chastised myself. *What do you think, that Ryan followed you all the way over here? Please. Get it together or Max is going to think you're crazy.*

"Come on," he said. "Let me show you around."

I cast one last glance at the windows before taking his hand and letting him lead me through the big, empty house.

CHAPTER THIRTY-THREE

AUDREY

Seven bedrooms, nine bathrooms, and at least four fireplaces later, I had forgotten about the scratching noises outside. The house was immense and elegant, like nothing I had ever seen—and certainly like nothing I expected to find in an urban environment. As nice as some of the ritzy town houses on the Upper East Side, but more spacious, it seriously tempted me to break my self-imposed Instagram moratorium. Max concluded the tour on the master bedroom's balcony, a space that was almost as large as my entire apartment. It was covered in potted palms, giving it a lush, tropical feel that nearly obscured the fact we were in DC—until I looked ahead.

There's this rumor that no building in the District can be taller than the Capitol Building, and while Cat has told me that's not strictly true, the city nonetheless lacks the vertical diversity I became accustomed to in New York—and lacks some of its views. But standing on the balcony of this gorgeous, private home atop a small hill in a quiet neighborhood, I could see the dome of the Capitol glowing like a luminary against the darkening sky and the Washington Monument shimmering white.

"Wow."

"I thought you'd like it," he said, smiling shyly. "Monument views like this are rare."

"Is this some sort of guerrilla marketing attempt to sell me this home? Because, I have to tell you, it's working."

"Am I that obvious?" he joked. "For the low, low price of four million dollars, all this could be yours."

"Four million, huh?" I said, surveying the private yard and swimming pool below. "That's actually not as much as I would have guessed. I'd have to sell a hell of a lot of presets, though."

"A lot of what?"

"Presets. They're basically filters," I explained. "I've been developing a collection of them, and, once I've launched it, my followers will be able to essentially adjust their Instagram photos to look just like mine."

He drew his thick brows together in confusion. "Now, admittedly, I don't know much about Instagram because—"

"The Russian porn bots," I supplied helpfully.

"Yeah," he said, grinning. "Those. So maybe this is a dumb question, but why would people want to make their photos look like yours?"

I smiled and shrugged. "For the same reason people buy Kylie Jenner's lip kits and Michael Jordan's sneakers.

They don't actually believe wearing Kylie's branded lip color will give them a pout like hers, or that Air Jordans will enable them to dunk a basketball, but they want to believe in the dream. And the dream that I'm selling is a perfectly curated, perfectly aesthetic life."

He tilted his head, warm brown eyes searching mine. "Is your life perfect?"

The honest answer was no. Of course it wasn't perfect. Whose was? I was lonely and living in a basement and losing my mind over the sound of some tree branches. But that wasn't the kind of thing I could say aloud to the adorable, thoughtful man who had presented me with a breathtaking view of the city. It wasn't even the kind of thing I could say aloud when I was alone in my own home. *Be as if.*

"I don't have too many complaints."

He smiled crookedly, his expression telling me that he saw through my charade but was too polite to call me on it. Finally, he said, "Tell me more about these presets. How do they work?"

"It's easier to show you," I said, pulling my phone from my bag. I snapped a quick photo of the view, capturing the glowing obelisk of the Washington Monument on the right side and a border of the balcony's foliage across the bottom, but otherwise taking a photo of the velvety twilight sky over the roofs of buildings. I glanced at the photo and then showed it to him.

"Very nice," he said, nodding appreciatively. "You have an eye for composition."

I looked at him out of the corner of my eyes to gauge the legitimacy of the compliment—that was the kind of thing Nick might have said mockingly—but he looked earnest. I smiled and quickly added my chosen edits. Instantly, the sky was an inkier blue, the plants a more vibrant green, the monument whiter. I held the phone out to Max for his inspection.

"What about now?"

"Wow," he said, looking impressed. "It's a subtle change, but a powerful one."

"Thanks," I said, uploading it to my Instagram grid before I remembered that I wasn't sharing images from this date. I shrugged it off. At least my caption—an emoji of the smiling moon—was ambiguous.

"So here's where I admit that the rest of the night will be far less photogenic."

"Careful," I teased. "I'm grading this date on its Instagramability."

"Then I'm afraid I've failed," he said, wincing comically as he led me to a small table in the corner of the balcony, almost completely surrounded by potted palms. A blue Dutch oven sat in the middle of the table, alongside a bowl heaped with brown rice.

"I don't know what you're talking about," I said. "This tableau is lovely."

"I made curry," he said as he lifted the Dutch oven's lid. "I promise it tastes good, but I'm aware it looks rather . . . underwhelming." He paused, then gave me a concerned look. "I should have asked if you liked spicy food."

"I *love* spicy food," I assured him as I pulled out a chair. "I can't believe you cooked for me."

I COULDN'T RECALL the last time someone other than my mother had cooked for me. For that matter,

I couldn't remember the last time that *I* had actually cooked for me—and I certainly never made anything half as delicious as the silky lemongrass curry Max had prepared. Over glasses of dry Riesling, we talked nonstop, covering topics ranging from our undergraduate experiences (I'd attended a state school with one of the nation's largest student populations, whereas Max had gone to the private, urban University of Chicago) to our opinions on the Washington, DC, metro system (I found it a pale imitation of the NYC subway, while Max offered, "At least it's not on fire all the time anymore," which sounded ominous and horrifying) and our favorite Netflix shows (I advocated for *The Crown*, and Max preferred *Black Mirror*).

"That was amazing," I told him, setting down my fork. "If I cooked at all, I'd ask for the recipe."

"It's just as well, because if I gave you the recipe, I'd have to kill you." He rose and offered his hand. "Come on, let me refresh your glass and I'll clear the table."

I took his hand, but he tugged slightly too hard and I stumbled on my wedges as I stood, landing against his chest and spilling the rest of my wine on his shirt.

"Sorry—" he began.

And I kissed him.

It was, hands down, the most awkward kiss I had ever experienced, including the kiss Tommy Neulander planted on me at the eighth-grade dance, when he aimed for my lips and caught my eye instead. Max was still speaking as I pushed my lips against his, his voice reverberating in my mouth. We stood like that, mashed together, for a split second before I pulled away, cheeks flaming with embarrassment.

"I need to . . ." I said, trailing off as I fled indoors to

the nearest bathroom. I shut myself inside and stared hard in the massive, sparkling mirror, wondering what the hell had overcome me. We'd been having a lovely, nearly enchanted evening, and then I had gone and done *that*. I had *jumped* him like some sort of sex-starved teenage boy, right after falling over my own feet, no less. It wasn't my style at all.

Get a grip, Audrey, I commanded myself.

CHAPTER THIRTY-FOUR

AUDREY

When I returned to the balcony, once again fully in possession of my cool, I discovered Max had cleared the dishes and relocated the candles from the table around the space. He had turned up the music that had been playing in the background during dinner, and I recognized the current song as "This Must Be the Place" by the Talking Heads. I smiled to myself. The song was a good omen; it had always been lucky for me. In fact, I had been listening to that song when I got the call from Ayala offering me the job. I hoped it portended good things for the rest of the evening.

"Hey," I said, joining Max at the edge of the balcony.

"Hey," he responded, handing me a freshly poured glass of wine.

As I sipped the wine and considered how to reenergize the lively conversation we'd been having before my graceless attempt at a kiss had destroyed the mood, I felt my phone buzz in my purse. Grateful for the distraction, I pulled it out and checked the notifications.

It was only Nick: Watch out for bags of zip ties and collections of sharp instruments.

As I read his message, my phone vibrated again, this time with Nick sending me one of my own Instagram posts for the Hirshhorn, a close-up of the final, bloody Rosalind diorama. I shuddered.

"Is everything okay?"

I glanced up at Max, who was looking at me with concern. I put my phone facedown on the balcony ledge and drove Nick—and Rosalind—from my mind.

"Better than okay," I said. "That dinner was delicious, and this view is incredible. You know, it might be my New York bias showing, but I never thought of DC as a particularly attractive city. You've gone and proved me wrong."

"It's not as flashy as New York, that's for sure. It has more of a quiet beauty, the kind that sneaks up on you. Someday you'll find you're in love with it without knowing what happened."

"Maybe you could show me some of the best parts," I suggested.

"I would be honored," he said seriously.

Then, holding my gaze, he cupped my face in his warm hands and lowered his mouth over mine. The tenderness of the kiss, its sweetness, caught me off guard. It was so different from kissing Nick—Nick was a technically proficient kisser who left me panting, but he didn't *touch* me like this. I never felt as though Nick needed *me* specifically to create a knock-your-socks-off kiss; all he needed was a willing mouth. Here, though, with Max, I knew that I was a part of things—my lips, tongue, desire all integral components in this gentle but irresistible kiss.

I wrapped my arms around him, surprised to find that his body felt firm and well muscled beneath his ill-fitting, slightly rumpled shirt. As I leaned into him, my phone vibrated noisily on the ledge. Max stiffened and pulled away, looking almost accusingly at my device.

Nick, if that's you, I'm going to put your *head in a freezer*, I thought viciously. I tried to ignore the phone, tried to guide Max's soft mouth back to mine, but he wasn't compliant.

"Do you need to get that?"

I shook my head, willing him to kiss me again. He watched me carefully and licked his lips, but that was all. We remained like that, he with his hands loosely on my hips, I with my arms draped around his torso, staring at each other, for one moment too long. I finally realized that we might be standing there like that all night, and, after my awkward, lunging kiss earlier in the evening, I was not going to be the one to make the first move. I dropped my arms and took a half step away.

"Well, I should probably get going," I said, hoping he would ask me to stay. "But this has been lovely. Thank you so much for inviting me."

He nodded, his expression unreadable. "Maybe I'll see you again."

I hope so, I thought.

I COULD STILL FEEL Max's soft lips against mine, could still taste the cinnamon Altoid he must have popped when I went to the restroom, as I climbed into bed with my laptop. Almost as soon as I opened the lid, an iMessage appeared up on my screen: Make it home safe and sound?

I rolled my eyes. I didn't know why my ex-boyfriend from seven years ago had suddenly decided he was my keeper, but it was no longer cute. I ignored Nick's message and started browsing Netflix.

Seriously, Aud. I just want to know that you're safe in your own bed.

Annoyed, I responded, I bet you'd like to know that.

Immediately, three dots appeared as Nick typed a reply.

Good night, Nicky, I wrote, and logged out of Messages.

Beside me, my phone buzzed. I glowered and reached for it, ready to cut off Nick's mode of communication there, too, but saw instead it was a message from Max: I had a really nice time tonight.

A smile spread across my face. I snuggled down in bed and typed out, I did too.

Another text from Nick arrived: Don't do anything stupid.

I rolled my eyes and turned off my phone, thinking, *You're the only stupid thing I do.*

CHAPTER THIRTY-FIVE

CAT

I slipped through the crowd loitering on the sidewalk, narrowly avoiding the tip of someone's burning cigarette and brushing against someone else's sweat-covered forearm. I wrinkled my nose in disgust and clutched my bag more tightly against myself, wondering whether I should just go home. I really didn't want to be pushing myself into this packed bar at nearly midnight on a Friday night, still in my work clothes and carrying a stack of Westlaw printouts in my shoulder bag.

But Audrey had insisted I meet her there, and I was sickeningly eager to hear about last night's date with Max Metcalf. I'd sat by the phone the entire night, consumed with anxiety. When I didn't hear from her, I couldn't decide whether it was a good sign or a very, very bad one.

What if Max had told Audrey about camp? What if he had happened to mention there was this nasty rumor that . . . I'd hardly been able to sleep as panicked thoughts swirled through my mind. Finally, at seven in the morning, I could stand it no longer and texted Audrey. I typed and deleted dozens of permutations before finally landing on: How'd it go?

It took her two hours to respond, and in that time I nearly died a thousand deaths.

Great! she responded. Can't wait to tell you about it!

Lunch? I typed eagerly.

Can't, have a meeting. Going out tonight for Lena's birthday, meet me there and I'll tell you everything!

And so there I was, elbowing intoxicated strangers in this overcrowded bar as I searched for Audrey rather than drawing a bubble bath and relaxing after a long week. *Where is she?* I wondered as I wiggled farther into the crowd. *If she left without telling me . . .* Finally, I spotted the bright flag of her hair, and I pressed toward her. I tapped her on a bare shoulder and she whirled around, beaming.

"Cat! There you are! Look who I found!"

I blinked when I recognized the man Audrey was talking to as the tattooed bartender from our usual trivia bar. "Oh. Hi. It's . . ."

"Eric," he supplied, his face turned to me but his eyes still on the dangerously low neckline of Audrey's flimsy white dress. "You're Cat, right?"

"That's right," I said, shoving my hand at him in an attempt to force his gaze anywhere else. "Nice to officially meet you."

He snickered and shook my hand. "Yeah, you too."

"Isn't Cat a riot?" Audrey giggled, throwing an arm around me and inadvertently sloshing her vodka soda on my arm. "Whoops! Sorry, Kitty-Cat."

"Okay," I said, taking her firmly by the hand. "We need to get you some water." I looked pointedly at the bartender to discourage him from following us and said, "Goodbye, Eric."

"See you around," he said, his eyes once more on Audrey.

"You should loosen up, Cat," Audrey said as she followed me to the bar.

"Look, Audrey, I'm tired," I said. "I came out to see you, but I didn't know that meant I was going to have to babysit you while you drunkenly flirted with some bartender."

"Don't be such a martyr," she teased. "Besides, I'm over this place anyway. Let's go home."

I sighed with relief, and together we began cutting our way through the noisy, sweaty crowd. Halfway to the door, Audrey stopped suddenly and twisted her head around.

"What?"

"I don't know," she said, sounding confused. "I just had a really strong sensation that someone was staring at me. But I don't . . . Let's just get out of here."

I glanced around the room. Out of the corner of my eye, something caught my attention, but before I could focus on it, it was gone. *What was that?* I wondered uneasily as I followed Audrey out of the bar. I'd had the impression it was a familiar face, but it had moved too quickly for me to recognize it.

Probably just Audrey's new friend Eric, I thought drily as I stepped outside.

ONCE WE WERE OUTSIDE in the fresh air, Audrey seemed to sober up a modicum.

"So you won't believe what happened," she began. "This was a birthday party for my colleague Lena, right? And I think I've told you how much she hates our other colleague Lawrence."

"He's the one that assaulted you, right?" I cut in.

"He's the creep who couldn't keep his hands to himself," she said blackly. "So Lena didn't want him there, and everyone knew it, especially him. And then who do you think showed up?"

"Really? He did?" I said, feigning surprise even though I couldn't care less about Audrey's office gossip. All I wanted to know was how the date had gone with Max, whether Max had said anything about me. Whether I needed to worry.

"He totally did. Lena made him leave and—" Audrey cut herself off and glanced over her shoulder.

"What?"

"Nothing, I just thought . . ." she muttered. Abruptly, she brightened. "Oh! So let me tell you about your friend Max."

My stomach jumped and I wasn't sure whether I should correct her on the term "friend." But before I could decide, she squealed, "First, there was this *mansion*."

As Audrey launched into a detailed play-by-play of the date, I began to relax. If anything about camp had come up, Audrey surely would have said something by now. She wouldn't be describing every piece of artwork in that house or blathering on about some text messages Nick had sent.

"Wait," I said suddenly. "Nick kept pestering you while he knew you were out?"

She laughed. "Nicky's just so insecure."

"I've met Nick," I said, frowning. "'Insecure' is not a word I would use to describe him."

She laughed again and leaned toward me, her voice loose as she said, "You didn't hear this from me, but Nick hasn't always been Mr. Suave."

"What do you mean?"

"I was his plus-one to a family wedding this one time, and his brother was telling me—" She broke off into laughter. "No, I shouldn't repeat it. Nick would kill me."

"You can tell me," I insisted. "I'm your best friend."

"I know," she said lightly. "But I really shouldn't. Let's just say that Nick hasn't always been the best with the ladies and leave it at that."

"I—"

"Did you hear that?" Audrey interrupted.

"Hear what?"

She looked over her shoulder anxiously. "I think someone's been following us."

I turned around and studied the sidewalk behind us. There were a handful of people coming and going, none of whom seemed to be looking at us in particular. "I don't see anything suspicious. Let's just get home, okay?"

Audrey nodded and stepped up her pace. "Oh, and did I tell you Max has already texted me to ask for a second date?"

"That's great. What are you guys going to do?"

She wagged a finger teasingly and said, "I said he asked, not that I accepted."

"But I thought you were just telling me what a great time you had."

"Well, yeah. But I don't want to seem too eager," she explained, as though it was the most obvious thing in the world. "That's how you scare a guy away."

Briefly, I flashed back to the night of the preview at the Hirshhorn, more than a week ago. As Connor and I shared an Uber back to Dupont Circle, I had suddenly blurted out an invitation to come over for a drink. *Eager. Way too eager.* Connor mumbled something about an early call, and we avoided each other's eyes for the rest of the ride. Since then, our conversations had been stilted and awkward. Audrey was right; that was how you scared a guy away.

"Anyway, I won't leave him hanging for too long," she said as we turned onto the path leading to her building. "Do you want to come in?"

"Thanks, but I should really get home. I'm exhausted and I have a lot of work to do tomorrow."

"All work and no play—" Audrey began, but the sound of shoes scuffing on the quiet sidewalk made us both turn around. My blood went cold as I saw the edge of a shadowy figure dart behind a tree.

"Come on," I said quietly, grabbing her by the arm. "You're not staying here tonight."

I kept my fingers wrapped tightly around Audrey's sculpted upper arm as we ran down the darkened street together, both of us panting in fear. *Audrey was right.* Someone *was* following her. I threw a glance over my shoulder, terrified that I would see the figure chasing us, but the street was dark and silent. I stared hard at the tree, searching for human movement, and saw none. I began to wonder if my eyes had been playing tricks on me.

When we reached the corner, Audrey wrenched her arm free from my grasp and shouted back down the street, "I'm not afraid of you!"

As her clear voice rang out, I was certain a head peered around the corner of the tree. I caught my breath and squinted, trying to make out any identifiable features, but it was too dark. I thought I saw the outline of a baseball cap, but I couldn't be sure. And then it disappeared.

"Did you see that?" I whispered.

Audrey nodded, her eyes wide and fearful in the moonlight. "Do you think he was following us? I mean, do you think that was random or that he was after *us*?"

I shook my head uneasily, not wanting to say what I was thinking: *He wasn't after us. He was after* you.

CHAPTER THIRTY-SIX

AUDREY

The day that *The Life and Death of Rosalind Rose* opened, I was too nervous to consume anything other than coffee and a banana. I knew the exhibit would be a success—the preview had gone well, we'd gotten positive coverage in the *Post*, and the images I'd been sharing online were generating tons of engagement—but my stomach still swarmed with butterflies, their wings furiously beating a chorus of *Don't screw this up, don't screw this up, don't screw this up.* I needed to prove myself to Ayala, not just for the promotion but also so that I could finally, definitively show her and everyone else that I was made for this line of work, that my lack of an advanced degree meant nothing.

I spent the entire morning in the gallery, streaming microinterviews with museumgoers and uploading crowd shots. After spending so many weeks virtually alone with Rosalind, I felt oddly protective of her. When I overheard someone dismissively say "that fame-hungry bitch deserved what she got," rage clouded my vision and I wanted to stomp over and demand they show some respect. I took a deep breath, restrained myself, and instead cheerfully suggested they check out the accompanying video from the artist—in which Irina Venn discussed how easy it was to blame ambitious women for their own demise, and how that was something she hoped to confront in the exhibit.

That misogynist was the outlier; almost everyone else who walked through the gallery seemed to understand the gravity of the dioramas before them. Some were affected by it more than others. I watched as one woman with long, silky black hair stared into the final glass case, in which Rosalind's small body lay dismembered. She had been frozen in place for several minutes wearing an expression of muted horror, and as I watched a tear well in her eye and her lips press into a thin line, I suddenly understood: this hit too close to home for her.

I was about to approach her when I felt a hand on my shoulder. I stiffened. Brandon, the so-called president of my fan club and Senator Potts's son, had been skulking around the gallery earlier, giving me his usual dead-eyed grin from underneath his hat. I prepared a fake smile befitting a major donor and spun around.

The smile dropped from my face when I saw it was Lawrence, wearing his orange shirt and an irritatingly casual smile.

"Amazing turnout, huh?"

I gritted my teeth so hard they squeaked. Since the preview two weeks ago, my surprise and disgust with Lawrence's behavior had simmered and concentrated until it was thick, viscous rage. His appearance at Lena's birthday party had only further cemented my anger. I was furious with him for cornering me like that and furious with him for trying to laugh it off like it was just a joke, and I was furious with myself for not reporting him. I knew that if it had happened to a friend, I would be shocked they hadn't called their boss immediately and had not relented until the aggressor had faced consequences. But it hadn't happened to a friend; it had happened to me, and I was all too aware that Lawrence had been working at the museum for years, while I was just a newly hired, underqualified Instagrammer angling for a promotion she didn't deserve. I didn't want to hold him accountable at the expense of my own career.

He squinted at me. "Everything okay?"

"Yep," I said tersely.

"Are you sure?" he asked, reaching out to touch my arm.

His fingertips grazed my skin, and my vision tilted as I remembered the way he'd laid his hands on me that night. I snatched my arm away and growled, "Keep that hand to yourself if you want to keep it at all."

"Whoa, who pissed in your coffee this morning?"

All my pent-up fury gathered on the tip of my tongue, and I felt myself on the verge of lashing out. I forced myself to swallow my anger before I caused a scene and risked the credibility I'd been working so hard to build. This scumbag was *not* going to cost me my promotion.

"I don't want you to touch me," I said, keeping my voice quiet and professional.

"Audrey—"

"*No.* I didn't want you to touch me the night of the preview, and I don't want you to touch me today, tomorrow, or ever. Got that?"

Without waiting for a response, I turned purposefully on the metal heel of my favorite pointy-toed pumps and marched toward the door. As I strode out of the room, pulse thundering, the black-haired woman caught my eye and smiled.

I WAS READY TO COLLAPSE by the time I left the museum. My feet, legs, and back ached from stalking the gallery all day in four-inch heels, and my eyes felt glazed from staring at my phone screen as I posted images and responded to comments. I'd planned an indulgent evening of self-care: a long, hot shower; a crisp glass of cool wine—I'd sprung for a twenty-five-dollar bottle of New Zealand sauvignon blanc from the cute wine shop on my street—and testing out an overnight hydrating mask (which had been sent to me by a new organic skin-care company) while watching Netflix in bed. I was already thumbing through the programming options on my phone as I walked home.

I looked up as I neared the apartment, and my stomach sank. Ryan, wearing a T-shirt with the sleeves cut off and with his brown hair hanging lankly around his shoulders, sat idly on the steps, drinking a canned energy drink and smoking a cigarette. As if he had been waiting for me, he raised his head and met my eyes. Holding the cigarette between his thumb and first finger, he took a long drag and then smiled, letting the smoke escape from the gaps in his teeth.

"Hello, neighbor."

"Hi, Ryan," I said faux brightly as I continued to my apartment.

He leaned over the stairs as I unlocked my gate, and I said a silent prayer that he wouldn't ash that cigarette on my head.

"What are you doing tonight?" he asked in his cagey way.

Why, so you know whether it's safe to break in or not? I thought. I flashed him a saccharine smile and said, "Sharpening my knives."

He burst out with a shrill, hyenalike cackle. I shuddered and hurriedly let myself into my apartment. As I carefully engaged each of my three locks, I could still hear him howling with laughter. Hoping to drown out the unsettling noise, I opened my laptop and chose a Spotify playlist heavy on my current favorite band, Ted and the Honey. I turned up the volume until I could hear nothing other than the music, then hopped in the shower.

I emerged refreshed and relaxed, and, still wrapped in my towel, headed to the kitchen for that sauvignon blanc. I'd just finished pouring a glass when my buzzer sounded.

I jumped, sloshing wine onto the tile. I glanced uneasily toward the door. *Ryan?*

The buzzer sounded again, this time holding its ear-splitting note for an extended period.

Goddamn Ryan, I thought angrily. *How would he like it if I went up there and harassed him?*

I was looking for Leanne's contact number on my phone when it vibrated in my hand with a text from Nick: I can hear you in there. Let me in!

I cautiously opened the door to find Nick, tanned and grinning. Ocean-colored eyes twinkled as they surveyed my towel-clad body, still beaded with water, and he let loose a slow wolf whistle.

I swatted at him. "Stop it."

"Nice of you to get dressed up for me."

"Yeah, well, if I'd known you were coming, I would have baked a cake," I said sarcastically. "What are you doing here?"

"What do you think?" he said, tossing me a wink as he sauntered in. "Jesus, babe, you have the worst taste in music. If it's not that seventies post-punk garbage, it's this pretentious indie rock crap."

"We can't all stan for Maroon 5," I teased, snapping shut my laptop before he could start messing with my carefully curated playlists. The last time Nick had gotten his hands on my Spotify account, he'd snuck a bunch of Maroon 5 and Coldplay songs into my playlists and it had taken me weeks to root them all out. "Hands off."

"That's not what you usually say," he said with a smirk, and then gestured to my wine. "What's a guy got to do to get a drink around here?"

"Be an invited guest?"

He put a hand over his heart in a mock-wounded gesture, and I laughed. I gave him a hard time, but I was secretly glad he was there. It had been a busy day, and I missed being able to come home after days like that and discuss them with Izzy.

"How about this?" I offered. "I'll pour you a glass of wine, but you have to listen to me talk about my day."

"Sounds fair."

While Nick worked his way through two glasses of

wine, I told him about the opening of the Rosalind exhibit and how the possibility of promotion was tied up in it.

"That promotion is as good as yours," he assured me, leaning over to kiss me. "You always get everything you want."

My response to Nick was, as ever, Pavlovian. All he had to do was brush my skin and I melted into a mindless puddle of lust. I tilted my face to his, our lips meeting. With his hands tangled in my still-wet hair, Nick pressed his body against mine and walked me backward to my bedroom, his mouth trailing down my neck as he did so. The backs of my legs hit the edge of my mattress, and Nick moved one of his legs between mine, the fabric of his jeans rubbing against my bare skin. My body automatically sloped toward him, closing the already postage stamp–sized distance between us. Leaving one hand in my hair, he moved the other to loosen the towel still knotted around my chest.

"Stop," I said suddenly, surprising us both.

Nick froze in place, his body still tight against mine, the heat of him still burning through the cloth between us. His mouth just inches from the tender skin at the base of my throat, he asked, "What's wrong?"

The sensation of his breath on my flushed skin made me shiver and I almost gave in. After all, what *was* wrong? I hadn't intended to say "stop," hadn't even realized the word was forming. As I wildly searched my brain for an explanation, Max's face appeared in my mind's eye. I almost laughed. *Max?* We had been on exactly one date, and I was choosing him over Nick? Nick, who had been in my life for a decade? It couldn't be—and yet that's who I was picturing as Nick's fingertips nestled themselves into my flesh.

"Audrey?" Nick asked, pulling away slightly to look me in the eyes.

"I'm really tired," I said, a half-truth that would buy me more time to sort out my feelings.

Nick laughed and looked at me expectantly, waiting for the punch line. When none was forthcoming, he blinked. "You're kidding."

I took a step away, his fingers falling from my side, and forced a yawn. "I'm just so, so exhausted. I really need to sleep."

He cocked his head at me and licked his lips. "Aud, babe, give me, like, fifteen minutes, and then you can have all the sleep you want."

I shook my head. "Sorry, Nicky. Not tonight. Rain check?"

"Yeah, sure," he said, brow wrinkled in confusion. He shoved his hands into his pockets and rocked back on his heels. "Hey, Audrey, you . . . you would tell me if something was going on, right?"

I hesitated. *Was* something going on? But I couldn't tell Nick about Max, not before I had even committed to a second date, and so I looked him in the eye and said, "Of course."

He nodded and lingered in my bedroom doorway, as though I might change my mind and ask him to stay.

"Okay," he finally said. "I'll see you another time then, I guess."

What's with me? I wondered, slumping down in my bed as Nick's departing footsteps echoed through my apartment and he let himself out. In the last seven years, I hadn't ever refused Nick, not even the time I was nearly delirious with a fever.

But I also hadn't ever been intrigued by anyone quite like I was intrigued by Max.

UNABLE TO FOCUS ON WORK after Nick left, I curled up in bed with a fresh glass of wine and my laptop. I was working my way through a binge session of *Gossip Girl* when I heard a now-familiar scraping noise in the alley. I paused the show and listened intently, partially believing it was just that damn cat and partially worried about that shadowy figure who may or may not have followed Cat and me home from the bar.

I caught my breath as I heard not just a scraping but a shuffling.

Shit.

Someone was out there. Terror climbed my throat, and I tried to think rationally. Last time I had confronted someone in the alley, I'd made the mistake of charging at them with that shoe. They'd fled into the night, and I'd been left without even a description of the creep to give to the police. This time I needed to be more shrewd. I would sneak out there, capture this disgusting Peeping Tom on my phone, and then call the police. Even if he booked it before they arrived, at least then I could give them a suspect. Maybe they would catch him and I could finally relax.

I opened the front door and gate as quietly as I could, but nearly blew my cover when I tripped over a random cardboard box in my walkway. I covered my mouth to mask my surprised inhalation, shoved the empty box out of the way with my foot, and began creeping along the building to the alley. Once I'd reached the alley gate, I took a deep breath and readied the camera on my phone. With my pulse thundering in my ears, I peered through the gap between the gate and the building.

There was no one there.

Confused, I threw open the gate and stepped into the alley, turning around to see every corner of it.

It was only when I pivoted back around that I realized the gate at the other end of the alley was ajar, swinging slightly on its hinges as though someone had just gone through it.

CHAPTER THIRTY-SEVEN

AUDREY

I woke groggily, consciousness sticky with the remnants of a sleeping pill. Unnerved by the incident with the near miss with someone in the alley, I'd been unable to sleep. At two in the morning, exhausted but wired, I swallowed an Ambien and fell into a dark, dreamless slumber.

I reached for my alarm-bleating phone and found that it wasn't charging in its usual spot on my cardboard box–slash–nightstand. Only after riffling through my tangled sheets did I find it in bed beside me, along with my laptop. Rubbing my eyes, I plugged in my phone and set about my first task of the day: checking the Hirshhorn social media accounts. I gave a cursory glance to the hundreds of comments that had appeared on the posts about the Rosalind opening, promising myself I would read them more fully once I was at the office and had consumed some caffeine—preferably enough caffeine to give half the city the jitters.

Next, I checked my personal account and found a bunch of messages about *Gossip Girl* (Chair 4ever!, You're prettier than Serena!, I ♥ GG!), including one from Nick: That's what you're doing instead of me? Lame, Aud. Lame.

I lay back on my pillow and turned the camera on myself, fanning my hair out around my head like rays of the sun. I experimented with a few different angles before taking a selfie using a filter that gave me puppy ears. I uploaded it to my Story with an animated GIF of a dancing cup of coffee.

That's enough procrastination, I told myself sternly. *Time to get out of bed.*

I was just setting down my phone when it buzzed with a text message from Cat: Lunch?

I hesitated. Cat had been really weird lately. She seemed incredibly invested in my accepting Max's invitation for a second date, so much so that it had made me a bit hesitant to respond. Was there some history between the two of them that I didn't know about?

I sighed and pressed a hand to my tired eyes, promising myself I would text her later.

I REALLY SHOULD HAVE *followed Nick's advice to buy a coffeemaker*, I thought as I finally left my apartment, still feeling bleary and disoriented. As I swung open the gate, I noticed the empty cardboard box I'd stumbled on last night was still on the lawn. I leaned over to grab it for the recycling and paused, noticing for the first time that my name was scrawled across the top in thick, black letters.

I crouched to investigate and gently lifted one of the unsealed flaps. Flower stems. The box wasn't empty after all. I smiled, thinking back to the beautiful orange blooms I'd found on my gate last month. My secret admirer had returned. I eagerly tossed open the other flap and froze. Stupefied, I stared at the contents.

Someone had decapitated the entire bouquet.

ACROSS THE TABLE from me at Sweetgreen, Cat's jaw hung open as she stared at a picture of the flower-less bouquet on my phone. That morning, I had snapped a photo and then promptly disposed of the stems—box and all—in the dumpster behind my building. As the heavy lid slammed shut, I'd felt eyes on me and looked up to see the dark curtains in Unit 1 swaying. Anger flooded my body as I imagined Ryan standing behind them, laughing to himself about scaring me with his childish prank. I'd thrown an infuriated double-middle-finger salute at his window and stormed away, already reaching for my phone to text Cat that we were on for lunch.

I'd barely waited for her to sit down with her salad before I thrust my phone in her face.

"Wow," she finally said. "That's intense."

"Right? Headless flowers? I'm totally creeped out."

"Is there any chance this was just trash that somehow got kicked toward your door?"

"Nope," I said, shaking my head firmly. "They were in a box labeled 'Audrey.' They were for me."

"That's so disturbing," Cat said, her thin shoulders

shuddering. "What kind of person would do something like that?"

"Well, my landlord's dirtbag grandson, Ryan, is the obvious suspect. He was lurking around when I got home from work last night, and he watched me throw the box away this morning."

"You don't sound convinced."

"It's just that . . . Ryan is more of a ring-the-buzzer-until-it-breaks kind of creep. This feels more calculated." I toyed with my fork. "You know, I can't help but wonder about my colleague Lawrence."

"I still think you should report that guy to HR. I know you're worried—"

"Let's put a pin in that," I interrupted. "Anyway, I've been avoiding being alone with him at work, but yesterday he came up to me, chatting like nothing had happened. I snapped at him a bit—not as much as I wanted to, of course, since we were standing in the gallery in full view of patrons, but enough that he seemed upset."

"Upset enough to do something like this?"

"I don't know. Maybe." A thought suddenly came to me, and my spine straightened, each vertebra tingling. "Wait. You know what? Rosalind got headless flowers, too."

"The doll? Someone sent the doll headless flowers?"

"In one of the dioramas," I clarified, grabbing my phone and opening the museum's Instagram account. I quickly found the photo I had in mind: the little blonde doll standing in her doorway, looking befuddled as she held a paper-wrapped bouquet of stems.

"Here. Look at this."

Cat's eyes widened. "Audrey, you posted this yesterday. That can't be a coincidence."

"I know," I said, nodding. "I'm wondering if Lawrence used it as inspiration."

"Have you talked to Lena?" Cat asked, taking the phone and beginning to scroll through the comments. "Hasn't she had problems with him, too?"

"Yeah, but . . ." I trailed off as I saw the color drain from Cat's face. "What is it?"

"Have you seen this?" she asked, turning the phone to face me and pointing to a single comment: *Roses are red, violets are blue, some flowers are headless, you could be too.*

"Jesus Christ," I gasped, my hands shaking as I snatched the phone from her. "I can't believe I missed that."

"Missed it? Do you have to approve the comments?"

"No, but part of my job is to read them all and delete things that are inappropriate. You'd be shocked how many morons think our posts are the best venue for a dick joke. I delete hundreds of trash comments every day. But last night I blew them off because Nick was over, and then this morning I was exhausted when I was reading through them. I must have just glossed right over this."

I tapped the name of the offending commenter, someone calling themselves "zoomie098." They used an avatar of a sunglasses-wearing wolf as a profile picture and a Chris Farley quote as their bio, and their grid was a mishmash of reposted memes in a bad imitation of Fuck-Jerry. I relaxed slightly. I was almost certain this was just a lame attempt at a joke. *Almost.* I screen-capped the profile for reference and then deleted the comment.

"Nick came over?" Cat asked sharply.

I looked up, surprised. "*That's* what you're focusing

on right now? Someone posted a rhyme about cutting off my goddamn head and you're on my case about Nick?"

"I just don't understand why you waste your time with him, especially since I thought you were interested in Max."

"Nick just dropped by to hang out," I said with a shrug.

Cat gave me a dubious look.

"It's true," I insisted. "When he went to kiss me, I actually sent him away."

"You sent Nick away? That's a first."

"Trust me, he was surprised, too."

On the table between us, my phone vibrated. We both looked down and read the text that popped up from Nick on the screen: How about some real fun tonight?

"Speak of the devil," Cat muttered.

"God, Nick, take a hint," I said, rolling my eyes as I dismissed the notification. "Needy is *not* a good look on him."

"Audrey," Cat said slowly. "You don't think . . . you don't think *Nick* might have left those flowers?"

"Oh, please," I said, bursting out laughing. "I don't think Nick even knows how to find a florist. The man has never once sent me flowers."

"Maybe there's some poetry in starting with dead flowers."

"No way. I don't know who left those flowers, but it couldn't have been Nick."

"If you say so," Cat said, but she still looked doubtful.

CHAPTER THIRTY-EIGHT

HIM

'd felt electrified as I used the shears, snipping the head from each orange rose and setting the stems carefully in a box. My hands had been bloody, my body still vibrating with a dangerous mixture of anguish and righteousness as I placed the box in front of her door, and I had walked away certain my message had been conveyed. But then the night had taken a turn, and I was no longer sure it had been the right thing to do. In fact, as I replayed the action on a loop in my mind, I became more and more worried I was only going to drive Audrey away from me.

You know he just drives everyone away. My niece's mocking words came back to me as I sat before a cheerful blue row house in Capitol Hill on a set of concrete steps I'd climbed dozens of times before.

Across the street, I saw a sandy-haired woman lean over a high-end stroller, cooing at the infant inside. With a start, I realized this was the same woman who used to waddle up and down these streets, her hands cupping her massively pregnant belly. I wanted to rush across the street to congratulate her, peer underneath the awning of the stroller to see whether the baby had its mother's sharp features, tickle its fat little feet. I restrained myself. The last time I had seen this woman, I had been shouting some things I wasn't proud of, and I didn't want to alarm her.

But, oh, how seeing her and her infant made me smile. My body went warm and fuzzy as I imagined Audrey's slight form swelling with the fruit of our union. Her small face would grow rounder, glow, as she carried our little one within her body, and when our beautiful child finally made its way into the world, she would look up at me from the hospital bed with a bursting smile and say, *I love you. I love this life you've given me.*

I was stroking the downy head of our perfect infant and planning its future when I realized my ex-girlfriend Aly was standing at the base of the steps. Her cheeks were white and her shiny brown ponytail trembled; one thin hand clutched at the lapels of her navy suit jacket while the other drew her NPR tote bag across her body like a shield. Irritation flared within me. Aly had always been so dramatic.

"What are you—?" she began, looking around wildly as if searching for help. Her dark eyes landed on the new mother across the street, and she opened her mouth as if she was going to call out but then seemed to think better of it. She looked back at me, tightening her grip on her bag. "You shouldn't be here."

"Nice to see you, too, Aly," I said, standing up. "It's been a while. Six months, right? Since you unceremoniously dumped me over text message?"

She took a step backward, and something inside me clenched. For a split second, I envisioned grabbing that ponytail in my fist and using it to smash her plain face into the concrete. That would really give her something to be frightened of.

I held up my hands to show her my palms. "Relax, I'm just here to talk."

"There's nothing to talk about," she said, taking another step away from me.

"That's not true," I said, fury swirling hot in my gut as I remembered the cold message Aly had sent to dismiss me. *I no longer see a future for us. Please don't call again.* I'd ignored her edict and called, and then I continued calling, my anger growing in intensity each time I heard her voice mail. And then I'd found myself on these same steps one night, waiting for her to come home, my fists like spring-loaded rocks at my sides.

I swallowed hard, forced my hands to unclench. "Aly, I just want to know what I did wrong. I don't want to make the same mistake again."

"Again?" she repeated, her eyes narrowing. "Are you dating someone?"

"Don't look at me like that," I snapped. God, how could I have forgotten how *suspicious* Aly was about everything?

"I'm not—"

"You were. You were looking at me like I could never have a relationship. I know that's what your friend Leigh thinks, but she's wrong. You're wrong. You're *all* wrong."

She tightened her mouth into an almost invisible line. "Don't take another step."

I looked down, surprised to find that I was now standing only an arm's length from her. "Aly, I—"

"You need to leave."

"Aly," I started, softening my voice.

"I'm going to take a walk around the block. When I come back, you can't be here." She stared at me so intensely her eyes bugged slightly. "Do you understand?"

Do you understand? Like I was some sort of simpleton, incapable of comprehending basic language. The men from the Overexposed forums had been right about Aly: she was nothing but an uptight bitch. She would never be happy, and I deserved much better than her.

"I understand," I sneered at her.

"Good," she said, nodding abruptly. She pivoted on her heel and marched off, without looking back even once. I watched her go, her strong runner's calves bobbing from underneath the hem of her skirt suit. Aly was so *severe*. It was hard to imagine that I had once thought she was something special.

I paused and looked back at her building. Within a week after sending that impersonal message, Aly had changed the locks on her home. It had been performative; the lock she had installed wasn't anything special. I could easily break the glass panel beside the door, snake my arm through the newly created hole, and let myself inside her apartment. I could smash the mason jars she used to serve drinks, an affectation that drove me mad; knock all the pretentious biographies and all the books of political analysis she said I didn't understand off her flimsy IKEA shelves; burn those expensive candles that smelled like sugar until there was nothing left but crumbling wicks. I could wait in the shadows of that dark row house until she returned home and—

No.

That wouldn't get me any closer to Audrey, and she was all that mattered. Everything else was just a distraction.

CHAPTER THIRTY-NINE

CAT

Bill Hannover summoning me into his corner office on a Friday afternoon could mean only one thing: my weekend was about to be consumed with some research project or motion drafting. In the four years I had worked at the firm, I could count on my fingers the number of times I'd had a completely clear weekend. It wasn't something that bothered me. I knew that sacrificing my weekends was a necessary step on my path to the partnership, and I was happy to hand them over. Since Audrey had parachuted back into my life, however, I'd started carving out more time to spend with her, checking out new restaurants, visiting the museums, and acting as her photographer so she could pose in front of interesting backdrops from the Lincoln Memorial to that house on Q Street that was painted to look like a water-melon.

That weekend, though, I was free to do all the work Bill might pile upon me. Audrey had a second date with Max Metcalf, and I'd felt both relieved and queasy since she announced it. Their relationship seemed like a catch-22. If things didn't work out, would Max hold me accountable and make good on his "a person never forgets camp" threat? On the other hand, if they *did*, would Camp Blackwood come up in their conversation? Would Emily Snow? And once Audrey learned about that summer, what would she do with that knowledge? She'd never demonstrated discretion with other people's secrets (for example, I knew exactly how many men our mutual friend Jasmine had slept with, even though Jasmine had never once revealed a partner to me), and she had a platform that could reach more than a million people in an instant. I couldn't decide which scenario was worse.

I shuddered and pushed the unpleasant thoughts from my mind as I took a seat before Bill's modern glass desk. Work first, then I would worry about Audrey and Max.

"Catherine," Bill said, looking up from a thick binder and rubbing his neatly trimmed gray beard. "Thanks for coming by. I have to jump on a call in a minute, so I'll make this brief. I've been impressed with your work."

I held my breath, hoping Bill wouldn't add a "but" and go on to mention the memo I had flubbed after Audrey kept me up all night.

"You're the kind of diligent, conscientious associate I want in my corner. Do you have time to join my team for the Phillips litigation? I'm not going to sugarcoat it, it'll be round-the-clock work for a while, but it's an interesting case and we'll be arguing it before the Southern District in October."

"I have the time," I assured him, chest expanding with pride. "Count me in."

"All right," Bill said with a decisive nod. "Glad you'll be joining us. My assistant will reach out later to schedule an on-boarding meeting for the full team."

Bill picked up his pen and turned back to his binder, dismissing me. I rose from the chair and floated out the door, nearly running directly into Connor. He looked behind me to Bill's office, then gave me a quick smile and, with an inclination of his head, indicated I should follow him down the hallway. Butterflies burst into my stomach. This was the most significant interaction I'd had with Connor since the uncomfortable night at the Hirshhorn two and a half weeks earlier, and I had been craving a return to normalcy with him. I missed our jokes, the way his hazel eyes twinkled when he smiled, the slight imperfection in that otherwise gorgeous smile.

"So," he said, voice low, as we walked down the hallway. "Coming from Bill's office, huh? And with a smile on your face? Let me guess: Good news about the Phillips team?"

I nodded, straining hard to remain professional. "I've been killing myself to get staffed on that case. You know how most of the cases I work on settle, so I'm excited to get in the courtroom. And there's no denying that this is an interesting case. The libel allegations alone—"

"Yeah, definitely. Well, congrats. It'll be fun working with you."

My heart skipped a beat, part thrilled at the prospect of working alongside Connor, part offended Bill had chosen him before me. "I didn't realize you were on the team, too."

"Yeah, Bill asked me this morning. Sounds like there'll be a lot of all-nighters in our immediate future."

Against my will, my heartbeat resumed and stepped up to a double-speed pace as I imagined long nights in the office with Connor, the two of us holed up in a conference room, chugging coffee and sharing vending machine candy, discussing the finer points of our legal arguments. Our hands would meet atop a stack of binders, and everything that had happened since Audrey had begun messing in our relationship would melt away. This would be our chance to start fresh, to recapture the intellectually stimulating atmosphere of when we first met.

"Oh, well," I said, forcing a casual shrug. "That's just part of the job."

THAT NIGHT, I dreamed about Connor. I awoke flushed, my whole body tingling from the sensation of dream-Connor tracing his long fingers over and inside my body. My cheeks grew hot and I pulled my covers back up over my face. I was relieved it was Saturday and I wouldn't have to go into the office, where I was sure the indecent scenarios my sleeping brain had conjured would be glaringly obvious. My only conversations with Connor that day would be over email, and for that I was grateful.

The dream continued resurfacing during the course of the day, popping into my head when I was in the middle of reading a case or blending a smoothie for lunch or responding to Audrey's texts about what she should wear on her second date with Max. Memories of the dream (the feel of his soft lips meeting mine, his hands being assuredly placed on my hips, then stroking the skin there lower and lower and lower . . .) kept me so mellow I didn't even feel any anxiety over what Audrey and Max might talk about on their date.

I was still luxuriating in my secret fantasy as I walked to my usual Saturday afternoon nail appointment. I could already hear Monet teasing me about the blush in my cheeks, and I was debating whether to tell her some version of the truth when I thought I saw Connor's tall form on the sidewalk in front of me. I stopped short, certain my overactive imagination had created this apparition. I watched the Connor-like image as it walked ahead of me, certain it would soon fade into the nothingness it assuredly was. But when it pulled open the door to Columbia Brews and disappeared inside, I realized it wasn't some sort of shade. It was Connor, in the flesh.

Sweat tickled my palms. This was my perfect opportunity to casually chat with him outside of work, to try to repair some of the damage that had been done to our relationship. All I had to do was walk into the coffee shop, act surprised to see him there, and then . . . what? My inclination was to talk about work, but I knew Audrey would chastise me for that. *Let him see you as someone other than his colleague,* she had said to me, and that advice rang through my ears. But what should I say? What would Audrey say in this situation? I closed my eyes and tried to imagine myself as her, imagine what she would say if she happened upon the object of her affection while out. She would clap her hands joyfully, the gold bracelets she often wore tinkling with the motion, and she would make a joke about him stalking her. Or would the joke be about *her* stalking *him*? Audrey did self-deprecation better than I did; she always managed to seem humble yet still glittery.

Just say something, I told myself, and took a deep breath before following Connor inside the coffee shop. It was crowded, and it took me a moment to spot him. When I did, I caught my breath. He was seated at a two-top in the back, across from a petite woman. I couldn't see her expression, but the way Connor was looking intently at her and leaning forward made the nature of their meeting obvious.

Connor is on a date.

Unbidden, the dream slipped back into my consciousness, flooding my mind's eye with false memories of dream-Connor's warm body pressed against mine, his breath in my ear, his voice, low and soft, saying my name. Tears stung my eyes, and I whirled around, racing out of the coffee shop. If he saw me spying on him on a date, I would never live down the humiliation.

Just outside the door, the tears began to fall in earnest. Swiping futilely at them, I hid inside a nearby bus shelter and called Audrey.

A date, I thought as the phone rang. *He is on a date. How long has he been dating? How am I ever going to fix this?*

I tapped my foot anxiously as I waited for Audrey to answer. She would know what to do. She had more experience with dating than I had; she would know how to advise me. Refreshed tears blurred my vision as her voice mail picked up and I lowered my phone in defeat.

That's right. She's out with Max.

I frowned bitterly. This was partially Max's fault.

When he walked out of my past that night at the Hirsh-horn, I had been so worried about what he might tell Connor or Audrey that I'd dropped my eye from the prize. The almost-date Audrey had arranged had been ruined in part because I'd let Max Metcalf get under my skin. And he was out with Audrey right at that moment, getting exactly what he wanted. It wasn't fair.

CHAPTER FORTY

AUDREY

Roses are red, violets are blue, some flowers are headless, you could be too.

The unsettling rhyme had been looping through my brain for days. Even though I'd gone all twenty-first-century Nancy Drew on the comment's author and was 99 percent certain he was a bored Nebraskan teenager making a bad joke about Rosalind, I couldn't completely banish the uneasiness the vague threat had inspired. Even now, sitting in the passenger seat of Max's silver Prius, singing along to a Beatles station on satellite radio as we cruised downtown on a sunny Saturday afternoon, the unpleasant little ditty popped into my head.

I rubbed my arms to banish the sudden gooseflesh

and chastised myself, *Stop being ridiculous. No one is going to cut off your head.*

But I couldn't shake the unease that clung to me like a cobweb. So that edgelord wannabe poet hadn't left me those headless roses, but *someone* had. Someone had gone to the trouble of buying a giant bouquet, cutting off each flower's bloom, and then leaving the thorn-studded stems on my doorstep. It was clearly a message of some kind, but I had no idea what that message was or who it was from.

"Is everything all right?" Max asked, bringing me back to the present.

I banished all thoughts of those awful stems from my mind and stretched my gloss-covered lips into a smile. "Absolutely. Just wondering where we're going."

He adjusted his Ray-Ban aviators and smiled mischievously. "If I told you, that would ruin the surprise."

WE DROVE INTO VIRGINIA over the Fourteenth Street Bridge and out past the airport before looping back toward the city and eventually pulling into a crowded parking lot.

"Where are we?" I asked as I climbed out of the car. I couldn't see much of anything other than an expanse of grass hidden by some trees, a strip of water, and a row of porta potties. Near us, a rowdy pack of teenagers were chasing each other and waving a Frisbee in the air. Beyond them, I saw mostly sneaker-wearing couples pushing toddlers in strollers and people dressed in padded shorts and helmets walking bicycles. I looked down at my chambray sundress and platform sandals and sincerely hoped Max wasn't expecting me to engage in some sort of physical activity.

"So many questions," he teased, unloading a pair of reusable Trader Joe's tote bags from the trunk.

"I don't like secrets," I said, grabbing the edge of one of the bags and peering inside. I spotted a cutting board and baguette and looked up triumphantly. "Aha! It's a picnic."

"You were the kind of kid who searched for her Christmas presents, weren't you?" he guessed with a laugh. "But, yes, you caught me. It's a picnic. Now that the weather is finally cooling down, I thought it would be nice to spend some time outside."

I took one of the bags from him and together we began walking toward the grass. "I haven't been on a picnic in ages. When I first moved to New York, I used to try to convince my roommates to picnic in Central Park with me. I'd get all this stuff from Zabar's, but they weren't really into eating, so—"

The rest of my words were drowned out by a sudden roar from above. I snapped my head up and saw an enormous airplane careening toward the ground in front of us. I froze, veins crackling with terror, unable to look away from the impending disaster.

"Oh my God," I croaked out, clutching Max's arm. "It's—"

Before I could finish my panicked sentence, the plane landed gracefully on what I now recognized as a runway leading toward the airport. Fingertips still digging into Max's biceps, I turned to him in shock.

"Holy shit, did you *see* that? That couldn't have been normal, right?"

"Normal, expected, and the entire reason we're here," he said, dimples popping as he smiled impishly. He pointed across the water to where the plane was still taxiing. "That's DCA over there. This park is called Gravelly Point, and people come out here to watch the planes land and take off."

"That was wild. I had no idea this was out here."

"Most people don't. I know I promised to show you the most beautiful parts of the city, and this is not really beautiful or technically within the city, but—"

"It's amazing," I interrupted. "And a total rush. Thanks for bringing me here."

"Come on," he said, taking my still-sweating hand in his and leading me toward the grass. "Let's set up that picnic."

"THIS LOOKS INCREDIBLE," I said, admiring the feast of crudités, baguette, grapes, and a variety of cheeses that Max had arranged on a red-and-white-checkered blanket. "I mean, what are you even doing with that blanket? It's a *perfect* picnic blanket and makes the whole thing look like something out of a magazine. Which, I'm sure you realize, is total catnip for me. I've got to take a picture of this."

"You said you rated dates on Instagramability," he said, grinning. "And I'll confess, I bought the blanket especially for this."

"I knew it!" I laughed, swatting at him. "The only people with checkered picnic blankets are suburban moms from the fifties and influencers."

"And those who want to impress them."

"Well, it worked," I teased while I snapped a photo and quickly applied my preset filter. As I was typing out a caption, the sky broke apart with the thunderous sound of another plane arriving. Even though I knew what to expect this time, my heart jumped as I looked up to see the belly of a red-and-blue plane flying low above us.

"Wow," I said. "Where do you think this one's coming from?"

He tilted his face upward and the sunlight caught his blond curls, turning them golden. He thought for a moment and then decisively said, "Dallas."

"No way," I protested. "Not Dallas. Somewhere more exotic. Thailand, maybe."

"Maybe," he said slowly. "Although that would be unusual, considering DCA doesn't service international flights."

I wrinkled my nose and stuck out my tongue, making him laugh.

"Here, look, there's this app where you can see what planes are coming from where," he said as he pulled out his phone. He tapped on it briefly, then held it up in the air and beckoned me to look at it with him. "You can view planes that are coming and if you tap on them—see, like this? It'll tell you where they're coming from and where they're going."

"Okay, that's pretty cool," I said begrudgingly. "Not quite as cool as Thailand, but pretty cool."

He smiled and lowered his phone. "Have you ever been to Thailand?"

"No, but it's at the very top of my bucket list. I've been planning my fantasy vacation there for years. Seriously, I have this Pinterest board crammed full of articles on the best places to eat in Bangkok and the best islands for snorkeling."

"You should stop planning and just go. I went a few years ago, and it was one of the most incredible experiences of my life. I spent a few days in Bangkok, a few more in Chiang Mai, and then a week island hopping. I can give you all sorts of recommendations."

"Maybe I'll take you up on that someday. If I ever find someone to go with me."

"I'm sure you won't have trouble finding a travel companion. What about Cat?"

"Oh, come on, you know Cat. Can you honestly imagine her taking time off work?"

"She *is* a little tightly wound," he allowed, smiling crookedly. "Here, tell you what: if you can't find someone who wants to go, I'll go with you."

I laughed. "Sure. We just met, let's fly to Asia together! It can be our third date. What could go wrong?"

He laughed with me, but soon our laughter faded and we were left looking at each other with goofy half smiles on our faces. Max's tongue darted out to wet his lips, and then he leaned toward me. I closed the distance between us, our lips meeting in the middle. He cupped my face in his hands, the slightly rough pads of his thumbs stroking my cheeks, and warmth spread like molten lava through my limbs. Dimly, I heard the roar of another plane, but all I could focus on was Max, on the connection of our mouths and the smell of his skin.

Roses are red, violets are blue, some flowers are headless, you could be too.

I shivered involuntarily as the rhyme resurfaced suddenly and without warning, and Max pulled away, his eyebrows knitted in concern.

"Is something wrong?"

I shook my head and reached for him, but he held me off.

"Are you sure? Was I too forward there? I was just kidding about—"

"Nothing's wrong," I promised. "Just some online stuff I thought about for a second. It's nothing."

"Online stuff?" He tilted his head. "You mean your . . . what did you call them? Presets?"

"Not them, actually. I haven't quite finished them yet. I'm getting close, though. I actually used a trial version when I shared the picture of the picnic earlier."

"Really? Can I see?"

"Sure," I said, grabbing my phone and opening Instagram. I tapped on the new photo in my grid and started to hand Max the phone, glancing offhandedly at the comments as I did so.

One in particular caught my attention: *Who are you with?*

My skin prickled. I could feel Max's eyes on me, and, not wanting him to think something was amiss, I quickly deleted the comment and handed over my phone with a bright smile.

"Here you go. See how bold the colors are? Particularly that blanket." I winked. "It was a good investment."

"I knew it," he said faux seriously. "But, Audrey, really, this looks incredible. You took my dumb little picnic and made it look like . . . I don't know, like *art*. I can see why you have so many followers."

I put on an amused smile, but I couldn't stop thinking about the Instagram comment. *Who are you with?* It could be innocuous, but it felt menacing. I rubbed my hands over my arms, quelling the sudden outbreak of gooseflesh, and surreptitiously glanced around. Was someone watching us?

CHAPTER FORTY-ONE

HIM

We had only just sat down to dinner when Arielle placed one of her spray-tanned, acrylic-tipped hands across her flat stomach and said, "No wine for me, thanks. Tag and I are expecting again." Both of my parents leaped from their chairs with the kind of enthusiasm they reserved exclusively for congratulating inseminated daughters-in-law and began lavishing attention on Arielle, who basked in it. At one point, I swear my mother was petting her like she was some sort of prized cat. I muttered a halfhearted "Congratulations" to Tag and stabbed a fork into my endive salad.

I should have been grateful that Arielle was commanding all the attention, leaving no one to harass me about my love life, but it was a Pyrrhic victory. Pregnant

Arielle was even more insufferable than nonpregnant Arielle. She acted as though she were some sacred vessel, even though I and everyone else in the room knew that Arielle was not the only woman to carry Tag's progeny. It was an open secret that our father had given Tag's high school girlfriend an undisclosed sum of money to go away and pretend the baby wasn't his. It was nausea inducing.

I tuned them out, hoping I could just get through one dinner unscathed.

And then I heard Arielle's voice, dripping with fake sweetness, ask me, "How are things going with your secret girlfriend, Peanut?"

I glared at Arielle. Her innocent act was such bullshit. My fingers itched to close around my steak knife, to lunge across the table and jam it through the exposed orange flesh of her neck. I could imagine her eyes widening in surprise as the blade plunged in, could almost hear the sound of her skin ripping as I dragged the serrated edge downward. Everyone would back away in shock, and no one would ever, ever interrogate me about my dating habits again.

"Yeah," Tag added. "How are things going? Did you ever take my advice to send her flowers?"

Without meaning to, I burst out laughing.

Simon and Tag exchanged a look.

I composed myself and said, "As a matter of fact, yes, I did."

"That's great," Simon said. "What did she say?"

"She definitely took notice."

"So what's the harm in telling us about her?" Arielle pressed. She threw a look at Leigh and added, "Is it someone we already know?"

I pressed my lips into a thin line, and Arielle laughed. "Is that a yes?"

Leigh cut her pale eyes at Arielle and shook her head. Sometimes, when I imagined slicing open every one of their worthless torsos and stringing their entrails along the banister like a festive garland, I spared Leigh. She was the only one of the lot with a single kind bone in her body.

I turned my attention back to my dinner, keeping my face tilted to my plate and chewing diligently, and eventually they moved on to other topics that weren't me. It didn't take long. Narcissists can't help but talk about themselves.

AS MY MOTHER led everyone out to the porch for after-dinner drinks, Leigh pulled me aside in the hallway. She pushed her mousy brown hair behind her ears and drew her thin face into a worried expression before saying quietly, "I know you saw Aly."

Her pale eyes searched mine, plainly looking for some sign of guilt, some admission that I'd done something wrong. I wouldn't give her that satisfaction.

"Yeah. So?"

Leigh shifted, looking uncomfortable. "You know Aly doesn't want to see you."

"Then why did she call me?" I challenged.

"Oh, Peanut," she sighed. "Aly didn't call you. Don't forget that she and I are friends; she told me all about you going to her house."

"She *did* call me," I insisted. "Yeah, I stopped by her house the other day and she told me she didn't want to talk, so I left. But she called me yesterday morning and asked to grab coffee."

Leigh stared at me, her expression unreadable. I stared back, daring her to call me a liar. I knew she wouldn't. She was too sweet. There was a reason Leigh was the only member of this family I would spare in a massacre.

But I understood her doubt. Leigh had set us up, and Aly had always run to her with all sorts of complaints about me, from my alleged clinginess to the time I shattered her bathroom mirror. (The latter was a simple misunderstanding, but that hadn't stopped Aly from spinning a tale for Leigh about my supposed rage issues.) I was sure Aly had called Leigh to report my uninvited appearance, but hadn't bothered to later correct the record when she called me. Because she *had* called. Saturday morning, her voice supplicating, Aly had phoned and asked if I still wanted to talk. When I said of course, she suggested meeting at a coffee shop. *Neutral territory*, she'd said.

Territory. As though we were warring nations rather than onetime lovers who had drifted apart. Christ, Aly could be so dramatic.

She met me at the coffee shop wearing white, something that irritated me for its connotations of purity. Aly was not the innocent one here, and I was about to tell her so when she opened her mouth and apologized.

"I'm sorry," she said, looking me straight in the eye. "I've thought about it, and I think I overreacted. I was surprised to see you, that's all. After how we left things."

And I smiled. How had I forgotten that while Aly could be theatrical and irrational, she was also quick to say she was sorry? I graciously accepted her apology and offered my own for not calling ahead, all the while hoping she would give me what I really wanted: a playbook to help ensure I didn't make the same mistakes with Audrey, didn't drive Audrey away like my family thought I did Aly.

But Aly had nothing to say she hadn't said already, just one more chorus in the song of "it wasn't meant to be." Why had she called me, then? To assuage her own guilt? What a self-serving waste of time.

Sitting across from me, she had smiled encouragingly, her too-pink lipstick clashing with her olive complexion. "You'll find someone someday. I know you will."

I bit my cheek hard enough to draw blood, and smiled at her while the inside of my mouth went copper. If only she knew.

CHAPTER FORTY-TWO

AUDREY

I sat straight up in bed, blinking my eyes in the dark as my heart thundered against my rib cage. *What was that?* I remained perfectly still, not even breathing as I listened for whatever had awakened me. Nothing. Carefully, I pushed myself out of bed and padded to the window. I lifted the edge of the curtain and looked out into the alley. It was empty. I exhaled, sagging with relief.

Maybe I'm just talking to myself again, I thought as I reached for my phone to check the Luna Listen app. Only after I had opened it did I realize I hadn't set it. I was about to put down the phone when I noticed two unheard recordings from weeks ago, both from the same date: the day *The Life and Death of Rosalind Rose* opened. Between the thrill of finally sharing the dioramas with the public, the confrontation I'd had with Lawrence, and the unexpected visit from Nick, that day had been a whirlwind—I couldn't imagine what kind of nonsense I would be mumbling about in my sleep.

Curious, I pressed "play." The recording started with a muffled *thud* followed by a series of soft taps. Footsteps? I shuddered before I remembered that I was listening to a recording of the *inside* of my apartment. The footsteps had to belong to me. *That's new,* I thought. *No one's ever accused me of sleepwalking.*

But then I remembered swallowing a sleeping pill late that night, and also an article I'd once read listing some genuinely strange things people had done after taking sleeping pills: calling friends, eating, having sex, even driving. Apparently I was a sleepwalker when under the influence of sleeping pills. Who knew? I turned up the volume on my phone, wondering what else I might hear.

"Hi."

My voice on the recording was so loud and clear I almost laughed. Most of the nocturnal chatter I'd captured with the Luna Listen app had been either sleepy murmurs or terrified shouts. This was a chipper, wide-awake greeting.

Then I heard something else, something that stripped the smile from my face. A shushing noise, possibly rustling of some sort? I rewound the recording and listened, trying to determine if it was more movement or perhaps just me in my sheets. I had to listen to it twice more before I realized what it was, and when I did, I dropped my phone in horror.

A voice, low and hushed, saying, "You're dreaming."
Someone had been in the apartment with me.

THERE WAS NO CHANCE of sleep. With my sharp-
est knife—a beautiful, shiny butcher's knife I'd purchased
purely for the aesthetics and had used only once for a
staged photo of slicing fresh veggies—clutched in my
hand, I ripped my apartment to pieces, searching every
nook, cranny, and possible hiding place. I pushed open
the bathroom door and froze, my eyes fixed on a shadow
on the shower curtain. *Someone is in there.* I nearly
blacked out with fear, but gripped the knife and forced
myself into action. With a primal yell and my arm poised
and ready to stab the hell out of an intruder, I thrust the
curtain aside to find the shower empty. I staggered out of
the bathroom and collapsed in the beanbag chair, surveying the apartment.

There was no one there but me . . . at the moment.

You're dreaming.

Just remembering those words made me feel like
I'd been dipped in ice water. Who had been in my apartment? And what had they wanted? After hearing that
muted voice, I forced myself to keep listening, terrified
of what I might hear, but there was nothing else on that
recording. The second recording, time-stamped just over
an hour later, was brief and familiar: the same soft taps
followed by the same muffled thud. As incomprehensible
as it sounded, it seemed someone had come inside and
watched me sleep.

But what kind of sicko would do something like that?
Ryan, I thought immediately. It had to be Ryan. I

hadn't seen any indication of a break-in, and no one else had access to the keys. There was no other . . .

Oh, I thought, suddenly remembering what had happened after Nick left. I'd heard the footsteps in the alley and had gone to explore. Exhausted and distracted, I must not have locked the door. I'd practically invited the intruder in. But what kind of intruder just came in to watch you sleep?

The kind that wants to be sleeping with *you*.

I shook my head to clear the thought. I knew Cat thought Nick was the one who left those headless flowers that night, but she was wrong. That wasn't the kind of thing he would do, and he certainly wouldn't break into my apartment to watch me sleep. It couldn't be Nick . . . could it?

NICK WAS WAITING for me in the Hirshhorn lobby, lounging in one of the sleek chairs as he typed on his phone. Light poured in from the huge windows, illuminating golden highlights in his hair, and my stomach twisted. This was Nick—Nick, a man I'd slept beside hundreds of times, a man who'd held my hand through tattoos and turbulence, weddings and funerals. I couldn't believe that I was about to accuse him of something so deranged it seemed ripped from a horror movie. The idea should have been laughable, but things had gotten weird between us since I had moved to DC.

I had to ask, and I had to ask him face-to-face. I'd known Nick long enough to tell when he was lying (tugging on his right ear while saying "No, Audrey, I didn't sleep with that freshman" meant "Yes, Audrey, I *did* sleep with that freshman—more than once, in fact"), and I needed to watch his reaction.

"Hey," I greeted him, my bitter anxiety making my throat feel tight and constricted. "Thanks for meeting me."

"Sure thing, babe," Nick said, looking up from his phone with an easy grin. He clocked my expression and his smile faded. "What's wrong?"

You're being crazy, my inner voice scolded. *Nick is your friend. Don't accuse him of this.*

But I'd come this far, and so I took a deep breath and lowered myself into the chair beside him. "I need you to be honest with me, okay?"

"Always."

"The other week, that night I wouldn't let you stay over—"

"You've come to your senses and want to apologize?" he broke in, cracking a smile. "It's okay; I forgive you. You didn't need to call a summit for that."

He paused, clearly expecting me to laugh. Any other time I would have, but instead I shook my head and said, "Let me finish. After you left, you went home, right?"

He cocked his head to the side. "Are you asking me if I hooked up with someone else?"

"No, I don't care about that." Nick looked offended and opened his mouth to say something, but I cut him off. "Wherever you went when you left. You didn't come back, right?"

"No, of course not. You know I didn't."

The tightness in my body started to subside. There was no ear tugging, no shiftiness, no indication he was lying. Nick's face was an open book—a confused book, but an open one nonetheless. He had no idea what I was talking about.

"And you didn't . . . linger in the alley before you left?"

"*What?* Why would I do that?"

"And the flowers . . ."

"Audrey, what's going on?"

"Something really weird happened," I admitted, pulling my phone from my bag and opening the Luna Listen app. "Here. Listen."

Nick clicked the "play" button and held the phone between us. The *thump* of the door sounded, followed by a brief silence.

He turned to me curiously. "What is this?"

I shushed him as the footsteps started.

Hi, my voice said on the recording, loud enough to make my body erupt in goose bumps. I would never get used to hearing myself talk in my sleep.

"That's you," he said. He glanced down at the app's interface and started to smile. "Wait a minute, I know what this is. This is one of those sleep-tracking apps. Are you sleep—"

"Listen," I commanded.

You're dreaming, the soft voice said. My stomach rolled unpleasantly and I looked to Nick, but he didn't even flinch.

Oh, my voice said.

"There you are again," Nick said. He smiled triumphantly and pumped his fist. "I've been telling you for *years* that you talk in your sleep. Vindication at last!"

Too preoccupied to correct him that I'd never doubted I talked in my sleep, only that I said the filthy things he claimed I did, I said, "You didn't hear it?"

"Hear what?"

"Really listen this time," I admonished him, using my finger to rewind the audio and restart it.

Nick gave me a strange look but obeyed. When the recording finished, he looked at me and shrugged. "I don't know. All I hear is some noise, and then you saying 'hi' and 'oh.'"

"You heard nothing between my words? Nothing at all?"

"Maybe some mumbling, I guess. Nothing clear." He frowned. "Was I supposed to hear something?"

"You have to listen again," I said, starting to rewind it once more.

"Audrey."

I startled when I heard my name behind me, suddenly aware that I was in the lobby of my place of employment, playing a recording of me talking in my sleep for anyone within listening distance to hear. I swiveled in my chair to find Lawrence hovering behind me. He was staring hard at my phone, and the expression on his face made my skin crawl.

"Sorry to interrupt," he said, looking pointedly at Nick. "But do you have a minute?"

"Not right now," I said, struggling to modulate my tone of voice. Even though I hadn't forgiven Lawrence for the way he'd behaved at the preview, I was trying to maintain a professional relationship with him. "But I'll come find you when I do, okay?"

Lawrence nodded tightly, cast another look at Nick, and then turned to leave. I felt my body sag with relief as he walked away.

"Nice bow tie," Nick said, snickering. "Listen, Aud, as

much fun as we're having with whatever this is, I have to get to work. Why don't you just tell me what's going on?"

"Just one more time, Nicky. Please."

He rolled his eyes good-naturedly and held the phone close to his ear as the audio played once more.

"Okay," he said, frowning. "Yeah, okay. I heard it that time. You say, 'Hi, you're dreaming, oh.'"

"You think *I* said all that? You think *I'm* the one who said 'you're dreaming'?"

"Who else would it have been?"

"That's kind of the question. I've got this recording, which sure makes it sound like someone was in my apartment, but nothing's missing. And it sort of sounds like they just stood there, so—"

"Hold up," Nick interrupted. "Is *this* why you were asking me if I went home? You think that's *me*? You think I'm some sort of weirdo who gets off on watching you sleep?"

"That's not—"

"I've got news for you, babe. I have better things to do than watch you toss and turn."

I arched an eyebrow at him.

He snorted and shook his head. "The ego on you."

"That's why you love me, though, right?" I said, hoping to lighten the mood.

A slight smirk appeared on his face. "That and that ass of yours."

"Well, my ass and I were totally freaked out. Honestly, I didn't know what to think. It hadn't even occurred to me that it might just be me."

"It's totally you," he said with a shrug. "But maybe I should come over tonight and see if it happens again."

One of Nick's golden eyebrows was crooked seductively, and I was suddenly very aware of the way his striped dress shirt strained slightly across his broad shoulders, the way his gray slacks hugged his firm thighs. Warmth pooled in my stomach, and I bit my lip.

And then I thought about Max—sweet, floppy-haired Max, who sent me the recipe to his lemongrass curry as though I might actually make it myself. Since our picnic, we'd started texting throughout the day and chatting every evening before bed. It was something I had started to look forward to—curling up at night and telling him about my day, listening to him describe his. He was sweet and thoughtful, and I was starting to think that I might really be falling for him. I couldn't ruin what we might be building by letting Nick into my bed again.

"Not tonight," I said.

Nick squinted at me. "First you wouldn't let me stay. Then you don't respond to my messages. And now this. Are you mad at me or something?"

"No, not at all."

I considered leaving it at that, but thought better of it. I didn't owe Max anything—we'd only gone out twice and had certainly never had any conversations about being exclusive—but it seemed like there was definite possibility there. Maybe we could really be something, as long as I didn't leave a door open for Nick.

"Actually, Nick, I've"—I paused to take a deep breath—"started seeing someone."

Nick smiled, as though it might be a joke. "What?"

I nodded. "Yeah."

"Huh," he said, leaning back in his chair, brow furrowed. "So is this the guy you had that picnic at Gravelly Point with?"

"How do you know about that?"

"Audrey, you post your life all over the internet. I'd be surprised if there was anyone on the Eastern Seaboard who didn't know about it." He sighed and drummed his fingers on his knee. "Well, shit. I'd say you don't know what you're missing, but you do."

"The ego on *you*," I shot back teasingly.

"We're a pair, huh?" He screwed up his mouth. "I have to admit, I'm a little surprised to see Audrey Miller interested in monogamy."

"It's just something I'm trying." I offered him a smile. "You never know, maybe I'll be calling you next week."

He scoffed. "Maybe you'll be calling me tonight."

"Nick—"

He waved me away and stood. "See you around, Audrey."

CHAPTER FORTY-THREE

AUDREY

Cat frowned down at my phone, which sat on the table between us at Sweetgreen, buffeted by our salads. The Luna Listen app was open, its eerie recording playing at top volume.

"I don't know," Cat finally said. "I'm not sure what I'm hearing."

I rewound slightly and lifted the phone toward her ear. "There. At the end. Do you hear someone say 'You're dreaming'?"

"Maybe," she said uncertainly. She took the phone from my hands and listened to that portion again. "I don't know, Audrey. Is that you?"

"Really?" I asked hopefully. "You think that's my voice?"

"I don't know. It's really hard to tell if it's even a voice at all." She frowned. "Do you remember waking up last night?"

"This isn't from last night," I clarified. "This is from a couple of weeks ago. The day the Rosalind exhibit opened, actually. I was so wired that night that I took a sleeping pill, which is why I didn't notice this recording right away. I hadn't even realized I'd turned on the app."

"Oh," Cat said slowly. "That was the night you heard someone in the alley, right? And saw the box that had the headless flowers in it?"

I nodded grimly. "Exactly. Do you think it was all the same guy? Whoever was in the alley and left those flowers later came back and came inside? I just don't get why he would leave the flowers outside if he could come inside."

"Maybe he didn't know he could get inside when he left the flowers," Cat suggested. "Or maybe he didn't want you to know he was inside. Or maybe it's not the same person at all."

"Or maybe you were right and the voice is me, and the flowers are just a weird coincidence."

"I don't know," Cat said doubtfully. "When I said it might be you, I didn't know what day we were talking about. It would have to be a pretty big coincidence for all this to happen on the same night and not be related."

"Stranger things have happened. Besides, you're not the only one who thought it was me. Nick thought so, too."

"You played this for Nick?" Cat asked, raising her eyebrows.

"Yeah, this morning."

"This morning?" she repeated sharply.

"Get your mind out of the gutter. Nick met me before work to listen to this. I . . ." I stalled, not wanting to admit to Cat that I had been on the verge of accusing Nick. ". . . I wanted his opinion."

"Wait," Cat said, pursing her lips. "The night of this recording. The night before you found those flowers. Wasn't that also the night that you sent Nick away?"

I nodded reluctantly. "I know what you're thinking, and I've already thought of that. But it wasn't Nick. He flat-out denied it."

"Audrey, this is the guy who lied to you about denting your car's fender right after you watched him do it. He would hardly admit to breaking into your bedroom at night."

"That was one time almost ten years ago, and totally different. Besides, Cat, you don't know him like I do. I can tell when he's lying, and I'm sure he was telling the truth."

"All right," Cat said uncertainly. "But maybe you should stay with me for a while."

IT WAS SWEET OF CAT to invite me to stay with her, but there had been a hesitation in her voice that told me the offer wasn't entirely sincere. I was sure it had to do with work—I knew something big was going on, and all conversations with her gradually morphed into discussions about how stressed she was, how many cases she had to read or pages she had to write, and whether I thought it meant something that Connor had brought her a cup of coffee while they'd been working. I didn't want to add to her pressure—and I didn't exactly relish the idea of sitting alone in her apartment while she worked late. I needed to get out, to *do* something, anything that would take my mind off that recording.

Luckily, I knew just the person to call.

MAX WAS WAITING FOR ME at the bar at the Dabney, where he'd somehow managed to score last-minute reservations, looking slightly rumpled and wearing those god-awful Vans. Fashion ineptitude aside, my heart cartwheeled when he directed those warm brown eyes toward me and smiled, showing off his dimples. *A comb, an iron, and decent footwear*, I thought to myself. *That's all he needs.*

"Audrey," he said, kissing my cheek lightly. "I'm so glad you called."

"I would have called sooner if I knew you had these reservations in your pocket," I quipped. "I've been dying to try this place."

"There was a cancellation," he said with a shrug. "I just got lucky."

If I had been with Nick, I would have said *We'll see about that*, and he would have winked, and then he would have been putting his hands on my knees under the table. It would have been hot, but somehow there was something almost hotter about this: standing across from this man and feeling the attraction buzzing between us, wanting to touch him but not doing it; the uncertainty and anticipation of what might happen when we left the restaurant.

I rocked forward on my tiptoes to return the kiss, my lips lingering on his cheek as I inhaled the clean scent of his aftershave. "I think I'm the lucky one."

* * *

OVER SHARED PLATES of fire-roasted peppers and charred romaine salad, Max and I talked nonstop about our respective jobs, the incredible food, the people on a clearly terrible first date next to us, something he'd read in the *Post* about track work on the Metro—everything other than the one thing that I couldn't get off my mind.

You're dreaming.

Was it possible that it was just me? I couldn't say; I'd never heard myself whisper like that. Then again, I'd never heard myself talk so plainly in my sleep. Everything I otherwise caught had been shouts and yelps.

If it wasn't me, though, who could it have been? I'd initially thought it was Ryan, but my unknown guest had stood silent for nearly an hour, and I'd never seen Ryan remain still for more than a half second. Maybe if he had been super-stoned? It was hard to believe him leaving without taking anything, though. Then I'd wondered about Lawrence. After all, he *had* been upset with me that day, and I still suspected he was the one who had left me the orange flowers. But why would he break into my apartment and then just stand there? It didn't make sense.

Could it be Brandon from the museum? Or Eric the bartender? He'd seemed laser-focused on me the night of Lena's birthday, and I wondered if he had been the one to follow Cat and me home from the bar. Or what if it was someone else entirely, someone I didn't even know? I kept thinking back to an evening last year when Izzy had come charging into our apartment, cheeks flushed and angry.

"Some girl outside just shouted 'Hey, Izzy' at me," she

said, flinging her oversized Tory Burch bag down on the couch.

"So?" I asked, looking up from my laptop, where I was editing some photos.

"So I don't like the idea of random people knowing who I am and where I live just because you overshare online."

"How do you know this has anything to do with me?"

"Be serious, Audrey," she'd said, casting a withering look at me. "I work in finance and keep all my social media accounts private. Random twenty-year-old girls carrying fake designer bags aren't going to know who I am . . . *unless* they've seen me on your posts."

"Again, I say 'so'? What do you think that girl's going to do, other than shout your name a few times?"

"Just because *she's* not dangerous doesn't mean that someone else *isn't*. People know where we live, Audrey. It isn't safe."

I had rolled my eyes and told her she was overreacting, but what if she was right? What if I had been too careless with my personal information, and someone was using it against me? What if the creep who had peered through my window, left those headless flowers, and been caught on the recording was a stranger? Or, more terrifying, what if it was *three* strangers, all of whom had found me because of what I posted?

"Audrey?" Max asked, breaking into my thoughts. "You seem like you're someplace else."

I caught my bottom lip with my teeth, scraping away some of the gloss. I wanted to tell Max about what I'd heard, confess how frightened it made me. There was something about him that made me feel as though I could confide in him; I knew he wouldn't blow me off like Nick had, so quick to tell me it was nothing, or get overly dramatic about things like Cat had. I knew he wouldn't give me a lecture about privacy or calling the police, as I was certain my sister would.

But that was just a feeling. I trusted my intuition about people, but I didn't really *know* Max. What if it was too much for him? I mean, I wouldn't blame him for walking away. What kind of person would want to date someone who was in the midst of being stalked? Or who shared so much online that random strangers might be creeping into her bedroom at night?

I opened my mouth, prepared to say something safe about being distracted by the wood-burning oven on display, but the lie stuck in my throat and suddenly I heard myself saying, "Have you ever used a sleep tracker?"

"A what?"

"A sleep tracker. It's this app you can use to monitor your sleeping habits." I paused, debating whether I should tell him the full truth or only say that I heard myself talking in my sleep, turn it into a funny anecdote. I met Max's soft eyes and took a deep breath. "I've been using one, and I think I may have captured someone breaking into my apartment."

"*What?*"

"Yeah. Needless to say, I'm a little freaked out."

"What happened? Tell me you weren't home at the time."

"I was, actually," I said with a grimace. "I slept through the whole thing, which is why I can only say that I *think* someone was breaking in."

"Nothing was taken?"

You're dreaming.

I shuddered and shook my head. "No, that's the really weird part. It sounds like whoever it was just . . . *stood* there, watching me sleep."

Max's eyes widened so much I could see the whites all around his irises. "That's straight out of a nightmare. Are you okay?"

"I mean . . ." I trailed off, unwilling to say *No, I'm not okay* even though it was the truth. "Here's the thing: I don't use the app every night. So this apparently happened a couple of weeks ago, but I just listened to the recording today. And now I can't stop wondering if this has happened other times. What if someone has been in my apartment more than that—what if they're in there *regularly*—and it's only by chance that I heard it this once?"

"God," he muttered, rubbing his mouth with his hand. "You're not still staying there, right?"

"Cat said I could sleep at her place, but I don't know. She's been so busy with work lately, even more than usual. I mean, you know how she is."

"She can be intense, I know, but, Audrey, you can't stay in that apartment. Not until the police have caught this creep."

I turned my attention to my Negroni, rattling the ice in the glass. "I haven't called the police."

"*What?* Why not?"

"You'd have to hear the recording to understand, but . . . two people I trust thought it might just be me. So, I mean, if both of these people think it's me, what are the police going to think?"

"But you don't think it's you," he said slowly. "I can tell by the look on your face."

I forced a shrug. "It's hard to tell."

"Listen," he said, taking my hand across the table. "If you think someone was in your apartment, I believe you. And I know I'm just a guy you barely know, but if you don't want to stay with Cat, you're more than welcome to stay with me."

Butterflies fluttered in my stomach when Max's hand closed over mine, and I involuntarily licked my lips. I met his eyes, looking at me seriously from underneath bovine lashes, and lost interest in discussing what had happened in my bedroom all those weeks ago. I was suddenly much more interested in what might be happening in Max's bedroom that night.

I cracked a grin and teased, "Max Metcalf, are you trying to get me into bed?"

His cheeks flushed scarlet. "That's not what I meant. I mean, you can have my bed. I'll sleep on the couch. I just—"

"Shut up," I said gently. "Why don't we get the check?"

"THIS IS INCREDIBLE," I said, heading directly for Max's wall of floor-to-ceiling windows. My nose bumped the glass as I admired the vantage point from his seventh-floor unit. I stepped backward as a slight wave of vertigo swept over me, and turned to Max. "That mansion you took me to had an incredible view, but this one is an extremely close second. I mean, you can see the Washington Monument!"

"A sliver of it," he amended. "But it is a nice view."

"That's the understatement of the year. I would *kill* for these windows." I paused to flash him a devilish grin. "I might kill *you* for them."

"Is that my cue to hide the knives?"

"Depends on whether you're feeling lucky."

"I'll take my chances," he said. "Can I get you anything? Wine? Water? Another Negroni?"

"Oh, man, a Negroni sounds amazing, thanks."

"I can't promise it'll be as good as the one at dinner," he said, pulling a bottle of Campari down from his open kitchen shelving. "In fact, I can guarantee it won't be."

"As long as it has alcohol."

"I can handle that," he said with a grin. "Hey, do you want to put on some music? I've got Apple Music hooked up through the TV, or, if you're feeling old-school, you can put on a record."

He pointed to the wall behind me, and I turned, squealing in delight as I discovered a bookcase stuffed with records. "Look at your vinyl!"

He blushed. "I know you're so digital that you probably think records are archaic, but I've got a real soft spot for them. They force you to listen to the songs in the order the artist intended. No skipping around, no playing just the singles. You get to hear the entire album in context."

"No, I totally agree! I love listening to songs on demand and making playlists just as much as the next person—probably more, actually—but I've always said you don't really understand an album until you've listened to it in full." I turned back to his record collection and began running my fingers along the spines, noting the presence of old albums from the likes of the Beatles, the Who, Talking Heads, as well as more contemporary bands like Arctic Monkeys, the White Stripes, and the Strokes. I stopped suddenly as my finger lit upon Ted and the Honey's first album, *No Lessons Learned*, which was three albums before they finally hit mainstream success.

"Get out! You're a Ted and the Honey fan?"

"That band is great," he said defensively. "If you've never—"

"No, no!" I interrupted him. "I *love* Ted and the Honey. I hate to sound like one of those assholes, but I saw them play in New York way before they were cool."

"Well, I hate to tell you, but that does make you sound like one of those assholes," he teased.

"What can I say? My true colors had to emerge sometime."

"I like your true colors," Max said quietly as he crossed the room and handed me the brilliant orange drink.

Our fingers brushed as I took the glass from him, sending a small thrill up my spine, and I smiled. "You don't know how happy I am to hear you say that."

FOR THE FIRST TIME IN WEEKS, I awoke feeling content. Sunlight was streaming through Max's huge windows and warming my face, and I smiled and stretched like a cat. *This*, I thought happily. *This is what I needed. A good night's sleep and some sunshine.* I glanced over at Max, still asleep beside me, his lanky body curled like a shrimp and his mouth hanging slightly open. I reached over to brush aside one of his dark blond curls, and he didn't stir as my fingertips grazed his forehead.

I shivered. Had I been this dead to the world when the intruder was in my apartment? Did the intruder *touch* me like I'd just touched Max?

I looked down at Max again, suddenly realizing how

vulnerable he was at that moment. How could he sleep so soundly after what I'd told him last night? If Max had been the one sitting across from me blathering about some weird recording and a possible stalker, I sure as hell wouldn't have let him into my home, no matter how cute he was. The story sounded too outrageous to be true, and I would have wondered about the mental stability of the person telling it.

Max, it seemed, was more trusting than I was, and for that I was glad. I reached for my phone and snuggled back down into his fresh-smelling, blue-and-white-striped sheets. I kissed him gently on his bare shoulder and then opened Instagram to start my morning routine. I checked the Hirshhorn's accounts first, interacting with some posts and tweets before moving on to check my own. I responded to comments, deleted a few obvious bot comments, and then checked my tags.

I blinked when I saw my most recent tag, wondering if I had somehow clicked back to the Hirshhorn account. But no—there was a photo of one of the Rosalind dioramas, Rosalind in a tiny sparkly dress, out dancing with some of her friends while her masked stalker lurked in the background, and there, right on Rosalind's little blonde head, was the tag for my personal account: @audreyvmiller.

That doesn't mean anything, I told myself as my mind began to spin. *All it means is that this user @an0nYmiss knows you're the Social Media Manager and is trying to get your attention.*

But then I read the caption: *Your apartment misses you.*

"Jesus," I said aloud, shuddering so violently that Max blinked and sat up.

"What is it?" he asked, rubbing his eyes. "What's going on?"

I glanced down at the offending post in my trembling hand. I knew that Max would put his arms around me, tell me it was all right. But what would he really be thinking? Would he start to wonder what kind of trouble he'd invited into his bed? I sure would. I wouldn't want to see someone whose stalker plainly knew when they weren't there. What if he knew I was *here*?

I quickly turned off my screen and grinned. "Nothing. I was just catching up on some celebrity gossip. Sorry if I woke you."

"Don't apologize," he said with a sleepy smile as he leaned over to kiss me. "You didn't do anything wrong."

That's right, I thought to myself as I returned the kiss. I didn't do anything wrong. There was no reason I needed to tell him about that post. No reason to worry him.

CHAPTER FORTY-FOUR

CAT

Every once in a while, you meet a couple so well matched, so clearly perfect for each other that you can't help but believe in destiny." Priya paused and looked around, her eyes misty. "Tonight, we're gathered to celebrate one of those couples. Jessa and Lamar, we love you and couldn't be more thrilled that you're engaged. Everyone, please join me in raising a glass to the happy couple. Congratulations, you guys!"

I lifted my plastic champagne flute into the air along with the three dozen other people assembled on the roof of Priya's apartment complex. She'd rented the entire space, complete with a wet bar, fire pits, and an unobstructed view of the Capitol, for the party, and decorated it with gold balloons spelling out Jessa's and Lamar's names.

Priya was streaming some pop music I didn't recognize through unseen speakers, and everyone was toasting and refilling their champagne and hugging and laughing.

I shouldn't have come, I thought.

I almost hadn't. I was happy for Jessa and Lamar, of course, but I had already congratulated them, had heard the story of their engagement at least twice, and would send the appropriate gifts at the appropriate intervals. Was it really necessary for me to *also* make small talk with friends of friends instead of tackling the mountain of work I had at home? Since joining Bill's team, I'd been even more buried under work than usual, and I knew that taking tonight off would mean I had to work all weekend. I had been formulating an excuse for Priya when Audrey texted me See you tonight at Priya's! I'd paused. If Audrey was going, so should I. After all, these weren't her friends. I didn't want her to feel alone.

But the party had been in full swing for more than an hour and Audrey had yet to make an appearance. I pulled out my phone and started composing a message reprimanding her for being so inconsiderate to my friends, but then I stopped and sighed. It wasn't like it mattered. Audrey could blow off the party completely and my friends would forgive her. People like Audrey were always forgiven.

"GORGEOUS NIGHT, HUH?" Connor said, materializing at my side. "Thank God we're not trapped in the office."

A shiver ran through my body and I nodded, not telling him I'd just been planning my exit so I could get back to work.

"Priya always has known how to throw a party. Remember that wild come-as-you-are party first year?" He chuckled. "Nice toast, too. That bit about destiny . . . What did you think?"

I glanced at him out of the corner of my eye. Was he asking me whether I liked Priya's toast or whether I believed in destiny? And, if it was the latter, was it some sort of sign? I thought back to a night earlier in the week when Connor and I had been reviewing a stack of potential exhibits in a conference room at two in the morning. He leaned over me, putting his hand on my shoulder, and . . . *squeezed*, sort of. In the moment, I had frozen, and then I'd spent the intervening days wondering whether it was a pass of some sort. And now this question about destiny? My heart fluttered.

I swallowed and then answered honestly. "Nothing in life is preordained. Destiny and fate are just excuses people use when they're too lazy to put in real work."

He burst out laughing. "God, Harrell, you're such a pragmatist. I suppose I should have expected you to say something like that, though. I've never met anyone who works harder than you."

Heat rushed to my cheeks and I mumbled, "I take pride in my work."

"I meant it as a compliment," he said gently, chucking me lightly on the shoulder. Then he paused, eyes trained somewhere behind me. "I didn't realize Audrey was coming. Who's that with her? That friend of yours?"

I turned and saw Audrey stepping onto the deck. She was wearing a short floral dress and a too-large men's fleece jacket, and she was hand in hand with Max Metcalf. It suddenly felt as if the champagne were burning a hole in my stomach. Why had she brought Max here? It was bad enough Audrey was spending time with him, but she had to introduce him to all my friends? To Connor? One offhand mention of camp and everything could fall apart. If Connor learned about Emily Snow, what might he do with that information? I could certainly say goodbye to any chance of a romantic relationship with him. And what about work? We were friends, yes, but we were also competitors. Only one of us would get to argue during the Phillips trial, and down the road, we would be vying for partnership at the same time. Connor might seem affable, but no one went to a top-ten law school and worked at a Vault 50 firm without being at least a little cutthroat.

I forced myself to breathe. I was getting ahead of myself. Emily Snow would not come up. Camp Blackwood would not come up. Why would it? There was no reason for anyone to even be talking about me, not with Audrey right there.

QUICKLY I REALIZED my earlier concern about Audrey feeling alone at the party was unfounded. I watched from across the rooftop as she flitted around with a flute of champagne in hand and Max in tow, chatting with complete strangers as though they were intimate friends. I'd always envied her ability to do that.

If I was honest, a small part of me also envied the way Max was looking at her as though she were the most beautiful creature to ever walk on two legs. No one had ever looked at me like that, whereas almost every man who came into contact with Audrey was immediately smitten. Even Nick, who usually seemed so cool and detached, lost his mind over Audrey. I'd never forget the night sophomore year I awoke to hear someone jiggling our door handle. Audrey had still been out, trawling the bars with Jasmine, when I'd gone to bed, and I assumed she'd forgotten her key. It wouldn't have been the first time. I was crossing the room to the door when I heard a high-pitched keening noise on the other side.

I froze. The noise sounded more animal than human.

"Audrey?" I tried.

The handle rattled again, and with my heart in my throat, I cautiously opened the door. The shadowy figure of a broad-shouldered man loomed in the darkened hallway, and I screamed and jumped back.

"Audrey?" the man said hopefully, his voice thin and his breath smelling like beer, as he lurched forward toward me.

Panicked, I put up my hands to ward him off. "No!"

"But . . ." he said, staggering backward, wiping at his eyes with the backs of his hands.

That was when I recognized the shadowy figure as Nick, whom Audrey had been casually seeing for only a couple of weeks, and also when I realized that he was crying. I shuddered as I realized *he* had been the one making that inhuman noise.

"You can't be here," I said, trying to keep the alarm from my voice. "Men aren't allowed upstairs after seven p.m."

"I know," he moaned. "But she's not taking my calls. Where is she?"

I hesitated, worried about his reaction if I told him Audrey wasn't there. Before I could come up with a plausible lie, the hallway was suddenly drenched in light and our house mom, Nancy, was pointing a sharp pink finger-nail at Nick.

"You," she growled. "Out. Now."

Nick blinked in the light, his eyes red-rimmed and bright with tears. He opened his mouth to say some-thing, but then seemed to notice Nancy's expression and shuffled away. Audrey had laughed when I'd recounted the story to her, and Nick had never once hinted that he remembered the incident, but I had never been able to forget the image of Nick crying outside our room like some third-rate Romeo.

I wonder what Nick thinks about Max.

"HEY," AUDREY SAID BREEZILY, dropping onto a cushion beside me as I sat around a fire pit with Connor, Priya, and some of Priya's work friends. She sat so close to me that she was practically on my lap, forcing me to brush strands of her hair from my eyes and scoot away, and then she glanced up at Max and patted the sliver of cushion beside her. "Come on, sit down."

As Max awkwardly lowered himself onto the precari-ous seat, Audrey turned to the rest of us and, completely oblivious that she was interrupting our conversation about our predictions for the upcoming Supreme Court term, said, "Have you all met my boyfriend, Max?"

Boyfriend? I felt my cheeks grow hot. Since when was Audrey calling Max her *boyfriend*? And why hadn't she told me first? We were best friends. Or we were supposed to be.

"Hi," Max said, waving self-consciously.

"Nice to meet—" Priya began.

"So," Audrey said, cutting Priya off as she leaned forward. "Do you guys want to hear a scary story?"

"Baby," Max said softly, putting a hand on her shoulder.

I almost felt bad for him. He would learn soon enough that there was no stopping Audrey once she got going, and even if there were, a soft "baby" wasn't going to do it. *Baby.* As if Audrey Miller stood for anyone calling her "baby." I gave Max another week, at most.

Audrey shrugged him off and launched into a dramatic retelling of the sounds she'd heard on her sleep-tracking app. She'd always been a good storyteller, and this was no exception. My friends were hanging on every word, their faces a combination of amused and horrified.

"Holy shit," Priya said when Audrey finished. "Holy *shit.*"

"How are you not more freaked out?" one of Priya's friends demanded. "I don't think I'd ever sleep again."

Connor cleared his throat. "Let's hear it."

"Connor," Priya scolded. "I'm sure Audrey doesn't want to have to listen to that again."

"Oh, I don't mind," Audrey said, already holding out her phone, the star-spangled interface of the app visible. She looked around the group, arching her groomed brows, before hitting the "play" button. "Prepare to freak out."

Everyone leaned in as if pulled by a centrifugal force, even me. I thought back to that night in the sorority house, Nick trying to get into the room where Audrey was sleeping. She'd said she'd turned him away that night. Could he have come back?

"Totally creepy, right?" Audrey said after the recording ended, her voice artificially bright.

"Yeah, it's creepy," Connor agreed. "But not for the reason you think."

She tilted her head, her hair cascading over her shoulders. "What do you mean?"

"That's not another voice," Connor said, pointing to her phone. "That's you."

"That's not me," she protested. "Weren't you listening? The voices are obviously different."

"Hear me out. One of my brothers talks in his sleep, too, and he does that thing where he changes voices. It's creepy if you're not expecting it, but it's just him." He leaned over and patted Audrey on the hand. "I get why it weirded you out, though."

His hand lingered over hers, and I glanced at him sharply. My stomach bottomed out when I recognized the look in his eyes. It was the same hungry look he'd had the night he tried to kiss her at the bar, the same look that Max wore and the same one I'd seen on Nick so many times.

Don't be surprised, I chastised myself bitterly. *It's not like you didn't know that Audrey takes everyone.*

I concentrated on remaining calm and keeping a bland smile on my face, but when Audrey pointed a grateful smile at Connor, I heard myself snapping, "Well, I've heard Audrey talk in her sleep plenty of times, and that's not her."

"What?" Audrey said, turning to me with eyes wide. "You have? When?"

My cheeks burned as I realized I'd never told Audrey I heard her talk in her sleep. I'd always been embarrassed, feeling as though I'd overheard something that was private. But now I had admitted it in front of an audience, and everyone was looking at me like I was some sort of freak.

Once a freak, always a freak, Emily Snow giggled in my ear.

"You know," I said suddenly, rising. "I have a lot of work to do. I should get going."

I expected Audrey to stop me, but she just waved. "See you later, Kitty-Cat."

CHAPTER FORTY-FIVE

HIM

Sweat popped along my hairline when she started the recording, and I was certain that she would recognize my voice. I felt exposed, as if I'd been turned inside out and my organs were on display. I waited for her to turn to me with her mouth a perfect O of horror and point at my misshapen, bloody heart as it beat vulnerably before me. *Oh my God*, she would say, recoiling. *That's you.*

But it never happened. She never recognized my voice. She had no idea that I was the one in the room with her that night. It was almost a shame because not knowing I was there meant not knowing what I did. And I was sure that if she knew what I did for her, that expression of horror would fade from her delicate face, and it would be replaced by one of gratitude. She would thank me profusely, and for the rest of our lives, she would know exactly how much I loved her.

That night, after I had deposited the box with the meticulously snipped flowers on her doorstep, I hadn't been able to stop myself from peering through her windows. I hadn't been cautious enough at first, and she'd chased me from the alley. I'd stood on the other side of the gate, heart pounding, listening to determine whether she would explore the alley or return to her apartment. I should have gone then, but I was still buzzing with fury and wondered if she'd encountered the flowers. I reasoned that I couldn't walk away now, not without knowing what she thought about them, and so, with my baseball cap pulled down low, I carefully, quietly snuck back to her window.

I sagged with disappointment to see her lounging quietly in her bed. She hadn't seen the flowers. But still I kept watching, her heart-shaped face beckoning to me like a siren. Slowly the electricity in my veins fizzled and dissipated, leaving me calm, content.

And then I saw her shake a pill from an orange prescription bottle and wash it down with that glass of wine she'd been refilling all night. Instantly, I was on alert. From my vantage point, I couldn't see the label on the bottle or the shape of the pill, but I knew Audrey took both Xanax and Ambien, neither of which should be mixed with alcohol. She'd just recklessly put herself in mortal danger, and she needed someone to watch over her, someone to stand sentry. I was her only option. I would be her savior. I had to be.

So I watched.

I watched even as cramps developed in my legs and my limbs grew cold. I would suffer through personal discomfort to protect her. I would do anything for her.

I squinted into her bedroom, realizing it had been a while since I had seen her move. She was resting on her back in the center of her messy bed, her body twisted in the tangled sheets. She looked beautiful, peaceful. But did she look *too* peaceful? And weren't overdose risks not supposed to sleep on their backs? I leaned closer to the window, searching for confirmation that her chest was moving. It was impossible to tell.

My heart sang with the certainty that Audrey needed me, and I grabbed at the bars that covered the window, testing their resilience. They didn't budge. I raced for the front door. Anyone with an internet connection knew that Audrey had had problems with that lock since she moved in, and there was a chance it might be open. A small chance, but one worth pursuing before I was forced to consider a more drastic course of action. Scarcely daring to hope, I pushed on the iron gate in front of her door. I expected it to remain firmly in place, but it swung open with a light creak.

Fate. I was fated to be there that night, fated to be the one to save her. I grasped her doorknob, certain that it would turn easily in my hand.

It did.

My blood tingled as I entered her darkened apartment. I paused to inhale the distinct smell of her home: the lingering aroma of her coconut shampoo, a citrus-scented candle, a slight twinge of dust. I looked toward her open bedroom door and remembered my mission. My heart climbed my throat, threatening to choke me.

I turned toward her bedroom, fearful of what I might find in there. If, God forbid, something had happened in the time it took me to get inside, I knew I would never recover from discovering her corpse, from seeing her skin waxen and her summer-fruit lips blue. I reminded myself that fate had steered me to her window, that it wouldn't let me get this far and then snatch her from me, and stepped into her bedroom.

Audrey sat straight up in bed, her eyes flying open like a doll's.

I froze, too startled to move.

"Hi," she said pleasantly.

Heart pounding so hard it rattled my rib cage, I stared at her. Something was wrong. Her eyes were unfocused and lacked their usual sparkle. She was looking at me, but she wasn't seeing me. She was either asleep or seriously out of it from the pills.

So I said the only thing I could think to say: "You're dreaming."

"Oh," she said agreeably, before lying back down and closing her eyes.

I exhaled, pressing a fist to my mouth. *Holy shit.*

I remained rooted to the floor, afraid to move, to do anything that might awaken her. And so I just stood there and watched her sleep, her pale chest rising and falling, her heart-shaped lips open. It took everything I had not to cross the room and kiss those lips, but I didn't. I wouldn't. I wasn't some sort of weirdo.

CHAPTER FORTY-SIX

AUDREY

In my nearly thirty years, I've only ever thought I loved two men. The first was Charles Newton, whom I dated my senior year in high school. He was the captain of the soccer team, and had perfect chestnut waves and a sound system in his used Toyota that was loud enough to qualify as a public nuisance. We were making out on the couch in his basement, Fall Out Boy playing in the background, when he whispered wetly in my ear, "I love you." Overcome by hormones and emo music, I said it back. Two weeks later, he broke up with me via text, and one week after that I was dating his best friend.

The other was Nick. I couldn't remember who said it first or feeling that sort of all-consuming passion I assumed one felt when they were in love; I just thought that I *must* love him since we had dated for so long. It wasn't until after we broke up that I realized the truth: I was never in love with Nick. I enjoyed his company, and we had incomparable sexual chemistry, but we were never truly in love.

There was a third man to whom I had said the three magic words. His name was John or Josh or possibly Jeremy, and I had met him at a party shortly after I moved to New York. My blood brimming with MDMA, I confessed my love to this stranger on a makeshift dance floor in someone's Williamsburg apartment. He responded by licking my cheek. I did not consider him one of the great loves of my life.

Max, though. Max might be different. I didn't *love* him, of course—I'd only known him for five weeks—but I thought I might be able to see myself falling in love with him someday. Possibly someday soon. I wasn't sure. All I knew was that I had been staying with Max for two weeks, ever since I first heard the eerie voice on the Luna Listen app, and it just seemed *right*. His apartment felt more like a home than my own—which, sure, could be because I'd never bothered to fully unpack, but maybe it was also because Max made everything so cozy and welcoming. At my place, I had fallen into the habit of eating frozen Trader Joe's meals while perched on my beanbag chair, drinking wine and streaming something mindless on my laptop. At Max's, I sat at his kitchen island while he cooked dinner— real dinners, like that curry and this fantastic chickpea-and-Swiss-chard thing—and we chatted about our days. And, unlike Nick, he really *listened* when I told him how things were going, even asking thoughtful follow-up questions. Then he would pull me into his strong, soap-scented embrace, and we would snuggle together on the couch, listening to records or watching something together, until we couldn't stand the closeness a second longer and would fall on each other like lust-driven animals.

Cat kept asking me to stay with her instead, kept saying I was moving too fast with Max. "I'm worried," she'd told me over the phone. "Someone's going to get hurt." But what did Cat know? She had been obsessed with the same man for the last seven years and had kissed him exactly once. By that yardstick, sure, Max and I were moving fast, but that was hardly a reasonable standard.

BUT AS MUCH as I loved living at Max's, our relaxed routine was proving detrimental to my personal brand. I slipped in posting content, even neglecting my Instagram Stories. My loyal followers began sending me direct messages expressing their concern, asking if everything was okay. I assured them it was, but I couldn't continue like this much longer—not if I wanted to maintain the social media presence I had worked so hard to cultivate.

Max nodded agreeably when I told him I was going to take care of some personal things after work, but his eyes had widened when he realized I intended to go back to the basement apartment.

"Audrey, are you crazy? That's not safe."

"It'll be fine," I assured him. "I've been back a bunch of times for clothes and stuff."

"With me at your side," he countered.

"I don't need a white knight," I said gently. "Listen, Max, I'll lock the doors, and I won't stay after dark. I'm talking an hour, two, tops."

"That's an hour or two too long. Please, baby, work here. I promise I won't bother you."

"I can't work here," I told him, running a finger along his soft lips. "Too many distractions."

He kissed my fingertip and then took my hand. "Then go to a coffee shop. Don't go back to that apartment."

"I can't live my life in fear," I told him. "Anyway, everything will be fine. You'll see."

He sighed heavily. "I want it noted for the record that I don't like this at all. Be careful, okay? And don't answer the door for anyone."

MAX'S ADMONISHMENT CAME back to me when the buzzer rang thirty minutes after I'd arrived home.

It has to be Ryan, I thought darkly as I approached the door. *He's noticed that I'm back and decided it was time to harass me for fun.*

I cracked open the door, ready to tell my least favorite neighbor where he could shove it, and instead found Nick, grinning wolfishly at me with his golden hair in disarray.

"Let me in, Rapunzel," he said, rattling the gate.

"Rapunzel lived in a tower, not a basement."

"Semantics," he said, swaying slightly. "Come on, babe. Let me in."

I sighed and unlocked the gate. "You can come in but you can't stay. I have work to do, and besides, I have a firm policy of not entertaining drunks."

"I'm not drunk," Nick protested as he sauntered into my apartment.

"Like hell you're not," I said, shutting my laptop and

preventively moving it out of his reach. "I can smell the tequila coming out of your pores."

He lifted an arm to his nose and sniffed. I laughed despite myself.

"You're ridiculous. It's a Wednesday evening and you're thirty years old. What have you gotten into?"

"Going-away party for a colleague. Former colleague, I guess. We went to happy hour."

"And then you thought of me. How nice."

"I always think of you."

"Oh, Nicky," I said with a laugh. "You're so cute when you lie."

"I'm not lying," he said, looking indignant. "I do think of you. More than you think of me, obviously. You haven't answered any of my texts recently."

"I've been busy," I said vaguely.

"That boyfriend of yours, right?" he demanded, leaning toward me.

Something dangerous flashed in the blue of his eyes, and I suddenly remembered one Halloween night years ago. We had gone to a bar together but had drifted apart: I went to dance with my friends, he went to drink himself stupid with his. I was singing along to a Katy Perry song when Nick suddenly grabbed me by the arm and whirled me around, red-faced and shouting something about my kissing another guy. It only took me a few minutes to realize he'd seen some *other* woman dressed as a mermaid locking lips with someone, but in those few minutes I had been genuinely afraid of him. I never figured out if he'd taken something or if he had just been excessively drunk or if he really did have a dark streak that he usually kept hidden beneath all that charm, but it was the only time Nick had ever looked at me like that.

Until tonight.

"Come off it, Nick," I said, pushing him away.

"I don't get you, Audrey," he said, shaking his head. "I always thought we had something special."

"We do. We have a really special friendship, and—"

"I love you."

I blinked in surprise. "What?"

"I love you," he repeated, reaching a clumsy hand for me.

"Nick, no," I said gently, intercepting his reach. "You don't mean that."

His handsome face contorted and he snatched his hand out of my grasp. "Who are you to tell me what I mean? Seriously, Audrey, who the fuck are you?"

"Come on, Nicky," I said lightly. "You think after all these years that I don't know you better than you know yourself?"

"Fuck you," he said, his voice growing loud. "You always want to control everything, including how everyone else behaves. News flash: you can't fucking *curate* other people. You can't just play with us like we're fucking dolls."

I sucked in my breath. "Nick, you're drunk."

"That doesn't change *shit*. And you know the worst part? I still love you even though you're a manipulative, image-obsessed bitch. I tried to forget you, okay? I dated other women, and then you moved here and fucked me up all over again. Fuck you. I love you. Fuck you."

"I think you should leave now," I said, trying to keep my voice from wavering.

"You don't want to hear it tonight, that's fine. But, Audrey—"

"No," I said. "Nick, it's not like that. Okay? I enjoy spending time with you, but I don't love you like that. And I'm not going to."

"You loved me once," he insisted, shaking his head. "You'll love me again."

"Nick, please. Do me a favor. Go home and sleep it off, and we'll pretend this never happened."

Nick's expression turned hard and he sneered, "Sure. Whatever Audrey Miller wants, Audrey Miller gets, right?"

"Nick—"

But he was already slamming my front door.

CHAPTER FORTY-SEVEN

AUDREY

M anipulative bitch.

I couldn't stop obsessing over Nick's insults. In all the years I'd known him, through all our ups and downs and stupid fights, he had never spoken to me so harshly, not even that Halloween. I wanted to believe that he was just drunk and lashing out, but what if there was more to it? What if that was how Nick really felt about me, deep down?

What if there was a bit of truth to it?

I was still thinking about it the next night as I returned to the apartment. Max had disapproved, insisting that I could work at his place, but I'd needed the quiet and the space. I hadn't told Max about the incident with Nick—I mean, how would I even begin to explain my complicated relationship with my ex-boyfriend to my new boyfriend?—and I wasn't sure that I wanted to give him cause to wonder whether I really was a "manipulative bitch."

I was almost to the building when I suddenly remembered Cat wanted me to join her for trivia. I'd meant to do so, I really had. It didn't take some sort of mentalist to realize Cat was pissed that I'd brought Max to the engagement party the other week, and so I'd promised myself I would make more time for her. Which I would, but not that night. I absolutely needed to get some work done, and besides, I had zero interest in spending another evening with Cat's terminally boring friends.

Sorry, Kitty-Cat, I started typing as I neared home. I've got a bunch of work to do tonight. I don't think I'm going to make it. Sorry!!!

Immediately, dots appeared to indicate Cat was typing. They disappeared and then reappeared before finally disappearing once more. No response came. Whatever Cat had planned on saying, she'd decided against it. I felt a smidgen of guilt but brushed it off. If anyone would understand bailing on social engagements to work, Cat would.

Just as I came to the front of my building, I heard a familiar scratching sound coming from the alley. I snapped my head in that direction, fully expecting to see that damn cat sauntering out . . . but also terrified of coming face-to-face with my stalker, whoever he might be. As I stood frozen, I realized that it was more than scratching—it was footsteps, too. Someone was undeniably moving through the alley. I held my breath as the alley gate swung open, and then Ryan came skulking out. His perpetually greasy hair was hidden beneath a bleach-stained baseball cap, and there was something dark smudged across the front of his loose V-neck T-shirt.

He stopped when he saw me staring at him and curled his lips into a predatory grin. "Hello, neighbor."

"What are you doing in that alley?" I demanded.

"Walking," he drawled as he continued past me to the stairs. "What's it to you?"

"I'm barely here anymore," I said. "So you can stop wasting your time."

He paused partway up the stairs and turned to me, sucking on his teeth.

"And I loved those flowers," I continued, hoping to catch him off guard. "Cutting off the heads was a really nice touch."

He barked in laughter. "What are you on?"

"Just leave me alone," I muttered.

"Sweet dreams," he said, still laughing as he let himself into his unit.

I shuddered and continued walking up the path. I reached out to unlock the iron gate outside my door and found that it was standing open.

My stomach crashed to the ground.

"Ryan!" I shouted angrily, but his door was closed.

I looked back at my apartment and noticed that the front door was ajar as well. Fear tickled the back of my brain. I wanted to believe it was just Ryan burglarizing my unit again, but why would he have been sauntering through the alley, empty-handed? I swallowed my rising panic and backed away from the building, not stopping until I was on the other side of the street. I stepped behind a massive tree and called 911. I was tired of feeling unsafe.

* * *

AFTER THE DISPATCHER assured me help was on the way, I called Max. My fingers gripped the phone tightly as I waited for him to answer, already anticipating his soft, calm voice telling me that he would be there soon, that everything was going to be all right.

Hi, you've reached Max Metcalf. I'm not available right now. Please leave a message.

I pulled my phone away from my ear and stared at it in disbelief. Max had *never* not answered when I called. Once he'd even answered while on the treadmill. Where was he now, when I really needed him?

Where are you? I texted him.

As soon as I saw the texting dots appear, I dialed his number again.

"There you are," I said when he finally answered.

"Yeah. What's up?"

In a rush, I said, "Someone is in my apartment. Or they were, I don't know."

"What?" he asked, suddenly animated. "Audrey, are you okay?"

"I'm okay, just rattled. I was walking up the path when I saw my creepy neighbor coming out of the alley, and then after he left I noticed my gate and front door were open. I don't know if Ryan was in there or it was someone else, but I don't care. I'm so, *so* over this shit. I'm never, ever coming back to this godforsaken apartment again."

"Of course not. Have you called the police?"

I sniffled an affirmative.

"Okay, good. I'm coming over." He paused. "You want me to come over, right?"

"Yes," I sobbed. "God, yes, Max. Please come. I need you."

NO ONE WAS INSIDE the apartment. But someone certainly had been. Every cabinet and drawer in the kitchen had been opened and its minimal contents strewn across the floor. My boxes were upended, the cardboard torn. My closet had been riffled through, my clothing pulled from the hangers and piled on the floor, my carefully organized shoes ripped from their boxes and thrown around the room. Everything that could have been disturbed was, right down to a roll of paper towels, which was unwound and stretched around the room like a demented streamer.

For all the destruction, nothing seemed to be missing. The vintage Chanel flap bag I'd painstakingly sourced from eBay sat untouched on my bed where I had left it the day before; the real pearl necklace my parents had given me for my sixteenth birthday was under my overturned jewelry box.

After the officers had taken their report and left, I surveyed the wreckage of my belongings. If I weren't standing right in the middle of it, staring at the slashed and gutted remains of my beanbag chair, I wouldn't have believed it had really happened. Why would someone terrorize me this way? What did they *want*?

"Someone must be really mad at you," Max said quietly beside me.

"But *why*?" I asked, my voice catching in my throat. "I don't get it. What have I done? I'm a good person, Max. At least I try to be."

"Hey," he said, kissing me on the forehead. "You *are* a good person. You didn't do anything to deserve this, okay?" He paused and looked around. "Unless . . . unless you can think of someone who might *think* you did."

"No, not really. I've had some problems with my neighbor, but he would have robbed me. There was an issue with a colleague at work, but that's behind us and, anyway, I can't imagine he would tear my home apart. There's this creep who hangs around the museum, but . . ." I trailed off as I realized something. "Jesus, Max, this must be the same person who was in here that night. To think they had so much *violence* in them and they were standing there, watching me sleep . . ." I choked back tears, unable to continue.

"Come on," Max said, wrapping a protective arm around my shoulders and drawing me in close. "Let's go back to my place. We can talk about this there."

"Yes, thanks," I said, collapsing against him. "I think it's time I get serious about finding a new apartment."

"Agreed," he said, bending down to kiss me gently on the top of my head. "But, Audrey, you can stay with me for as long as you want. You'll be safe at my apartment, I promise. Whoever this creep is, he won't find you there."

CHAPTER FORTY-EIGHT

HIM

An excess of adrenaline was still surging through my veins, leaving me amped and on edge. I couldn't concentrate on anything; all I could do was think back to the moment I'd stepped inside Audrey's apartment that afternoon. I'd let myself in with the key I'd sweet-talked from the landlady weeks ago, and stopped to appreciate the warm sunlight streaming through her windows. The small unit looked cozy and inviting, even with the mess of moving boxes Audrey had let overtake the space. Every single time I came by her place, I expected to see at least some of them unpacked, but she had yet to make a dent. She really was such a slob. It was impossible to know that about her from her carefully composed online presence, but I had realized she would live in filth if left to her own devices.

Just another example of how she needed me.

I lifted a sticky wineglass from the floor beside her beanbag chair and hesitated. I imagined the shock and horror she would experience; I almost put down that dirty glass and left. I didn't want to traumatize her. But I had to make a point.

You're doing this because you love her, I reminded myself as I flung the goblet against the wall. It shattered in an explosion of cheap glass. I grabbed a fashion magazine splayed open on the floor and ripped its cover, tore its glossy pages into confetti. I felt a thrill as I threw them in the air. I was panting; my heart felt outsized.

And then I let myself go.

There was something cathartic in trashing her apartment. All the emotion I had been feeling coalesced into one swirling vortex of destruction. I lost track of time and myself as I flung clothing around the room, ripped her sheets from her bed, smashed palettes of makeup.

Afterward, I stood in the middle of her living room, dizzy, panting, looking at the devastation with wonder. Had I really done all that? There was no way she could misunderstand the depth of my emotion now. Satisfied, I staggered out the front door, not bothering to shut it behind me.

CHAPTER FORTY-NINE

AUDREY

After everything that had happened, I was in no hurry to live alone again. I could find another apartment, but how could I be certain that this maniac wouldn't follow me there? I felt safe at Max's, high above the street, protected by a doorman, and wrapped tightly in Max's comforting arms. There, I could almost forget all the unsettling occurrences that had plagued me since I moved to the city.

Almost, but not quite.

Naked in Max's bed, streaming Ted and the Honey's new acoustic album and ranking our favorite songs, I was outwardly laughing and smiling, but my mind was still stuck on the other night. Even as I argued the pros of my perennial favorite, "This One's for You," I could see my destroyed apartment: my clothing strewn about, wineglasses smashed on the floor, my pricey Harry Josh hair dryer cracked. Involuntarily, I shivered.

"Come on, baby, the lyrics aren't *that* good," Max said gently, kissing my shoulder. "What are you thinking about?"

"My apartment," I admitted. "I'm still really freaked out."

"That's understandable. I can't imagine how it must have felt to see your place torn apart like that. There was so much anger there. Have you thought any more about who might be that upset with you?"

"Only Cat," I said, half laughing.

"You don't think—" Max said haltingly.

"No! Of course not. I'm only teasing. Well, I'm not teasing about Cat being mad. She wouldn't admit it, but I think she was *pissed* that I brought you to that party the other week. And then I know she was upset I didn't go to trivia with her last night. But there's no way Cat would do something like that. I mean, can you imagine her making that kind of mess? She's so pathologically neat she would have stroked out on the spot."

"Right," Max said thoughtfully.

"Hey," I said, trying to change the subject. "I'm famished. Let's have lunch. Is there any more of that curry?"

"No, sorry. But I could run out and pick up some Thai food."

"Don't go," I said, twining my arms around his neck. "We'll starve and die together. It'll be romantic."

"You're an odd woman." He laughed, kissing me and slipping out of bed. He stepped into pants and pulled a shirt over his toned chest, then pointed at me. "Don't you move a muscle. I'll be back with pad thai before you know it."

"I'm not going anywhere," I promised.

JUST AS I HEARD the front door shut behind him, the album we had been streaming finished its last song and began again. I rolled over and reached for his laptop on his bedside table. I was scrolling through Spotify, considering the options—Max had such great taste in music, and I wanted to impress him with the perfect playlist when he came back—when something in the upper right-hand corner of his desktop caught my eye.

A folder titled "Audrey."

A smile tugged at the corners of my mouth. What could he be keeping in a folder with my name on it? Maybe something for my birthday next month? Maybe those tips on Thai travel he'd promised me? Normally I wouldn't open someone's personal file—or, at least, I would feel slightly guilty about doing so—but this one had my name on it. He was practically begging me to open it. I double-clicked the folder.

My smile faltered.

The folder held hundreds if not thousands of photographs. As far as I could tell from the thumbnails, they were all faraway shots of a woman. I enlarged the first and saw myself walking down Fourteenth Street, sipping an iced latte while wearing a light blue dress and round sunglasses. I frowned. Something felt wrong. Maybe it was the way I wasn't looking at the camera. I didn't remember Max taking a candid of me while I was walking.

Suddenly, my heart skipped a beat as I recognized the

dress I was wearing. It was the blue flowered Madewell dress that I had accidentally spilled red wine on in mid-July, nearly a full month before I met Max. I loved that dress but I hadn't been able to get out the stain, and I'd had to throw it away.

Why did Max have a photo of me wearing it?

I opened the next photo, and it was another shot of me in the same outfit, seemingly taken mere seconds later. The next photo was more of the same. I kept clicking open photos until I realized there were at least fifty of me in that same outfit, walking down the same street, sipping the same drink.

What the fuck?

I opened another photo at random and saw me, clad in black Lululemon and with my hair in a sweaty ponytail, digging in my bag, as if searching for my keys. The viewpoint was from across the street, as though the photographer had been watching me from afar.

Not "the photographer," I corrected myself. *Max.*

Cold reality drenched me as I realized what that meant: Max had been taking surreptitious photos of me long before we met. Max had been watching me. *Max had been stalking me.*

I shot out of bed and fumbled for my clothing. My limbs shook as I stepped back into my jeans, pulled my shirt over my head. *Max is stalking me.* All those times I'd heard someone in the alley, all those times I'd thought someone was behind me . . . it had been Max. Jesus, what if he had been the one in my apartment, too?

I checked the time on my phone, trying to judge how long he had been gone. How long would it take him to pick up our usual order of pad thai and papaya salad and return to the apartment? I had to get out of there before he returned. In a panic, I closed the folder and replaced the laptop where I found it, and then grabbed my bag and began shoving my loose belongings into it: my laptop, my wallet, my sunglasses.

Just get out of here! my brain screamed at me. *Leave your stuff behind!*

I was halfway to the door before I paused. I looked back into his familiar apartment, noticing the empty LaCroix can I'd left on the counter, the *Atlantic* Max had been reading last night splayed on the arm of the couch. The door to his bedroom stood open, his soft bed with its sheets probably still warm from my body heat just beyond it. Ted and the Honey continued playing from his laptop, as though I hadn't just discovered something life changing and horrible on it. How could everything still seem so normal?

Max is the stalker.

I raced out of his apartment, opening the Lyft app as I did so. I hesitated when it asked my destination. I couldn't go home. Home wasn't safe. Besides, it was the first place Max would think to look for me. I plugged in Cat's address. Cat would help me. I could always count on her.

CHAPTER FIFTY

CAT

As I carried the pale pink nail polish to Monet's station, my phone buzzed for the fifth time. I glanced down to see Audrey's name on my caller ID once more.

Maybe I should answer, I thought. *Something must be wrong for her to call this many times in a row.*

But just as quickly, I reminded myself of all the times in college that Audrey had acted like the sky was falling when she and Nick had had a quarrel. She'd probably had some minor spat with Max. If I came running every time Audrey called, I would never get anything done. And, with the Phillips trial fast approaching, I had a *lot* that needed to get done.

I sank into the chair opposite Monet and turned on its vibrating massage feature. I wasn't going to let Audrey and whatever was going on with Max ruin my weekly ritual, my one chance to unwind.

"This color again?" Monet said, clucking her tongue. "What is it this time? A client?"

"I'm going to New York for a trial next week," I said with no small amount of pride. "I'm actually going to be making an argument in court."

"Well, look at you!" she exclaimed, holding up her hand for a high five. I laughed and slapped her palm. This was more of a reaction than I'd gotten from Audrey when I'd relayed that same news to her. I'd had to do it over text message, since she couldn't be bothered to disentangle herself from Max for more than two seconds, and she'd responded by "liking" my message. She hadn't even taken the time to type "Congratulations." I'd stared at the phone, waiting for something else, some sort of personal message, but none was forthcoming.

As Monet began to remove last week's polish, my phone went off again. I apologized and reached to silence it, noticing the text on its screen as I did so: CAT PLEASE ANSWER OMW TO YOUR PLACE HELP I NEED YOU.

I hesitated. What if Audrey really did need me? What if she'd learned something more about the person who had been in her apartment? Or if she'd had some sort of other encounter? Doubt gnawed at my stomach, and I realized that my nail appointment was already ruined.

I sighed and pulled out my wallet. "I'm sorry to do this, but I'm going to have to reschedule."

Monet's eyebrows jumped in surprise. I didn't blame her; it was the first time in four years that I had canceled on her like this. "Is something wrong?"

"I'm sure everything's fine. One of my friends just needs to be talked down from a ledge."

AUDREY WAS WAITING on the steps outside my building when I arrived home, and she looked terrible. Her face, devoid of makeup other than smudgy, leftover eyeliner, looked almost gray, and her eyes were glassy and wide. I immediately felt guilty for not answering her earlier calls.

"Are you okay?"

She shook her head violently and drew her arms more tightly across her chest, as though she had to physically hold herself together. I hurried her into the apartment and poured her a glass of water, which she ignored.

"What's going on?"

She swallowed hard and turned frightened, wet eyes to me. "Max has photos of me."

I sipped my own water, waiting for more. Audrey papered the internet with images of herself; of course her boyfriend had some.

"Photos of me," she repeated significantly, as if that might help me understand. "On his *computer*."

"Okay," I said slowly.

"No, Cat. Not *okay*. He has photos he shouldn't have."

"Oh!" I said, my cheeks burning as I suddenly caught what she was saying. "You mean he has *intimate* photos."

"No, not nudes. Photos of me just . . . doing stuff. Drinking coffee, walking, coming home from exercising." She drew a ragged breath and when she spoke her voice was a squeak. "I think . . . I think Max has been *watching* me."

"Audrey, *everyone* has been watching you," I said.

"You post photos of yourself online all day long. So Max saved some of them to his computer. I don't understand what's so upsetting about that."

Her eyes widened, their blue-green color brilliant underneath the sheen of tears. "Are you even listening to me? These aren't photos I've posted. These are photos I've never seen of myself, photos that are like . . . I don't know, like *paparazzi* shots or something."

I felt a bubble of inappropriate laughter rise in my throat. Of course Audrey assumed she had paparazzi, like she was some sort of celebrity. I could see she was distressed, but phrases like that made it so hard for me to take her seriously.

"Breathe," I instructed, taking her hands. "I'm sure there's a reasonable explanation. What did Max say?"

"He doesn't know I saw them. He went out to pick up lunch and left music running on his computer. I went to change the album and . . . I saw them. Just sitting there on his desktop in a folder labeled 'Audrey.' I mean, what the hell, Cat, it's almost like he wanted me to see them." She paused and pressed a hand against her mouth. "I freaked out. I mean, wouldn't you? I picked up and left, and I haven't answered any of his calls or texts. I can't. I don't know what to say. I don't know what any of this means, other than that he's the one who's been stalking me."

"Audrey, no," I told her gently. "You know that's not true. This is *Max*. Come on, you just have to talk to him. I know you said you've never seen them, but you post so many photos, how could you ever keep track?"

"I didn't post these pictures," Audrey said stubbornly.

I doubted she could be so certain, but saw no point in continuing to argue with her.

"Okay," I said placatingly. "You didn't post them. You still have to talk to him. This is your *boyfriend*, Audrey. Do you really believe he's the one who's been stalking you?"

"No. Jesus, Cat, he's so *nice*. I can no more imagine him tearing apart my apartment than I can you doing it."

"There you go. Haven't you always said that you trust your gut?"

She tapped her manicured fingers together in thought. "You've known Max longer than I have, Cat. Can you imagine him doing something like this?"

A person never forgets camp.

"No," I said firmly, curling my bare nails into my palms. "Just talk to him. There has to be a reasonable explanation for this."

"TELL ME THERE'S a reasonable explanation for this," I hissed on the phone to Max. He had started calling me almost as soon as Audrey had, but I waited to return his call until Audrey had retreated to the bathroom with a glass of wine and a jar of my best bath salts.

"I've been calling—"

"I know," I interrupted. "Audrey's here, and she told me what happened."

"Then you know more than I do," he said, his voice distraught. "What's going on?"

"She found your little photo collection."

There was silence on the other end of the line.

"Max? Did you hear me?" I drew a breath and closed my eyes. "Please tell me this is all a misunderstanding. Please tell me you didn't take those photos."

"I didn't take those photos," he said quietly.

"Why don't I believe you?"

"Because liars always assume everyone else is lying," he suggested, a nasty undercurrent to his voice.

"What?" I gasped.

"Cat, I didn't take those photos," he said emphatically. "Does Audrey think I did?"

"She thinks that you took them, and, more than that, she thinks you've been stalking her. She thinks you're the one who's been terrorizing her."

"Oh God," he murmured. "That's not true. Let me talk to her."

"I don't think she wants to talk to you."

"Please, Cat," he said desperately. "I have to talk to her. Please."

I sighed. "I'll tell her you want to talk to her, but I'm not promising anything."

"Please, Cat," he said again. Then his voice hardened as he added, "It's what's best for us. For *all* of us."

CHAPTER FIFTY-ONE

AUDREY

I sat at an otherwise empty communal table at Columbia Brews, my hands cupping an almond milk latte I was too nervous to drink. I kept my eyes on the door, and my stomach jumped every time a blond man walked in. I almost got up and left four separate times, unable to believe I'd let Cat talk me into meeting with Max. She was so certain those photos were innocent. *What do you have to lose by talking to him?* she'd asked. *Just talk to him, and you'll know whether he's telling the truth or not.*

I knew Cat was referencing my sixth sense for judging character. I was rarely wrong. Sophomore year in high school, for example, my friends all said I was crazy when I turned down an invitation to senior prom with Bobby

Kendall, indisputably the best-looking and most sought-after boy in our whole school, simply because I had a "bad feeling"—but then Bobby Kendall drove himself and his date into a tree after a post-prom party. And then there was the time I told Izzy I was getting a bad vibe from the cute guy she'd met on the Q train; she soon discovered his apartment was filled with taxidermied rats.

But lately my radar had been malfunctioning. I'd been completely surprised by Lawrence's behavior; I was shocked to discover Nick was harboring some sort of unrequited love. And so I didn't trust my gut when it came to Max. My instinct was to believe that someone who looked at me as tenderly as he did couldn't be anything other than genuine, but then I remembered those creepy surveillance photos of me on his computer and I wasn't sure of anything.

I was about to push myself back from the table a fifth time when I looked up to see Max loping into the coffee shop, looking more rumpled than usual. My heart twisted, and I had to fight my natural inclination to greet him with a kiss.

"Hey," he said uncertainly, lowering himself into a seat across from me. He flashed me a quick smile that didn't reach his red-rimmed eyes. "Thanks for meeting me."

My fingers longed to reach out and touch the soft edges of his vintage Ramones T-shirt, the one I had worn to sleep so many times I could practically feel it now on my body, but I held myself back. I lifted my chin and looked at him squarely, keeping my voice steady as I said, "You should be thanking Cat. She's the one who convinced me I should hear your side of things."

He nodded mutely.

"I trusted you, Max," I said quietly, my voice betraying me and breaking. "I don't know what to think."

"Help me out, Audrey," he said, his eyes searching mine. "I don't know what we're talking about. What happened? When I left, you were naked in my bed, and when I came back, you were gone and no longer taking my calls. What changed?"

"I found the pictures."

"What pictures?" he asked, his expression so bewildered that for a split second I wondered if I had imagined the whole thing. But then I recalled the shock of opening that folder and seeing rows upon rows of digital images of myself, and anger flared inside me.

"Come on, Max," I snapped. "You know what pictures I mean. The ones on your computer. The ones of *me*."

"Oh," he said, casting his eyes down to the scratched table. "Those."

"*Those*."

He nodded dumbly. "Yeah. Jeez, Audrey, I can understand why those might have freaked you out. But they're not what you think."

"Then tell me what they are," I said, allowing myself a flicker of hope that there might be an innocent explanation, that I hadn't been so wrong, so completely and utterly wrong, about this man.

"Don't freak out, okay? But I found those online."

"What? Online where?"

"When we first started dating, I . . . well, I googled you. I really liked you, and I wanted to know what I was getting myself into." He smiled weakly. "I didn't want to fall in love with you only to find out you had a secret husband or were wanted in six states."

I refused to let myself smile at his joke. "There's no way you found those photos in a simple Google search. I've had a Google alert set up for my name for years, and I've never seen them."

"I didn't find them right away. I had some trouble with my search at first. There were more people named Audrey Miller than I expected, so I had to try something different. I pulled some images from your social media profiles and did a reverse image search. That was when I found them."

"I still don't understand. Where did you find them?"

He shook his head. "A gross site you don't want to know about."

I shuddered, not wanting to imagine what kind of site would be so gross that Max couldn't tell me about it. "Are they still there?"

"No, I took care of it. I called one of my friends who is . . . well, he's a hacker. He broke into the site and removed your pictures. I also asked him if he could trace where they originated, but he hasn't been able to do so thus far."

"Max . . ." I started, unsure what I wanted to say. It's not like I didn't believe him. Of course I *believed* him; he was my boyfriend. But . . . there was something that felt sketchy about his explanation. There was something he wasn't telling me.

"I don't like you keeping things from me," I finally said.

"I know," he said miserably. "And I'm sorry. I was just afraid you were going to think I was some weirdo for looking you up."

"Of *course* you looked me up. I did the same to you. Googling someone before you date them is normal. Finding out that person has a fucking *stalker* and then keeping that information to yourself, however, is *not.*"

He nodded, swallowing so hard I saw his throat move. "I know. I'm sorry."

"Sorry isn't good enough. You knew how scared I was about everything that had been happening at my apartment, and you had additional information that you kept to yourself. You should have told me. We could have given that evidence to the police, and this creep, whoever he is, could be behind bars right now."

"The police don't have the resources my friend does," Max protested. "I told you, he's working on it."

"Excuse me if I don't trust your nameless, never-before-mentioned friend with my life. I mean, for God's sake, Max, this is *serious.* Don't you remember what happened to Rosalind?"

"Audrey, that's *why* I couldn't tell you. You were so consumed with that exhibit that I knew you'd see parallels where there were none and freak out." He took a deep breath and leaned across the table, taking my hands. "I messed up, I get it. And I'm sorry. But you have to know that I love you. I love you so much, Audrey. I would do anything for you. *Anything.* I made a mistake, I see that now, but you have to believe me when I say it was a mistake that I made for you."

I love you. I hadn't known until the moment he said those words just how much I'd been dying to hear them. My heart trembled and fluttered, but there was nothing I could do. Everything about the circumstances was all wrong, so completely, totally wrong.

"Okay," I said softly, pulling my hands away.

"Okay?" he echoed, eyes round with hope.

"Okay, I hear you," I clarified. "But I need some time to think."

"Okay," he said, so quietly I almost didn't hear him as he hung his head. "Okay."

I pushed my chair away from the table with an ear-splitting scrape and rose, slinging my purse over my shoulder. I started toward the door, but then doubled back and pressed my lips to the crown of his head, inhaling deeply and smelling the aroma of his sandalwood-scented shampoo.

"I love you, too," I whispered into his hair.

Before he could respond, I walked briskly out of the coffee shop.

CHAPTER FIFTY-TWO

CAT

It was almost eleven o'clock by the time I left the office that night, and I'd eaten nothing other than a handful of almonds since that morning. In less than seven short hours, I would be meeting Bill, Connor, and the rest of our team at Union Station to take the six o'clock Acela to New York; the Phillips trial was scheduled to start the next morning. I had just a few final hours to practice my portion of the argument, pack, and get some sleep. The latter seemed out of the question, considering my anxiety over the argument, but I would have to try. I dreaded falling asleep on the train, drooling and head bobbing, in front of the partner I needed to impress and the man I still secretly loved.

"Cat."

I jumped at the sound of my name and I whirled around on the darkened street. There, leaning against the side of the building with his face mostly obscured by shadows, was Max.

"Max," I said uneasily. "What are you doing here?"

"Looking for you, of course," he said, flashing me a quick, humorless smile. "I need your help."

"I don't know what else I can do. I already convinced Audrey to meet with you."

"I know, and thank you for that. But things are still all twisted. And, look, I know it's my fault. I should have told Audrey about those pictures the second I found them, but I was so embarrassed about searching for her. And then once I got my friend involved and he hacked into that site, things got more complicated. But that's no excuse. And I get it now. I messed up in a major way, and so I need to apologize in an even more major way."

I shook my head. "That's between you and Audrey."

"I don't need you to do much," he insisted. "Just tell Audrey you're taking her out to dinner, and instead bring her to the location of our first date. I'll have the same meal prepared, and flowers and music and all the things I know she likes. She'll see how much I love her. I just need your help getting her there."

"Your first date was in an empty building," I reminded him. "And I don't think Audrey is going to feel comfortable being in an empty building with you right now."

"Jeez," he moaned, rubbing a hand over his face. "I can't believe how badly I've ruined everything."

His obvious anguish was uncomfortably reminiscent of how I had felt after the Hirshhorn event, when I realized I'd squandered a chance with Connor and made everything between us worse instead of better. I reached out and patted him tentatively on the shoulder. "It'll be okay."

He caught my hand and held it tightly, compressing the bones. "Please, Cat. You have to help me. I love Audrey so much."

"I'll think about it," I promised, carefully extracting myself from his grip. "But it will have to wait. I leave for trial tomorrow, and I'll be out of town for the rest of the week, maybe longer."

"Okay," he said, his disappointment clear. "I guess that will work. It'll have to. Unless . . . Is Audrey going to be at your apartment while you're away?"

I hesitated. "Um . . . I think so."

"Maybe you could give me a set of your keys? I could surprise her with flowers."

"I don't know," I hedged. "Audrey hasn't had the greatest experience with flowers lately."

"Something else, then. Air plants. Champagne. Animal crackers."

"I'm sorry, but I don't think surprising her with anything is a great idea. Not right now, at least. After everything that happened with her apartment and discovering she has a stalker, she's been really on edge. She needs someplace she can feel safe."

Max's expression darkened. "And you're the only one who can make her feel safe? With the way you're trying to keep her to yourself, it almost makes me wonder if *you're* the one who's been stalking her."

My mouth dropped open in surprise. "Max, that's ludicrous."

"Is it? I've seen the way you look at Audrey."

"I don't know what you're insinuating, but—"

"You look at her like you want to *be* her. Like you want to take her skin and wear it as a suit."

"Audrey is my best friend," I said, aghast. "I certainly don't want to *skin* her."

"Are you Audrey's best friend, though?"

I sucked in my breath. Max had hit me right where it hurt, the tender spot I didn't think anyone else knew about. Ever since she'd taken my hand on Bid Day, Audrey had been my best friend, my only friend. I'd always known our friendship didn't mean as much to Audrey as it did to me, and I had accepted that. Just getting to have a piece of Audrey was enough for me. And then she had moved to DC, and I had glimpsed behind the glimmering curtain, seen what it was to have Audrey's sparkling attention focused solely on me. But just when I was starting to fully appreciate it, Max had swooped in and snatched her away from me.

"If you were, she would have accepted your repeated offers to move in," he added.

My stomach lurched as I imagined Audrey telling Max I had asked her to live with me, and then the two of them laughing about it together. *Cat's so pathetic, she's always trying to force a friendship*, Audrey might have said. *Careful*, Max might have cautioned, *you know what happened to the last girl who wouldn't be her friend.*

"Maybe it was you," Max continued. "Maybe you ransacked Audrey's apartment to scare her into moving in with you."

"By that logic, *you're* the one who trashed her apartment," I countered. "After all, she moved in with *you*. How do *I* know that *you're* not the one stalking her?"

"I would never do anything to harm Audrey," he said, sounding offended. "*Never.*"

"Neither—"

"Besides," he interrupted. "I'm not the one with a history of violent jealousy."

I had been expecting something like this, but it felt like a blow to the stomach. "That was an accident."

"Sure it was, Cathy." He cocked his head slightly. "What do you think Bill Hannover would say about it?"

My mouth went metallic. "Are you threatening me?"

"What would make you think that?" he asked, sneering slightly.

Time stood still as he held my eyes, daring me to call his bluff. I swallowed hard. "Max, if I give you these keys—"

"Everything will be fine."

"It better be," I murmured. I felt sick as I handed him my key ring, but what else could I do? If Max told Bill about Emily Snow, my future at the firm would be over. Legal careers were built upon reputation, and any connection to that kind of unpleasantness would be catastrophic. I had to protect myself.

CHAPTER FIFTY-THREE

AUDREY

I briefly fantasized about tagging along to New York with Cat, going back to the city where I'd always felt safe and maybe never returning, but I knew I couldn't. I couldn't go there with the way things were—me practically homeless, estranged from my boyfriend, and in possession of nerves so shattered that I jumped every time the wind blew—without feeling like a colossal failure.

Instead, I helped Cat pack. As I handed her a pair of pantyhose, covering up my anxiety about her leaving with a joke about Cat being the only woman other than the Queen of England who still wore hose, she suddenly seized my hand.

"Why don't you call Nick?" she suggested, her expression serious.

"Who are you and what have you done with my friend?" I asked, taken aback. "You *hate* Nick."

"I'd feel better if you weren't in this apartment alone," she'd said, forehead creased with worry. "Even if that means you're staying with that awful ex-boyfriend of yours."

"You're sweet to worry," I said, patting her hand. "But I don't trust any men right now, Nick included. They all look like goddamn stalkers. I'll be fine here. Truly. Your apartment is so much more secure than mine."

Cat opened her mouth as though she was about to say something, then closed it and nodded. "Just be careful."

"I will," I promised. "Everything will be fine."

It was something I believed—or at least *wanted* to believe. Still, I lay awake that entire first night alone, every innocuous creak or thump sending an electric current of terror through my body. I checked the lock on the front door at least seven times and did a sweep of all the windows twice. Everything was in order, but sleep still eluded me. I rolled my bottle of Ambien between my palms, tempted to take a pill but terrified to do so. I hadn't had one since hearing the strange voice on the Luna Listen app, hadn't been willing to numb myself to the world when there were creeps in it who wanted to watch me sleep. Instead, I stared at the smooth ceiling of the guest room until the first rays of morning light stretched across it, at which point I finally drifted off.

My alarm sounded ninety minutes later, and I raised my head long enough to call in sick before going back to bed for the rest of the morning. Six hours later, I awoke energized and more than a little embarrassed at how frightened I'd been. Cat's apartment was plainly harmless in the daylight, and I considered whether I should just go full vampire while Cat was away. I made up for my unproductive morning by responding to emails and planning some future Instagram content, and then I took a Reformer class and picked up a salad from Sweetgreen on my way home.

Despite the postexercise endorphins in my system, I felt a twinge of loneliness as I climbed the steps to Cat's building. I really hated being alone. I'd been that way ever since I was a baby—my mother loves to say I only learned to crawl so I could follow my sister around. And after Maggie was promoted to her own bedroom, I used to sneak in and sleep on the floor by her bed, curled up on her pink shag rug alongside the cat. I no longer slept on the floor like someone's pet, but I'd never gotten over my dislike for being alone.

So I was lonely without Cat around, sure, but as much as I hated to admit it, I missed *Max*. I missed eating home-cooked meals at his side while listening to his impressive record collection, and I missed nestling into the crook of his elbow and snacking on his brilliant concoction of Tabasco-dressed popcorn while we watched television. I missed the feel of his soft lips on mine, the way his mouth always tasted faintly of cinnamon. I missed him pressing his face into my hair and telling me I was beautiful.

But could I ever forgive him for keeping those photos a secret? How could he not have told me about them? And what kind of website had they been on? Something gross, he had said. I should have pressed him on that. When I first moved into the basement apartment, I hadn't always remembered to draw my curtains before undressing— years of living far above the street had made me lax about such things—and what if this creep had seen me? What if he had posted *naked* photos of me?

I shivered and wished desperately there was someone I could call. A side effect of only showing the best and most beautiful bits of my life to everyone meant that I felt like I couldn't reveal my messier, more complicated emotions to anyone other than a trusted few. But I'd lost Izzy to Russell, Nick to his own hang-ups, and Cat to work, at least temporarily. The only other person I could think to call was Maggie, but I knew how that conversation would go: she would imply this was my fault for sharing too much online, and then she would start telling me about something adorable her children had done, and I would hang up the phone feeling vaguely envious, even though there was no way I would trade Maggie's life for mine. Me as an accountant in Ohio with two children under the age of two? No, thank you.

You'll have Cat back soon enough, I told myself, stepping into her apartment. *You can hold it together for a few more nights.*

I was about to drop Cat's extra set of keys on the front table when I heard footsteps. I froze, every nerve in my body signaling danger.

Was someone in Cat's apartment? Had my stalker followed me there?

I dismissed the notion as ridiculous—besides, I was *certain* I had just unlocked the door, and Cat didn't have a creepy Ryan with an extra set of keys. Unless . . . When Cat had come home the night before her trial, she had needed me to let her in. She said she must have forgotten her keys back in her office, but what if she had dropped them along the way home? What if someone had found them and used them? Or . . . what if someone had *stolen* them from her purse?

Don't be absurd, I thought. *It's most likely that Cat's work thing ended early and she's home.*

"Cat?" I called.

There was no response. There was nothing at all. I relaxed, determining I must have imagined the earlier sound. I set down the keys and crossed to the kitchen. I was lowering the salad onto the counter when I heard another noise, a *thump*. I froze. Where did that come from? Was that inside the apartment?

"Cat?" I tried once more, my voice just a squeak now.

A floorboard creaked. Awash in panic, I thought, *Someone is in the apartment.*

I spun on a sneakered heel and raced out of the apartment, barely pausing to grab the keys off the table as I did so. I flew down the exterior stairs, my feet slipping on the wrought iron, and burst onto the sidewalk, fumbling with my phone to call Cat. I was panting and must have looked totally wild, because an elderly couple walking a Yorkshire terrier actually crossed the street to avoid me.

"Hello?" Cat answered.

"Where are you?"

"New York," she said slowly. "Audrey, are you all right?"

"I just came home from Pilates and heard someone in your apartment."

"What do you mean?"

"I mean *I heard someone in your apartment.* I thought it must have been you, but it's obviously not," I said, my voice rising with each syllable. "Jesus, Cat, do you think my stalker followed me to your place?"

"Stay calm," she commanded. "Did you look through the apartment?"

"Hell no. I'm not trying to get murdered."

"I just . . . Audrey, don't panic. I'm sure it's nothing. Just—"

I hung up on Cat and dialed 911. It wasn't *nothing*. There was someone in that apartment, undoubtedly the same someone who had been in my apartment. *Someone was after me.*

THE TWO POLICE OFFICERS who responded to my call were both overweight, middle-aged men who obviously thought I was some hysterical girl, afraid of her own shadow. I went over the sounds I had heard once again, struggling to keep my voice calm, trying to force them to take me seriously, even though one of them was blatantly ogling me in my cropped exercise shirt and mesh-paneled leggings.

"I don't know what to tell you, miss," the one who was exhibiting a modicum of professionalism said. "There are no signs of a break-in. Nothing appears to be out of order."

"But I *heard* something," I insisted. "Footsteps. Creaking."

"These old buildings can be funny," he said kindly. "Maybe you heard the downstairs neighbors. You mentioned you're staying here because of some problems with your apartment. Maybe you're more on edge than usual."

"Of course I'm on edge," I said, frustrated. "Someone is *stalking* me. Wait, did I tell you about the pho—"

"There's no evidence of an intruder," the other one interrupted, tearing his eyes away from my chest. "The door wasn't forced open, and we found no open windows. I don't believe anyone was there."

"You think I'm making this up?" I demanded.

"No one thinks you purposefully made anything up," the first officer said gently. "I'm sure you heard something that frightened you. But, miss, there's no one here. Try to relax, get some sleep. You'll feel better in the morning."

"Thanks," I said sarcastically. "Thanks for the help."

"Just doing our job, ma'am," he said, giving me a quick nod. "You have a good night."

As I watched the utterly useless police officers depart down Cat's front steps, my fingers itched to call Max. *He* would believe me. *He* would know that I wasn't just being jumpy. He would whisk me away to safety, put his comforting arms around me, and help me forget all of this mess.

But what the fuck was he doing with those photos?

I had to know more about them, had to figure out where they had come from. I grabbed my laptop from where it sat open on the coffee table and sank onto Cat's large couch. Max said he stumbled across them while doing a reverse image search, so I tried to re-create his steps using the profile picture from my Instagram account. I didn't get any immediately obvious results, so I began trying other combinations: my Twitter profile picture, other images I'd uploaded to my various accounts, plus adding in search terms like my name, "summer," and "candid." No matter what I tried, Google only returned the expected results in the form of my own social media, the *Glamour* piece, some other articles that mentioned me. I was still combing through pages of results, looking for anything that might be close to what Max had described, when my computer's screen suddenly went dark.

Shit.

All at once, I remembered leaving my charger at Max's apartment when I'd rushed out of there last week. I'd been sharing Cat's since I'd been at her place, but of course she had taken it with her to New York. *Stupid*, I chastised myself.

Leaving my brick of a computer and my phone on the couch, I stood and crossed to the corner of the room Cat used as her home office. I turned on her desktop computer, exhaling with relief when I saw it wasn't password protected. I opened Google and resumed my search. I couldn't rest until I had some answers.

CHAPTER FIFTY-FOUR

HIM

Where did she go?

She'd been there, on the screen, looking a bit pale and worried. It was an expression I'd seen more of lately, ever since I had left my mark on her apartment. I'd gone too far that night; I understood that now. I'd wanted her to understand how deeply I loved her, how crazy she made me, but that hadn't been what had happened. I had to do something to atone, something to set things right. Something that would make that sweet mouth curl into a smile once more.

I looked into her distraught face and saw her aquamarine eyes were brimming with tears. Daggers stabbed through my heart, and I knew I needed to do something right away. I'd jumped up from my couch and rushed out to buy her another impressive bouquet of orange flowers. I would surprise her with them that night. Maybe I would even leave her a little note, a bit of poetry perhaps. I was thinking over my options as I picked up my laptop again, the flowers at my side, only to find that she was gone.

I immediately grabbed my phone to check her Instagram, sure there would be a Story about an exercise class she was taking or a friend she was meeting, but there was nothing. She was uncharacteristically silent. A flicker of disquiet sparked in my stomach.

She must be in the shower, I told myself. *She'll come back soon.*

But she didn't. Hours passed and Audrey didn't reappear. I remained glued to the couch, staring dumbly at the blank screen while the flicker in my stomach turned into an inferno. Where had Audrey gone? Had she discovered the RAT?

You ruined this, my family's collective voice said in my head. *You drove her away.*

Aly appeared in my mind's eye, her eyes narrowed as she nodded sagely, agreeing with them. *You're not fit to date anyone.*

Sabrina, her hair longer and redder than it had really been, appeared beside her, laughing. *Pathetic.*

"Leave me alone!" I bellowed, upending my coffee table, sending the coffee cups and container of animal crackers atop it flying. The mugs shattered; loose legs and torsos scattered everywhere.

It was physically painful to admit, but my abhorrent family was right. It was my fault. It was *always* my fault. I drove everyone away: Sabrina, Aly, Audrey, all the minor players who had left me in between. What was the common denominator there? Me. It was fucking *me*.

I picked up my laptop, where her screen was still black in the RAT desktop, and shook it, screaming, *"Where did you go?"*

CHAPTER FIFTY-FIVE

CAT

The man across the aisle from me loudly cracked open another pistachio, his twenty-sixth. I'd been glaring at him since the third, hoping the intensity of my stare would shame him into eating a quieter snack. Instead, he reached for another.

Sitting alone in the Acela's Quiet Car, scowling at a stranger and counting nuts, was not how I envisioned my return to DC after the Phillips trial. Then again, it wasn't technically "after" the Phillips trial. The rest of the team remained in New York, preparing for the next day's work, while only I returned in shame. I blanched as I remembered what had happened in court that morning. It had been time for me to speak, making a jurisdictional argument that was technical and a bit dry, but nonetheless important. As I rose from my chair, nylon-clad legs shaking underneath my skirt suit, I heard Connor whisper, "Go get 'em, Harrell."

I took a deep breath and glanced down at my notes. On the table beside my legal pad, my phone screen lit up, Audrey's name visible. Messages started appearing on the screen, one after another. I tried to ignore them, tried to focus on my notes, but the word "help" caught my eye.

"Catherine," Bill whispered to me. "You're up."

I lifted my gaze sharply, reminding myself of the import of what I was about to do, but my concentration was shot. I couldn't stop thinking about that "help." Did Audrey need me? Did this have something to do with the noises she claimed she'd heard in my apartment? I had assumed they were Max, depositing his flowers or whatever he had decided to do, but what if it wasn't? What if Audrey was in trouble?

The argument I'd exhaustively practiced left me; it simply vanished from my head. I felt Bill's eyes burning holes through the back of my suit jacket, no doubt wondering why he had entrusted something so important to such an awkward loser.

Cat got your tongue? Emily Snow taunted.

I opened my mouth and forced out words. They weren't the words I'd planned to say, and my voice was thin and tremulous, like that of a child rather than a competent professional. More than once, the judge had to ask me to speak up. When I flubbed a case holding and the judge interrupted to correct me, I knew it was over. I wanted to melt into the floor. It took every ounce of fortitude I had to finish the argument. As I returned to my seat, I looked to Connor for sympathy, but he couldn't even meet my eyes.

And the worst part was that when I checked my phone and read Audrey's text messages, they were just something about not being able to sleep and needing to talk about Max.

Goddamn Audrey.

She was my savior and my executioner. Without her, I never would have gotten along in the sorority, never would have had any friends or any fun. But without her, I might have succeeded today. If she hadn't distracted me at the last minute . . . She *knew* how important this trial was to me. She *knew*, and still she texted me with this self-obsessed nonsense. I didn't know why I was surprised. Audrey always thought about herself first and foremost.

She would never change. So I had to.

CHAPTER FIFTY-SIX

AUDREY

I was exhausted. After last night's scare, I hadn't slept well, and had claimed a migraine headache so I could leave work early and spend several more hours unsuccessfully scouring the internet for amateur paparazzi photos of myself. I sent Cat another text, begging her to call so I could talk this through, and then opened a bottle of wine I found in her kitchen. I drank one glass of the velvety cab before pouring a refill and carrying it upstairs to the bathroom. I drew a warm bath, sprinkled in some lavender bath salts I pilfered from her cabinet, and then eased into the claw-foot bathtub, exhaling audibly as I leaned my head against the gentle slope.

I closed my eyes and tried to relax, but all I could think about were those damn photographs. I'd been unable to re-create Max's reverse image search, and I couldn't decide whether that should reassure me or not. On the one hand, it was a relief to not find any creepy stalker pictures of me on the internet. On the other hand, where the hell had they come from? If I couldn't find them in a concentrated search, how could Max have innocently stumbled upon them? Either he did a much more intensive dive into my online footprint than he wanted to admit, or he was lying about their origin.

Beneath the warm water, my skin prickled in gooseflesh, and I gulped at the wine and returned to the question that had been nagging me ever since I first opened that folder. *What if Max took those photos?* It was so hard to believe that someone who looked at me as sweetly, as *tenderly* as Max did could be the one stalking me. But was that any harder to believe than his story about how he'd found them and enlisted the help of some superhacker?

I knew I was too emotionally invested in this and needed someone to help me think rationally. I needed Cat. Impatiently, I glanced to the floor for my phone—surely Cat would return my text messages soon—and realized I'd left it downstairs.

I was debating getting out of the tub to fetch it when I heard the unmistakable sound of a door closing. My spine went rigid and my mind imagined a hundred different horrible scenarios—most of which involved my meeting a bloody end at the hands of my stalker, Rosalind-style—before I realized who it must be: Cat. She must have seen my messages and recognized how much I needed her. I relaxed. Thank God for Cat.

"Cat?" I called.

She didn't shout hello, but I could hear her moving through the apartment downstairs.

"Cat?" I tried again. "I'm up here!"

Footsteps sounded on the spiral staircase, and pitch-black fear oozed through my veins as I realized they were too heavy to be Cat's. *You're wrong,* I told myself. *It has to be Cat. You locked the front door.* The footsteps continued, each footfall sounding heavier and less like Cat than the last, until they came to a halt outside the bathroom door.

I was paralyzed, afraid to even blink. There was no more movement in the hall, but I could hear breathing—no, panting. Someone was *panting* outside that door. The wine turned unpleasantly in my stomach. Whoever was in the apartment was now between me and the only exit.

Get out of the bathtub, my mind screamed at me. *That door is going to open in five seconds and you are going to go the way of Janet Leigh in* Psycho *if you don't get out of the bathtub right fucking now.*

And then what? Even if I were able to leap from the tub and lock the door before the heavy breather in the hallway threw it open, then what? I would be trapped inside Cat's bathroom with no cell phone and no way out.

The doorknob clicked slightly, a soft but ominous sound, as though someone had gripped the handle on the other side but not turned it.

Yet.

Forget thinking three steps ahead. Survival was all that mattered. Mind nearly blank with terror, I flung myself out of the bathtub. Lavender-scented water splashed over the tiles as I lunged for the door, and my feet slipped out from underneath me. My knees smacked the ground hard enough to bring tears to my eyes, and I cried out in pain. My hands flew to my mouth, as though they could shove the noise back in, as though there might remain some mystery about where I was. The doorknob turned, and I squeezed my eyes shut in a panicked, pointless attempt to prevent the inevitable.

"Audrey?"

His voice was so calm, so *normal* that I almost believed it was an auditory hallucination. Slowly, I opened my eyes. Max was standing in the doorway, wearing his favorite Ted and the Honey T-shirt and an expression of concern.

"Are you okay?" he asked, setting down a paper Whole Foods bag and holding out a hand to help me up from the floor.

I scrambled to my feet without assistance and grabbed a thick towel, wrapping it protectively around my body. "Max? What are you doing here?"

"Checking on you. I knew you were here alone, and you weren't answering my calls. I was worried. I wanted to make sure you were okay." His voice dropped as he looked at me closely. "*Are* you okay?"

I ached to fling myself into his arms and let his gentle hands soothe my rattled nerves, but I took a step back instead. I still had some serious questions about those photographs, and, besides, I'd told him I needed time to think. He shouldn't have just come barging into someone else's home looking for me.

Someone else's locked *home*, I remembered with a start.

"How did you get inside?"

He tilted his head slightly. "The door was unlocked."

"No, it wasn't."

"Yeah, it was. When you didn't answer after I knocked, I got concerned. I tried the knob and it opened."

He was lying. I had locked that door. Or I *thought* I had locked that door. But if I had, how had he gotten inside?

"I was right to worry, wasn't I? You look scared."

Of course I'm scared! I wanted to scream. *Someone has been stalking me and I'm afraid it's you!*

"I heard someone in here," I finally said.

His eyes widened. "What? *Here?* Audrey, why are you still here?"

"The police came and said no one was here. They said I was safe." I cleared my throat and watched him carefully as I spoke. "But now I wonder if maybe they missed something. Maybe there's another entrance. After all, you got in."

He blinked. "I told you, the front door was open. You don't really think . . . Christ, Audrey. I know you're still mad at me, but there's no way you think I would *break into* Cat's apartment to see you, right?"

I couldn't answer. I focused instead on the Whole Foods bag at his feet, one of Nick's bad jokes from my first date with Max coming back to me: *Watch out for bags of zip ties and collections of sharp instruments.*

"What's in the bag?"

"Oh," he said, brightening. "I almost forgot. I brought you something."

With a flourish, he pulled out a bouquet of fat orange roses. My blood turned to ice and I stumbled backward.

"Why did you bring me those?"

"I thought you'd like them," he said, looking hurt. "I

made a mistake, and I know it. I want to make it up to you."

"No," I said, voice trembling. "Why did you bring me *those*? Why did you bring me orange flowers?"

"Because orange is your favorite color."

"But how do you know that? I never told you that."

"Sure you did."

"No," I objected, although suddenly I wasn't certain. We'd spent so many hours talking about so many things— it was *possible* I had mentioned my favorite color. But I couldn't ignore the coincidence between these flowers and the orange bouquet tied to my gate. I'd found that months ago, long before I met Max . . . but around the time the strange photos on his computer must have been taken.

"Baby, come on. This is ridiculous. Here, I'll go put these flowers in water."

"You're lying," I blurted. "You're lying about that, and you're lying about those photos."

He froze, his face an unreadable mask. "What?"

"I searched online for them. They're not there, Max. I don't think they ever were. And you know what? I've thought about it, and even if you *had* come across them on some random website, why would you download them? I could see one or two, maybe, as evidence or something, but *all* of them? There must have been thousands."

He swallowed audibly. "I love you."

"You took them, didn't you? *You* took those photos."

It was no longer a question in my mind, but I was still surprised when he whispered, "Yes."

"Jesus," I murmured, staggering. "I don't understand. But how . . . ? Why?"

"Because I love you," he said, his voice plaintive and

his eyes going liquid. "I've loved you for more than eight years, Audrey."

"Eight . . . ?" I choked out.

"That was when I first laid eyes on you. I really did come across your photo on a dodgy site, but it was just a screengrab from your Facebook. When I saw it . . . Audrey, you hit me like a bolt of lightning and I just *knew*. I knew we were destined."

Destined? I gaped in horror at this man I thought I knew, this man who I was just now realizing was completely unhinged.

"I've read everything you've ever posted," he continued earnestly. "All your blog posts, Facebook statuses, tweets, Instagram posts and Stories. I've listened to all the playlists you've made on Spotify. I've watched every movie you've ever recommended, read every book. I know everything about you, and I love every bit of you. Every last, incomparable bit."

I shuddered and clutched the towel more tightly around my body. Naked desperation was shining in Max's eyes, and I knew I needed to be anywhere other than alone in an empty house with him. I glanced toward the staircase, my only escape route. It was just five feet from me, but he was standing in front of it. I took a minuscule step toward it, hoping I might get past him if I moved slowly enough and kept him distracted.

"What about those other orange flowers?" I asked. "The ones tied to my gate? Were you the one who left them for me?"

He nodded proudly. "I knew you'd like them."

"They were beautiful," I allowed. "But what about the others? The headless ones? Was that you, too?"

"I needed to send a message," he said, his expression darkening. "You were ignoring my requests for a second date, and then you had over that knuckle-dragging ex of yours. I know what you do with him. It's disgusting."

My mouth dropped open in surprise. "How do you know about Nick?"

"I told you, Audrey. I know everything about you." At his side, one of his fists began clenching and unclenching. "I've done so much for you, so much that you don't even know about, and then you just ran back to that meathead's arms? That *hurt*. I had to show you how you were destroying something beautiful."

"I'm sorry," I said weakly, inching toward the stairs. "I didn't understand."

"I know," he growled. "If you had understood, you wouldn't have kept running back to him time and again."

"I didn't," I protested, shaking my head wildly as if this—this misunderstanding—would be the thing that cleared up this whole nightmare. "I swear. I wasn't ever with Nick after we started dating."

"You're lying," he snarled, his fists tightening, knuckles going white. "Just like you lied then. You told me you had to work, but then you invited that pompous ass into your home. So I had to teach you a lesson. I had to show you, once and for all, that you shouldn't leave me."

"Oh my God," I murmured, suddenly understanding. "You trashed my apartment. But how . . . ?"

"Your landlady is sweet," he said, meeting my eyes defiantly. "And a little daft. All I had to do was tell her that I was your boyfriend and that you'd locked yourself out, and she gave me the key off her own ring."

"Jesus, Max, I trusted you. And it's been you this

whole time, hasn't it? Following me around, creeping in the alley."

"I had to see you," he said, voice softening. "You get that, don't you? You're everything to me, Audrey. My sun, my moon, every last one of my stars. I'm sorry if I scared you, but—"

"*If* you scared me?" I said incredulously. "I've been terrified, and you *knew* it. You were scaring the shit out of me. For God's sake, Max, you stood over my bed and *watched me sleep.*"

"That wasn't what you think," he started.

"And tonight?" I interrupted. "When I thought someone was here earlier? That was you, too, wasn't it?"

"No," he said firmly. "I swear."

"How do you expect me to believe you? You've been *stalking* me, Max. I can't trust you at all."

"You *can.* I promise you can. Just listen—" he started, reaching for me.

I sidled out of his grasp, closer to the staircase. "Not another inch."

"Please, Audrey. Listen. I know you'll understand. I've loved you from afar for so long. And then when you moved here, to my city, I knew it was fate. We were *fated.*"

"That's not fate." I paused as a thought dawned on me. "What about Cat? Does she know about . . . all this?"

"You being friends with Cat was just a happy coincidence." He smiled slightly and took a step toward me. "See what I mean? Fate."

I looked behind him to the stairs. They were so close now—with just one large step I was certain I could be on them—but Max was standing within grabbing distance.

There was no way I would ever make it past him and down those stairs without him stopping me.

"Max—" I started.

He reached for me suddenly, and I instinctively tried to dash past. My bare foot slipped at the top of the spiral staircase, and I grasped desperately for the railing. It was too late; my balance was too far off. Max's face contorted, his mouth opening in a cry as he grabbed for me, and then everything went black.

CHAPTER FIFTY-SEVEN

MAX

All I had wanted was to see her. She had disappeared from my screen, and I just wanted, *needed*, to see that she was okay. I'd grabbed the flowers and headed to Cat's apartment, the keys she'd given me jangling a happy tune in my pocket. Those flowers (orange, her favorite color, which I knew because two years ago she posted a photo of her open palm filled with orange Starbursts captioned as such) would get me through the door, I was sure of it. Then we would start talking, and then she would realize how awful I felt that she'd had to find those photos. I felt sick whenever I thought about how easy it would have been to store that folder anywhere other than on the desktop.

But then she was looking at me as though I was a

stranger and asking questions I didn't like in an accusing voice, and it was clear she didn't understand. I had done *everything* for her. I'd been a devoted follower for years, made her my religion. I'd decorated my apartment with art she would appreciate (I even sourced a print of her favorite Jackson Pollock after reading about it in a blog post titled "Let Me Tell You Why Jackson Pollock Is the Bomb," posted May 21, 2014) and peppered my shelves with books she liked, from *Gone Girl* (*WTF?!* ♥, she had captioned an image of the book on September 3, 2012) to a dog-eared, secondhand copy of Edna St. Vincent Millay's *Collected Poems* (finding the poem that had inspired her tattoo and flagging the page with a bookmark, so that she might stumble across it, then flip over her wrist to show me the very same lines indelibly marked on her body).

I'd kept a detailed spreadsheet of all the music she posted about or added to public playlists, and then I used that as a guide while I painstakingly assembled a record collection from scratch. That first Ted and the Honey album had been hard to find (there hadn't been many pressings, and with the band having hit mainstream success, people weren't parting with theirs) but I did. Knowing how much she loved them, I even listened to their entire catalog despite the lead singer sounding like he had a mouth full of gravel and the whole thing being a bit too noise-rock for my liking. I knew which songs were her favorites, and I learned the lyrics, would be able to sing along if the situation demanded. I even threw out all the animal products in my kitchen in case she decided to open my cabinets. How could she not *understand*?

Did she have *any* idea how much effort I had put into

our first meeting? I'd originally planned to "meet" her at bar trivia, hoping I could catch her alone at the jukebox. *How about something from* Abbey Road*?* I'd planned to say. When she asked what my favorite song from the album was, I would say "I Want You" both because I knew it was her favorite ("Unpopular opinion: 'I Want You' is the best track on Abbey Road," she had tweeted last April) and because the words were true. I imagined her catching the double meaning and the corners of her glistening, bitable lips curling up, and then the two of us discussing the finer points of Lennon's songwriting and debating which Beatle had the most successful solo career, conversations that I had researched and prepared for. But then that idiot Connor had tried to swoop in on her and ruined the evening.

Even so, fate had offered a silver lining: that night I saw Cat Harrell in person and realized Audrey's best friend was the same Cathy from Camp Blackwood. Later, when I observed Audrey and Cat discussing the Rosalind preview through the RAT, I realized that would be a better venue for our first meeting. Audrey would be primed and in her element. All I needed was to get myself in the room and I could let Cat do the rest.

I agonized over the perfect location for our first date, knowing I needed something that appealed to Audrey's aesthetic interests but that also looked effortless. Audrey liked things that were lovely but easy, and I knew hitting that sweet spot was the key to charming her. That Kalorama Heights mansion ticked all the boxes, and it wasn't hard to extract the lockbox code from Tag. Then there was everything I had done to make the setting perfect for her: the small fortune I'd spent on candles and foliage, the recipe I'd carefully selected based on her expressed desire to go to Thailand (and the travel blogs I'd read about Thailand so I could pretend I had been there), the way I had practiced making that damn dish three times a day for *days* until I knew I had it down. By the time the date arrived, I had never wanted to look at tofu curry again.

Everything else—the picnic carefully selected to be as photogenic as possible, the Tabasco I sprinkled on popcorn after noticing her multiple tweets over the years about loving spicy food, the Negronis I'd learned how to mix after seeing a Story in which she raved about them, the donation I'd made to the Hirshhorn to gain access to the Rosalind preview, the anonymous comments and posts I'd made in a deliberate attempt to unsettle her so she would seek shelter in my arms, and so much more— had all been done because I loved her. Why couldn't she see that? I had done *everything* for her, had bent myself completely into a knot in the service of pleasing her.

But she didn't understand that, and so I knew I needed more. I needed to *touch* her. I just needed to take her small, soft hands in mine and kiss her rosebud lips, and then everything would be okay again. She would feel the electricity crackling between us and understand we were destined. Our love was unbreakable; it could survive anything.

But she kept evading me, and as I reached for her, certain that *this* would be the magical touch that reaffirmed our connection, suddenly she was slipping, falling head over heels down that spiral staircase, leaving a trail of water and blood behind her.

For a moment, nothing seemed real. I stared down at

her perfect body crumpled at the foot of the stairs, and I thought, *She looks just like a beautiful, broken bird.*

And then I saw the pool of dark red blood forming around her head and spreading across Cat's pristine floor. My stomach twisted at the sight. I clambered down the stairs so fast it was a miracle I didn't fall myself, and pressed both hands against the wound on Audrey's head. As her sticky blood seeped through my fingers, I was entranced and sickened by the sensation of having her life pulsing beneath my hands.

"Audrey," I said gently. "Are you okay?"

Her eyelids didn't even flutter.

"Audrey," I said again, more loudly, more desperately. "Audrey, please."

But she wasn't waking up.

My body began to cave in upon itself. This wasn't how things were supposed to be. We were supposed to spend an eternity together; we were supposed to live happily ever after. We were *fated*.

CHAPTER FIFTY-EIGHT

CAT

As I climbed the steps to my apartment, holding the extra key I'd left at Priya's for emergencies, I desperately hoped that Audrey was elsewhere. I hoped she'd followed my advice and called Nick, or that Max's ill-conceived plan to win her over through surprise flowers had worked. I couldn't face her after my catastrophic failure in court that morning; I couldn't handle her faux sympathy and her *Oh Kitty-Cat*s, especially when she was the reason everything had fallen apart. If only she hadn't distracted me with those texts.

God help me, I thought as I twisted open the front door. *Audrey, if you're here, I might actually kill you.*

I stepped into my apartment and stopped short. I

blinked, hoping that the gruesome scene before me was just a manifestation of my subconscious.

"Oh my God," I managed, dropping my suitcase and taking an involuntary step backward. For all the wishing Audrey away I had done that afternoon, I never wanted this.

Max Metcalf was crouched at the base of my narrow spiral staircase, cradling Audrey's lifeless, naked body in his blood-streaked arms. Dark red dotted both of them and was smeared on the floor beneath them.

"What happened?"

Max raised his head to look at me, and I shuddered. With a slash of blood on his cheek and almost feral eyes, he looked wild and dangerous.

"She fell," he said, his voice hoarse.

"She *fell*?" I repeated dubiously.

He nodded, gazing down at Audrey and stroking her face, leaving a ruby smear along her pale cheek.

"She'd just gotten out of the bath," he said quietly. "Her feet were wet. She slipped. I tried to catch her, but it happened too fast. She hit her head and . . ."

As he trailed off, my eyes traveled from Audrey's wan face to the dark blood matting her hair. A memory flashed through my mind: another head wound, another beautiful girl's hair streaked a sticky red. Spots swam in my vision. This couldn't be happening. Not again.

I grabbed at the entry table to steady myself and forced myself to think pragmatically. Audrey dying like this, on my floor and at Max's hand, would lead to questions I didn't want to answer. I would have to explain how Max had come to have the keys to my apartment, and it would be impossible to explain my connection to Max without Camp Blackwood coming up. It was only a matter of time before someone noticed the parallels between Audrey's unfortunate demise and what happened that summer. It *wasn't* the same, of course, it *wasn't* my fault, but would anyone believe that? My future with the firm, already on thin ice after that morning's dismal performance, would be destroyed. I would be lucky if I escaped with my law license intact. Everything I had worked so hard for, gone. All because of Audrey.

Audrey had ruined too many things for me already; I couldn't let her take my career, too. I had to do something. *Think, Cat, think.* How could I prevent the truth about Emily Snow from emerging?

Hiding Audrey's body was out of the question. I wasn't a criminal lawyer, but I had watched enough *Law & Order* to know I would never be able to completely rid my apartment of the evidence. A murder investigation would begin and end at the base of those stairs.

But what if it was just an accident? It was plausible. Those stairs were a hazard under the best of conditions, and Audrey had been wet. I glanced around the room and noticed a half-empty wine bottle on the kitchen counter. *Of course.* Audrey had been drinking, she was in the bath, and she had fallen. It was tragic, but sometimes life was.

It would have been a perfect explanation, if not for Max. He couldn't be here. He was unpredictable, and, more than that, he was the connection to what had happened at camp, the reason that Audrey's accident would seem like something more sinister. My only shot at salvaging this awful state of affairs hinged on extracting Max from the situation before anyone learned he was there.

"When did this happen?" I asked. "Have you called an ambulance?"

"I just wanted to talk to her," he said, still stroking Audrey's face.

"That's a nonresponsive answer," I snapped. "Tell me: Have you called 911?"

"No," he said hollowly. "I was trying to stop the bleeding. My hands were . . . But you. You can call. Now."

I looked down at Audrey, so pale and still in his arms. There was so much blood, even more blood than . . . I had to turn away, a lump forming in my throat.

"Max, it's too late."

"What?" he said blearily. "No. No, it can't be. We can save her. We just have to—"

He began shifting Audrey's body in his arms, reaching one bloody hand into his jeans pocket for what I assumed was his phone. Panic leaped in my chest. I couldn't let him make that call, not until we were on the same page.

"Max," I said as sternly as possible. "No."

"Are you out of your mind?" he demanded, looking at me incredulously.

"Look at her," I commanded. "No one could recover from a head wound like that."

His expression turning vicious, he snarled, "And you know something about head wounds, don't you?"

"Now is not the time—"

"I know what you did," he growled, leaning forward while still clutching Audrey to his chest. "Emily Snow didn't just *happen* to fall off that trail. She didn't *stumble* and wind up brain damaged. You *pushed* her."

I shook my head quickly, automatically. "No, I didn't."

"I saw you, Cathy. *I saw you.*"

Something snapped rubber band–like in my brain, and I struggled to keep my voice level as I said, "That's impossible."

He laughed coldly. "Is it? Because I twisted my ankle at the start of that hike and had to wait for the rest of you to finish. Do you remember?"

My stomach dropped because I *did* remember. We had only been a couple of yards out when Max had tripped over a root and fallen to the ground with a sharp cry of pain. Emily Snow had tossed her white-blonde hair and laughed, saying, *Walk much, Max?* I'd felt bad for him as he limped back to the trailhead with one of the counselors.

"I was resting in the picnic area," he continued. "Do you remember where those picnic tables were? Level with the parking lot, above the trail. There was this great view of the river, and I was sitting on one of the tables taking pictures. I heard you all below, so I hopped to the edge with the idea I would get some shots of everyone. I was doing that when I noticed Emily stop to tie her shoe. You hung back with her, which I thought was weird because you two weren't friends. And then you pushed her."

The edges of my vision faded, and for the briefest of seconds, I could feel the fabric of Emily's camp T-shirt beneath my palms, the sharpness of her shoulder blades as I gave her a quick shove. She hadn't screamed, hadn't even shouted. There had only been a sudden, shocked inhalation as she fell wordlessly off the trail and tumbled down toward the riverbank.

I hadn't meant to cause permanent injury. I hadn't even meant to cause minor injury. At most, I thought she would roll down the slope and into the river, emerging wet, muddy, and embarrassed.

Which was what she deserved. She should know humiliation for once. Emily Snow had spent the first part of the summer tormenting me, calling me "freak" and "loser," yanking chairs out from underneath me and slamming doors in my face. As camp wore on, I'd grown numb to her abuse, and so, like the pretty little sociopath she was, she'd changed her tactics. She'd started pouring on the sugar, lending me her fashion magazines and inviting me to play truth or dare with her group of similarly pretty friends.

I fell for it. When she offered to do my makeup one afternoon, I sat eagerly on her lower bunk, thrilled to be welcomed into her inner circle. As she dusted pink blush across my cheeks, she'd told me that Dylan Carter, the cute camper from Texas, had a crush on me. In retrospect, I could hear how she was swallowing her laughter, could see her friends hiding smirks behind their hands. But I'd been oblivious, and had taken her advice to approach Dylan that evening in the cafeteria.

He had laughed in my overly made-up face. *Everyone* had. I spun around, vision blurring with tears, and discovered, to my ultimate mortification, that even the camp counselors were laughing.

Four days later, that humiliation still fresh in my mind, Emily had paused on the trail to tie her shoe. I was lagging behind the group, wanting to fade into the forest, and when she saw me, she asked in a singsong voice how Dylan was.

All I wanted was for people to laugh at *her* for a change. Instead, she cracked her head open on a jagged rock, and then she proceeded to strike more rocks as she rolled down toward the riverbank, leaving a bloody trail behind her. *Freak accident*, everyone said. *What a tragedy.* One-in-a-million chance that she ended up brain damaged, but that's what happened.

Emily's friends accused me of pushing her. *It's the weirdo's fault!* they screamed, pointing pink-polished fingernails as mascara-blackened tears stained their cheeks. Everyone else shifted their eyes away when I insisted she had tripped and fallen. The same counselors who had laughed when Emily tricked me watched me warily and wouldn't let me be alone with anyone else. Even my father, when I opened my mouth to tell him my side of the story, had shushed me with the admonishment "Some things are better left unsaid." I knew that everyone thought I pushed her, but no one knew for certain.

Except, apparently, Max.

"I didn't mean to hurt her," I said. "Just like I'm sure you didn't mean to hurt Audrey. These were both just accidents. Unfortunate, tragic accidents."

"They're not the same at all," he protested. "You pushed Emily. Audrey *fell*."

"Think about how this looks, Max. You were stalking her, and—"

"I wasn't stalking her."

"No? Explain those photographs. Explain how she's dead in your arms, with you covered in her blood. No one will ever believe you." I paused to allow the weight of my words to sink in and then pointed to the open bottle of wine on the kitchen counter. "But maybe it was an accident. Maybe she was drinking and fell. Maybe you were never here, and she died alone."

"She's not dead!" he shouted, yanking his phone free from his pocket. "Fuck, Cathy, what is *wrong* with you?"

I couldn't let him make that call. I couldn't have the police coming here before I'd convinced him to leave, couldn't have them finding him blood-soaked, manic, and babbling about Emily Snow. I would do anything to stop him.

I lunged for him, managing to smack the phone from his hands before slipping on the blood-splattered floor and landing hard on my back. Sharp pain radiated from my spine and I struggled to catch my breath. Before I could gather myself, Max threw his body over mine, pinning me against the floor while he reached for the phone, which remained just out of his grasp.

"Get off me!" I grunted, struggling.

"She *trusted* you," he barked, saliva flying from his mouth and landing on my face. A vein bulged in his forehead as he stared down at me, his expression one of twisted rage, and then he grabbed a fistful of my hair, painfully yanking my head up before smashing it down against the floor. Stars burst in my vision, and I cried out.

He made another grab for the phone, and despite the mind-bending pain in my head and the room swirling around me, I forced myself to take advantage of his momentary distraction. I threw my body weight at him like Audrey and I had learned to do in self-defense class, knocking him off-balance, and then scrambled atop him, using my knees to hold him down. He spluttered with fury, fingers grasping at the edges of the cell phone, sending it spinning out of his grasp.

"You bitch," he growled, turning on me. Clawed hands shot at my face, scratching my skin and reaching for my eyes. I looked around desperately for something that could subdue him. The wine bottle. It would mean releasing him, but at least then I would have a weapon.

I slapped him hard across the face to distract him, and then jumped to my feet and snatched the bottle from the counter. I whirled around and brought it down on Max's head with all of my strength. The bottle didn't shatter as I had envisioned, but it did make a satisfying *thump* as it connected with his skull. He collapsed, blood trickling from the contact point.

I sagged against the counter. With the scratches on my face and the bloody scene at the base of my stairs, no one would question me if I claimed I hit him in self-defense. *He murdered my best friend, and then he came for me. I had no choice.* The partners might be displeased with the attention it brought to the firm, but they wouldn't fire me over it. I was the victim, after all. And there would be no one to tell them about Emily Snow.

I turned my attention to Audrey's motionless body. My heart twisted, and I was surprised to feel a flicker of relief. I would never find myself under Audrey's manicured thumb again.

"Rest in peace," I whispered.

Then I saw her chest rise shallowly. I blinked. So Max hadn't been delusional; she *was* still alive. I crept closer to her and peered down at her waxy face, shockingly pale and surrounded by blood. Her lungs were still working, but what about the rest of her? How could she ever be the same after a head wound like that? I knew Audrey. She wouldn't want to be a vegetable, to have to be spoon-fed and wear diapers for the rest of her life. She wouldn't want to live like Emily Snow.

Killing her would be a mercy, the last thing I could do for her as a friend.

In a daze, I crossed to my couch and selected one of

my plumpest throw pillows. I remembered how Audrey had admired the gray-and-cream-striped fabric, had complimented me on it. I returned to her body and knelt over it, holding the pillow in my lap.

Even smeared with blood, she was beautiful.

Her eyes fluttered open, unfocused and dull. She rasped, "Help me."

My throat closed. *God, she was awake.* How long had she been conscious? Had she heard me telling Max not to call for help? Had she heard the truth about Emily Snow? Had she seen the scuffle between Max and me, seen me crack him over the head to stop him from calling 911?

I fingered the fringe on the edge of the pillow. I could still end this. I could still walk away a victim.

"I need your help, Cat," she whispered. "Please."

I need your help.

How many times had Audrey said that to me before? How many times had Audrey asked for my assistance with no regard for how it would impact me? Hadn't she done that that very morning? Hadn't she ruined my career prospects without a second thought? The truth was that Audrey wasn't a very good friend. She never had been. She had hurt me, casually and without remorse, time and time again, and I knew she would never stop.

Unless someone stopped her.

"I can't help you," I said quietly, and pressed the pillow down over her face. "Not anymore."

She struggled weakly, her pale limbs barely moving. My stomach shifted queasily. Was this really how Audrey Miller, the most sparkling, vivacious woman I had ever known, was going to go out? Not with a bang, but with a whimper? I closed my eyes, telling myself it would all be over soon. Then I could start putting the pieces of my life back together. I would make myself a priority, much like Audrey had always made herself a priority.

Dimly, I heard a scraping noise behind me. Still holding the pillow over Audrey, I opened my eyes and turned toward the sound just in time to see the bottom of the wine bottle swinging at my face.

CHAPTER FIFTY-NINE

AUDREY

Nick set a cardboard box bursting with my clothing down in the center of the empty floor and looked around. "This is a nice place. Much better than that hole in the ground you used to call home."

I set down my own box and surveyed the space, happiness flooding my body. My new apartment in a recently constructed building on the waterfront had floor-to-ceiling windows, which were a welcome change from the small, ground-level, bar-covered windows at my old place. More important, these windows were on the fourth floor—meaning no aspirational stalkers could be peering through them, watching me sleep.

"I know," I said. "I should have held out for something

like this the first time around. The doorman alone is going to be worth the cost of rent."

"Just getting out of that basement is worth it. I always hated staying over there, and that was before I knew that nutjob was hiding in the shadows."

I glanced at him. "I didn't know you hated staying over."

"It was the location, not the company," he said, tousling my hair.

"Careful," I said, bringing a hand up to protect the still-tender spot on my scalp.

"Sorry, babe," he said, wincing. "Are you okay?"

"Yeah." I nodded. "But . . . hey, Nick, are *we* okay? I feel like we've been waltzing around the elephant in the room."

"Yeah," Nick said, suddenly very interested in the toe of his sneaker. "I mean, if you can forgive me for calling you a bitch and all that other stuff I said, then, yeah, we're okay."

"I'll forgive you for that if you forgive me for thinking you broke into my apartment."

He looked up and laughed. "I don't know, Aud. That was pretty fucked up."

"Leave me alone," I protested, pinching him. "I was really scared."

"I know," he said, catching my hands and looking at me seriously. "And I'm sorry I wasn't there for you. I got caught up in my own bullshit jealousy. But you can count on me from now on, I promise."

"Thanks, Nicky," I said, stretching up on my tiptoes to kiss him on the cheek. "I missed you."

"And now that all your new DC friends are in jail, you need me, huh?"

"Max isn't in jail," I corrected him. "Cat, on the other hand . . . well, let's hope she's not getting out anytime soon."

"Good riddance," Nick said with an elaborate shudder. "That chick always gave me the creeps. I hated the way she used to follow you around all the time in college."

"I thought Cat was sweet," I said, my voice catching as I remembered our decade-long friendship, all the fun we'd had together, the secrets we'd shared. When I thought of all the nights we'd slept together under the same roof, I got chills. Had she ever stood beside my bed, pillow in hand, before? When she said she'd heard me talking in my sleep—had that made her want to smother me? How many other times and other ways had Cat wished me harm over the years? And how had I never known how she really felt about me?

"Christ, Audrey, the bitch tried to *murder* you. She wasn't *sweet.*"

"I said I *thought* she was sweet. Listening comprehension, babe. Try it."

"Whatever. You sure can pick 'em. Her and that psychopath you were sleeping with."

I flinched, getting the same strange feeling in the pit of my stomach that I always did when I thought about Max: a mixture of fear, disgust, and pity. The extent and dedication of his fixation with me was alarming, and I still felt like throwing up when I thought about him standing in my apartment that night, watching me while I was completely vulnerable. But there was something *sad* about it. Max had truly believed he loved me. His feelings had been real—and, for a time at least, so had mine. It felt insane to admit, but a part of me actually *missed* Max.

"Be fair," I said softly. "Max isn't a psychopath. He's . . . well, he's not wired right, that's for sure, but he's not a psychopath. It's not like he was going to hurt me."

"You don't know that. Just because he *didn't* hurt you doesn't mean he *wouldn't* have."

"He never would have hurt me," I said with certainty. "He's not violent. And he loved me too much."

"I worry about you, Audrey. You're too trusting."

"Not so trusting I didn't get a restraining order."

"The first smart thing you did since moving to this town," Nick said, shaking his head. "But, seriously, I'm glad you're sticking around. I was worried you were going to pack it up and head back to the Big Apple. I wouldn't have blamed you, but I would have missed you."

"Real talk, if I hadn't gotten that promotion, I might have considered it." I punched him lightly on the arm. "But, let's be honest, we both know I couldn't let a couple of head cases run me out of town."

"That's my girl," he said with a smirk, wrapping his arm around my waist and pulling me close.

"Hold that thought," I said, pressing a finger to Nick's lips and pulling my phone from my purse. "I want to Instagram this sunset."

CHAPTER SIXTY

MAX

One month after that horrible evening when everything unspooled into a bloody mess, Leigh pulled me aside after dinner. Her plain face arranged in a mask of sympathy, she patted my arm as though I were terminally ill and solicitously asked, "How are you doing, Peanut?"

"Fine," I said through gritted teeth, counseling myself not to yank my arm away.

"Really? You're not still . . . obsessed with that girl?"

"Of course not," I said stiffly, because I *wasn't* "obsessed" with Audrey.

I had never been *obsessed* with her. Calling it obsession made it sound dark and one-sided, and that hadn't been the case at all. I *loved* her, could feel our connection in every single cell of my being, and she loved me, too.

No matter what she said now, no matter what she told that judge, I knew she loved me still. Her soul called out to mine.

But Leigh, who was ordinary in every sense of the word and married to my equally unromantic older brother, wouldn't be able to understand the transcendent bond between us. None of my family would, and neither would the new therapist my father had arranged. I felt sorry for them, knowing they would never experience the same kind of love, being consumed from the inside out.

Besides, I knew it was only a matter of time before Audrey and I were reunited. Leigh and the rest of them might argue that a restraining order was a clear indication our relationship was over and she never wanted to see me again.

But that wasn't the case. How could it be, when she continued to open her laptop and stare directly into the camera, biting her plump bottom lip enticingly? They could say she didn't know about the RAT on her computer, that she had never seen those forum posts, particularly the ones hidden within the VIP section—but then why did she look straight into the camera? Why did she point those sparkling, soulful eyes right at me?

It wasn't over. It couldn't be. Not when she posted online about her favorite snack, popcorn with Tabasco, a creation I introduced her to. Not when she created a public playlist of her favorite Ted and the Honey tracks and included "Everything," the song I had told her was my favorite, the song that contained the lines "I've done everything for you / everything you ever wanted / everything you never knew." Not when she continued to drop bread crumbs about her new apartment's location, like that photograph of the sunset taken from her window.

Not when she still googled my name.

The signs were unambiguous, the conclusion inescapable: Audrey still thought about me. She still loved me. We were still inevitable.

This time, though, I wouldn't rely so much on fate. I had allowed too much room for error, and everything had fallen apart. I couldn't let her get away again.

ACKNOWLEDGMENTS

I owe an enormous debt of gratitude to the brilliant team that helped me transform this story from a pile of loose notes into the novel you are holding in your hands. Massive thanks to my exceptional agent, Lisa Grubka, who has been there for me at every step and who is the best sounding board, beta reader, and advocate I could ever ask for; my outstanding editor, Lauren McKenna, who can always clearly see the story even when I can't and whose guidance and encouragement were invaluable to this book; Jackie Cantor, for her assistance; everyone at Gallery Books who helped make this book a reality (Jennifer Bergstrom, Maggie Loughran, Meagan Harris, Jessica Roth, Abby Zidle, Bianca Salvant, Anabel Jimenez, Lisa Litwack, Steve Breslin, Jaime Putorti, Caroline

Pallotta, Allison Green, Mike Kwan, Jane Elias); everyone at Fletcher & Company who has supported it (Christy Fletcher, Melissa Chinchillo, Gráinne Fox, Elizabeth Resnick, and Brenna Raffe); and Michelle Weiner, Michelle Kroes, and Olivia Blaustein at CAA. Thank you, thank you, thank you.

I am also deeply, deeply grateful for the family and friends who continually support and encourage me. My most heartfelt thanks to my husband, Marc Hedrich, without whose unending support none of this would be possible; my mother, Mary Barber, who has always believed in me and who, with my late father, Richard Barber, has always nurtured my creativity; my brother, David Barber, who is always game to bounce around an idea (or a tagline!) and whom I can always count on for sage advice when I start feeling stressed; my in-laws, Philip and Laurie Hedrich, and also AJ Hedrich and Kevin Hedrich, who have all been wonderfully supportive of me; and all the friends and family who encourage my writing. I love and treasure you all. A special thank-you is due to those who came out to watch the baby while I was on deadline (Mom, Phil, Laurie, and AJ), and to the little bear himself for being such an agreeable fellow.

I also have to thank the writing communities that have welcomed me online and off: the crime writers in DC (Ed Aymar, Christina Kovac, Angie Kim, Louis Bayard); the Women's Fiction Writers Association; the 17 Scribes; and of course Kristin Rockaway, Suzanne Park, and Chelsea Resnick for always being there to celebrate or commiserate via group message. Also a big thank-you to the women who foster online reading communities, notably Kristy Barrett of A Novel Bee; Barbara Bos of Women

Writers, Women's Books; and Andrea Katz of Great Thoughts Great Readers—and to the readers themselves!

Finally, thank you to Hilary-Morgan Watt for taking the time to meet with me and tell me what it's like to work in a museum—I hope you're not too horrified by the liberties I took in service of the story! Inaccuracies and fabrications are 100 percent on me. Also, acknowledgments are due to the *Murder Is Her Hobby: Frances Glessner Lee and The Nutshell Studies of Unexplained Death* show at the Renwick Gallery, which partially inspired *The Life and Death of Rosalind Rose*, and to Nate Anderson, the writer of the Ars Technica piece cited in the author's note that so freaked me out that I wrote a whole book about it.